RUN TO GROUND

By Stuart Johnstone

Out in the Cold
Into the Dark
Run to Ground

RUN TO GROUND

STUART JOHNSTONE

Allison & Busby Limited
11 Wardour Mews
London W1F 8AN
allisonandbusby.com

First published in Great Britain by Allison & Busby in 2022.

Copyright © 2022 by STUART JOHNSTONE

A CIP catalogue record for this book is available from
the British Library.

First Edition

ISBN 978-0-7490-2878-7

Typeset in 11.25/16.35 pt Sabon LT Pro by
Typo•glyphix, Burton-on-Trent DE14 3HE

FSC
www.fsc.org
MIX
Paper from
responsible sources
FSC® C171272

For Lindsay

CHAPTER 1

Amateur Hour

Dillon's hands trembled as he gripped the slick bat. His bottom lip trembled too, though not from the cold rain that was bouncing off the mud at his feet. *Pull yourself together*, he thought. *Was he fucking crying? Get a hold of yourself, Dillon, fuck sake.* He was suddenly very glad of the darkness and the downpour to hide his cowardice. Small floodlights beamed down from high on posts at seemingly arbitrary spots in the yard, showing clearly the ferocity of the downpour directly in front of their bulbs, but it was easy enough to stay clear of the areas they highlighted.

Were the others scared too? If they were there was no sign of it. Tavish at the front of the line, raised his hand, which meant stop, a signal agreed upon in the van. *What did he think this was? Commandos infiltrating an enemy camp?* Dillon turned to look at his brother, bringing up the rear, wiping his eyes before he did. Davie was looking nervously around the scrapyard, but when he saw Dillon's face he winked and gave what he must have thought was a reassuring nod. Ahead of Dillon, between him and Tavish (*on point?*), Sal was fidgeting and trying to see past Tavish's shoulder.

Dillon waited for whatever it was Tavish had them paused for and listened to the rhythm of the metal graveyard in which they stood. Metallic thuds of the heavy raindrops striking the roofs and bonnets of the discarded vehicles, some piled four or five high, sounded in a relentless beat.

Dillon was being pulled low by his brother. He looked ahead and Tavish was urging them down with a swatting hand. No sooner had Dillon ducked to his haunches, leaning against the side of a rusting Transit van, than the roar of an engine flew past them. A Range Rover, coming from seemingly nowhere, charged through the scrapyard and was gone as quickly as it had appeared. Tavish responded with a curl of his hand, urging the group on.

Dillon followed the line, the fear rising again in his chest as they turned the corner of a monolith of rotting hatchbacks, avoiding the circles of light from on high. Ahead, through the driving rain was the row of portacabins they had cut a hole in the fence to visit. Tavish gave the signal, tapping at his mouth with an open hand. Dillon pulled his scarf up over his nose, the others covered their faces in similar ways. *This is it. Shit, this is it.*

Tavish was running across the patch of earth between them and the cabins. Then Sal was and his legs took him without thinking, his brother was right at his shoulder.

They stopped at Tavish's signal. He was peering through a small window in the nearest of the three cabins, discreetly at first but soon cupping his hand at his eye to remove the glare from the overhead light.

He moved on to the middle cabin. A dark blue BMW was parked at the bottom of a small ramp that led to a blue door at the cabin's centre. A light above this door showed Tavish clearly, all attempts at stealth now apparently abandoned. Again, he was at the window, though this time he quickly ducked and began urging the others to come.

The four of them congregated on the ramp. Tavish approached the door at a crouch and tried the handle. The door remained closed. Now Tavish was on his feet facing the door. He appeared to be contemplating using the crowbar in his hand to jemmy it, but then it was lowered and he was taking a step back before launching his foot at the handle. The door was thrown open and Tavish was inside. Sal was moving in too. Dillon's legs betrayed him until he received a shove from behind and he too was out of the rain and into a blindingly bright room full of shouting.

It took a moment for Dillon's senses to settle and take in what was going on around him. He raised his bat, ready to swing at anyone he didn't know. There was nobody to hit. The shouting was coming from Tavish and one man he had pinned backwards over a desk. The laptop that had been there lay in pieces at their tangled feet.

'Shut up. Shut the fuck up,' Tavish hissed. The guy, prone on his back, was yelling through Tavish's hand across his face and mouth, his own hand pushing into

Tavish's chin. He was being forced into the desk surface, unable to get any purchase to fight back. 'Listen up, prick, I'm going to take my hand away and you're going to sit up. Any shit from you and you get another slap with this,' Tavish said, shaking the crowbar with his free hand.

Dillon moved to get a better look, his pulse racing and what felt like vomit sitting in his throat. As the guy on the desk sat up, his hands held up in defeat, Dillon saw a significant cut at his left temple, blood pouring freely. It ran down the guy's face and dripped from his chin onto his Brown Leather Jacket.

'That's better,' said Tavish. 'And if you think about running or doing anything stupid, it'll be a lot worse than a tap with a crowbar. Cover him.' Sal stepped forward and lowered both barrels at the man's chest. 'Now, where's the shit?'

The man coughed into his fist and then dabbed at the cut on his head gingerly. He examined his fingers and moved to reach into the pocket of his jeans before Sal cleared her throat and bobbed the barrels at him. He paused, then continued going into his pocket, albeit slowly with his other hand raised. He produced a handkerchief and held it to his head before raising his eyes. He took each of the four interlopers in, his gaze lingering on each for a few seconds. The words that came out of his mouth were calm and even, despite the threat contained within them. 'Just what in the name of fuck do you think you're doing?' he said, his accent vaguely Liverpudlian. He pulled his right foot up to rest on his left thigh. To Dillon, the guy in his well-fitting coat, well-groomed dark hair, wearing a genuinely inquisitive expression on his face, looked like the one in charge of the situation.

Dillon's pulse was still on fast forward. He lingered by the door listening for any noise of an engine, but all he could hear was the steady drum of the rain on the roof of the portacabin. His breath was released in small clouds of steam through the saturated scarf at his mouth and nose. Sal was the same, she fidgeted and was breathing hard.

The question seemed to throw Tavish for a moment as he looked around first at Davie and then at Sal, but then he was laughing. 'What do *we* think we're doin'? *We* think we're robbing you of a copious amount of illicit substances, that's what. Now where the fuck is the stuff?'

'And what stuff would that be?'

Tavish scratched at his head and his gaze went to the door and then back. He raised the crowbar and advanced on the bloodied man again.

'All right, all right,' the man said holding the red-blotted handkerchief up in surrender. 'You need to stop waving that thing around, mate. You'll have someone's eye out. Look,' the man started, then paused, a small smile blooming. 'I don't know how you found out about said substances, but trust me when I tell you that you don't want any part of this. Any of you.' His eyes again searched out each individual, though Dillon felt they hovered on him longest. 'Clearly – I mean quite clearly – you have no idea to whom said substances belong and if you don't know, well I'm not going to be the one to enlighten you. Just trust me when I say that the intelligent thing to do is leave and do it quickly and then you run and don't stop running for a while and maybe, just maybe, I'll start to forget about this.' He removed the handkerchief from his head and inspected the red blotch. 'Though no promises,' he said as if to the stain.

'Time for you to stop talking and start telling. Where's the shit?' said Tavish, the crowbar bobbing eagerly in his hand.

'Look, if you're quick, you might just about get out of here before my colleagues return.'

'You mean the mob in the Range Rover? Nah, they were out of here in a big hurry. Whatever they're going to, looks important. When they get back, we'll be long gone. Now, the shit, last chance.'

'No, mate. This is *your* last chance.' The man uncrossed his legs and cleared his throat. 'If you insist on this, it will become the biggest regret of what remains of your short life. All of you. You get an A for enthusiasm and gratuitous violence, in your circles that will probably take you far, but right now you're more out of your league than you can imagine. You couldn't possibly have known that my colleagues were going to have to step out for a minute and so my guess is you were planning on doing this with all of us here, in which case you'd already be dead. As it is, you got lucky, but luck doesn't last long. You're amateurs trying to run against professionals and—'

'We know what the fuck we're doing,' Sal cut in, pushing both barrels towards his face.

The man's attention turned on her. 'The evidence suggests otherwise, sweetheart. Maybe in the schemes you lot run around in, someone might be fooled into thinking you were holding a shotgun on them – you know, if you smashed in quick and made a lot of noise – but me? No, I see a couple of pipes taped together in the same half-arsed manner as the rest of this ill-conceived evening you're having. I see a thug whose ambitions are way bigger than his capabilities,' he said returning his eyes to Tavish, then they turned to Dillon. 'And I see a scared shitless kid who seems to be the only one realising the magnitude of—'

There was a thud of the crowbar, a low groan from the man whose chest had been struck a fierce blow and a further thud as he slid from the table to the ground. He lay there writhing, gulping in air as if surfacing from a deep dive.

'You talk way too much,' said Tavish. He crouched down next to the man and began rifling through his pockets. First, he produced his phone, which he slid across the floor to Davie who kicked it past Dillon out of the portacabin door. Then he pulled a set of keys from the man's jacket. Tavish held them up, giving them a victorious rattle. 'Go see what you can find next door,' he said and tossed them over to Davie.

'C'mon,' he said to Dillon.

They stepped out into the rain once more. The downpour had intensified. Dillon stared out into darkness looking for any movement while Davie tried keys in the door of the first portacabin. A clunk of a lock and a judder of a door sounded and they were inside.

'Check that side for a light,' said Davie. They both set about patting the unlit walls until Dillon's hand landed on the switch. Overhead lights blinkered into life and Davie voiced the thought in Dillon's head. 'What the fuck?'

This cabin was a twin of the other, but in place of office furniture and a beaten man were stacks upon stacks of large brown packages. Three wooden pallets were loaded with these soft brown bricks. They stood, staring for a moment before Davie stepped forward and lifted one. He turned it over in his hands before tossing it to Dillon.

Dillon caught it in both hands, his bat rattled to the floor. One knee bent slightly as he absorbed the weight of it. It was about two feet in length and the contents were wrapped in thick layers of cellophane and brown tape. Through the wrap, it was clear to see that the tightly packed powder within was brown and not white.

'W-w-what is it?' he asked, but his brother had already darted out of the door. Dillon placed the package back amongst the others and had begun counting them amongst the three pallet loads when he heard a heated conversation out in the rain growing louder. He lifted his bat again as Davie re-entered followed by the leather-jacketed guy, pushed harshly into the room by Tavish.

'What is so fucking interesting I needed to "see for myself"?' Tavish said. Dillon realised he was blocking the view and stepped aside. Sal closed the door over. She'd dropped the shotgun ruse and instead held the pipes as if ready to take the guy's head off if he tried anything.

Tavish said nothing for a full minute as he slid his hand over the top layer of packages, almost sensually.

Davie approached him and whispered angrily into his ear, but in the small cabin he might have well been shouting.

'Kilo of MDMA, you said. What the fuck is this?'

Tavish picked up a package. He turned it over, even gave it a sniff before turning back to Davie. His mouth and nose were hidden under the Hibs scarf, but his eyes were smiling. 'What does it look like? Fucking jackpot, is what it is.'

'S-smack? What do w-we know about smack?' Dillon said.

The guy in the Brown Leather Jacket was chuckling to himself somewhere behind him.

'He's right,' said Davie. 'Pills we can shift, but not this. What are we gonna do with this? Fuck it, let's get out of here before that lot in the Range Rover get back.'

'Trouble in paradise boys?' Brown Leather Jacket said. 'Your information was a little wide of the mark, eh? More than you bargained for.' He laughed, but stopped as Sal threatened to take a swing. He held his hands up, palms out at his chest. 'All right, love, take it easy. But seriously boys, maybe you weren't listening before, and maybe you'll listen now. That enormous amount of grade A heroin over there belongs to a very bad man. A man you don't ever want to meet. Now, time to think very carefully about the next step.' The three boys were looking at one another as Brown Leather Jacket continued. 'If you take even a single gram of that there stash, he will follow you to the ends of the earth. Now, I'm appealing to your sense of reason here. Turn around, crawl back through whatever hole you made to get in here and run. Run until morning and then run some more.'

'Go get the van,' Tavish said to Dillon. Davie breathed a heavy breath.

'Y-you're not s-serious?'

'A kilo of MDMA might have kept us going for a few months. This, this is life-changing. There's no way we're letting this opportunity slip through our fingers. Get the van and we'll figure the rest out. All right?' Tavish said, first looking at Sal, who nodded. 'All right,' he said, this time to Davie who hesitated, but then with that same heavy breath, said:

'Okay.'

Tavish's gaze returned to Dillon. 'Now go.'

Dillon was still for a moment. Then made for the door. 'This is a m-mistake,' he said under his breath. He was halted as he reached the door, Brown Leather Jacket's hand grasping his wrist.

'That's a t-terrible s-stutter you have there, lad. You're not going to be very hard to f-f-find, are ya?'

Dillon pulled his arm free, stared deep into the eyes of this man for a second and then left.

Nobody said a word on the way back into town. After a few minutes someone in the front even turned off the radio. Dillon, in the back of the van, bracing himself between enormous piles of heroin, was imagining what was going through the heads of those up front. Tavish's tiny quota of grey matter would be doing sums and then spending the totals. Davie, if he had any sense, would be contemplating the enormity of what had just happened, and Sal? Well, she was anyone's guess, maybe the evening's events, maybe what she was going to have for dinner when they got back. She wasn't tuned to the same frequency of

15

most people. Dillon's thoughts revolved around a man in a Brown Leather Jacket and the central question: how in God's name did he allow himself to get talked into this?

They rolled into the scheme a little after ten. The rain hammered on, though Dillon was only too glad to step out of the van when Davie opened the back door.

'We're going to stash this lot,' he said. 'You stay.'

'Davie, what the fuck?' Dillon said, a little under his breath and waving a hand at the van's contents.

'Not now, Dillon.'

'Davie—'

'Later. It is what it is.' Davie was looking over his shoulder. He turned back and forced a smile.

Dillon shut the doors to the van. It was pointless arguing. Davie was right, there was no going back.

'Later,' Sal said. She lifted her hood against the rain and walked off towards the other end of the circular scheme. Dillon started towards his own flat. He was alerted by a shrill whistle. Wee Cammy was standing next to a car idling in the street. The kid was holding up his phone. Dillon pulled his own and checked the text that had arrived:

Gd, yr back. This guy wants HalfW 1GMD

'Fuck off, Cammy. Not right now,' Dillon said to himself. He heaved a breath, thinking about how much cash he had left. He texted back:

5mins

In the flat he checked the drawer. Cash was low, but so

was product. Their code wasn't a complicated one, and if the cops ever pounced and confiscated their phones they wouldn't need a think tank to break it, but it helped them feel a little more secure. He didn't have the 'half' ounce of weed, but the one gram of MDMA was fine. Another text to Cammy:

Only QW. 80 all in

He waited for a response. That was the last of the weed, a quarter. Four wraps of MDMA to make up the gram was exactly half of what they had left. Beyond that just pills that went for pennies. His phone chimed:

Sound

Dillon met Cammy at the door. Handed back a tenner of the cash for the kid along with the stuff.

'You eaten?' Dillon asked.

'Aye. Chippy earlier. Where were yees?'

Off making an enormous mistake. How was your night? 'Just a thing we had to do. Nothing,' Dillon said.

'Awrite,' the kid said. And spun on his heels. 'See you later.'

'Aye, later,' Dillon said.

The thought turned in his head. *See you later.* What had the guy said exactly? 'You're not going to be very hard to f-f-find, are ya?'

Dillon shut the door over. He was hungry earlier but not now. He went to his bed where he knew he would lie awake most of the night.

CHAPTER 2

Tulliallan

A tangible sense of dread flushed through me as I pulled the car off the main road and through the gates of the Police Scotland Training College. Tulliallan to the general public, more affectionately known to surviving recruits as Castle Greyskull.

A group of new intakes were being put through their paces on a field to my right. Circuit training. One lot doing burpees while another did press-ups and a third sprinted between two plastic markers. Poor bastards. I could see a training sergeant leaning down next to someone struggling to lower themselves into another press-up. I couldn't hear what was being said, but it was surely words of crushingly cruel encouragement. The muscles in my arms twitched in response.

DCI Templeton, in the passenger seat, looked up from her phone as the front tyres dipped over a speed bump. 'What a cheerful place,' she remarked almost too quietly

18

as the main building of Tulliallan Castle came into view. Grey, turreted and imposing, it loomed over the well-kept grounds. Purchased post-war and converted into the training centre for police recruits, it made for an intimidating place to begin life in uniform. In addition to new starts, it also hosted training for road policing and detective training. We parked and made our way across the gravel drive towards the castle. Another troop of recruits ran past us, all in white T-shirts and black shorts.

'You must have endured something similar when you joined the Met?' I asked.

'Hendon, yes. Same idea, just a little less . . . Arthurian.' She looked along the turreted roof of the place. 'What have they got you doing, anyway?' she asked.

'A course on crime pattern analysis.'

'Oh fuck, bad luck.'

'How about you, ma'am?'

'I don't really know. Some shit about senior investigators. Also, some delegation is over from India, so it's likely to be a schmoozing exercise, as if we've fuck all better to do.'

I smiled and hoped she hadn't noticed. I'd been working in her presence for a few months, but her plummy English accent and contrasting gutter vocabulary I was still finding amusing. She paused at the step of the building. A young recruit had spotted us approach and was holding the door open, which had me urging to get inside, but DCI Templeton was busy fishing into her handbag. I exchanged an awkward smile with the young lady who looked like she didn't know whether to stick or twist. DCI

Templeton surfaced from her bag with a pack of nicotine gum. She cracked two from the blister tray and popped them into her mouth. 'All right,' she continued, 'let's get this over with. I'll find you at lunch if I can get away. Can't stand senior officer chit-chat. If not, I'll see you at the car at five.'

'Ma'am. Sir.' The young lady holding the door addressed us individually with a small nod as we stepped past her. She had that air of excitement and terror I recalled from my time here. DCI Templeton's warrant card hung in full view from her neck, my own was hidden beneath my coat. As a rule, if there's ever any uncertainty of someone's rank, or even if it's not clear if they're even police, the clever thing to do was to err on the side of most respectful moniker as she had done.

After wandering around the old halls that had terrorised me as a fresh-faced probationer, with every passing recruit making a great point of nodding and addressing me 'sir', the feeling of having exorcised the place from my jar of bad memories started to kick in. There was a point to it all, I supposed, to break down new recruits to a state of intimidated compliance and thereafter rebuild with a sense of discipline and respect. The police, after all, had its structure roots in the military and while, inevitably, a lot of that discipline would fall away in time, enough should remain to retain respect of rank. Though having seen DCI Kate Templeton in the presence of her superiors, unafraid to tell them to shut up, or even fuck off with nothing but a wry smile to suggest at playfulness, it wasn't universally the case.

My reminiscing, if that was indeed the right word, stretched on longer than intended and I ended up speed walking around to the more modern annex of the training centre. Finding the appropriate classroom, I entered, stopping the white-shirted officer in his sentence.

'Sorry . . . Inspector,' I said, getting a quick glimpse of the pips on his shoulder.

'It's fine, take a seat, we just started.' I shuffled through the room. A quick glimpse of the faces of those seated showed they weren't much older than those in the halls. I guessed they were predominantly new DCs and that I might be the only one present of any rank above. Bags were being dragged out of my way as I took a desk roughly in the middle. Somewhere behind me a throat was cleared loudly, perhaps annoyed at my interruption. I sighed as I removed my coat and saw we were all looking at a PowerPoint presentation. A yawn began growing in my jaw as I read the title: Crime Pattern Analysis – Systematic Approaches and Theory.

'What's your name please?' the inspector asked as I pulled a pad of paper from my bag. He held a clipboard and began checking it when I said:

'Sergeant Don Colyear.'

'Ah, okay. DS Colyear.' I was still getting used to this title. I still felt like looking back over my shoulder anytime someone addressed me as such.

He made a mark on his board and continued the lecture. A tedious three hours followed that felt like six.

I was first out of the room as the inspector thanked us for our attendance and attention. I snatched a handout from him and cursed DCI Templeton under my breath. I would always blame her for my transition to CID, even if she had sort of saved my career by making it happen.

I returned to the main building, half using my memory and half my nose to find the cafeteria. The catering staff were just setting out ahead of lunchtime and so I had first dibs of what was on offer. Things hadn't improved much, I saw, as I looked across the various catering trays. Slices of beef swam in oily gravy, macaroni swam in an orange cheese sauce and pieces of broccoli could be seen in the vegetarian curry, swimming.

I elected a drier option. The lady in the white overalls never looking at me as she spooned and passed the plate under the heat lamps. I poured tea from an industrial-sized machine and took a table as far from the new recruits' section as was possible. They would soon swarm in like black locusts and devastate the stainless-steel pasture.

I dragged a fork through my stir-fried vegetables and noodles, chop suey they'd called it. Not fully convinced at my choice, I started instead on the chips and with a heavy breath I read through the handout I'd been given. I was on to the reverse side of the sheet when a voice interrupted.

'Carbs, with a side of carbs? No wonder you've put on weight since I last saw you.'

I lowered the sheet, and it took a second to recognise the young lady in the grey suit standing there, her arms folded and sporting a small smile.

'Rowan, bloody, Forbes. Holy shit. How are you?' I stood and stepped around the table. I pulled her into a firm hug. Her head only just reached my chin, despite some height in those well-polished shoes. 'What the hell are you doing here?'

I released her and returned to my seat. She took the one opposite.

She snatched up a chip and said: 'Same as you. Some detective you make. I was sat two rows behind you in class. I even tried to get your attention.'

I laughed, remembering someone clearing their throat. 'I almost didn't recognise you. Your hair.'

The last time I saw Rowan we were being shuttled out of a West Highland village in a convoy of detectives and senior officers. Her hair was short then – a pixie cut, I'd thought of it as. Now her auburn locks almost reached her shoulders.

'You made it, then, CID. I knew you would, just a matter of time. DC Forbes has a ring to it.'

'TDC Forbes. The *trainee* tag will have to remain for a year at least.'

A silence settled for a moment. I studied her face as she ate the chip in small bites. 'You're not in the least bit surprised to see me in a suit,' I said.

'Which means what?' She leant forward and after scrutinising my plate, selected another chip.

'Well, since I never once expressed an ambition towards CID, it means you already knew.'

She smiled while she chewed. 'Your observation skills are shit, but there's nothing wrong with your deduction. Course I knew.'

'How?'

'What do you mean, *how*? This is Police Scotland. A

tighter clique of gossiping fishwives you'll never meet. At the end of the summer your name was being passed around like a dirty secret, even as far as Dumbarton.'

'That so?'

'Yes, that is so.' She pointed the half-eaten chip at me. 'You're not going to ask what I heard, are you?'

'I honestly don't care.'

'Well, I know you and so I believe you there, but I'll tell you anyway.'

'You're going to tell me in the hope I'll clarify the true events. Like a "gossiping fishwife".'

She grinned again. 'There's various stories doing the rounds, but the one I like best suggests that you undermined Edinburgh CID by single-handedly solving the Star of the Sea killings. And that they were so embarrassed that they made you join to save face.'

The double killing of a ten-year-old boy and a Catholic priest earlier in the year had been given this title by the Edinburgh press, named after the church where the second body was found, and had been used extensively during the trial.

'Well?' Rowan urged.

I gave my head a micro-shake, hoping she'd get the message to shut up, but it was too late.

'I think single-handed is an exaggeration of the most perverse proportions.'

Rowan dropped what was left of her chip. Wiped her hand on her trousers and stood. Her face was flushed scarlet. I wanted to clap it was so delicious to see Rowan squirm with such embarrassment.

'I'm sorry, ma'am. I was just catching up with Don, with uh, Sergeant Colyear. We're, uh, old friends?' she said, looking at me to see if this was an appropriate description.

'Ma'am,' I said, trying not to laugh. 'This is—'

'TDC Forbes. Yes, I'm aware.'

I stopped short. Rowan was wearing her ID, but it had flipped at her chest, the details hidden. *How did she. . .?*

'Ma'am, I just wanted to say thank you for this opportunity. I aim to make the most of it. I won't let you down.'

My eyebrows furrowed. I was aware my mouth had fallen open again.

'I'm sure you'll do fine,' DCI Templeton said to Rowan before she turned to me, or rather my plate. 'Dear God, what the fuck are you eating?' I was about to attempt a description, maybe an explanation, when she continued, 'What class do you have this afternoon?'

'Uh, interview techniques, I think, why?'

'I'll find whoever is taking it and make your excuses. I need you back in the city.'

'What's happened?' My pulse quickened a little. I stood and brushed a crumb from my tie.

'Take your time, finish your – lunch?' she said with a hint of a sneer. 'It's a drugs death. I just need the usual boxes ticked.'

My pulse settled. 'Sure. I'll get on it,' I said, trying to sound even about it.

'Control will give you the details. I'll need the car key.' She held out her hand and when I didn't move for a moment she began curling and opening her fingers. I shook my head a little and fished the key from my inside pocket and handed it over.

'Uh. How am I supposed to . . . I mean, you want me to attend this call now?'

'After your meal, yes.'

'Yes, but if you have the car. How am I supposed—'

'Well, I'm making the leap that TDC Forbes drove here?'

Rowan and I exchanged a glance. Then Rowan answered. 'Yes, ma'am. Of course.'

'Great. I'll see you both at Gayfield when you're done, for an update.' She spoke the end of her sentence into her phone as she began checking it. I watched her cross the room as recruits busily started to pour through the door. Dressed head to toe in black, the murmuration ducked, weaved and separated around her. DCI Templeton failed to respond to the chorus of *ma'ams* as she passed them.

I turned to Rowan who had returned to my plate. She picked up on the expression on my face. 'I'll explain in the car,' she said. She stood and snatched up a small handful of chips. I followed her out of the room.

CHAPTER 3

No Suspicious Circumstances

'You work for the same Police Scotland as I work for, right?' I said as I poured myself into Rowan's car. A Fiat Spider, a modern incarnation of a classic little two-seater sports number.

'You mean this?' She tapped the dashboard affectionately. 'It wasn't as expensive as you think.' As she said this, she started it up and a throaty growl erupted below our bottoms as if the car itself was saying, *aye right*. 'Besides, everyone has their thing. Some go on long-haul holidays and others have five-bedroom detached homes. I stay in a crappy flat and haven't been abroad in three years. But I have this. She pumped the throttle and raised and dropped a single eyebrow to echo the rise and fall of the din. I laughed. I'd missed her and hadn't realised.

A few unapproving faces turned in our direction as Rowan exited the car park with a bit of a skid. I'd have told her to slow down, that the call we were attending wasn't urgent, but this was just the way she drove and she could no sooner change that than the sarcastic edge to her chat.

'Here's how my day is going,' I said, when Rowan reached the main road and I could hear myself talk once more. 'This morning I turned up at work and found out that my boss also had a module to attend at Tulliallan, so I had to endure uncomfortable chat and even more uncomfortable silence as I drove us both here in a pool car. I sat through an excruciatingly boring lecture and before I could manage more than a bite of my lunch, I find myself being driven, in excess of the speed limit, back to the city in Rowan Forbes' hairdresser's rocket and attending a call with this same person whom I haven't seen in, what? Nearly three years? And who, for all I knew, was busy advancing her career on the opposite coast of the country. My question to you, TDC Forbes, is, how the hell did my day take such a bizarre twist?' I turned in my seat to look at her.

'That's easy, you're just a lucky bastard.' I gave her a sardonic smile and waited for a proper answer. She turned her head to look at me and then back at the road. 'All right, where do I start. Well, first, I didn't know I'd be seeing you today, though I did know it was possible. You're aware I've been angling to get into CID for some time now?'

'Uh-huh.'

'Well, I always thought it'd be Glasgow I'd be going to if I ever did manage to find my way in, so for a while now I've been, I don't know, researching, I guess. And Kate

Templeton quickly became something of a hero of mine. That sounds stupid probably?'

'No, I think I get it. Strong, ambitious and takes no shit. Sounds familiar.'

'Right,' she said, smiling and gesturing at herself. Again, I chuckled. 'So, I've been pestering the shit out of her for months about getting a TDC position. We exchanged a few preliminary emails and this is all before the Star of the Sea killings. As soon as that kicks off it all goes quiet. Fair enough, right. Major inquiry and all that. Then finally she responds. She says she's looked at my file and even had a chat with my sergeant, all good stuff. Problem is, she's transferring over to E Division, but she'd be happy to speak to someone in Glasgow about getting me started.'

'And you think, why not follow over to the east?'

'Well, yeah. I've got no binds in the west, so why not.'

'And this has nothing to do with me?'

At this she raised both eyebrows and turned. 'Check the ego on DS Colyear. Remember this is a two-seater, I don't think there's room for the three of us.'

'I didn't mean it like that. It's just a . . . breathtaking coincidence. I still can't believe we're heading to a call together.'

'Coincidence, maybe, but *you're* the common denominator here.'

'How do you mean?' I braced so I didn't fall into her as she took a left turn too quickly.

'Rumour has it—'

'Ugh, enough with the rumours.'

'*Rumour has it*, that Kate stayed in Edinburgh to keep an eye on you. That she doesn't trust you. If that's true, then it's all your fault we're working together again. Well?'

'Well what?'

'Is it true?'

'Don't be ridiculous,' I said, but only after I'd laid the question next to certain insecurities I'd had since trading the uniform for a suit.

'You hesitated. Come on, spill. It's me.' She knocked my elbow with her own.

I tutted and voiced the thought: 'The . . . possibility had occurred to me; but to give it oxygen puts me at risk of succumbing to paranoia or indulging in arrogance. I'm sure she's in Edinburgh because it's exactly where she wants to be, nothing more.'

'Buuut?'

'Buuut, she has been micro-managing me like you wouldn't believe. I haven't seen her do it with anyone else. She sits on my shoulder like a bad conscience. Also, I'm surprised she's allowing us to work together. For all intents and purposes, I'm also a TDC. You should see the cases I've been assigned.'

'Basic stuff?'

'Put it this way, I've seen more action when I was working in the Community department. Speaking of, hold on.'

We were reaching the outskirts of the city and I hadn't yet accepted the incident. I called the control room and assigned us both to what I was told was a sudden death in a homeless hostel, near to the shore.

'Shopliftings, minor assaults, and these.'

'What?'

'The cases I'm being assigned. A spate of thefts, a couple of set-to's outside of nightclubs, and these sudden deaths that are just an exercise in bureaucracy. That's what I've got to show for my first couple of months in CID.' I fished my notebook out of my jacket pocket and scored through Tulliallan training 9 a.m. to 5 p.m.

'You have to start somewhere, I guess. But to assign a DS to that stuff, well, I get your point. Maybe after you complete the detective course, she'll give you a longer leash?'

'We'll see. Meantime, this is my third drugs death this month. They're beyond tedious.'

Rowan gave the steering wheel a small slap as we hit city traffic, she'd be forced to drive like a human the rest of the way to Leith. 'I thought the detective course was all online these days,' she said after a bit of a silence I was beginning to enjoy.

'I thought so too, especially in a time of harsh budget cuts, but apparently they're trialling returning the course back to the training college. Something about networking and encouraging force-wide unanimity. Still too many older cops doing things the way their old force used to.' It had been eight years since the amalgamation of the police forces across Scotland to form a single entity, but it would be at least another eight before procedures were fully unified. You didn't have to travel far to find cops who just didn't see the point in reinventing the wheel, when it had turned well enough for them for a long time before they changed the logo on the uniforms.

Rowan handed me her phone as we reached London Road. Traffic was heavy, but the lane turning left onto Easter Road was at least moving. 'Put the address in. This is about as close to Leith as I've ever been.'

'We're in *your* car. We'll stop at Leith Station and walk.'

Rowan screwed up her face. 'I thought I was going to be sat in classroom all day, I'm wearing heels. I'm walking no place.'

I laughed. 'Fine, but we'll pick up a pool car.'

'Ach, nonsense. We're driving now and uniform will already be wondering where the hell we are.'

'This isn't *Starsky and Hutch*. You can't go around solving crimes in your own cool car,' I said, but the angle of Rowan's eyebrows told me my reference did not compute. 'Fine, it's your insurance.'

There was a marked Transit parked outside the four-storey building on Parliament Street. It was a fairly unassuming place. Large, as it took up the entire block, but if you weren't looking for it, you'd walk past without registering.

Men, who might be residents of the hostel, lingered and smoked on the pavement, their hands tucked under the cuffs of their hoodies against the cold wind that whipped October leaves in squally gusts. We parked further down the street. Two teenagers eyed us, our warrant cards and the car as the Fiat chirped to confirm it was locked. Rowan glowered at them until they were out of sight.

The wind buffeted and I buttoned my suit jacket against it. I was struck again, as I had been on multiple occasions in the past few weeks, of how utterly naked I felt without my body armour and assorted accoutrements. I kept a set of handcuffs within the jacket, but they did little to allay the sense of vulnerability.

The bored-looking uniformed officer at the door of the building nodded, muttering 'second floor' as we passed.

We entered into a reception area, something inserted in modern times to make the place secure. A desk with a small office sat between the front door and a security door giving access to the hostel proper. The receptionist, a lady in her early thirties, was having an animated conversation with a man it became clear was a resident. He was being denied entry, not only because of why we were there, but because he was clearly drunk.

'Come back tonight, Charlie,' the lady was saying. 'If you've sobered up a bit. You know the rules fine well.'

The conversation continued for a short time, and I was just wondering whether to get involved when she folded her arms and shook her head at him. The conversation was over as far as she was concerned and as it turned out, he knew it too. He trudged past us back out of the building, a sour smell of wine followed him.

'Sorry to keep you,' the lady said, turning her attention to us. 'He's a chancer, but he's harmless. But you're here about poor Mr Salisbury. I'll take you up. I'm Annie, day supervisor.' She unlocked the office door and led us into the building.

'This happens often? The deaths?'

'Often enough. They're not allowed to use in the rooms, but we're not about to cavity-search residents.' Her tone was in no way disrespectful, but it was nonchalant, considering we were here about a body.

'Did you find him?' Rowan asked as we began climbing the stairs.

'I did, this morning. Rooms need to be vacated by 9 a.m. His door was still locked. When there was no answer, myself and Tony opened the door and found him there. I'm afraid we had to move him. He was lying against the door.'

'Door was locked from the inside? And the room's on the second floor?' I asked.

'That's right.'

I exchanged a look with Rowan, one that said nothing for us here.

'We'll need to get a statement,' Rowan said. 'From Tony too, he's your colleague?'

'He is. You can come find us in the office when you're ready. I'll put some tea on.'

When we reached the second floor, Annie pointed down the corridor to our left, though she needn't have. The other uniformed officer guarding the room was a decent clue. We stepped up to the room.

'Thanks for covering. We can take it from here,' I told the PC.

'I have a list of everyone who's been in,' she said.

'Great, could you photocopy your notebook and send the pages to Gayfield?' I said.

She agreed and left us to it.

'Shit,' I said, patting at my pockets.

'What?'

'No gloves.'

Rowan rolled her eyes and dug into the pocket of her

jacket. 'I've only the one pair, so we'll have to do this one-handed.'

'Thanks. In my defence, I thought I was only going to be shuffling paper all day.' I pulled on one of the gloves. My hand felt like it had been shrink-wrapped; I held it up to her. The cuff of the glove barely made it past the base of my thumb. I had a sudden image of O.J. in the dock.

Rowan laughed and covered her mouth with her own gloved hand, hers fitting neatly. 'I steal these every time I go to the hospital. We only have mediums, but they have a choice of sizes.'

'Ready?' I said.

She nodded, taking a breath as she did.

I turned the handle and pushed the door. The swing was interrupted about three-quarters of the way by striking a foot.

I stepped into the room by stepping over Mr Salisbury. He lay flat out. His shirt was pulled open and sticky connectors were attached to his chest where paramedics had attended earlier to confirm what was blatantly obvious. Those who had been in the room before us had done well to disturb him as little as possible, a fact confirmed by the needle still hanging from the skin in the bend in his left arm below a band of rubber tubing wrapped around his bicep. A trail of blood ran modestly from the needle down his forearm. Small smears of it painted the section of floor around him where he'd moved away from the door.

'What is that smell?' Rowan said, walking around me.

'I think Mr Salisbury may have released his bowels at

some point in his final ride of the dragon.' The stench of shit hung heavy in the air. I opened the window, secure in the fact that this was no crime scene, just an ignominious end to a miserable life.

'How old do you think he is, was?' said Rowan, she was standing above him, her nostrils gripped.

I took a good look at the lad. His arms first, they demanded attention. The one he'd injected into sported a scattering of needle marks and bruising ranging from midnight plum to faded amber. The other had similar marks, though it was hard to see past a sore on his forearm that dug perhaps half an inch into his flesh. Even now it looked angry and wet. His face was drawn, accentuated by his open jaw. The teeth within were broken and filthy. 'In his twenties, I think, though hard to be specific. We'll see what info the desk have for him,' I said.

'Here,' said Rowan. She'd moved away from the body and was riffling through a backpack she'd found by the bed. She removed a canvas Adidas wallet and pulled something from it. 'Provisional licence. Mark Salisbury, his date of birth makes him . . . twenty-five, no twenty-six. Shit, he could be forty-six.'

'Come on, let's get this over with.'

'What?' Rowan was looking at me as if I'd suggested she give him a cuddle.

'You know the score. We need to check the body. His back, at least. The gaffers don't like it if you call in an accidental drugs death and they find a knife in his heart when he goes for a PM.'

* * *

36

A box-ticking hour passed with SOCO attending to do their thing and then the morticians for the body. We noted statements while they worked, which left only one last job for the day. Save the worst for last.

A PNC check of Mark Salisbury showed a history of petty criminality, though only one small jail sentence. He spent three weeks, probably gripping his knees in his cell dealing with withdrawal symptoms, at HMP Edinburgh for unpaid fines, though I didn't know anyone who used its official name. To everyone the prison was simply *Saughton*, named after the corner of town in which it sat. Other than this, there was nothing too sinister about Salisbury. Just a familiar pattern of sustaining a heavy habit.

When we returned to the car, daylight was fading and the air temperature falling. I was busy updating control as I sat in the passenger seat. I paused my short report as Rowan hissed: 'Fuckers.' For a moment I didn't see what she was so irked at and then I did. Two extremely well-baked globs of spit were oozing south down the windshield. Those responsible had really worked their noses and throats to produce these prize horrors.

'I told you—'

'Yeah, yeah, Scratchy and Hutch or whatever.' She held the washer on until it wheezed dry.

Control were running a check for me on the phone. Various addresses were held over the ten-or-so-year story that could be surmised from the entries under his name and date of birth. We were heading to the first that had been recorded, an assumption that had been vindicated by a voter's roll check that confirmed the Salisburys still lived there.

The Spinney was a cul-de-sac in the Gilmerton area of town. Pairs of semi-detached homes in a stretched circle in an area some might consider a little rough, but the street was perfectly quiet and a million miles from the squalid room in which the boy who grew up here took his last breath.

Two boys bouncing a ball at the kerbside stopped to watch us trundle by, enviously eyeing Rowan's pride and joy.

'Twenty-two. This is it. Have you done this before?' I asked.

Rowan's face dropped. 'Once, and it was awful. Come on, Sarge, if you do it, I'll do all your paperwork for a month.'

'Nope, you're up, Forbes.'

'Two months.'

'Come on.'

'A year,' she called as I hauled myself out of her car. I could hear a slap of her hand against the dashboard.

'Just be succinct, professional.'

'Succinct, professional,' Rowan was muttering as I pressed the doorbell.

The door was answered by a man in his fifties or early sixties. His face was paint-flecked as were his trousers, the kind that have more pockets than any single piece of clothing ought to. Various tools poked out from here and there.

'Mr Salisbury?'

'Uh-huh,' he replied to Rowan. He squinted at her ID and his face dropped.

'You're here about our Mark? You better come in.' He looked around the street before closing the door and leading us through to the kitchen where Mrs Salisbury, I assumed, was loading a dishwasher. She smiled as she turned and then withdrew it when she clocked the warrant cards.

'What now?' She clutched the cup she was holding like she might launch it at us.

'Maybe we could sit down for a minute,' I said.

'What's the point?' Mr Salisbury said. 'There's nothing you can say will shock us any more when it comes to Mark.' He took the cup from his wife. 'What is it this time? Thieving, I suppose? Whatever it is, he can stay in jail and deal with it himself. We're not bailing him out any more. That's right, isn't it, love?'

Mrs Salisbury nodded. 'We talked about it and aye, it's tough love from now on. He won't learn otherwise. So, where is he?'

'He's, uh. Well . . . on his way to the morgue,' said Rowan.

The cup crashed to the kitchen floor so that Mr Salisbury could dash to catch his wife.

'Jesus,' I breathed. Succinct she was, but she could have been a little less so.

A painful half hour followed with Rowan backtracking and apologising at the end of every sentence. She explained that he'd died of an apparent overdose, but that a post-mortem would be required to confirm and his lab-work might take a week, perhaps ten days to complete. Mrs Salisbury sat on the living room sofa staring out into middle distance. Mark's dad nodded along to the information but was likely taking in as much as his wife. I gave my card, knowing that questions would start to occur to them in a day or two and we left.

Rowan stopped when we got to the car. 'I fucked that up,' she said.

My instinct was to soften it a bit, but it's not what she would have wanted.

'Maybe think about how you'd want to receive that kind of information next time,' I said. She unlocked the car, but checked her phone before she climbed in. 'Shit,' she said.

'What?'

'Check your phone. Do you have the same thing?'

I fished mine from my pocket. 'Shit,' I echoed. A dozen or so missed calls from Kate Templeton. I rang back immediately.

'Ma'am, it's DS—'

'I know who it is. Where the fuck have you been?'

'Ma'am, sorry, we were delivering a death message.'

'Get your arse back to the office. No, in fact head to the Royal Infirmary. I'll see you there.'

CHAPTER 4

Possession

Wee Malky felt a knock on his elbow. He'd been a million miles away, thinking about dinner, one of those fat haggis burritos from Los Cardos on the way home, maybe. Not maybe – now that it was in his head, it wasn't going to be denied.

'Awrite,' the guy said, gently dancing, one foot to the other, his jaw pounding a piece of gum. He was talking to Malky, of course, but his eyes were everywhere else.

'Many?'

'Three.'

Malky deftly palmed three wraps from his right coat pocket, shifted them into his left hand and into the opposing pocket. The guy, he didn't know his name, but a regular enough customer, reached in when Malky removed his hand.

'Cheers.'

'Aye.'

Malky casually looked around, though there was little need. He couldn't be in a more public place, at least not in this city, but hiding in plain sight had worked for him for years now. He walked the short distance to the public telephone box. Closed the door behind him and lifted the receiver. It never failed to surprise him that there was a dial tone. Who used public telephone boxes any more, at least for the purpose for which they were actually designed? Surely these days someone squeezing themselves into one of these boxes was far more likely to take a piss than a call? A theory supported by the smell rising from the booth floor.

Maintaining the pretence of a conversation, Malky reached down into his stowed rucksack and replenished the sold packets, examining the roll of cash left by the last customer. There was little need to check it. If he'd been short-changed the guy could no longer use his services and junkies, the liars, thieves and frauds they may be, were actually the most loyal of clientele. *Don't fuck with your supply chain.* He left the booth then with his full quota restored, five wraps. Enough for the vast majority of transactions and few enough to ensure a possession charge as opposed to supply, if the pigs swiped him. He returned to his spot.

His day was going well. He'd shifted three hundred quid's worth in little more than three hours. A steady drizzle was falling and threatening to turn to proper rain. Another five or six and he'd pack up early.

He stood in the doorway of the shoe shop, though he'd have to move soon. The art of invisibility was not standing still for too long. A random guy staying out of the rain for a few minutes goes unnoticed, an hour though draws the attention of staff. Besides, any doorway was fine. His clientele knew he would be somewhere in this short stretch of Frederick Street, between Princes Street and George Street. He liked this patch, the castle in full view and the foreign girls stopping to get a picture could be ogled.

Shit, he thought as someone caught his eye from across the street. *Was he fucking waving? And clearly off his tits.*

A taxi blared its horn as Dingo stepped, or rather stumbled into the road. 'Arsehole!' the driver yelled as he pulled around the space cadet who was making a beeline for Malky.

He tripped on the kerb on Malky's side, but through some miracle kept his feet. 'Awrite, man. How's it goin'?'

'Dingo, what's up?'

'Nuttin, nuttin, man. Just was wonderin' like—'

'Sorry, Dingo, no can do.' The stench from him was shocking. Sweat, cheap wine, and his breath as he leant in to keep their conversation private, was like garbage from a fish restaurant sitting in the sun for a month. Malky tried to get around him, but he was penned into the shoe shop entrance.

'Just a couple tae next week. You know I'm good fur it, man.'

'I don't do tick, Dingo. You know—'

'For punters. For punters you don't,' he almost yelled. Eyes flicked in their direction. Dingo lowered his voice. 'But I'm a mate, eh? You can do it fur a mate, eh?'

Back in the day Dean Gordon was the type of guy who demanded your respect. Tall and solid, he was once even a bit of a star at the local boxing club and always unpredictable, hence the wild-dog bastardisation of his name. Until he found heroin. There's a fine tipping point, when it came to smack, about which side is in control, user or needle. In the ring, Dingo was formidable, by all accounts – Malky had never seen him box – but in the battle with the brown, he stood no chance. 'Dingo, if I do it for you, word gets out and suddenly I'm chasin' debts and that's no what—'

'You, fuck off.'

The interrupting voice ended the conversation which might have been a blessing, except that . . . 'Fuck,' Malky breathed. The two men who had appeared out of nowhere were clearly plain-clothes cops. Were they watching him when he last went to his rucksack?

'I said FUCK OFF,' the guy in the Brown Leather Jacket repeated, this time with emphasis and right in Dingo's face.

'Right, right, aye. Catch you later, Malky.' For a second it looked like Dingo might stand his ground; of course, he was still as tall as ever he was, but almost all that teenage muscle he used to throw with accurate violence in the ring was gone, leaving a gangly shadow. His eyes seemed to focus and as wasted as he was, some primordial survival instinct sobered him sufficiently.

'Aye, see you, Dingo.'

There was a moment of peace as the three men involved in this little dance waited for the fourth to shuffle out of sight. Malky knew the steps well enough. A car, or a cell van would appear in a minute and then there would be a cursory search, little more than pocket emptying and then it's cuffs on, *keep your fuckin' hands where I can see them* and off to the cop shop for the unsavoury part of the afternoon. *Turn around and grab your ankles, Malky.* 'Fuck,' he breathed again. There really is nothing quite like being told to spread your arse cheeks to put you off a haggis burrito. He was *this* close to packing up for the day. 'So where to, boys? St Leonard's? No, it'll be Gayfield, right?'

The two guys exchanged a look. One smirked. What was that about?

The car arrived, just as it always did. Not a marked car, though. It was usually a marked car. This was a black . . . it was a black Range Rover. What the. . .?

'Move.'

The rear door was pulled open by Brown Leather Jacket and Malky was tossed, like a toddler being removed from the scene of a tantrum, onto the back seat.

By the time he sat himself upright, he'd deciphered what should have been obvious from the beginning. 'You're no police,' he said.

'You're a sharp one,' the driver said. An English accent. His blue eyes switched in the rear-view mirror from him to the road and back. 'Sharp is good. It might save you from a fate worse than jail, Malky.' The back of his bald head turned left and right as he drove the Range Rover hard, up and over George Street towards Queen Street. The man sitting silently in the front passenger seat was rectangular, making this huge car look small.

'What's this about?' Malky said to the bald head. He turned to the guy in the Brown Leather Jacket sat next to him on the back seat when no response came. This guy was handsome, like movie handsome. The dark hair and stubble were carefully kept. Even the paper stiches above his eye just made him all the more screen-star-ish.

'Information, Malky,' this guy said. He slid along the seat and put an arm around his shoulders. His accent was also English. 'You answer a few questions and we drop you off safe and sound. That is if the answers are correct. Think of it like a game show. You'll even get a cash bonus if you win.'

'Why me? And how do you know my name?'

'You're a filthy little drug dealer, *Malky*,' the driver said, lingering on his name. 'Now don't take that bad, there's nothing wrong with it. Some of my best friends are filthy little drug dealers, Malky.'

Malky's hand drifted to the pocket and the five wraps.

The arm around his shoulder hugged him. Brown Leather Jacket began patting his shoulder. 'We don't want your drugs, mate. We want *our* drugs.'

'I-I don't have—'

'We know that. That's why we're only talking and why you're still breathing. With the chance to walk away with a large amount of cash, I should remind you.'

Malky looked at the hand tapping his shoulder and up into the handsome face. 'Cash? What are we talking?'

'Oh, I don't know. That depends on the quality of the answer. But I think we could stretch to, what, five grand, for the good stuff.'

Five grand. The words rang around his head. 'And what if I *can't* help?'

'You mean the booby prize? Oh, you don't want the booby prize.' Brown Leather Jacket leant forward and slapped the shoulder of the front seat passenger, drawing a small, gruff laugh from the faceless bear. 'Just do your best, you'll be fine.'

Malky took a quick look out of the window. They were approaching the Picardy Place roundabout. They'd have to stop for sure. He could try the handle, make a run for it? But if he pulled and the door stayed shut, that would probably be the end of the game. Besides, they knew his name. And five grand? What choice did he have? 'What do you want to know?'

'Good lad,' the driver said, then he handed back over to Brown Leather Jacket.

'What do you know about an enormous amount of product appearing in town?'

'Product?'

'Smack, Malky. A huge dump of smack. Maybe you've been offered a large amount for a suspiciously low price?'

Malky could feel his head shaking in negative response. He thought hard, but had to tell the truth. 'Huge amount? No. Sorry, I–I've not heard anything.'

Brown Leather Jacket sucked air through his teeth. 'That's a wrong answer, Malky.' The guy in the front passenger seat made a blare sound like from a TV game show then laughed. 'Don't let there be another, now.'

'I'm sorry. I really haven't heard anything.'

The car moved forward into the roundabout on the

inside lane. The driver pushed through a red light and they were back on George Street.

'Now, what can you tell me about a lad with a stutter?'

The way Brown Leather Jacket said 'stutter' helped Malky place the accent. He sounded like Steven Gerrard and Paul McCartney. Liverpool.

'A stutter?'

'Did *I* fucking stutter? Yes, a stutter. Young lad, well built, with a fucking stutter.'

Fuck, Malky had no idea. A stutter? Like a stammer? *Fuck*. 'I, ah. Look, I'm not sure. I, uh—'

'If you don't know, you don't know, Malky. It's all right,' the driver cut in.

'Really?'

'Noooo. No, no, no. That puts you in serious trouble, my little junkie supplier.' The driver slapped the shoulder of his front seat passenger with the back of his fingers. The bear took his cue and turned in his seat. His head was as rectangular as the rest of him. He grinned at Malky with absolutely no humour whatsoever.

'Look. I can help. Large amount of smack, uh, product. Kid with a stutter. I can find out. Really. I have, you know, connections. Give me a few days, I'll find out. I swear.'

There was a silence, or would have been if the sound of the Range Rover's engine wasn't roaring.

'What do you think? Can we trust little Malky here to come good, or do we just rip his arms off now and save ourselves the hassle?' the driver asked the other two.

'I like him. Look at this little face. How can you dislike a face like that?' Brown Leather Jacket was squeezing

Malky's cheeks together between his teeth, not gently. Malky didn't resist.

'All right. You have two days. If I have to come searching for you, the deal's off. You'll be here, in your grubby little spot as usual. And don't let me down, *Malky*,' the driver said as he pulled the car over and came to a sudden stop that almost had Malky sliding into the front seats.

Brown Leather Jacket reached across Malky and pulled the door handle. The door wasn't locked, after all. It was pushed wide.

'And the cash. I still get the cash if I get the info?'

'Don't push it, Malky. Just do a good job and we'll see.' And with that Malky was himself pushed. He rolled onto the pavement outside the shoe shop. By the time he got to his feet the Range Rover was turning back onto George Street.

The guy stood, one hand on his chin, the other supporting the opposite elbow as he eyed the package on the fold-out table, still speckled and marked from wallpaper paste and emulsion, now reutilised for a bit of business. The guy was making a show of his indecision now, a counteroffer was on its way, he sensed their desperation. Dillon had never been involved in a . . . transaction before, but even he saw it coming.

'I'll take a quarter kilo, but I'm no payin' a penny over four.' He went into his pocket and produced a serious pile of cash. He removed the elastic band and began counting out fifty-pound notes next to the half kilo of wrapped smack they'd separated for this sale. His cohort, a short but bullish man in a tight black T-shirt, stared into his phone next to the Porsche Cayenne they'd rolled up in. The phone lit up his face in the evening gloom.

'Nah, fuck that. I checked. Smack goes for twice that,' said Tavish.

'Well, I don't know you from Adam, pal, and I don't know what the quality is like. So, take it or leave it.'

This guy, 'Call him Kelty' as the contact of a contact of Tavish had advised, was holding all the cards. A dealer from Fife who they'd been promised was a real player and so a chance to shift a serious amount of the stash. The half kilo was supposed to be for display purposes only and the quarter kilo he was interested in was laughably short of the twenty Tavish had insisted was a minimum to expect. Just under three million, he calculated the entire score at the going rate. This was the third sale and even if it was concluded successfully, they'd still be sitting with more than eighty-four of the eighty-five kilos they'd swiped.

'Naw, at least six. I'll take six for it, but no four – fuck, you kidding?' Tavish stood, arms folded, in the doorway of the lock-up on Orchard Brae, a long way from home, but perhaps that was no bad thing. It had been rented from persons unknown by Dillon and Davie's father. However, since the day Dad had managed to clip the verge on the A71, miraculously missing oncoming traffic as his van spun across the carriageway and slammed into a farmer's wall (while four times over the legal limit), killing him instantly thanks to the seat belt he never once wore, it had been theirs. At least, until whoever owned it realised rent was no longer being paid and came to change the locks. But since Dillon had been ten when this had happened, he doubted they were going to have to give it up any time soon.

'Have it your way,' Kelty said. He gathered together the notes he'd laid out like playing cards and gave a small whistle out the side of his mouth. 'We're out of here,' he said, prompting a nod from the driver, his face suddenly disappearing as he switched off the phone.

'Wait, wait. All right, look. Since it's our first . . . interaction, I'll let you have it for five, but it'll be six next time when you come back for a lot more. And you will be back for more, it's good shit. Go ahead and test it.'

Kelty laughed. 'You watch too much television, pal. You think I walk around with a wee science kit that tells me your shit is what you say it is? Or maybe I rub some on my gums? This is smack and I'll take a quarter kilo of it for four thousand. And if I do come back for more, the price will be the same. What'll it be?'

'A sale's a sale, Tavish,' Davie said. He sealed up the remainder of the stuff in its plastic and placed it back into the pile at the rear of the garage, covered by a tarp.

There was no response from Tavish. He stared out from the lock-up into the now darkness drawing from his cigarette and blowing out into the cold.

Sal placed a hand on his shoulder. 'Davie's right. It's something.'

'It's fuck all,' Tavish said and knocked her arm away.

'At this rate we'll be stuck with this sh-shit for years,' Dillon said and regretted it almost instantly.

'You shut your mouth, you ungrateful little prick.' Sal's hand was back on Tavish's shoulder, this time drawing him back from Dillon. 'What are you doin' to shift this lot? Huh? What am I even paying you for? To stand in the background and make stupid fucking comments?'

'Tavish, leave it,' said Davie.

'And you. What the fuck are you doin' for your quarter? I'm the one setting up the deals, I'm taking all the fucking risks.'

'Risks?' Davie was on his feet now, not exactly squaring up to Tavish, but the chest was pushed out. All posturing of course; they would never come to blows. Tavish was shorter than Davie and Dillon by an inch or so and inferior physically to both of them too, but everyone present was well aware that it was not Tavish's physique that made him dangerous, it was his ambivalence to violence. Dillon had been in plenty of scraps in his life, but to punch another in the face was always adrenalin inducing, sickeningly so. Not to the likes of Tavish, who might beat a man into the hospital for a wrong look in the pub as soon as shake his hand. It was nothing to him. Tavish was a class A prick – however, Dillon, Davie and Sal were the only people close to him in the whole world, he'd never endanger that by letting his temper spill over entirely. They'd grown up in the same crappy housing estate and were, for all intents and purposes, family, and like family, you didn't get to choose. 'There's a fuckload of smack in *my* garage, Tavish. If anyone of these people you're selling to squeals to the police, I'm the one going down. Don't you fucking talk to me about risks.'

'Fuck this,' Tavish said, flicking his fag at Davie's feet and turning on his heels. Sal was again swatted off.

They watched him walk off into the dark of the evening, saying nothing until he was out of earshot. Sal turned to Davie, placing her arms around his neck and rolling her eyes. 'I'll talk to him,' she said and kissed the corner of his mouth. She stepped out of the garage, pulling her long blonde hair into a ponytail, securing it with a band from her wrist.

'Help me with this.' Dillon gestured at the opposite end of the blue tarp. Davie helped to pull the thing tight around the brown bricks sitting on the pallet, securing it with a bungee cord. They then started replacing pieces of old furniture and Dad's old gardening equipment in front of it. Stuff they should have tossed years ago, but it had some sentimental value and neither brother, Dillon knew, wanted to be the one to suggest it. It was how Dad had made a living, or scratching something close to it, and pretty much all he'd left behind, except for the CDs, early nineties rock that Davie cherished and Dillon had no interest in. Dad had no training or qualifications in gardening or horticulture, he just bought a van one day and some tools and Marshall Landscaping was born, though never announced to HMRC, of course. It was a move necessitated by mum's death. She'd worked two different checkout jobs after Dad had lost his with a security firm. They were never told why, but it probably had much to do with the faint smell of alcohol that never left him. Mum's illness was mercifully short. The cancer had spread wide before she'd even seen a doctor and

Dad was left to figure things out. Dillon wondered if the industrial-sized strimmer would even work these days as he laid it against the tarp. A token gesture if anyone came for this stuff, but it was the best they could do.

'I don't l-like it.'

'Don't start. I'm not in the mood.'

'Davie, we need to t-talk about it. This is p-prison if we get caught and the fucking morgue if whoever we stole this from ever f-f-finds us.' Dillon made a fist and beat it against his thigh. His stammer was normally pretty mild. He'd worked hard in primary school with a speech therapist, doing the exercises, and it had brought what felt like a wild animal in his mouth largely under control, but in times of stress or anger, it slipped its tether and ran away from him.

'You think I don't know? I haven't slept since that night. Every time I hear a sound in the flat at night, I'm convincing myself it's either the cops or that cunt in the leather coat coming for us. I've barely slept a wink in weeks,' Davie said. He moved to the front of the garage and began flicking off lights.

'You've no slept in weeks because you're up all night shagging.' Dillon's brother turned to look at him with an expression of mock shock. 'Seriously, Davie, the walls are thin and Sal's a sc-screamer.' Dillon gestured over his shoulder at Sal who was at the end of the row of garages with her hand again on Tavish's shoulder. The boys looked at one another and burst into laughter.

'What?' Sal said.

CHAPTER 5

Results

Edinburgh's Royal Infirmary was a maze of modern buildings. It was dark as we turned off Dalkeith Road into the complex in Little France. Even at twenty miles per hour, the signs lit up by the headlights, offering some sense to the place, came too quickly. In the end Rowan selected a car park at random, figuring it would be easier to find this lab on foot.

The theory was sound enough, but proven false by half a dozen bemused faces when asked for directions. In the end we were sent to a thoroughfare in the main building. Bleary-eyed medics in scrubs hurried around. People in pyjamas and coats wandered slowly towards the exits, sparking up cigarettes before they'd quite made it outside. In the middle of this a large, round desk was manned like the hub of a spacecraft by a solitary staff member who juggled questions from concerned relatives, ringing phones and his radio, crackling on the desk in front of him.

We stood, waiting, for a few minutes, but when an elderly man in his dressing gown cut in front of us, I leant past him and presented my warrant card to the space captain.

'Pathology lab. Doctor Patience,' I said, pondering the irony.

Like asking a local in a European village on holiday, he gave us overly complicated, almost unintelligible directions, but somehow they were enough to find us in a lower level corridor, silent but for Rowan's heels clicking like a metronome. The light here was different, more subdued than the floors above, or perhaps that's just how it seemed.

We were in the mortuary section. Rowan pushed up into her toes to peer through every door we passed.

'You're hoping to see bodies?'

'Well I don't know if "hope" is the right word, but you can't blame me for being curious.'

'You're a ghoul.'

'I'm a dedicated detective who's so far led a sheltered career.'

'CID out in Dumbarton? You must have had some interesting cases?'

'Shoplifters, mainly. Serial shoplifters, but yes, that's about it. I did work a serious assault. Guy lost an eye in a barfight, but I was only doing productions. No interviews. I didn't even get to see the cyclops.'

'And now you've hit the big time, working drugs deaths with me. Sounds like you walked under a ladder, tripped and fell through a mirror shop.'

'Excuse me,' a voice said from behind us. We turned to see a woman in her twenties, carrying her coat and hurrying along the corridor towards us. 'You wouldn't happen to know where I can find Dr Patience would you?'

'Join the search party, we're going to the same place,' Rowan said and introduced us both.

'I'm Eileen McLellan, fiscal depute. I've never been sent to anything like this before. I'm not really sure what to expect.'

I stopped dead and looked at her. 'You're from the fiscal's office?' She nodded. 'What did they tell you? What are we doing here?'

Her eyes narrowed and her mouth pursed as she formulated a response but another voice, this time from the opposite end of the corridor, cut her off.

'About bloody time. Get your arses in here.' Kate stood, gesturing at us to hurry up. Though not directed at her, Eileen rushed along beside us like chided schoolchildren.

We followed her into a room that was a sort of antechamber for labs further on to the left. Signs warned to go no further without appropriate lab protective gear, but our route took us right to an office, which was home to around a dozen desks, but which was empty except for two people at the far end sitting at a screen.

'Grab a chair,' Kate said, then suddenly clocked Eileen at the back of us. 'I don't know you.'

'Ah, no. I'm from the fiscal's office. I'll be honest, I'm not sure what I should be doing,' Eileen said. Despite the poor light in this place, she was clearly red-faced and flustered.

'You're a depute?' Eileen nodded. 'Just graduated, new to the job?' She nodded again. For a moment I thought Kate might send her back out the door, but instead her tone softened. 'That's okay. Take a seat, take notes and pass on what you learn here to your boss, okay?'

'Yes. Thank you.'

The two women in front of the computer monitor had been muttering to themselves the whole time we had entered and formed a semicircle around them with our chairs. At last, the older of the two exchanged a nod with Kate and she turned and smiled at us collectively.

'Thank you for coming in this evening. My name is Holly Patience. I'm a senior clinical scientist here at the Royal. We're here to chat about a particular sample that was tested today. A blood sample collected during the autopsy of a young male; toxicology requested by the investigating officer . . .' She looked through a pad of paper she lifted from the desk. 'Sergeant D. Colyear?' She looked at Rowan and me. I nodded. 'The sample was run by my colleague here. It's my job to sign off all samples that come through my lab and when this particular result was put on my desk, I had to assume there had been a mistake, even though that would be very unlike Anne here.' The ladies smiled at one another. 'I asked that the sample be run again and when the result confirmed the findings of the first, it was time to call you in.' Dr Patience now addressed me. 'This was a routine drugs death?'

'Sorry, Doctor, I'm still playing catch up. Which O-D was this?'

'Yes, sorry. The deceased's name was Mariusz Wozniak?' Dr Patience said, taking care with the pronunciation.

'Yes. Four or five weeks ago, I think?' The lad was originally from Poland, but had been working in Edinburgh for over eight years. According to his flatmate, he'd had an intravenous habit for as long as he'd known him, but he was functional with it. Somehow. Never missed a day of work. 'Twenty-nine-year-old, if I remember right. Overdosed in his own flat. No suspicious circumstances. Unless you're about to tell me otherwise, of course.' It had been the first case I'd been assigned since moving from uniform into CID and it had set the trend since.

'Well, that depends on how you interpret these results. That's where my job begins and ends.'

'What exactly are we looking at, Doctor?' Kate said, though not impatiently.

'Well, the overdose is confirmed. No argument there. It's just that the amount of heroin in his system was beyond anything I've ever seen. And if you're telling me he was a functional user, that would suggest at a relatively low dose when he used?' I looked at Kate and we both nodded; it was a reasonable assumption. A phone on a nearby desk began to ring. Anne wheeled herself over to it and answered in a whisper to allow us to continue. 'I've seen plenty of overdose samples come in, many from heavy users, and this is way beyond that. This young man either made a mistake or was fully intending to take his own life. That is, if you're confirming someone didn't do this to him?'

'No, there's no evidence to suggest he didn't inject himself.'

'The other possibility is the heroin itself. Was there a sample of it when you attended the scene?'

I had to think about it. There had been a few of these and they had a tendency of bleeding into one another, but, 'No. No drugs on him or in the flat. He used whatever he'd brought home with him.'

Dr Patience now turned to Kate. 'Have there been further deaths in recent weeks?'

'Well, yes. But these things are pretty common.' She looked at me. 'You've been dealing with these. How many?'

'We had our fourth today, since I started, ma'am.'

'Which is what time period?' Dr Patience asked.

'Six weeks or so,' I said.

'And is that figure high, would you say?'

I had to look to Kate, I wasn't sure.

'Maybe. I mean it might just be a bad month. I couldn't tell you how many drugs deaths we look at each month, but—'

'Thirteen hundred a year. Across Scotland. Highest rate in Europe, unfortunately. So, four in Edinburgh might not mean anything.' Dr Patience removed her glasses and rubbed at her eyes.

'What are you worried about, exactly?' I said.

'Sorry to interrupt,' Anne said. She held the phone clutched to her chest. She leant into Dr Patience's ear and they exchanged murmured words. The look on both of their faces was grim when they returned their eyes to us.

'When the result we've been discussing came in, I went ahead to look and see if you'd submitted any other samples lately. We ran the bloodwork of a case from ten days ago.'

'That would have been a young lady sleeping rough in Leith,' I said. The image of her leg sticking out from under a pile of cardboard at the rear of a takeaway place was still vivid in my mind, even if her name escaped me at that moment.

'The result was disturbingly similar. Massive amount of heroin in her system. I didn't hesitate at that point. That's when I called it in. But I also wanted to be thorough, so I had the sample run again and we've been waiting for the result. That was the call. They confirm the findings.'

'You're talking about a rogue batch of heroin?' Kate asked.

Eileen was scribbling furiously on a pad of paper. At some point in the conversation she'd also started recording on her phone, which now perched on the pad, a small green light flashing away at its top corner.

'Yes. I think so. You're aware, I'm sure, that almost all drugs are cut with one thing or another. In the case of street heroin, you would expect to see traces of paracetamol, fentanyl, caffeine, maybe even flour or chalk. When I first started here in 2010 there was some kind of market drought and so the samples we were seeing had a very low potency, around twenty percent or so. In recent years we're seeing purer samples, up around fifty percent. This fluctuation in purity is one reason the drug is so dangerous: users never really know what they're getting.

These samples,' she said, pulling some printouts from the desk and tapping the back of her fingers on them, 'I'd need a sample of the drug itself for an accurate assessment, but working sort of backwards from this bloodwork, in the assumption the user has taken a typical dose, it would place purity at over *eighty* percent.'

'Fuck,' breathed Kate.

'Yes, my thoughts exactly,' said Dr Patience. 'Which means you can expect to see more overdoses like these. A lot more.'

CHAPTER 6

CHIS

I was rostered off the following day, but either Kate was unaware or she cared little for any plans I'd made. She was setting up a meeting, she'd informed Rowan and I as we left the hospital, with those officers who were designated CHIS handlers.

In the old days anyone could develop a snitch, or so I'd been informed. You let someone off with a warning for some misdemeanour, making it clear what a huge favour you were doing them and thereafter present a promise of twenty quid or so for any information that they might think could be of interest to those of a uniformed persuasion and voilà, you had what was now a very regulated system of intel. No longer a snitch, but a covert human information source, paid for not out of your own wallet but the carefully guarded coffers of Police Scotland. All official and all recorded. To the point that only designated officers with the appropriate training could develop such a relationship with the criminal underworld. Not sexy, but I could see the sense in it.

Arriving at Fettes the next morning, I was expecting Kate's room to be filled with the sort of chiselled, too-cool-for-school detectives that someone like me would be far too intimidated by ever to approach for a little help. But other than Rowan and Kate, the only other person present was Adrian Geddes. He was bookish, short and closer in appearance to Jimmy Krankie than the Jimmy Dean I'd been picturing.

'Adrian will be taking you to see his CHIS this morning. A low-level dealer,' Kate explained after a short preamble, which was for the purpose of bringing DC Geddes up to speed on last night's developments. 'I have a meeting with the ACC on this issue, no doubt to spend pointless days developing a strategy, but in the meantime, I want you doing nothing else but heading this off directly. I don't care how you do it, I want that muck off my streets. Adrian has the only active CHIS at this time, I want to know what he knows. I've instructed the other trained officers to make contact with old informants and to get busy making new ones. For now, it looks like you're it.'

Rowan wasn't even trying to hide the smile spreading across her face. 'Uh, ma'am, I wondered if I could chat to you about that?' I said. Kate spread her hands, making it clear I had the floor. 'Uh, in private, if I may?'

'DS Colyear, is it lost on you how we're up against the clock here?'

'No, of course, but—'

'Then fucking spit it out, or get back to work.'

Rowan and Adrian wore the same expectant expression.

'It's just – I mean this is a big deal.'

'I'm glad you realise that. What's the problem?'

'Well,' – I could feel the thermostat in my collar begin to rise – 'since I joined CID you've had me . . . I mean I've been working these drug cases and, you know I don't mind, but suddenly—'

'I've been making you eat shit since you got here and now I've handed you some actual responsibility?'

She'd put it more succinctly than I could have. I suddenly regretted complaining to Rowan about the cases I'd been working. The truth was I felt unprepared for something like this.

'Not exactly how I would have put it, ma'am, but yes. I would have assumed you'd have someone with more experience working this?'

She backed up a little to rest her backside on the edge of her desk. 'It's no secret I have my reservations about you, DS Colyear. What happened last year will guarantee that will remain the case for some time. However, I don't believe in removing people from investigations. It happened to me several times when I was a DC. My inspector was a misogynistic prick and the second I made some progress on a case, or when it developed into something remotely interesting, he'd reallocate to one of his little boys' club favourites. That doesn't happen in my team. That doesn't mean I'm not watching you through a microscope and every development will be recorded and reported to me at every step of the way. Is that clear?'

'Yes, ma'am.'

'And . . . if you show any sign of not being up to the task, or do something remotely fucking stupid, then I will break my rule and remove you not just from the case, but from my team. We have a clear understanding?'

'You regret opening your mouth, right?' Rowan said quietly as we left Kate in her office.

'Yes and no. It never hurts to know exactly where you stand. And say what you want about DCI Templeton, she doesn't mince her words. You have to respect that.' I sat at my desk and watched with confusion as Rowan searched around and swiped a chair from a corner desk and pulled it over to sit beside me.

'What are you doing?' I said.

She shrugged. Her hands were on her knees and she was scanning around the room where six or so other detectives were quietly typing away. She looked like a teenager on work experience with no clue what to do with herself.

'Haven't you got work to do?'

'Nope. I cleared my caseload before leaving Dumbarton. Remember, this is effectively my first day on the job. So, I'm waiting for you to tell me what's what.'

She had a point. I'd been treated so much like a newbie myself since I'd arrived, I'd forgotten my rank. I was her supervisor.

'Okay.' I looked around the room myself. 'I guess welcome to Edinburgh CID where everything and anything can happen, but probably won't. Remember this is Edinburgh, not Glasgow.'

'This coming from the guy who was dealing with multiple murders not too long ago and now trying to track down heroin that could wipe out God knows how many junkies?'

'Well, yes. Point taken, but other than that, it's pretty quiet. Right now, I have an arson at a school and a few other enquiries, but that's all on hold according to DCI Templeton, so you might as well help me track the samples from yesterday and get it pushed through asap. You'll need somewhere to work. We're supposed to be using a hot-desk system, so in theory you can just grab any free computer.'

'In theory?'

'The reality is, people, especially cops, are territorial. On my first day I sat myself over there.' I pointed at a desk in the middle of the room adorned with family photos and post-its. 'I was chewed out by a DC in front of the whole room.'

'By a DC? Why didn't you stand up for yourself?'

'Ach. It's politics. I'm trying not to ruffle feathers. There's a general sense of me not having earned the right to be here and I figure it's better to play beta-dog right now. Besides, this particular DC has a thousand years' service. That kinda trumps the stripes at times. You know how it is. Sit there. The DC who uses it is fairly new and I doubt he'll kick you off, he's a bit of a nervous type.'

'And what? I'm scary.'

'Frankly, yes.'

Rowan snorted a laugh and took the desk opposite me; taking time to adjust her chair to its maximum height and then climbing onto it.

'How long are you planning to commute from Dumbarton? That's a hell of a drive.' I said to the back of her computer monitor.

'Actually, I won't be. I'm moving in with a friend. Someone I met at Tulliallan. There was a group of us got quite tight. She was super excited when she heard I was moving to town.'

'What part of town?'

'Uh, Bruntsfield?' she said, typing.

'Nice.'

'I'll take your word for it. I've only been there once, but it seemed fine.'

'What else is going on with you? Seeing anyone?'

At this she looked round from her screen with a glower. I knew fine she didn't like to share personal information, but I thought what the hell.

'Nothing . . . serious. How about you?'

'I'm not sure you'd call it serious either, but yes. I've been dating someone for a few months now.'

'Oh, check you. Colyear the ladykiller, all settled down?'

'Hardly.'

'What's the poor woman's name?'

'Marcella.'

'And what does Marcella do?'

'How did we switch this around to me?'

'Because you're no contest. Now tell me about the woman who took Donald Colyear off the market.'

'Uh, I don't know. She works in HR.'

'What does she do in HR?'

I stopped typing and thought hard. 'I have no idea. Whatever people in HR do, I suppose.'

'Ugh. You're such a bloke,' she said and disappeared back around her screen. 'I bet if I asked her about you, she'd give me ten full minutes on Sergeant Donald Colyear. In fact, I'll do just that when you introduce me to her.'

I laughed. 'Not a chance. If she met the weirdos I work with, she'd never stop worrying about me.'

'Are you ready?' Adrian called from the doorway, holding his coat and looking impatient.

'Where are we headed?' Rowan asked as she strapped herself into the back seat of the pool car.

'You'll see.'

Adrian pulled out of Gayfield station, and along tight cobbled roads until we hit Broughton Street, heading into the city centre.

I tried in vain to coax our driver into some conversation, but each attempt was met with a negative or affirmative grunt. It was a quiet trip then as Adrian took us up and over Queen Street to the Mound before cutting in to a loading area at the rear of the National Gallery. He cut the engine and placed a laminated card onto the dashboard. POLICE SCOTLAND with the force logo. I wondered how effective this would be against the notoriously officious Edinburgh traffic wardens.

We walked around towards the gallery cafe.

'Here? To meet a CHIS?' I said.

'It's where we always meet.'

'A bit . . . open, isn't it?'

'His choice. Reckon he figures it's the last place he's likely to bump into any of his clientele.'

We entered and Adrian scanned the room, his CHIS evidently had not yet arrived. We ordered and took our coffees, as well as a large hot chocolate spilling over with cream and marshmallows, to a corner table under a framed print of a Rembrandt. A self-portrait, the original apparently hanging somewhere within the gallery.

'How does this work?' I said. 'What does he get out of this arrangement? A blind eye turned to his dealing?'

'Oh God no. Those days are long gone. If he wants to deal in town, he takes his chances like anyone else. It's strictly financial. If he has some decent intel, he gets paid. If not he's just another scumbag dealer.' Adrian's eyes rarely left the entrance as he spoke. 'Here's the deal. I'll introduce you, you ask your questions, but don't write anything down. It makes them nervous. You will *never* contact him except through me. Even if you stumble across him in the street, or more likely in a holding cell at a station, you don't talk to him without me. That clear?'

'It's your show,' I said. Rowan widened her eyes at me with a micro-smile. The smell of the chocolate was dominating the table. I wondered how old this CHIS was.

There was a gentle buzz about the gallery cafe. Middle- and old-age couples mostly, ensuring a roaring trade in fruit scones for the place. They sat opposite one another in murmured conversation. Our presence, three suited adults, hadn't raised a single eyebrow, but as our guy entered, much of the chat faltered. His attempt at incognito was having entirely the opposite effect. His grey hoody was pulled up over the head and a green scarf covered his face from the bridge of the nose down. He wore baggy tracksuit bottoms. If he was like most of the dealers I'd encountered, he'd have a least a few more pairs worn underneath like a grubby Russian doll, his stash in the pair pulled on first. He wore these above bright red Nike hi-rise trainers. You didn't have to be in law enforcement to deduce this man's occupation. Every inch of him screamed drug dealer.

He stood with his hands in the pockets of his black coat, worn over the hoody, until he spotted us. He waited until he was seated before lowering the hood and removing the scarf.

He eyed us suspiciously as we were introduced in a whisper.

'And this is Malcolm, I'm assuming you don't need his surname,' Adrian said.

'Malky's fine,' our double-sided dealer said and pulled his hot chocolate to his chest. He fished out a molten marshmallow and pushed it into his mouth with fingers none too clean.

'He's all yours,' Adrian said before settling back into his chair with his arms folded across his chest.

'So, DC Geddes tells me you might be the man to ask for some information,' I said.

He shrugged and slurped his drink. 'Depends, doesn't it?'

I exchanged a look with Rowan that was designed to mean: *this is going to be a long day*. 'There's some – product, entered the market, Malky. Smack that's . . .

different. Dangerous.' I kept my voice low. The conversations around the room had resumed, but there were plenty of eyes on us.

'New smack?'

'That's right. Have you heard anything? Been offered anything?'

He looked to Adrian who held out a placating hand. 'It's all right, Malky, nobody is interested in you.'

'Well, what exactly are you looking for?' Malky said. He was sitting up straight now, his attention switched from his hot chocolate.

'Just as I said. There's new smack on the market and people are dying. I need it off the market sharpish. So, what do you know? Good intel will get you paid.'

'H'much?' he said, more to Adrian than me.

'Well, let's say this is time-sensitive and particularly important. So, double our usual fee.'

'Two hundred?'

'Only if the info leads us to the stuff,' I added.

Malky took another slurp. He pushed the mug away from himself and sat forward in his chair. 'Where's the stuff come from?' he asked.

'That's what we're trying to ascertain, Malky,' I said, a little confusion in my voice.

'Right, right, but what's the thinking? New player in town? And what's wrong with the stuff? Is it cut with some nasty shit?'

I glowered at him as his sudden enthusiasm was gaining fresh attention.

'The problem is it's not cut enough Malky. It's way too

strong,' Adrian said. I wasn't sure how wise it was to play all our cards face up, but there it was.

'Right, right. And what part of town is it showing up?'

'So far Leith and . . . Dalry,' I said, recalling the home address of the Polish lad who had succumbed.

'Okay. Two different areas. Not impossible it's from the same dealer, but I'd be surprised,' he said this as if pondering out loud.

'You don't have a clue, do you?' Rowan said. She looked like her patience was on its way out the door.

Malky shrugged. 'I'll be in touch,' he said and made to stand. Adrian pushed out a hand and urged him to sit.

'One last thing,' I said. 'I need a sample of what you deal. Need to rule it out.'

'I don't deal dangerous crap.'

'I'm not trying to insult you, I'm sure your heroin is a fine vintage. But I need that sample.'

He laughed. 'You don't really expect me to be carrying to a meeting with the fuzz, do you?'

'No, but the rucksack won't be far away. We just need a sample. It's not a trick,' Adrian said.

Malky chewed this over for a minute. 'Fine, but it's a tenner, same as everyone.'

Adrian rolled his eyes and opened his wallet, pushing the note across the table. 'I'll follow you out. You two all right making your own way back?'

Rowan started to complain, but I placed a hand on her wrist. 'It's fine. No problem,' I said.

We sipped at our coffees until the door had closed on the dealer and his handler.

'Worst CHIS ever,' Rowan said.

'I don't know. If CHIS stood for Covert Human Information *Seeker*, I reckon he'd be pretty good.'

'What do you mean?'

'If he knew anything, he'd have said and made a quick buck. But two hundred quid is nothing to a guy like him. He could make that in a quiet morning. What's with all the questions? Why does he want to go investigating on our behalf for a sum like that? It's dangerous work for a dealer to go around snooping. Extremely dangerous.'

'I don't know. Maybe he just likes feeling like a cop for a wee while?' Rowan said and began gathering her coat.

'Aye, maybe,' I said.

CHAPTER 7

Oxgangs

'How long have you been standing there?' he said. His hands were planted on his hips while he tried to catch his breath.

'Did you forget about tonight?' Priss said. She ran a thumb over Danny's glowing, sweat-damp cheek and kissed him.

He kissed her back, first wiping his palm on his jeans before placing it on the small of her back and pulling her in close. A wolf whistle sounded from behind him. He raised a middle finger in the general direction, but went on kissing her.

'Of course not,' he said, 'but it's only, what? What time is it?' He glanced at his watch and saw it was quarter to eight. 'Oh shit. I'm sorry, completely lost track.' Danny turned to the field behind him, to the game and his friends. He whistled through his fingers and then drew a flat hand across his neck, indicating he was done. There was a groan from the other players as Danny jogged over to collect his hoody.

Priss looked first at the autumn sky, bruised gold as the sun dipped behind trees, and then around at the other leaf-dusted fields of Edinburgh's Meadows, separated by bench-lined footpaths. Further casual football matches were being played along with a group playing ultimate frisbee, and beyond that lot there was a bunch getting set up with sticks and raised hoops.

'What are they up to?' said Priss. She hooked an arm through the crook of Danny's as he rejoined her.

He squinted in the direction she was pointing. 'Uh, looks like Quidditch.'

Priss, pulled on his arm. 'Piss off.'

Danny laughed. 'I'm perfectly serious.'

As they drew close Priss began to think he wasn't kidding. Some were holding sticks between their legs and there were a few scarves on show. 'Like the Harry Potter thing? No way.'

Danny shrugged with his free arm. 'Students,' he said, as if this were all the explanation required.

Priss didn't spend anywhere near the amount of time on the Meadows as Danny, as a lot of students, but she was no stranger to sitting on the grass with a few class friends while they passed around cans and gossip.

'What are you doing playing football in your jeans, anyway?'

'It's just a kick around. No tackling. So, come on, where is it you're taking me?' Danny said. He ducked behind Priss, placing his hands on her shoulders as they walked.

He kissed the back of her neck sending a bolt of pleasure down her spine that almost buckled a knee. Her hand reached around and found the back of his head. She stopped and kissed him again before taking his hand. She looked up into his deep-brown eyes and that ever-present smile.

'I do need to talk to you about that. If you're still sure about doing this, we're heading back to my old neighbourhood. It's not what you're used to and I don't want you to judge me.'

There was real concern in her voice. Danny stopped her, this time placing his hands on the front of her shoulders. He ducked to catch the line of her eye and then straightened, bringing her gaze with him. 'Priss, I don't care where you come from. And yes, I'm still up for this.'

There was that smile, perfectly white and broadening on his dark face. Utterly impossible to resist its gravity.

'Don't say I didn't warn you,' she said and took his hand again. They walked on, between two of the fields heading to the roadway.

'How bad are we talking? A little rough around the edges, or Gaza Strip?'

Priss laughed. 'Think somewhere in between.'

They walked uphill, through Marchmont. On the way his hands switched between her own, her shoulders and her bottom when they stopped in a quiet doorway. He slipped his hands under the skirt of her dress and briefly inside her underwear as their tongues danced. She moaned into his mouth and then pushed him off. Her eyes scowled, but her smile betrayed her.

This was new to her. She'd met Danny four months ago at a party a mutual friend had thrown. He wasn't her type, at all. Tall, athletic, with a face straight out of a magazine and seemingly strait-laced. It had crossed her mind, when he'd flirted with her in the kitchen, that it might be some sort of wind-up. Either way she'd given him the brush-off, but as the night drew on and the crammed flat had thinned to a few small groups, she found herself talking to him again and to her great surprise sharing a joint with him and then kissing him in the same kitchen she'd made it clear she wasn't interested. When she'd woken at his place the next morning, she'd told herself she'd done a lot worse with previous hook-ups and hadn't beaten herself up. She hadn't remembered exchanging numbers with him, but when a text arrived later that day asking her what she was up to, there was his face on WhatsApp. Three days later they hooked up again and soon on a regular basis. Then, and she couldn't remember when exactly it had happened, it wasn't all about the sex, at least not exclusively. Coffee, cinema, shooting the shit in the park. And for all that he looked like a poster boy for healthy living, he was open to anything, in fact, not just open but outright keen and curious. Priss had only once been with someone longer than three months, her high school boyfriend, which had lasted a year and a half, about a year longer than it should have, but she'd lacked the experience to know better. Now boys came and went, often quite literally, but this? And for him to be so into her after this length of time? It would be scary if she'd allowed herself to think on it too hard.

She looked up at the electronic board as they reached the bus stop, and waited for it to cycle through to the number five. 'Shit, twenty-minute wait.'

Danny didn't hesitate as he spotted a black cab passing on the opposite side. He pushed two fingers into his mouth once more and blew. The brake lights blared crimson in the failing light. The cab waited for traffic to clear and swung a U-turn.

'It's only twenty minutes, Mr Moneybags,' Priss said, but climbed in without further complaint.

'Where to?' the cabbie said through the rear-view mirror. Priss gave the address, or rather the street name. It meant nothing to Danny, but made the eyebrows of the cabbie jump.

They kissed and they talked. They talked about exams and mutual friends. They talked about the city.

'I reckon I'll stay when I graduate,' Danny said. He was watching the streets, the people and the buildings go by out of the window. He'd said this before, they'd discussed this before, but it wasn't some lapse in memory, Priss knew, it was him processing the decision. It was something you didn't have to think about until fourth year and not something Priss had to really think about at all. Edinburgh was home, always had been and would likely always be. She wondered whether she had lent any weight to this decision he hadn't quite made, Priss suspected, but was getting closer. The thought was as exciting as it was worrying.

'Well I hope you have a fancy job lined up for when you graduate. Even shoebox flats here go for crazy prices,' Priss said.

Danny was about to tell Priss something that she hadn't already heard, that he'd chatted with two of his current flatmates and that they'd expressed an interest in staying beyond uni too and that their flat-share arrangement might continue into the 'real world', as they'd dubbed approaching post-university reality, but the cabbie cut in before he could.

'Unless you're buying round here,' he scoffed. Even through the mirror Danny could see his face was twisted as if he'd just lifted an old piece of carpet he'd found in the forest.

'Oy, I grew up round here,' Priss chided, though there was no real ire in it.

'Sorry, love,' the cabbie chuckled. 'Where am I setting you down?'

'Just up here, on the right,' Priss said.

The cabbie indicated and rolled towards the kerb. 'Do you mind if I just slow to maybe twenty, let you jump and roll. If I stop the locals will take my wheels,' he laughed.

'You're talking yourself out of the tip,' Priss said.

'Just kidding.' The cabbie stopped and Priss exited while Danny sorted the fare.

The taxi rolled away and Danny scanned their surroundings in the twilight. A residential street and quickly Danny got the cabbie's joke. Rows upon rows of four-storey blocks of flats. Grey, square and uninviting. Small parking areas sat adjacent to each one. Some younger kids were kicking a ball on a small patch of grass to their right, under the dim light of a lamp post from the pavement. Further up the street and a group of older ones had gathered on bikes and it seemed they'd already attracted their interest. Most of the faces seemed to be pointing their way.

There was a chill creeping up Danny's spine, something like unease. 'Where are we exactly?' he said as Priss hooked his arm once more and led him along the road towards the older kids.

'Oxgangs. My mum lives a few streets away. Come on, we're fine,' she said, pulling on Danny's arm, evidently aware of his reticence as they drew nearer the group. 'It used to have a bit of a reputation, but trust me, it's not that bad. Not any more.'

'If you say so,' Danny said. He tried not to catch the eyes of the small crowd as they passed. Plumes of sweet-smelling vape smoke billowed from the circle of teenagers. The various conversations amidst the circle stopped. The chill in Danny's spine was threatening to ice over. Then one of them, a tall kid with face full of fuck-off gave Priss a small flick of the head. She returned the micro-gesture and the boys went back to their chat.

'Relax,' said Priss, laughing a little.

'What? I'm fine,' said Danny. He wanted badly to look back to check they weren't being followed, but that would only have revealed him a liar.

They stopped opposite one of these compact blocks of flats. Danny hadn't inspected every block in the street, but still, he'd swear blind that this was the worst one. All of the bottom windows, as well as one on the first floor had been replaced by metal shutters. Graffiti littered the stonework, various tags and insults to those in the know.

'EGGO – FUKIN GRASS' had been sprayed under one of the shutters followed by a crude skull and crossbones. Danny had no idea who 'EGGO' was, but he couldn't help feel a little sorry for him.

Priss turned to Danny and opened her arms to him. He embraced her, his arms around her waist, hers around his neck. They rotated slowly, Priss's lips brushing Danny's temple, Danny's face was amidst Priss's long dark hair, smelling the perfume of it. It was nearly a full minute before he realised this was not affection. Priss's eyes were open as they pirouetted on their joint axle. She was scanning the place. Danny pulled away, ready to ask what it was she was doing, but she was smiling at him, apparently satisfied with whatever that just was. 'Come on,' she said and took his hand.

They walked towards the front door of the block. It had been repaired several times, with screwed on pieces of wood here and there. It needed fresh attention, Danny saw, as the door swung free, its lock long since broken free. Despite the free access, Priss pressed and held a top-floor button on the metal panel. There was no audible reaction; still, Priss waited, her head poised close to the speaker. After thirty seconds or so, she pressed on it again, two, three, four times, holding the last down for a good ten seconds. When she released the speaker crackled into life:

'What?'

'It's me,' Priss said in a soft voice.

'Who's me?' the broken voice returned.

'It's Priss.'

'Who the fuck is *Priss*?'

'It's – it's me. Who the fuck is this? Is that you, Deek?'

'Aye, it's Deek,' the speaker confirmed along with a small laugh.

Priss hung her head for a moment, then went back to the speaker. 'Deek, I'm comin' up.'

There was no response to this.

Priss led the way inside to the stairs. There was no light, at least not a functioning one, and Danny's toe caught the first step, almost tripping him into Priss's back. There was an earthy smell about the place, unspecific, but nonetheless unpleasant. At the first-floor landing, Priss stopped. 'Listen,' she said, 'I didn't know Deek would be here. He's all right, but can be a bit of a dick when he's in the mood to be. Thing is, he's always been kinda sweet on me, and he might be a wee bit . . . prickly with you here. So, let's just keep the public displays of affection to a minimum. At least until I get you home. That okay?'

'Are we talking about an ex here?' Danny said, his voice was playful.

Priss chuckled and kissed Danny's lips. 'God no. You'll see why that's funny in a minute.'

She led on to the fourth floor. Here a hazy amber glow dimly lit the landing from a filthy plastic light case. As with the other floors, there were two doors. It wasn't difficult for Danny to guess behind which 'Deek' was waiting for them. This was a door unlike any other in the block. It was metal, but not like the shutters on the windows downstairs. The shutters told you: *nobody lives here any more. This door told a different story: people live here, but if you want to force your way in, it's going to make a lot of noise and take you a very long time, plenty of time in fact to calmly flush the toilet and flush it again.*

Priss knocked at the door. The sound was a dull series of clacks, which Danny doubted could even be heard from the other side, but soon a voice came, the same voice from the intercom but distant, as if from across a field.

'Who is it?' Deek said.

'Open the door. It's Priss.' Her voice was breathy, frustrated.

'I don't know a Priss. Try again.'

'Open the fucking door, Deek. Stop being a dick.'

It was faint, but that was definitely laughter from the other side. A series of clunks, clicks and rattling sounded and then the door, *vault*, Danny thought, opened.

Priss was right, the thought of this guy with her *was* funny. If you'd seen him from behind, you might have mistaken Deek for a child. Five-feet-not-much and painfully skinny. His once white, now grey, Sonic Youth T-shirt draped from his sharp shoulders and billowed lightly at a waist that struggled to meet the fabric. His skin was badly pockmarked, though much of it was partially hidden behind lank, black, curtain-parting middle length hair and a patchy beard.

'Who's this?' he said, putting out a hand in a failed attempt to stop Priss entering. 'You never said you had company.'

'You never asked. Come on,' Priss said and pulled Danny past the oily little man into a dark hallway.

'Hey, wait, I'm not to let anyone in. Barry said not to . . .' Deek was between minds, his hands moving from resecuring the door and following the visitors into the flat.

'Then why did you open the door? And where is Barry?' Priss said. She pulled Danny to the end of the hall.

'He's . . . he's out. Hey, wait.'

Deek fumbled with chains and then caught up to them, pushing into the room at the end of the hall ahead of Priss.

Danny followed the other two into a living room that had emerged from a psychedelic migraine from the seventies. One wall was dominated by a blue tie-dye fabric that sagged between the four nails holding it in place. The opposite wall, above a beaten burgundy sofa, hosted a collection of tour posters. The Velvet Underground, Pink Floyd and The Doors were the few Danny felt like he'd heard of. The music coming from an unseen stereo may have been one of these bands, though he couldn't say for sure.

There were at least three scents battling for supremacy. Rotten garbage, probably coming from the kitchen area at the far end of the room. Joss sticks, three of them burning from a small brass holder on a white-laminate coffee table, scarred from dozens of small burns. And weed. A fat joint sat in an ashtray next to the incense burner, its unmissable reek streaming into the air on an enthusiastic tendril of smoke. Danny stepped into a corner, trying not to touch anything, or perhaps not let anything touch him. Priss didn't hesitate to drop herself into the sofa and reach for the blunt, taking a long draw. She held the smoke in her lungs and held up the joint toward Danny. He thought on it for a moment before releasing one hand from the pockets of his hoodie and took it from her. Deek eyed him as he fell into the sofa beside Priss, touch-tight to her. She shifted along a little, rolling her eyes as Danny drew the smoke into his mouth and then heaved it into his lungs. He swallowed back hard the urge to cough with a grunt. This drew a small smile from Deek and he passed on the joint to him.

A few months ago, this draw would have had him on his knees coughing and spluttering, but Priss had an appetite for the stuff and so his own amateurish habit had become . . . semi-professional. Nothing compared to Priss. She could sample weed like a sommelier judging a robust Bordeaux, but he could at least now tell the good stuff from the pocket fluff some of his friends still passed around. And this was the good stuff. His whole body responded like a head to foot yawn. He looked around and sat in an armchair opposite the sofa, no longer caring about sanitary failings.

'So how d'you know Debs?' said Deek, his voice was chesty as he slowly released a cloud when he spoke. He passed the joint onto Priss who shot him a venomous glare. 'You do know her *real* name is De-bo-rah, don't you?' Deek pronounced the name in three delineated syllables, as if teaching it to an infant.

Danny raised his eyebrows to Priss. She calmly took a draw, blew and turned to face him. 'Priscilla is my middle name. Nobody's called me Deborah, or Debs, since I was fifteen. Except for this pleb.'

'Me and Debs go way back, like primary school age. Eh, Debs?'

'One more "Debs" out of you, *Derek*, and I'm going to punch you in the throat,' said Priss. She flashed Deek a large, but very brief grin, her face relaxing back into a scowl almost instantly.

Deek took the joint and gave a small laugh, one that said the joke had run its course. 'You two meet at uni, then?' he asked Danny.

'That's right.' Danny reached across the coffee table for the joint. As he did, Deek pointed at the emblem on the chest of his hoodie.

'"Edinburgh University A.F.C.?" What's that? Fitbaw?'

Danny sat back with the joint. His eyes flicked to Priss.

'Football,' she translated.

'That's right.' He drew on the roach, now wet. It would have disgusted him minutes ago, but he was comfortable now, very comfortable.

'You play for the university, like?'

'That's right.'

'Aye? What position?'

'Centre forward.'

'Striker, aye?'

'Aye.'

Deek seemed prickled by this. He sat forward in his seat.

'D'ye think it makes you better than the likes of us?'

'Deek,' Priss said.

'Come again?' said Danny.

'Wearing that university hoodie. Telling the world you're Johnny big-balls goin' tae Edinburgh Uni.'

'What? No, it's just a top. It doesn't mean—'

'Deek, I go to Edinburgh Uni. Nobody's trying to make anyone feel little.'

'Aye, but you're no pushing it in anybody's face.'

'It's just a hoodie, man. Here, it's yours.' Danny placed the joint momentarily into the ashtray as he removed the top, bundled it into a ball and tossed it on the sofa between the other two.

Deek seemed ambivalent for a moment. Priss would have expected him to throw it back, protesting the patronising gesture, but he'd lifted it and was now turning it over for a look at the back. Priss rolled her eyes and snatched the hoodie back. She stood and pushed it into Danny's lap before setting herself on the arm of the chair and taking the joint from Danny's lips.

'Aye, I don't want your top. I don't need badges to make me feel important.' Deek leant forward for the joint, but Priss was shaking her head.

'It's dead. Roll another, will you?'

He did as he was told, pulling a large hardback book from underneath the coffee table, an Atlas, Danny saw, and began the rebuild. He layered skins with practised precision. 'So, where you from?' he said as he began peeling a cigarette.

'Kent,' said Danny.

'Kent? What's that? London?'

'No, it's . . .' Danny began but Priss was tapping his shoulder. He looked up to her screwing her face. The gesture meant *don't bother*. 'Yeah, something like that,' Danny concluded.

As obnoxious as the little shit was, Danny couldn't

help but be impressed with him. He wasn't building the joint, he was conjuring it. He sealed the last few edges and sparked it up, seconds before Priss snatched it from his mouth and pushed herself into the seat of the armchair beside Danny. From the look on Deek's face, he'd not taken to this breaking of Priss's own no PDA rule kindly. Confirmed by what came out of his mouth next.

'So is your mum black, or is it your dad?' The words came out with a certain venom, as if he were asking which parent were to blame.

Priss coughed out a plume of smoke. 'For fuck's sake, Deek,' she strained to say. 'You can't fucking say—'

Danny was tapping her on the leg, he was laughing. 'It's fine,' he said. 'Actually, both my parents are mixed race.'

'Huh?' said Deek.

'Mum's half white, half Jamaican. Dad's a blend of British, African and Dutch.'

This seemed to confuse the hell out of the little man on the sofa. 'So, what's that make you, then?' he said eventually, just when Danny had thought he'd let the issue pass.

'Makes me Danny,' he said. He drew on the joint and passed it across to Deek who accepted it absently.

Deek fumbled with the joint as three slams of the front door sounded, followed by another one a few seconds later. Deek dropped the joint into the ashtray and leapt to his feet.

'Barry,' Priss said. She stood, smoothed out the front of her skirt and cleared her throat.

What was this? Was she nervous? Danny thought. He stayed seated but straightened himself up. 'Should I be worried?' he whispered as the sound of the front door being hauled open sounded.

'What? Oh, nah. Barry's a pussycat, if you know him. Don't worry.'

That pause before 'if you know him' ensured the opposite effect. Danny stared at the door frame waiting for the homeowner to enter the room. When he did, he wasn't the monster he'd been creating in his head. Still, there was something in the way this guy carried himself. That and the face tattoo, that was intimidating.

He wasn't thickset or obviously muscular but he was solid enough under the tight black jumper. He crossed the room, eyeing Danny, but heading for Priss. He placed a hand on her shoulder and kissed her cheek. Priss was tall, only a few inches shorter than Danny, but this guy towered over her. 'This is him?' he said.

'Yeah, this is Danny,' Priss said.

'Hey,' said Danny, but the hail got stuck a little in his throat. This seemed to amuse Barry, who smiled. Danny smiled back and tried to make out what it was that adorned this guy's neck and spread up over his chin and onto his left cheek. At first Danny thought it was some elaborate spider's web, but as Barry leant down to shake his hand, he saw that it was musical notation. Five lines with symbols and notes. Danny wanted to ask, but wasn't sure if he should and the moment quickly passed.

'Sorry, Barry,' Deek said from the doorway, looking like he might just turn tail and run. 'You said don't let anyone in, but you know, it was—'

'Priss. Of course, don't worry. I just forgot to tell you she was coming over tonight with her new friend.' Barry gave Deek a double, soft slap on the cheek. Then settled himself into the sofa.

'You have something for us?' said Priss. She sat once more on the arm of Danny's chair.

'What? No how you been, Barry? What's new with you? Seen any good movies lately?'

'You're takin' the piss, right?' said Priss, her eyebrows cocked.

Barry chuckled and went into the pocket of jeans. 'Course I am. H'many?'

'Three's fine. Tick all right?'

'Aye, your credit's good.' Barry leant forward and tossed three small plastic bags onto the coffee table.

Priss swept up the packets and gave one a little shake in front of her eyes.

'New batch,' said Barry. 'It's good, though.'

'You've tried it?' said Priss.

'Not yet, but nobody sells me shite.'

'Good enough.' Priss turned to Danny with a smile and clamped a hand on his knee. 'So, ready?' she said.

Danny was a little surprised to feel his heart rate kick into a new gear. He looked at the reddish-brown powder in the bag. Why was he suddenly nervous? This is why they had come.

'You okay?' Priss whispered in his ear, evidently reading his face.

'Yeah, course.'

'Come on,' she said taking his hand and, pulling him onto the carpet, they shuffled into the corner of the room. 'Stay here, I'll be back in a few minutes,' she said and headed for the kitchen area.

Danny pulled his hoody under his backside and tried to get comfortable. He was closer to the speaker now and he could clearly hear the droning melody. It was joined by a hypnotic baritone voice. He listened while he waited. Sounds of a lighter flint being rasped repeated from the kitchen area. He put it out of his mind and concentrated on the song.

'Maybe it's the weed talking. But this is really good.' Danny said, raising a single finger into the air as Priss returned with a tray spilling over with medical bits and bobs.

'What is?'

'The music.'

Priss sat and listened a moment. She laughed. 'Jim Morrison? Well, there's a man who could hold his drugs. You know, until he couldn't. But you don't have to worry. You're safe here, you know that, right?'

Danny took a second to look over at Deek, who was staring at them, but averted his gaze when discovered. Barry was busy building a fresh joint. Danny considered the question. He was sitting in a drug dealer's flat in a sketchy part of town, but, 'Uh-huh,' he said. He did feel safe. He felt safe because he was with her and there was no amount of worry on her face. That face. He leant forward and kissed her nose. She smiled, but widened her eyes, warning him again that public displays were to be suspended for the evening.

'It looks like you're building a lab here. Is all of this really necessary?' Danny said, gesturing at the tray and all of the apparatus it contained. Amongst it all he saw a string of syringes, held together by paper wrapping. One had been opened and sat on the tray with brown-gold contents ready for use. The sight of it made his heart pick up pace again.

'All right, give me your arm,' she said. Danny sat cross-legged. Priss pulled herself closer, one leg either side of his knees. She took a paper packet from the tray and tore it open. She swept the inside of Danny's forearm with the alcohol wipe she produced from the packet. Danny's hand hung between Priss's thighs. He shunted himself a little closer and moved the hand under her skirt, finding the front of her panties. He brushed a forefinger gently across the fabric, knowing a rebuke would follow. Only it didn't. As Priss wiped, she smiled and moved her bottom along the carpet a few inches, glancing behind her to check for jealous eyes. Danny massaged with his thumb, drawing a sigh from Priss who was busy tying off his arm with rubber tubing.

Priss moved Danny's arm around and inspected the veins. 'Okay. Ready?' she said.

Danny pulse rose one more level. He abandoned Priss's underwear and sat up. He nodded and moved his back against the wall.

'Look away if you want to,' Priss whispered.

'No, I want to see,' Danny quietly returned.

He watched as Priss rested her hand holding the syringe against Danny's wrist to steady it. Danny's own shook as he waited for whatever it was he was about to experience. *Nothing like it on God's green Earth*, had been Priss's description, her review, her promise.

He watched the needle enter his arm. He watched her thumb press on the plunger. For a second there was nothing. He was almost relieved but then . . . but then.

'Fuuuuuuu . . .' he heard himself say.

A heat rose from inside in waves. His limbs, his eyes, tongue, his soul, sang in glorious and exultant delight. His jaw fell open and he knew he would be unable to close it.

'Fuuuuuuu . . .'

Priss was giggling somewhere, but it was not in the warm, bronze world into which he was falling. He fell into a warm breeze that might have been a thousand hands gliding across every inch of his skin. The breeze grew warmer the deeper he fell. The intensity grew. Hot now and the hands had nails. They raked at him and the bronze world became a dark place. He fell and he fell.

'Danny. Danny!' Priss watched Danny's head fall to the side. His mouth hung and spit bubbled from the low corner. 'DANNY. Fuck. Danny, wake up.' She slapped her palm against his cheek, over and over, gently and then not so gently. 'DANNY.'

'What the fuck?' Barry was saying from behind her.

'Get. Someone. Get something.' Priss yelled. 'Call a fucking ambulance.'

CHAPTER 8

The Body in the Bin

In the dream someone was rattling a tin in my face. The charity collector's own face was featureless, except for a huge, clenched, toothy smile that feigned kindness, but in truth expressed unflinching determination. The collector stood on the pavement and no matter what I did, I could not move around them. I pivoted left and there was the figure, shaking the tin so close to my nose it had me leaning backwards. I shifted to the right, but this was anticipated and the rattling repeated. I could feel my body ache with frustration until the elbow in my ribs pulled me from the dream.

'It's yours,' said Marcella, her voice muffled by the pillow she'd pulled over her face.

'What?'

'Your phone. Answer or turn it off.'

It vibrated on the bedside table. The noise roused me enough to realise I was in Marcella's flat, not my own.

Fuck, what time is it? In her flat the blinds allowed daylight to spill through and the room was in complete darkness. The phone rattled again and Marcella's heel butted my calf.

I sat up and lifted the phone, checking the time on the display, just after 6 a.m., before I answered the call from DCI Templeton.

'Ma'am. What's going on?' I said softly as I left the bed and the bedroom in my underwear.

'I know you're not rostered on, Colyear, but I think you're going to want to see this. I'll let you wake Forbes. I'll text you the address. Bring coffee, will you?'

'Uh, sure. Yes, ma'am,' I said to the noise telling me she'd already hung up.

I called Rowan from the car. To my shock she answered immediately, fresh and lucid.

'I'm always up at this time,' she said when I asked.

'Of course you are, you little freak. I'm picking you up in fifteen minutes. Text me your address and be outside your building with coffees. One for Kate too.'

It took less than eight minutes in the early morning traffic. It was astonishing how quickly you could cross the city while it slept. The streets remained dark, but the castle up there on its rock was catching the first rays of day. It glowed like a golden palace from a story.

I sat by the pavement outside Rowan's address watching the door, but jumped when the passenger window was chapped. Rowan was partially hidden behind the three large Costa coffees she was struggling to hold. She climbed in, handing me a cup, and then set about finding holders for the other two, before taking the third back and drinking from it.

'What are we headed to?' she asked.

'I've no idea, but it's a sketchy part of town, so could be anything.'

It was still dark as we approached Oxgangs, pulling off the main road towards the housing estates. A flickering blue glow could be seen in the sky above the labyrinth of homes. We were stopped at a line of tape by a uniform looking cold and tired. Night shift it seemed, begging to be allowed to go home. I flashed my ID and we drove on slowly, past a series of marked vehicles parked roadside or abandoned on verges until we reached the centre of things. More vehicles, with lights spinning, the source of the blue glow, sat alongside a large bin lorry. An inner cordon of tape met us on the street. This time a flash of the warrant card was not enough to continue.

It was hard to see what the focus of all of this was. In my experience, you show up to fuss such as we found here and you're met either with people struggling in handcuffs, or people peering down at a body, but not here. Kate approached with the strident blue haze behind her.

'They're with me,' she told the uniform and we ducked under the tape. 'This way,' she continued, taking the coffee from Rowan without a thank you.

We followed her into the scene. Two SOCOs in overalls looked to be setting up, but setting up for what? Kate stopped at something in the middle of the road, in the middle of everything, in fact. A green wheelie bin sat ominously apart from everything else. I hadn't realised

I was cold until this moment. I shivered and thrust my hands into the pockets of my coat. Kate turned as she reached the bin. 'Gloves,' she said, and she began pulling on her own. We did as she said and my pulse quickened as she reached to the lid of the bin and raised it. She took a step to the side, urging us to take a look. I stepped forward and peered over the edge. The street lights failed to show more than a blur of the bin's contents, and I wished someone would turn off the emergency beacons flashing everywhere, they made the image shift and flicker. Then Kate flicked on a torch.

The first thing I saw were trainers, just below the edge of the bin, then legs as the body came into view. It had been stuffed head first into the thing. A young man. The light lingered on his face, pressed and contorted against the bottom and side of the plastic bin. There were fluids running from his nose and mouth, some of it blood, but mostly other stuff. His eyes were closed and I was grateful for that small mercy.

'Binmen found it an hour ago. It's only by chance that the guy looked in before he attached it to the truck. Unusually heavy, so he had a peek.' Kate nodded further down the street where a guy was scratching nervously at the edge of his grubby baseball cap as he gave a statement to someone I recognised from the office, but didn't know her name.

'Nasty. But why us?' I said.

'Look again,' Kate said and pushed the beam of her torch over the edge once more. I looked and it took a moment to see what she was getting at. Then I did. His right arm. It had rubber tubing tied tight, just above the elbow.

'Ah.'

'Yes.'

We stood and watched from the pavement, quietly sipping at our coffees as SOCO did their thing. Photographing and swabbing every inch before approaching and having a quiet conversation with Kate, at the end of which she gave her approval. Moments later a plastic sheet was laid out and the SOCOs upended the bin and pulled the poor lad from his grimmest of coffins. His limbs remained locked in the position set by the confines of the bin. The rigor mortis made it easy for the SOCOs to slide him onto the sheet. There was a further examination of the interior of the bin before they turned their attentions to the body. I was particularly interested in the right arm. SOCO did their best to straighten it long enough to get some pictures. There was a needle mark there all right, but no needle in the body or the bin. Daylight was upon us by the time the photography, finger scrapings and swabbing had been completed. Beside the body, on the sheet, were laid the contents of the lad's pockets. Phone, keys and a wallet. I approached and asked SOCO if I could now inspect the findings and was told, yes. I started with the phone, pressing at buttons, waiting for the screen to light up, but no charge. I went instead to the wallet. I brought it to the roadside. Rowan began noting details as I read from a driver's licence:

'Daniel Bakker. An address in Kent. Date of birth . . . uh,' I strained to read the small numbers in the pale light. 'Eighth of August, 2001. So, he's . . .'

'He's twenty,' Kate said. 'What else is in there?'

There was sixty pounds in notes and some change. Interesting in as much as they'd been left by whoever had dumped him, assuming he hadn't fallen in during his ill-conceived adventures in heroin. I fished out a couple of supermarket loyalty cards and a 'University of Edinburgh Library pass' I said, handing the yellow card over to Kate.

'Good. That's where to get started. Call me when you have a next of kin. I'll make the call. Assuming Daniel here has met the same fate as your other bodies, I think the cat is about to be let out of the bag. The bosses will want to start stroking their beards on this and how we deal with press and public, but don't get distracted. You've a job to do. Get on it, will you?'

'Yes ma'am.'

We were redirected twice before finding the correct office for student information. I'd assumed naively Mr Bakker's information would be easy to obtain, but the woman behind the desk, her grey hair tied back so tight she had an unadjusting expression of surprise, had other ideas.

'You have *heard* of data protection I assume?'

'Of course, but—'

'Do you have a – a warrant, or whatever?'

'I have one of these,' I said and tapped on the warrant card hanging at my chest, assuming it would be the trump card required to end this nonsense. Not so.

She pushed her glasses further up her nose and leant in to inspect it. She sat back in her chair, somehow managing to pull her face into a look that said she was far from impressed. 'I could knock one of those up in twenty minutes in our reprographics department, call myself chief constable, or, I don't know, Lord Commander of Earth and the solar system.'

I wanted very much to reach around her head and release her hair bobble and watch her face collapse into a puckered arsehole. Instead, I took a breath and considered the options. *Silly*, I thought, I did have a trump card.

'You're up,' I said to Rowan, softly.

She nodded, attached her most beatific smile and accepted being tagged in. 'Uh, Daria,' she said reading the name tag on the woman's bottle-green blouse, partly hidden by frills down the front. The unimpressed expression on Daria's face turned stony, *Let's see what this one's got*, it said.

Rowan reached over the desk and snatched up a notepad next to the phone. She had to stretch on tiptoes to do it.

'Hey—' Daria began, but Rowan cut in as she began writing.

'I'm going to write down the number for Edinburgh CID, but if you prefer, go ahead and dial the non-emergency number for Police Scotland and ask them to verify who we are.' Rowan returned the notepad.

'Well, it's not just verifying you are who you say you are, there's the small matter of data protection, as I've already mentioned. We can't just be handing out personal details of our students, even to the police. I'd have to check this with someone.'

'Please, go ahead,' Rowan said, her smile still attached, but peeling at the edges.

'Yes, but I'm most senior here today. No, I'm sorry, you'll have to come back another day.'

I thought about what Kate would say if we caved to this woman, what creative expletives she'd hammer us with. But I needn't have worried.

'Daria,' Rowan began, crumbling patience clear in her tone. 'The security and privacy of your students is incredibly important, I get that, *we* get that, but right now, one of your students is dead.' Rowan raised her voice a little at this point, ensuring the others in the office, two staff pretending to be typing at computers, but clearly eavesdropping, and a small group of students not even pretending they weren't watching events unfold, looked our way. 'His body is on its way to the mortuary as we speak, and it is imperative that we obtain details of his parents and his address in Edinburgh. Now, I don't care who you have to phone, whose day off you need to disturb, but if we don't get those details in the next few minutes, we're seriously going to start looking at charging someone with obstruction of a police investigation.'

There was a moment of silence and Daria's face relaxed back into perma-surprise. She picked up the phone and pressed a preprogrammed number button and a hushed conversation began. Words like 'police', 'dead' and 'data protection' repeated. One of the students was doing a terrible job at disguising she was taking a selfie with us in the background.

'Okay, but I want something on record to show that I'm doing this under objection, Iain. Uh-huh, fine.' Daria hung up the phone. 'Name of the student?'

'Death, taxes and they're always on the top floor.'

'What's that?' Rowan said, huffing in breath as we reached the top of the block of flats in Newington.

I sucked in a breath of my own and said, 'Something my tutor used to say. Three certainties in life: death, taxes and they're always on the top floor.'

I chapped the door of flat nine, ignoring the bell as I usually did, having learnt from years of showing up at other people's homes that you can't always tell if anything sounded within the place, and a good strong knock usually induces a sense of urgency in the occupant.

Certainly, the door was opened quickly enough and the young man who stood in the doorway, shirtless and dishevelled, looked like he was wondering where the fire was.

'Daniel Bakker lives here,' I said. It was not a question.

'What?'

'Go put a shirt on. We need to talk about your flatmate.' I pushed the door and walked past the lad. 'And put that joint away, we're still police.' The penny seemed to drop at this. He coughed and tossed the rollie he was holding into the communal stairwell.

'Hey, Danny's not here. If – if you've got a card or something, I'll, uh, get him to call you. Hey you can't go in—'

I pushed the door to the living room and entered. Not

a bad place, for a student let. Plenty of light coming in through the window that had a largely unobscured view of Arthur's Seat and Salisbury Crags. The sofas and armchairs were stain-free and the artwork on the walls was unexpectedly grown-up with framed prints of famous paintings, of which I could maybe name half of their creators.

The young occupant of the flat was pulling on a T-shirt, eyeing Rowan as he did before busily tidying away the contents of the coffee table, which included a hash grinder and elaborate glass bong.

'Can I get you something? Tea? A biscuit? Maybe a warrant?'

I moved a pair of jeans from the seat of the sofa to the arm and sat myself down. 'We're not here about some personal-use cannabis. We're here to talk about Daniel. Danny. You should take a seat,' I said.

'Like I told you. He's not here. I'll get him to call you if you want. What's it about, anyway?'

'Seriously, you should take a seat,' Rowan said and this time he seemed to sense the atmosphere.

He lowered himself into an armchair, bong and grinder still clutched to his chest.

'I'm going to ask you to keep this information to yourself for now,' I said. I sat forward in my seat, my forearms resting on my knees. 'The next of kin has almost certainly been informed by now, but for the rest of the day only tell who you absolutely have to.' I'd passed on all the details gleaned from the university office and Kate would have called Danny's parents as a priority.

'Next of kin? What the fuck?' The lad's voice was breathy with impending grief. I told him what was becoming apparent.

'Danny died. Sometime between last night and the early hours of this morning. I'm sorry to be the one to tell you. I assume you were mates, as well as flatmates?' He didn't answer, but the far-away look on his face, as his brain tried to absorb this information, told me they were close. 'I need to ask you some questions. I'd also like your permission to look through his room. I appreciate you might be uncomfortable with that, but it might be—'

'Whatever you need,' he said. His voice was small, cracking with emotion. 'What – what happened?'

Rowan and I exchanged a glance. I shouldn't really be telling this guy anything, but he needed to hear something. 'I can't go into the full details, but can I ask you, was Danny a regular heroin user?'

'What? Heroin? Are you serious?' I didn't respond, I just gave him time to process. 'We do a bit of hash, but . . . No, I've never seen him mess around with that stuff. He . . . overdosed?'

'Like I said, I can't really get into it at the moment. Who does Danny know in Oxgangs?' The lad's accent was mild, educated, but there was some Edinburgh in there for sure. I wouldn't have to explain the geography of the city.

He scoffed. 'Oxgangs? Danny would have to be seriously lost to find himself . . .' He drifted off. Something had occurred to him.

'What's your name?' Rowan said, softly.

'Uh, Brian.'

'What can you tell us, Brian? We're trying to make sense of this and we really do need your help to do that. What were you just thinking about?'

'His girlfriend, uh, Priss. I don't know anything for sure, but she mentioned once she was from a dodgy part of town. But Edinburgh has plenty.'

'Tell us everything you know about Priss,' I said.

My tutor constable John's assertion of the three certainties in life didn't hold up this time. That is, if Brian was correct in his recollection. There was no way I was going to dance the bureaucratic waltz again with Daria, particularly based on the vague information Brian could give us into Danny Bakker's love life. We approached the ground floor flat in Tollcross, the one Brian was 'pretty sure' was the one he'd attended a house party at and had met this new girl in Danny's life for the first time. 'Bit rough around the edges, but I can absolutely see what he sees in her – saw in her' had been his assessment of Priss no-surname-yet-ascertained.

'I'll leave you to it?' Brian said. He couldn't wait to be out of our company and who could blame him. A vague threat from me wasn't going to be enough for him to take us here and instead the good-cop routine, complete with some flirting from Rowan, had convinced him, but we were pushing the limits of his tolerance now.

'Maybe just a few more seconds, Brian. I'm assuming you weren't exactly sober the last time you were here? If it's the wrong place, maybe something else will occur to you,' I said and knocked hard on the blue painted door.

Ten seconds passed in silence and I knocked again and this time included a blast of the doorbell. Nothing. I turned and chapped the door behind us, the only other flat on this floor. It was answered quickly by a confused-looking, middle-aged woman.

'Sorry to bother you,' I said, flashing the warrant card at her. 'Do you know your neighbour who stays here?' I thumbed at the unanswered door.

'Not well. A couple of students. Young ladies.'

'Is one of them called Priss?'

She thought on this, but her head began to shake. 'I'm sorry, I'm not sure.'

'What does she look like?' Rowan asked Brian.

'Uh, she's kinda tall, uh . . .'

'Tell her,' Rowan said.

'Uh, she's tall, slim. Black hair, probably dyed. Has a sort of goth look with lots of dark eye make-up. Really pretty, though.'

'Yeah, that sounds like her. One of them,' the neighbour said, and I thanked her, allowing her to go back inside and probably watch from her peephole.

I rattled the door once more and this time had a look through the letter box. It was dark inside, curtains from what looked like a living room at the end of the hall glowed dully as they shut out the outside light. I cupped my hands trying to let my eyes adjust. Something slowly came into focus. Something on the floor. 'Fuck.'

'What?' Rowan said.

'Stand back.' I took two strides backwards, almost to the neighbour's door again, quickly assessed the distance and strode forward, launching my foot just below the door handle. The door resisted and a shockwave travelled up from my heel to my hip. I reset and went again. This shockwave was worse than the first, but a cracking sound from the door persuaded me into one last kick. This time the door conceded, swinging and crashing into the inside wall. 'Call an ambulance,' I said to Rowan. I flicked on the hall light and went to the leg I could see on the living room floor. Inside, the young lady Brian had just described lay. My first thought was she was dead for sure, another massive heroin overdose, but the several pools of vomit around her head and down her chin and chest demanded further assessment. I held my fingers to her neck, looking around the place as I did. Rowan was on the radio giving our location. 'Breathing, but unconscious. Very weak pulse,' I said for her to relay. 'Looks like an overdose, but pills.' I picked up one empty bottle and tossed it to Rowan for her to read the label to control.

Brian watched from the doorway, his hands in his hair.

CHAPTER 9

Headliners

As she stretched high into the kitchen cupboard, the T-shirt she was wearing, the iconic smiley-face Nirvana one of Davie's, rode up, revealing white panties and an incredible bottom. She strained higher, on one foot, and the corresponding bottom cheek tensed, gripping the underwear. The legs beneath the pert bottom were also fine. Milky white, athletic and—

'What the fuck are you staring at, ya wee perve?'

'Uh, n-n-nothin'. I was j-just . . .'

'Aye, aye,' Sal laughed and shook cereal into a bowl.

The fucking stutter always gave him away, evidently returning not just through stress, but also embarrassment. She did this on purpose, got some kind of kick out of it, he was sure.

She poured what was left of the milk into the bowl, tutting and tossing the empty carton into the sink. She approached the small table where Dillon sat and kneed his legs off the chair on which they rested, despite there being another two she could have taken. She sat opposite and raised her legs onto his thigh, slightly apart. She ate her cereal and swiped at her phone. The white panties begged for his gaze. He did his best to ignore this game of hers, until her heel began brushing the front of his jeans.

'Fuck off,' he said and knocked her legs away. She was laughing, and then he was too.

'What's the joke?' Davie said through a yawn as he entered the kitchen.

'Just that your wee brother is a pervert.'

'Aye, well, runs in the family. You can't blame him,' Davie said and kissed her neck. His good mood faded when he pulled the empty milk carton from the sink. 'Could at least have left me enough for a cup of tea.' He tossed the carton back and shook the cereal box, also empty. 'You're a pair of fucking animals.'

'That's why you love me,' Sal said. 'Here,' she handed Davie her bowl and stood. Davie took her seat and ate. 'Hey, Dillon?'

Dillon looked up from his phone. 'For fuck sake,' he said and averted his eyes. Sal stood with the T-shirt pulled up to her neck, shaking her tits side to side. She and Davie laughed. Dillon threw a tea towel at her back as she left.

'It's getting serious?' Dillon said, nodding at the now empty kitchen doorway.

Davie shrugged. 'I dunno. It's Sal. I hope so.' He said this last part in a whisper.

Dillon knew what he was getting at. Sal was feral, always had been. The idea of her settling down was somewhat laughable. Dillon couldn't recall the first time he'd met her. She'd been a permanent fixture of his childhood. She commanded an almost mythical aura, at least to the younger kids in the Wester Hailes housing scheme they called home and still did. She was faster, stronger, braver and knew more swear words than almost any boy. If he was honest with himself, Dillon would have to concede he'd always had a bit of a crush on her, but he was certain they'd all had at some point, even when she had been a skinny, snotty-nosed tomboy, and before she'd evolved into the striking, womanly tomboy. She'd always had that long blonde hair, the attitude and a knack for flirting. She'd been with quite a few of the older kids, including Tavish, though that was some time ago now. Davie had never been on her radar, though, not until this year. It wasn't clear what had changed, but Sal living with them in this shithole flat? That was something of a statement on her part.

They'd all been guilty of breaking a law or twelve, Dillon's own record consisting of three counts of possession. One of these had initially been an intent-to-supply charge, but had been successfully argued down by a court-appointed brief. However, of the four of them, Sal was the only one to have done time. Six weeks in Cornton Vale Young Offenders for, well, nobody knew exactly what, but they all remembered the night four or five police cars came screaming into the scheme. Dillon had been playing football under the street lights and had only just managed to get himself and his ball safely out of the way when they rolled up. They'd all gathered, he, Davie, Tavish and maybe a dozen others as Sal was dragged, kicking and screaming into a cell van. Two ambulances had also arrived by the time Sal was being shuttled from the street. Her mum and boyfriend left shortly after in one of the ambulances, his arm heavily bandaged. She had been asked plenty of times what had happened but had brushed it off. By the time Sal was released, the boyfriend was gone, leaving behind only sordid rumours.

'At least tell her to stop flashing her tits.'

Davie took Dillon's tea from him and drank half of what was left before returning the mug. 'What's wrong with her tits?'

'What? N-nothing's wrong with her tits, it's just—ach, stop being a prick.'

Davie was laughing again. His phone launched into 'Territorial Pissings', his favourite Nirvana song. Dillon knew this, not because he himself had any interest in the band, or any music really, but because his brother's eternal mission in life was to bring the band to the attention of anyone who dared be in the same room as him after a few drinks. As if they were some obscure hidden gem and not arguably the biggest band in the world in their day – Dad's day, that was.

There was a knock at the front door, hard, urgent. It made Dillon stop mid-gulp from his tea.

Davie motioned with his head, telling Dillon to get the door as he answered his call.

''sup?'

Dillon could hear the person on the other end of the

phone, it was the same raised voice that was coming from the other side of the front door.

'What? Slow down,' Davie was saying.

Dillon opened the door and Tavish entered, almost knocking him backwards. He hung up the phone when he reached the kitchen.

'What the fuck are you talking about, the news?' Davie said.

'Where's Sal?'

'In the shower, I think.'

'Get her. And get a laptop, or a tablet,' Tavish said to Dillon who swallowed his instinct to protest at being treated like a servant. Tavish wasn't in the mood.

Dillon could hear the noise of the shower in the bathroom. He chapped the door. 'Sal, get your arse out here. Something's going on.' He moved on to his room and scooped up his laptop from his single bed and pulled the power cable from it. When he returned to the hall, the sound of the shower was still hissing away. He chapped again and opened the door.

'Sal,' he said to the shower curtain.

Her head appeared round the side of it. 'You already saw my tits. That's all you're getting.'

'Tavish is here. Something's up.'

He returned to the kitchen and dropped the laptop onto the table. It was a silver Acer, a piece of shit adorned with stickers, most of which pertained to Hibs FC.

'I got a call this morning,' Tavish was saying. He pressed the power button and the laptop began its slow awakening. 'You remember that prick from Fife?'

'Kelty,' Davie said.

'Aye. He said to put on the news and he'd call back in an hour.'

'Meaning what?' Dillon said.

'Fucked if I know. It's why I'm here. Had a look on my phone, but couldn't find anything that made sense. How old is this fucking thing?' Tavish lifted the bottom of the laptop and let it slam down against the table. Dillon again swallowed his reaction.

Sal entered wrapped in a much-too-small-for-the-job towel. Her hair dripping onto the floor.

The desktop finally appeared, Hibs' crest backdropping a few dozen icons.

Tavish moved the cursor around, making frustrated noises.

'There,' Davie said and took over, drawing the cursor to Firefox before double-tapping.

The browser booted up, bringing with it a stream of tabs from the previous session, the last viewed being active on the screen. Dillon flushed with embarrassment as Pornhub loaded. The video section was blank but loading. Davie flicked him a disapproving glance and typed BBC Scotland News into the search bar, mercifully redirecting the tab.

'Such a perve,' Sal whispered and bumped the back of Dillon's leg with her hip.

The three of them read the headlines as Davie scrolled the page down. Articles on Brexit, focussing on a fishing dispute in the English Channel, dominated. But before long, something caught their accumulated attention. 'There,' Davie said.

Tavish read the headline aloud and clicked on the link: 'Rogue heroin batch killing Edinburgh addicts.'

Tavish scrolled down through the article, too fast for anyone to read much of it and clicked on the video attached to the story.

It took an age to load up, but when it did, a section of a police press conference played. A female officer in a sharp grey suit delivering a message. Her face, already pale, flashed white intermittently with photographers doing their thing out of shot.

'How do you turn it up?' Tavish complained. Dillion stretched over him and tapped at a button until the blonde woman's voice could be heard, the caption below her read: 'Detective Chief Inspector Kate Templeton.'

'. . . alert the public to a recent influx of heroin to the street market. So far, the incidents connected are in the Edinburgh area, but any users in Scotland should be aware of this particularly dangerous batch, which is significantly stronger than what can normally be expected. We are still gathering information and enquiries are ongoing, but at this stage there is enough concern to alert the public. If you are a heroin user, it is recommended that you search out safe drug-consumption spaces. Particularly, supervised environments where naloxone is available, sometimes known by the product name Narcan, which is effective in combatting accidental overdose. I'll take a few questions.' There was a murmured clamour off-screen as multiple journalists threw queries at the woman, but were not discernible on the audio. She answered the unheard question: 'So far we think we have four deaths connected, but we're pushing through toxicology of a few more that might well be included.' Another mumbled question was asked: 'We don't know the origin at this stage, no. Nor can we be sure how far-spread the issue is. Heroin has never been a safe drug, but our advice to users is be extremely cautious.'

The clip ran out and the four were left staring at the screen.

'Fuck,' Dillon said, at last.

'Means nothin'. How do we know it's our stuff?' Tavish said and slammed the laptop lid closed, but the look on his face confirmed what they all surely knew. The stuff being warned about in the news was the stuff in Dad's lock-up.

'Phone the guy, Kelty,' Davie said.

Davie took out his phone, tapped at the screen then laid it down on top of the laptop. The speaker buzzed a call dial.

'You saw it?' The voice on the other end said.

'Aye, so what?' Tavish returned.

'The bit about cases being in Edinburgh only isn't true. I've a customer in the morgue in the Victoria Hospital in Kirkaldy, and it's only a matter of time before they link these cases up.'

Tavish didn't respond to this. He looked around at the faces of the others. Then the voice was back.

'Ask me where I am.'

'What?'

'Ask.'

Tavish took a long breath in and out. 'Where are you?'

'Same place we last met. Be here in ten minutes or less, or I make an anonymous call to the pigs.' The call was hung up. Tavish fell back into his chair, rubbing his face.

'What's the plan?' Davie said. He was driving like a twat, but making good progress along Gorgie Road, overtaking when it was on and once when it really wasn't.

'You lot just stay in the van. If it kicks off, I'll be fine.' Tavish removed a fishing knife, the one Dillon had seen a few times, but never in action. Tavish pulled the blade from the handle and twisted until it locked in place.

'The fuck you will,' Sal said. She snatched the knife from him and collapsed it before shoving it back at him. 'We all show up. We got into this together, we'll get out together. Right?'

Davie grunted his ascent when Sal looked at him. She sat between him and Tavish in the front seat. Dillon was in the back of the van, gripping the bulkhead, trying to stay upright and feeling like a dog in a car boot.

'Right?' Sal repeated over her shoulder. Dillion nodded. What else could he do? He sat down, pressing his back against the bulkhead. This was the car yard all over again. Ill-conceived, undoubtedly dangerous. Plain fucking stupid. What were they driving to? And how the hell did it come to this? When this was over, surely it was time to sever ties with Tavish? If they made it out of today with their kneecaps in place, that was exactly what he would do. He'd have a chat to Davie, figure something out. Ironically, it was the thought of leaving Tavish and the scheme behind that had gotten him into this. Selling pills and weed to people you knew was one thing, this, this was quite another. *Need to talk to you about something*, Tavish had said, showing up at the flat at a crazy hour, not off his tits, but circling the drain. Clear of head enough to run his ridiculous plan by them. Tavish had refused to say where his intel had come from, just that it was kosher, that some new pricks had rolled in and were an easy target. Dillon had listened to nonsense, waiting for Davie to laugh in his face, and he might have done were it not for Sal. 'A kilo of MDMA? Just think?' Davie had folded like a pamphlet. Dillon was waiting to talk him out of it when he got Davie alone, but by the time he did, the promise of money was eating at his own resolve. Tavish had made it sound simple. Smash, grab, get the fuck out of Wester Hailes within a month. Now? Fuck only knew.

There was a bump of tyres on kerb and Dillon returned to himself.

'Here we go,' Davie said as he cut the engine.

'Everyone out,' Sal said – demanded.

The sunlight was in Dillon's eyes when Davie pulled the back door open. He stepped out, took a breath and came around to the front. The same Porsche Cayenne and hire-a-thug were there, along with a large grey Transit van and a couple more black-T-shirted men. If this kicked off, Tavish and his fishing knife weren't going to be enough, not nearly.

Dillion watched from the back. He could run from here, though he knew he wouldn't, not unless Davie did and he was too loyal, too in love with Sal who would sooner be beaten to death than break ranks.

118

'Awrite,' Tavish said to Kelty who was calmly leaning his back against the lock-up door. He was dressed as before, dark jeans and a blue suit jacket. He puffed at a cigarette and raised his eyebrows in response to Tavish's opener. 'So, what's the script? You're here for what? For revenge? To rob us? 'Cause I swear to you, you might get past us, but I'll take a couple of you cunts with me.'

Kelty raised his hands in mock surrender, which raised a collective chuckle from his crew.

'We didn't know there was anything wrong with the stuff,' Davie said.

'Oh, I know that,' Kelty said. He lowered his hands. 'You're not the brightest bunch, but you surely can't be so daft as to think you can sell me shite smack and get away with it.'

'So, what then?' Tavish's body language was jittery. He was as terrified as any of them, but he was also ready to go to war. For all that he was a prick, you had to admire the balls on him. His hand was in his pocket, no doubt fingering the knife within.

'Today's your lucky day,' Kelty said. He took a last drag of the cigarette before tossing it. Days gone I might have taken your balls and your stuff, but, I don't know, maybe old age is mellowing me.' Another collective chuckle from his crew. 'What I'm here to do is buy the rest of your shit.'

'What?' Tavish looked like someone had just tried to explain theoretical physics to him.

'You heard. So, how about it? Are you going to open your wee shop here and make a deal?'

'Wait. I'm confused.'

'Quite obviously. I doubt it takes much, but how can I be any clearer for you?'

'You said the stuff is dangerous—'

'The news said the stuff is dangerous, but you can let me worry about that.'

'What's the catch?'

'Are you open for business or not? I've not got all day.'

Tavish looked at Davie. Davie shrugged. Tavish thought on it for a moment and beckoned him over. Davie took out his keys and removed the padlock before heaving up the door.

This is where they rush us. This is where they do to us what we did to Brown Leather Jacket. But nothing was happening, yet. Dillon looked around at Kelty's men. They looked calm, uninterested even.

Davie was setting up the pasting table again, as if this was a car boot sale.

'H'much you looking for?' Tavish said.

'Like I told you. I'm here for the rest of it. I want all of it.'

It was Tavish's turn to laugh. 'You don't even know how much we—'

'It doesn't matter.' Kelty took out a brown envelope and calmly laid it on the table. He made a few small adjustments until it lined up perfectly square in the corner. 'However much you have, this will cover it.'

Tavish scoffed. 'And what if I was to tell you we've got over eighty kilos. You'd have to switch that envelope for a truck full of cash.'

Kelty raised his eyebrows at this, but he didn't seem shocked, or even particularly impressed. *What did he know?*

'Okay, eighty kilos? It's a deal.' Kelty pushed out his hand for Tavish to shake. Tavish didn't know what to do. His hand came up for a second, then he pushed it back into his coat pocket, back around the knife handle probably. He spun on his heels, looking first at Davie, then at Sal, even to Dillon. 'How much is in there?' he said, returning to Kelty. His voice was small, the confidence had left temporarily.

'You're welcome to check, but you'll find there's fifty-thousand exactly.'

Another scoff. 'You're a few million short, pal.'

'Oh, more, probably. See the stuff you're selling is almost uncut. See this shit wasn't meant for the street, not yet. So, you're probably closer to five million in value. The thing is, if you keep selling this in dribs and drabs, the boys in blue are gonna be all over this in days, maybe hours, depending on who you've been selling to so far. So not only have you no chance of making that kind of money, you're all also looking at lengthy jail time, just for trying.' Kelty stepped up close to Tavish. He tapped three times on the envelope. 'I could take all your shit right now, for free, but this – this is my insurance policy. It's also what you'd call a win-win situation.'

This time Tavish's scoff was half-hearted. 'Aye?' he said.

'Aye. See, if we make this transaction, you walk away with something, and I take the risk off your hands. That 50K means you don't go blabbing to the police. If they do catch up to you for this, you tell them whatever you like, but you leave my name out of it. Otherwise they'll be back for that money and take it under the Proceeds of Crime Act. You've heard of it?' The question was rhetorical, though Tavish's blank expression answered it anyway. 'If the police come looking for me, I let them know where I bought it from and for how much. They come back here and rip your life apart until they take every penny you've not pissed up the wall. So, what do you say? You want to get paid and get rid of this shit before you're locked up, not just on drugs charges, but also for manslaughter?'

Tavish was quiet for a moment. Dillon's heart was threatening to bask in relief, but Tavish was shaking his head.

'Fifty grand for three, or five, million worth? Nah, fuck that.'

'Tavish,' Davie said.

'Maybe you should have a chat with your colleagues, before deciding "fuck that" is your final word on the matter?' Kelty said.

CHAPTER 10

Painting a Picture

'Hey, it's me. Look, I'm sorry, I'm not going to make dinner tonight.' There was silence on the line. I lifted the phone from my face to check I was still connected. I was. 'Hello?'

'You're stuck at work?' Marcella said. Her voice was flat. Not angry, more like bored. Bored was worse.

'I'm sorry, really. I'm at the hospital and could be here for some time.'

'You're not hurt, are you?' Her voice rose, but only a little. She no doubt realised that if I was badly injured, it would be someone else calling her.

'No. A suspect. It was touch and go for a while, but it looks like she's going to pull—'

'Okay, well, I suppose I'll see you at the weekend. I better go, Don. I'll see you.'

The call was cut. There was no time to respond. '*I'll see you*'? There was something about the end of the call I didn't like. Not like *I'll see you later*, more like *I'll see you around*. Or maybe I was overthinking.

'Trouble in paradise?'

'Huh?'

Rowan broke off a piece of the chocolate bar she'd just bought from the hospital vending machine. She tossed it into her mouth and offered me the packet. The main cafeteria in the hospital was busy, but we discovered an area set aside for staff where only a few people were either reading or tapping at laptops.

'No thanks. Wait, on second thoughts, God only knows how long we'll be here.' I broke a piece and handed the packet back. 'I'm getting the feeling I'm on very shaky ground with Marcella.' I ate the chocolate and thought about what a lousy substitute it was for the reservation we'd made at a Thai place in Stockbridge.

'She's a Monday to Friday, nine-to-five type?'

I nodded, still getting the chocolate down.

'That's why I don't date normies.'

'Normies?'

'People with normal jobs. They just don't get it.'

'So, wait. You don't date cops and you don't date people with normal jobs? Doesn't that leave the pool a little – shallow?' I nodded at the table in the corner and we sat, Rowan's solitary chocolate bar sitting on the table between us.

'Who says I don't date cops?'

'You did.'

'When?' She broke off another piece of chocolate. Her face was twisted in confusion.

'Back in Stratharder.'

'Did I?'

I thought for a moment. It was a few years ago we'd met in the small highland village where she was still a probationer, but I was pretty sure she'd made this declaration. 'Yeah, you did. I asked about your previous relationship and you said you dated someone you met at the training college and that had put you off cops for life.'

'Are you sure?' She wrinkled her nose, her eyes searched the ceiling, either in an attempt at recollection, or she was being evasive.

'I might be paraphrasing, but yes. That's what you said.'

'Uh. If you say so.' She shrugged and popped the chocolate into her mouth.

'Wait. Does that mean you dropped this rule of yours at some point?'

'You're too old for me,' she said around the confectionary in her mouth. She was smiling, teasing me.

'One of a dozen reasons we'd be a complete disaster, Rowan. Now answer the question.'

Her arms were folded but she released one hand to point at her mouth suggesting I let her finish first. Before she did, my phone began buzzing in my pocket. A sense of relief grew. *Marcella*, I thought. Perhaps back with a more forgiving tone, but no.

'Hello.'

'DS Colyear, it's Simon, uh, PC Grant. You said to call you if you could get access? Well the doctor has okayed it.'

'Thanks, Simon, we'll be right up. We're on,' I said to the still-chewing Rowan. 'And this conversation is to be continued.'

'If you say so.'

PC Grant was reading a magazine, probably for the third time, outside of the room within the Intensive Care Unit. He dropped his reading and stood as we approached.

'Hi, Simon. What are the doctors saying?'

'Sarge. She's doing okay. Getting moved to High Dependency at some point. They said you can speak to her before they shift her, but not to overdo it. Whatever that means.'

'Is her mum still here?'

'I don't know. No fresh attempts to breach security, anyway.' There had been an awkward encounter with the woman the morning after her daughter had arrived at the hospital. We were just leaving, having been told Deborah 'Priss' Donaghy wouldn't be in any fit state to answer questions at any point in the proceeding twenty-four hours. The noise of a nurse shouting 'You can't go in there' was heard just before a diminutive middle-aged woman with the same bottle-black hair came running around the corner of Ward 118, having tailgated a staff member through the locked door. Rowan had put a tackle on her an All-Blacks forward would have been proud of. We'd done our best to convince her it just wasn't a good idea for her to see her daughter without spelling out the fact she was waiting to be questioned about a possible murder.

'Why don't you take a break. Go get something to eat. I'll call you when we're done.'

PC Grant didn't protest. He stretched his back and thanked us before taking his hat for a walk down the corridor.

'Fucking hated hospital watch,' Rowan said, voicing the thought in my head.

I pushed the door open and gave the inside a soft knock to gain the attention of the young woman on the bed.

'Hi,' I said in a small voice as we entered.

She made to sit up, but her wrist caught on the handcuff connecting her to the bed. She looked at it and then at us.

'Let me help you,' Rowan said and held a button to bring the bed up. The electronic whine seemed to last forever. I gathered a couple of chairs to sit by the bed.

'Has it been explained to you why we're here?' I said.

She nodded and began to cry. Her hand instinctively rose to wipe the tears, but again it was her right hand, the one tethering her to the bed. 'Fuck,' she said and yanked hard in frustration, something that must have hurt. She looked around, but Rowan was ahead of her, handing her a few tissues from a pack on the bedside table.

'I wouldn't be doing my job – Priss, right? – not Deborah?'

'Yeah, Priss,' she said and grunted the emotion out of her voice.

'I wouldn't be doing my job if I didn't spell it out and give you a common-law caution before we talk, okay.'

She nodded and dabbed at a fresh tear.

'Okay. Priss Donaghy you are currently under arrest on the suspicion of murder. You're not obliged to say anything at this time and anything you do say will be noted and may be used in evidence. Do you understand?'

She nodded again.

'Thanks, Priss, but I need to hear you say—'

'Yes, yes.' Fresh tears began.

'I also need to tell you that you have the right to legal consultation before I ask you questions into the crime.'

She sniffed and shook her head. 'It doesn't matter.'

I sighed. I was going to have to be officious again. 'I need you to confirm that you are waiving your right to legal counsel and to sign my notebook to that effect.'

'Fine. Whatever.'

While Rowan was setting up with the statement paper, I asked her about what the doctors had told her.

'That there's a good chance I've done some damage to liver and kidneys.' She shrugged. I wondered about what would happen when all this was over. The pills were not a cry for help. From what we could find discarded in the flat, she'd swallowed enough to kill herself a dozen times over.

'Are you comfortable enough now to do this?'

'Let's just get it over with. I'll tell you what I can, but there's a point I won't cross.'

'What does that mean?' I asked. I looked at her. She was pretty, as Danny's roommate had alluded to, but the past few days were written all over her face. Her glossy eyes were sunken, drawn into dark bowls. Her lips were dry and cracking. Her black hair had an unhealthy sheen and it stuck to one cheek, pulled in by the tears.

'I'm sure you'll see as we go.'

Rowan gave me a nod. I began.

'How long have you been a heroin user, Priss?' She followed my gaze to where subtle, but unmistakeable track marks showed.

She cleared her throat as she did the maths. 'Three years. Four if you count the period when I was just smoking it.'

'How long have you been seeing Danny?'

There was a long silence as she fought and ultimately lost the battle against the tears. She heaved in breaths between sobs and again yanked at the cuffs when she forgot they were there.

'How long, Priss?' I said softly when she'd just about composed herself.

'Ugh. I don't know. Four months maybe. But can we skip the getting to know you bit? I said I'll answer your questions. Don't torture me.'

'Okay. That's fair.' I quickly reshuffled the questions in my head. 'How many times had Danny taken heroin with you?'

She shook her head.

'This was the first time?'

She nodded and wiped at her face.

'What happened?' The attempt to open the interview up failed. She shook her head; she was only going to answer direct questions. 'Who prepared the syringe?' She looked at me and returned her eyes to the bedsheet at her legs. 'You prepared it?' She nodded. 'Who injected him? Did you inject him, Priss?'

'Yes. I did,' she said, which took me by surprise. Her responses had been meek, contrite, so far, but there was anger in this one.

'Where did this happen?'

She shook her head. 'No.'

'Priss—'

'I told you. Only so far.'

'Priss, trust me when I tell you that this is not the time to be protecting people.'

'And you trust me when I tell you I'm protecting myself, not others.'

I breathed a frustrated breath. *Double back, don't press right now*, I thought. 'When did you know he was in trouble?'

It took time for her to answer as she relived the moment. 'Right away. I knew it almost immediately.' She sobbed, but continued, 'I don't get it. I gave him such a small amount. I swear.'

'Why didn't you call an ambulance?' She was shaking her head again. 'You loved him. You must have wanted to?' The head was still shaking. I tried to picture the scene. 'You wanted to, but you weren't allowed to.' There was no answer, but the head was still. 'He went downhill so fast you were convinced, by persons unnamed, that it was pointless. You left, premises undisclosed, before or after his body was removed?' Nothing. 'I'm guessing it was before. You surely wouldn't have had anything to do with the undignified manner of his disposal.' At this she looked up at me. There was an unknowing in her wet eyes. 'Priss, I watched Danny pulled from a wheelie bin in the middle of the street.'

'No.' She clawed at her eyes with her free hand.

'You went straight home and tried to take your own life while someone was stuffing your boyfriend head first into that thing and dragging him far enough away from where he died as they felt was safe. As horrendous as that was, it was a convenient way for someone to remove a body. It might be that we'll get the information we need from fingerprints, Priss, but here's the thing. That heroin you gave Danny, it's part of a batch that I'm hunting down. It's not your fault that he OD'd. That stuff is uncut and Danny is not the first to die as a result, but I'm trying to make sure he's the last. I need to know where it came from.' The shaking head again.

I sat back in my chair. She would take what was coming to her, her conscience made sure of that, but she wasn't about to draw anyone else in, particularly a drug dealer she was afraid of.

'I need to paint you a picture of what's going to happen next, Priss. I'm not torturing you, but this isn't going to be easy to hear. It's a sad fact of society that the public don't really care about junkies succumbing to their habits. It rarely hits the news. But Danny? That's a whole different animal. He was a good kid from a good family, doing well at university with a bright future ahead of him. That was until he met you.' This much I'd learnt from DCI Templeton. I could only imagine how tough the conversation had been with Danny's parents, but at some point she'd managed to talk about his life in Edinburgh. Kate had warned me that the press would be all over this, and now I had to make it clear to this young lady. 'He's injected heroin for the first time by his junkie girlfriend and dies. His body is dumped into a bin in the hope it will disappear with the rest of the rubbish. Priss, I will need to chat your case over with the Crown Office and Procurator Fiscal Service for direction, but I'm pretty sure they will tell me to charge you with Danny's murder. This is going to be big news and there will be a lot of pressure on the judge and jury to find you guilty.'

'I'll kill myself before this ever gets to court,' she said, half yelled.

'Maybe. That's how you feel now, but I guess we'll see. Thing is, you can help yourself, at least a little. Information you have can help stop someone else dying from this filth that's on the street. If I can explain how you've helped in our enquiries, it will be in your favour. I won't make you any promises, but it might make the difference between a murder conviction and culpable homicide. That's years in terms of potential incarceration. Now, Priss, please. Where did this stuff come from?'

She let her head fall backwards onto the pillow. She was silent for a long time. I was beginning to think the interview was over when she sat herself up and cleared her throat.

'He stopped breathing almost immediately. I've seen an overdose once before and that started with really shallow breathing and then going downhill from there. The pale skin, then trouble breathing. But not Danny. His head lolled forward and by the time I got him onto his back I couldn't hear any breath from him at all. I was panicking. The—the people I was with were losing their shit. I did take out my phone to call someone, but he . . . It was taken from me. "He's gone," they were saying. "Look at him, he's gone." And he was. As soon as I realised that, I could hear myself screaming. Like I was out of my body, somewhere else in the room, listening to myself scream. I let them convince me to leave him there. I left him there.'

We waited for her to cry it out for some time. Her stuttered breathing began to gain rhythm once more and I could ask the question at last.

'Where is this room, Priss?'

CHAPTER 11

Bears' Den

Mercifully DCI Templeton decided it was best to wait until the morning to organise a warrant. It meant Rowan and I had the evening to get some sleep, though Rowan had other ideas.

'We need to go for a drink. I feel like I'm covered in something that no amount of showering will get off,' she'd said as we exited the hospital.

I'd agreed and let her choose the place. I went home, showered, called Marcella, thinking I might be able to recover the evening, but my call had gone straight to voicemail. I left a message that I hoped was leaning on breezy rather than pathetic. I was halfway through my first pint in Montpeliers, a nice, modern, little place in Bruntsfield where there were as many people eating as there were drinking, before Rowan showed. There was an awkward moment when I stood and suddenly wasn't sure why. I think perhaps I was about to kiss her cheek and then realised *why would I do that?* She was equally confused.

'Uh, sorry I'm late. I got a phone call I had to take,' she said and slung her coat over a chair.

'Don't worry, it's not like I had to cross the city to be here and you live a few hundred metres down the street.'

'You got an apology, get over it. Another?' she said, pointing at my glass.

'Sure.'

She returned with the drinks and I suddenly noticed what I'd failed to when she'd taken her coat off. 'Are you wearing a dress?'

'Wow. Good eye. You should be a cop.'

'Why?'

'Why what?' she said after a long draw from her glass. She'd also gone for beer and had drained a full third from that sip. Probably picturing it since we left Priss in such a state in her hospital bed.

'Why a dress? And, are . . . are you wearing perfume?'

'What if I am?' She leant away from me trying to get a sniff of her.

'What's the occasion?'

'Getting out of the house is the occasion. Doing anything but working, is the occasion. Just trying to feel human, and God forbid, perhaps even attractive – and don't worry, it's not for your benefit.'

'It didn't even enter my mind. I was just curious.'

'Yeah, yeah. Anyway, cheers.' She clinked my glass and emptied her glass beyond halfway, hiding a burp behind her fist when she laid it down again. She looked tired, really tired. I guessed that was why she got dressed up, try to break the cycle of work and recovery that can, if you're not careful, make you feel like a mouse on a wheel. The place had a nice buzz about it. Some soft music was overpowered, though not annoyingly so, by the hum of conversation.

'That was a tough afternoon,' I said. I thought it was time to bring up the reason for getting some alcohol inside of us.

She blew out a breath, 'Understatement. I'm not sure I could have interviewed her. You know, asked those difficult questions when it was clearly breaking her.'

'You think I should have approached it differently?'

She shook her head while she drank. 'No. Not at all. That was a really good result, and you kept your promise.'

'Promise?'

'That you wouldn't torture her. Nothing you asked was cruel. It was awful to see her relive it, but it was necessary. Do you really think her helping us will help her at all?'

My turn to take a long glug from my glass. 'I hope so. All I can do is make it clear on the report. Or ask the one who submits it, if Kate takes it off of us?'

'You don't really think that will happen, do you?'

'I don't know. It's not the first time I've been involved in a murder charge, but I've never reported one. Given the press this is going to get, it might be better handled by someone more senior, or at least by someone with more experience.'

'Surely that won't happen. You remember Kate's speech about being taken off of cases in her younger career. I don't see her doing that to you.' She put down her now empty glass and shifted in her seat to face me square on. 'You want her to take you off. Why?'

My mouth began forming a denial, but I quickly gave it up. 'Honestly, I'm still scratching my head a bit as to how I ended up as a detective sergeant, a sergeant at all. I was never so ambitious. Tracking down killer smack is one thing, but picking up a murder case is another.'

'Do you really think she'll face a murder trial?'

'I think that's what they'll charge her with. What *we'll* charge her with. There's legal precedence for it, injecting someone else with drugs, irrespective of the motivation. But I like to think her lawyer will negotiate it down, especially with her cooperation.'

'Fuck. Poor girl. Okay, I'll get them in. I want to drink until I don't give a shit,' is what she said, but as I laid a third round of drinks on the table half an hour later, she was pulling her coat on.

'What's going on?'

'Uh, sorry. Look, I got a call. I need to be somewhere.'

'That's . . . vague. You're okay?'

'Yeah. Of course. I just need to meet someone.' She was squirming. Cagey as a double agent as she always was when it came to her personal life. 'Don't hate me. This has been fun and we should do it again soon, it's just . . .' Her face was pulled into a painful grimace and her thumb pointed at the door.

'It's fine, Rowan,' I laughed. 'I mean running out on a friend should usually earn at least an explanation, but—'

'Thanks. You're a good sport. See you in the morning.'

'Six a.m., remember. So, keep that in mind for whatever it is you're running off to. For this mysterious thing you got dressed up for.'

She stopped for a second in her hurried exit, but she, in kind, gave up her attempt at denial and just smiled. I shot her a wink.

I felt self-conscious sitting on my own, but I was damned if I was going to leave two full pints behind, particularly at Edinburgh prices. I told myself to enjoy them and go home. I told myself this again while I pulled my phone from my pocket and started typing the message to Marcella. *Almost certainly a bad idea*, I scolded and yet, my finger was in a rebellious mood as it hit send. I switched to the BBC app and narrowed a news search to Scotland. And there it was, already. Lead article: STAR STUDENT KILLED BY ROGUE HEROIN. I clicked on the image next to the headline, and the picture enlarged to fill my screen. It was our Daniel Bakker, but unrecognisable from the twisted husk I saw pulled onto a plastic sheet in the middle of the street. It looked to have been cropped from a larger shot, the arms of his teammates still just about visible around his shoulders. He wore a dark green football shirt that suggested, from the mud stains on his chest, that this was a post-game celebration picture. He was the very image of athletic prowess and wore a smile of orthodontic perfection, the brightness of which contrasted so handsomely with his light brown skin. It was the ideal visual accompaniment to an article that described a young man whose immense potential would never be realised. It lingered heavily on him being top goal-scorer and vice-captain of the university football team, the highlight being scoring the winning goal the previous season that sent the team through to the third round of the Scottish F.A. cup. The team had gone on to play Dundee in the fourth round with no expectation of progressing, but had only lost by a single goal and had won the plaudits from supporters and pundits alike.

The article continued to his studies, describing him as a 'brilliant academic', though it cited no justificatory support, so who knew how accurate that was. I suspected it might be an exaggerated finger with which to better pluck at the heartstrings of readers. There was a link to the press event Kate fronted, which I'd watched from the sidelines.

There was no mention of the body being found in a bin, however. That horror headline would certainly have eclipsed the personal approach they were going for here. So that information was being retained by the force. The link to the 'rogue' heroin, though, was assumption, as Daniel's bloodwork still hadn't been returned from the lab, though nobody was expecting anything but confirmation that it came from my batch. *My batch?* I thought. I had a sudden flush of profound responsibility that unpleasantly wormed its way up my back and seemed to settle like a weight at the back of my neck. The article became increasingly political and read like the boy was murdered by the government's inability to tackle the country's 'drug shame'. *Did that include me?* I was pondering this when my phone buzzed on my lap, pulling me back into the room. I read the message below the one I'd sent and reached for my coat.

Hey. I'm in your neck of the woods having a drink with Rowan. Sorry again about today, but can I come over?

Fine. But I'm going to sleep. I have an early start.

It was a gruff reply, but better than I'd expected and perhaps deserved. I crossed from Bruntsfield and down through the millionaires' neighbourhood of The Grange, taking every opportunity to peer into gardens and windows to get a sense of how the other half live their lives. I always feel you can get a pretty accurate sense of house prices from the cars parked in drives and on the street and here there were more Range Rovers and Teslas than any area ought to have. The cars on the street switched from high-end to middle price to more like my affordability as I reached Newington and Marcella's flat. I found the key she'd given me on the ring of my others, thinking how close I might be to digging my nails into this split ring to remove it and hand it back.

It wasn't just recent cancellations; it was a theme since we'd started seeing one another. Twice she'd set up a dinner party with her friends only for me to get held on at work, which had resulted in our first fight, revolving around an accusation of my being uninterested in learning anything about her outside of her bed. It was harsh and untrue, but I'd been unable to offer much in the way of evidence to the contrary. *Normies* I heard Rowan say in my head. Even now I'd avoided dinner with Marcella and still was crawling into bed beside her. Which is where I found her. Tucked in her cocoon of a duvet with the lights off and the blinds drawn. I thought it absurdly unwise to try to instigate anything, so I undressed and slipped in beside her, giving her shoulder a kiss and readying to roll away from her. However, she moaned gently and moved herself backwards against me. Absurdly unwise or not, my body reacted, and thankfully so did hers.

I felt like I'd been asleep for minutes when my phone alarm sounded. Marcella may have had an early start too, but she was not pleased to be torn from her own slumber quite *this* early.

'Sorry,' I whispered. 'I'll see you later.' I made to kiss her shoulder again, but she rolled and pulled and I got a face full of duvet instead.

The office was busy with very broad men. I negotiated a labyrinth of shoulders and body armour to make my way into the room, holding my coffee high to protect against one of these bears turning around suddenly and robbing me of the caffeine I so badly needed.

'I feel like the ball in the middle of a rugby scrum,' Rowan said. She was perched against a desk near the front. I guessed she didn't want to sit on it and show everyone how far her feet were from the floor.

There was a floorplan being projected onto the wall behind DCI Templeton who was having a private conversation with what looked like the king of the bears. Older than the rest, grey, but covered in tattoos and in better shape than I could ever hope to be. The pips on his shoulders showed him to be an inspector with the Operational Support Division.

At last DCI Templeton cleared her throat and the room's many hushed conversations drowned away.

'Good morning, everyone. Thank you to OSD for attending today and assisting with this operation. I've had a quick chat with Inspector Reynolds and he's going to run through our property and approach before I hand you on to DS Colyear who is in operational charge today.'

It was all I could do not to spray coffee into the faces of men it would be very unwise to spray coffee into the faces of. I guessed that answered the question of whether Kate was going to leave us on this case.

'Okay, everyone. We're going as two teams. Alpha team is on the door, Bravo are on securing the property. The warrant has been checked and we're good to go as soon as we're done with this briefing. Information acquired by DS Colyear,' again my heart skipped as my name was mentioned, this time the bear king pointed me out to the rest of the room, 'suggests a reinforced steel door to the flat itself, but no resistance to entering the block. Alpha will do what they can to get the thing prised asap and then Bravo are in. Be systematic, but first in the door goes straight here.' Bear king tapped a finger at the image, indicating the bathroom. 'The steel door is designed to slow us down long enough to dispose of evidence. So be fucking sharpish. Thereafter secure any occupants to a single room. I'd suggest the bedroom?'

He tapped again at the image, but it took a second to register he was asking me.

'Uh. Yes. Bedroom. Sure.'

'You're killing it,' Rowan smirked as the inspector took up the briefing again. I shook my head at her.

He gave further instructions revolving around the fact that there was little likelihood of animals in the property, children or weapons, but to be vigilant. Then it was my turn.

I took a long sip of coffee – too long, as it threatened to burn my mouth. I stood up straight and walked to the front of the room. 'Uh, as Ka—uh, DCI Templeton says, thanks to you for helping us with this today. Beyond entry, the name of the game is evidence preservation. SOCO will follow us once we're clear.' I was winging it, and saying all the obvious stuff, but I hoped, at least I was sounding . . . commanding? 'That goes beyond drugs. The whole flat is a crime scene and so we need to disturb as little as possible – I appreciate that's impossible, but do what you can. According to our witness, our victim succumbed in the living room and so where possible, can we have no more than two people in there. Shoe coverings, masks and gloves should be worn.' There was a groan from somewhere at this. I assumed, from looking around the room that these guys, and it was all guys, a regular sausage factory of a set-up, joined the team not for delicate work, but entirely the opposite. Why open a door when it's so much more fun to kick it in? 'We are particularly interested in two sus . . . pects.' I faltered as the screen switched from floorplan to mugshot. Kate, I saw, was clicking at a mouse and had put this thing together. I suddenly felt like I should have been here hours earlier and made this presentation myself. *Was I in trouble?* I wasn't even sure which of our two suspects I was looking at. I gambled that Kate would have ordered them as I would have. And from what I'd read about the two, this one with the neck tattoo was surely Tobin. 'First is the homeowner, Barry Tobin. He's a horrible bastard with previous for every drug-related charge you could mention and for violence, though as the inspector said there is no PNC marker for weapons. However, this is his home – and there is a kitchen – so, you know, plenty of things to . . . you know, knives, or whatever. Just be vigilant.' I was losing where I was going. I looked at Rowan, she tapped her chest twice with the top of her fist, accompanied by a sarcastic wink. It wouldn't be long before she'd be taking briefings and I made a mental note to make sure I made her first particularly uncomfortable. 'Uh, next up,' – I paused and the screen switched to a greasy little man – 'is Derek, "Deek" Williamson. We understand he doesn't live at the address, but it's where he spends the majority of his time. We have a second warrant for his registered address, which is in the same neighbourhood. Perhaps entry team can divert if he's not present and move on that?' The inspector nodded. 'Both should be detained and arrested on suspicion of murder. It would be cleaner for the report if I or TDC Forbes did that, but if they resist or attempt to flee, you know what you need to do. I think that about covers it?' I looked at Kate who didn't nod an approval, but she didn't add anything, although did flick to one last image.

'Okay everyone. Rendezvous is here,' she said. The image looked to be a Google Maps image, screen-printed and projected. It circled a small parking area close, but not too close, to the address.

Once the room had cleared, and it felt like a cloud of testosterone had dissipated with it, I tested the water with Kate. 'Thanks for doing that, boss.'

'"Knives, or whatever"?' She didn't look angry, maybe amused.

'Sorry, ma'am. I guess I was a little underprepared.'

'Yes, well, word of advice. If it's your raid, get in early next time, yes?'

'Yes, ma'am.'

'All right. Let's get to it. Let them do the heavy lifting, but vest up all the same, will you?'

'Yes, ma'am.'

I had to concede it was impressive seeing these guys work. Once both vans and our car were parked we were all jogging into position within a minute. Alpha team trotted in time up the stairs of the block with a rhythmic metallic clunk-clunk, carrying equipment that might seem better fitted for firefighters. Bravo marched at their backs. Rowan, Kate and I waited at the bottom of the stairs. There was a quick update to control from the bear king in a hushed voice and then a yell that sent a wave of adrenalin through me.

'POLICE EXECUTING A WARRANT. STAND BACK FROM THE DOOR.'

I felt like a little boy watching some programme on TV. I wanted badly to climb the stairs to see exactly what they were doing. Rowan seemed to be of the same mind, staring as she was up through the gloom and around animated bodies to get a glimpse. Kate, on the other hand, was looking at her phone like this happened every other Tuesday.

There were a series of bangs, followed by an electrical whir and painful cracking noises. Someone yelled 'BREACH!' and all professional order seemed to have been abandoned. Above us was an indecipherable clamour of stamping, slams and shouting. Then, as quickly as it had all kicked off, it was over.

'I think we're up,' Kate said and put her phone away. We followed her up the stairs. Her lack of urgency was as frustrating as it was impressive. I imagined her pulse was steady as pond water while I could feel my heart slamming off the inside of the ill-fitting body armour I'd been handed.

Alpha team were congregated on the top floor landing, as calm as Kate.

'Safe enough?' Kate asked the Bravo at the front door; what was left of it. The metal outer was twisted and split, the wooden inner was shredded.

'Gimme a second, ma'am.' He went inside and returned moments later beckoning us in. There was some muffled yelling coming from somewhere. It grew as we walked into the dark place. There were doors to the left and right, open, and at least one Bravo standing guard. Further down the hall we were shown into the bedroom. Two terrified-looking plebs were sitting on the bed, both pairs of cuffed hands behind their backs. One I knew. Another familiar face was being mashed into the grubby grey carpet by the bear king who was applying cuffs, not gently. His right bicep bulged and a tattoo pulsed – some kind of fluttering, inscribed ribbon below a crest that I couldn't make out, but had me thinking of a forces regiment. The forearm the bicep was attached to was planted into the neck tattoo of Tobin and in the battle of the ink, there was only one winner. That said, there was a cut above the inspector's right eye, which was probably responsible for the 'reasonable force' he was applying to have a little seasoning on top of it.

'You I know,' I said to bed-pleb one. 'Deek Williamson. You and I are going to have many long and uncomfortable conversations.' He looked at me without any sense of bravado at all. That was good. Unlike the hissing and spitting Barry Tobin who still hadn't given up hope of somehow overpowering the enormous man on top of him and making good his escape past a dozen others. This was bad. This was a guy who was unlikely to offer information freely. *Probably looking at a 'no comment' marathon with him and his lawyer*, I thought. 'You I don't know,' I said to bed-pleb two. He was maybe late teens or early twenties. The handcuffs meant he was unable to wipe the tears running down his face.

'You want him taken in?' one of the Bravo asked.

'No. Just confirm his details and toss him. For now. What have you got for me, Mr Tobin?'

'Get fffucked,' he hissed and immediately after ate more carpet.

It must have been a lucky shot to have drawn blood from the inspector, but he was paying the price. 'Shut the fuck up and stay down,' the bear growled.

'Let's see,' I said. There was a phone in his back pocket. I plucked it out with a gloved hand and found it locked. 'I just need your assistance with something, Mr Tobin. Hold still.'

'What? Hey. You can't ffffuckn—' He took another large bite of pile while I peeled his thumb back and smeared it on the phone sensor. It clicked into life. 'Start filming this,' I said to Rowan. I had access to his phone now, and it would be forensically scrutinised later, but this was still time-sensitive and we couldn't afford the wait. I looked to Kate, wondering if she was about to pull the plug on this somewhat grey area of evidence gathering, but she only seemed interested to get a look at the screen. Rowan took her own phone and began recording. I went to recent calls. Blank. Everything had been deleted. This would be recorded by the provider and we'd get the information, but, again, in time. More bad news was followed by an empty messages log. Maybe the nerds could find something, but I thought it unlikely. No point in looking at emails, and if he'd ever had Facebook Messenger or WhatsApp, they'd been deleted too. I went instead to contacts. There was plenty here. I scrolled slowly so Rowan could capture more than a blur. Most of the names were nicknames or perhaps some kind of code. The very last one, though, rang a bell. 'Wee Malky'.

CHAPTER 12

Playing Both Sides

'Fife?' Are you sure?'

'I dunno, man. Just what I heard, eh?' Dingo was hurting. You didn't need to be a doctor or a distributor of narcotics to see he was in serious withdrawal. Even though the play park they were in was sheltered, surrounded as it was by buildings on Sloan Street and Dickson Street, it was nonetheless bitterly cold; and yet Dingo, shifting his weight from one foot to the other in an endless dad-dance was sweating like it was high summer. 'So, can I have some? It's good info, right?'

'In a minute, Dingo. Just tell me again exactly what you heard?'

'After, man. C'mon, eh? Let me just get fixed.'

His voice rose and he hovered on the 'fixed', drawing it out in a wretched plea. Malky looked around. A father guiding his son down a slide was looking over. This was why he didn't deal in places like this. It would take all of twenty minutes for someone to call the police. However, his usual spot was no longer an option. But this was where he knew he was likely to find Dingo. And as much as he was a colossal fuck-up, beggars couldn't be choosers. He'd take information from anywhere.

'One more time. From the beginning. And sit down, will you?'

'Fuck sake, man.' Dingo dropped himself into the swing next to him. With a scuff of his foot he sent himself into a shallow arc. Dad at the chute was pretending not to watch them. Dingo repeated the story. 'You cannae get smack anywhere right now. Everyone's like, nervous, or whatever. Even you disappeared.' This was true, but not because Malky was nervous of increased police attention, or dodgy product – after all, his own dealer had provided him plenty before people started OD-ing like it was suddenly a trend. He had been avoiding his spot because of the three text messages and several phone calls he'd tried to ignore. The last message arrived this morning and couldn't be avoided any longer. 'I tried scoring off a guy I know down here but he only had enough for himself. Says he went over to Fife tae get it. Says they've got plenty. Like some big score, you know? Also, cheaper than toon. But how the fuck am I gettin' over tae Fife? I've never been there before, wouldnae know where tae start. Anyway, telt him to get extra, I'll pay toon rates, know? He says maybe. Maybe's no good enough, man. I need something.'

Dad was leaving, making it look breezy. But there were plenty glances as he tossed the wee fella onto his shoulders. *Better wrap this up in case some sense of community made him reach for the nines on his phone.*

Malky took out a tenner-bag and slapped it into Dingo's hand.

The look of disappointment on Dingo's face was painful. 'C'mon, man. I need more. I'll pay for it.'

'You'll get more, Dingo. I just need you to think—' Malky paused as his phone vibrated in his pocket, sending a surge of fear up through his leg and into his chest. He tried to concentrate. This was something. The first mention of a score. '—think hard about what was said.'

'I telt ye—'

'Fife is a big place, Dingo. Is that all that was said? Think hard.'

That was and wasn't true. As a region, the 'Kingdom of Fife' was actually pretty small, but for someone like Dingo, who probably had spent only a few weeks of his life outside of Edinburgh, it was no doubt intimidating. And for Malky, he needed something more, somewhere to start. His life might be depending on it.

Dingo swung gently. His arms were hooked around the chains, his head slung low. 'Hang on,' he said. He brought his head up. The look of concentration was pretty much the same as the painful disappointment one, slack-jawed, brown-toothed, red eyes searching the grey sky. 'Like he said a place, and I was like "where's that, like?" and then he says "Fife". And I was like "Fife? How the fuck am I gettin' tae"—'

'Yeah, yeah. You said. But what was the place?' Malky asked, but held little hope that Dingo was going to pull that information from his opiate-deprived brain. The next thing would be trying to get Dingo to tell him who this fellow junkie was and where to find him and that was surely another wild goose chase, and more question-asking that could easily get him into as much bother as failing to gather this information at all.

'Aw . . . I dunno, man.' There it was. But then: 'A wee name, like Leith, know? But obviously not that.'

'So not like Dunfermline or Kirkcaldy or Glenrothes?'

'Nah. Much smaller. I've heard ae they places. I'm no stupit.'

'So . . . something like . . .' Malky searched his memory. He'd never really spent any time in Fife himself, but was aware of it and its reputation of being a mix of some of the best and worst towns and villages in Scotland, living shoulder to shoulder. For every Elie or St Andrews, you had a . . . 'What about Ballingry?'

'Nope.'

'Cardenden?'

'Nah. That's no—'

'Fuck, Dingo. Methil, Newburgh, fuckin' Kelty, uh, Leven.'

'Aye.'

'What do you mean, aye? Leven?'

'Naw, the other one.'

'Kelty?'

'Aye. I think so.'

Kelty? Fuck. Of course. He was about to ask Dingo whether he was sure it was a place he'd heard and not a name, but as he reached into his pocket and laid another four packets into Dingo's cold, but still sweat-slick hand, he thought it pointless, it amounted to the same thing, after all.

'Thanks, Dingo. I'll see you.'

Malky stood, letting the children's swing fall away behind him. Dingo didn't return the farewell, he was busy preparing. He was going to shoot up right there.

The text message that had arrived from 'Unknown Number' was more sinister than the preceding three:

Malky. Malky, Malky, Malky. Where is my Malky? You better call me before the end of the day, or I will come looking for my Malky and Malky doesn't want that.

He took a breath and called. It was answered immediately.

'You're alive. There I was thinking that some nasty mishap had befallen you. I was beginning to wonder where I should send the flowers.'

Malky recognised this Scouse voice as belonging to the large, bald driver of the Range Rover. The one in charge.

'Hi. Yeah, look, I'm sorry. I lost my phone and only just found it again. Left it at a mate's house.' He let out a little laugh, but he knew he was convincing nobody.

There was a pause and then: 'That so, Malky? I trust you used that off-grid time to find some useful information for me?'

'Actually. I think I have something for you.'

'Good boy. Where are you?'

'I'm uh . . .' Malky looked around; he was somewhere in the vicinity of Leith Walk. 'I just wanted to check there was still, you know, a reward for good info.'

Another pause, some breathing on the other end of the phone. 'I'll take care of you, Malky. Now, where are you?'

Malky sat at the bus stop on Easter Road. He thumbed through his phone to his missed calls. He scrolled past the ones from 'Unknown Number' to the one marked 'Pizza Hut'. Usually he answered straight away when that number flashed up, but he'd had nothing for him. Even now that he had something, it wasn't much, but it should still be enough to get paid. He pressed the call button and waited while it rang and rang. Eventually it went to voicemail. The familiar cheery, female voice spoke, completing the cover story in case he got himself into bother and someone got access to his phone. 'You've reached Pizza Hut. Have you tried our new flatbread pizzas? Or how about our range of vegan options? We're sorry we can't take your call right now, but please leave a message and a member of our team will get back to you as soon as we can.'

He cleared his throat and left the message for DC Adrian Geddes: 'Aye. It's Malky. Sorry I missed your call. Look, I think I have something for you, though. Uh, call me back.' Malky was about to get into a few tantalising teasers about what he could offer, at a price, when the Range Rover pulled into the bus stop at breakneck speed. Barely ten minutes since his call. The car somehow managed to stop without skidding. The guy with the

Brown Leather Jacket walked around from the back and opened the rear door. At least Malky was getting to climb in by himself this time. The guy climbed in after him and they were rejoining traffic before the door was closed properly. Malky was about to buckle himself in until this guy slid along the black leather seat and placed an arm around his shoulders.

'What have you got for us, Malcolm? I hope this has been worth the wait,' he said.

The occupants of the car were as before. Brown Leather Jacket, Bald Driver and Silent Gorilla in the front passenger seat. Malky wondered how many other street dealers had been cuddled so ominously in here. Surely he wasn't the only one canvassing the streets of Edinburgh for this information?

'Uh, well. I sort of heard a rumour.'

'Rumour?' Brown Leather Jacket tutted and shook his head. 'You better hope this is one accurate rumour, lad. After the calls you've been ignoring, we were expecting a lot more than hearsay.'

Malky knew it was a bad idea, but he was growing tired of threats. 'Look, I've been asking the question. Over and over and people don't like being asked questions when it comes to drugs, so I've been out here risking my neck. I'll tell you what I have and if it turns out to be shite, well it was the best I could do.'

'See that?' Bald Driver said, his eyes finding Malky in the mirror. 'Our boy here lost his phone, but he found himself a set of balls.' There were chuckles from the other two. 'Okay, what do you have?'

Malky gave Brown Leather Jacket a look. He returned a look of *Okay, you've earned it*. He removed his arm and slid back along the seat to give Malky some space.

'Things are pretty tense out there. Smack's not being dealt openly, everyone's assuming the cops are looking in pretty hard. That is, unless you're prepared to go to Kelty.'

'What's Kelty? A place?' The driver asked.

'A place, and a person. I've never dealt with him myself, he usually only operates north of the bridge, but he's a big player over there. I don't know his real name, but he has a chain of tanning salons in Fife. He's probably loaded, but he's Kelty born and bred, and at some point, people just started calling him that, or maybe he did, I don't know. Anyway, seems he found himself with a big score recently and he's not so nervous about selling it on.'

Driver looked around at the other two. Gorilla didn't move, but Brown Leather Jacket was nodding.

'Worth checking out. I'll put a team together,' he said.

'Team?' Driver said. 'Look around you, we have one, and with Malky on board with his big balls, we're all set. Now, where the fuck is Kelty?'

'Oh, I can draw you a map, or whatever, but no, you can just drop me anywhere.' Malky was trying to sound breezy, but his heart had just kicked into a canter, this was going horribly. 'And as for the money, well, let's just forget it. Happy to help.' Malky's 'big balls' were shrivelling. What the fuck had he gotten himself into the middle of?

'Malky, if your information's good, you'll get every penny promised, lad. Don't worry about that. Problem is, there's only one way to find out if you're full of shit. Now, where am I going?' Driver's eyes were on him in the mirror.

There was nowhere to go, no way out of this. He quickly ran through possible outcomes and could conceive of nothing that seemed good, or safe. 'You want to head out of town, west.'

'Here you are,' Brown Leather Jacket said. Handing his phone to Gorilla, who secured it on the dash for Driver. Google Maps showed the way. Malky settled himself in for the journey. He thought again of those outcomes. The one where this leads nowhere and the reaction to the disappointment. Or the other, where his information was good. That felt like a far worse outcome, at least while he was along for the ride.

The occupants, his captors, *let's be real for a minute, Malky*, he thought, chatted in their thick accents. Everything from football, to what they would be doing when this Scottish cluster-fuck was over. Apparently, Brown Leather Jacket had a girlfriend at home who was becoming increasingly convinced he wasn't caught up with work, but was busy banging some Scottish skank.

'You mean like that blonde thing I saw coming out of your room the other morning?' Gorilla said.

'Exactly like the blonde thing, yeah.' They laughed until interrupted by the sound of Malky's phone ringing.

Fuck, he thought and fished the phone from his pocket. He tapped at the red symbol, trying to shut the thing up, but in his haste, he was missing the spot.

'Let me,' Brown Leather Jacket said. He snatched the phone from Malky's slippery grasp. He checked the screen and for a terrible moment Malky thought he was going to answer it. 'Hungry, lad?' he said and cancelled the call from 'Pizza Hut' before tossing the phone back at him.

Malky was relieved at the engine sound, he'd be sure they'd hear his pulse otherwise. 'Yeah, I thought I was heading straight home, after like. And with a shit ton of money,' he laughed. 'Thought I'd celebrate with a takeaway, you know?'

'Sorry to mess with your plans. Plenty time for that later, eh?'

Malky smiled and put his phone away, turning off the ringtone before he did.

'When I was a kid,' Driver said. 'I begged my mother to take us here.' He was tapping at his side window. '"Why?" she asked. "Why do you want to go all the way to Scotland to see a bridge?"' They all looked out at the red structure to their right. There was a soft thump as the wheels of the Range Rover entered onto the new road surface of the Queensferry Crossing and the Firth of Forth appeared beneath them. However, all eyes were on the Forth Rail Bridge and all its Victorian engineering glory. 'You just have to imagine my bitter disappointment when she explained to me that the trains go straight across the middle, not up and down the peaks like a rollercoaster.' Malky joined in the polite laughter, though the chuckle was forced. When they got to the other side, to Fife, the small town of Kelty would only be minutes away.

And before he knew it, the Range Rover was exiting the M90 onto the slip. The sign directed them right, taking them high across the motorway they had just left and into the town limits.

'All right, Malky, where to find our Kelty in Kelty?' Driver asked.

'Actually, I've never been here before. Your guess is as good as mine.'

They drifted slowly along the main street, flanked by small, austere, council-built homes.

'This shithole doesn't look very big, boss. I'm sure we can find it,' Gorilla said.

This proved true. The small selection of shops that made up what passed here as a town centre did have one tanning salon. The window of 'The Tan Stand' was a riot of neon, making it stand out against the unremarkable stores on either side. They pulled up outside and Malky prayed he'd be told to stay where he was, and he was already contemplating a call to DC Geddes if he did. His hopes were dashed by a come-on curl of Brown Leather Jacket's finger.

Malky pulled himself along the seat and out onto the pavement. There was a chirp as the Range Rover doors were locked.

'Apparently he's got a chain of these shops,' Malky said, perhaps a last-ditch attempt to change this course. 'Good chance he's not here.'

'He's here,' Driver said, thumbing at the vehicle they'd just parked behind and he was being marched into the blue and gold-fronted shop. Inside, a small reception desk was being attended by an orange girl with impossibly straight black hair. She flashed a smile as she put down her phone that was almost as artificially bright as the shopfront.

'Hiya. Welcome to Tan . . . Stand,' the girl said. Faltering at the sight of these men who were unlikely to be here for ten minutes in the megaSun 8000 Hybrid.

Driver looked around the place and sat himself in a leather sofa adjacent to the desk. 'We're here to see Kelty, love. Go fetch him, will ya. And rustle up a cup of tea while you're at it.'

'Uh, Kelty? I think you might have the wrong—'

'DON'T MAKE A CUNT OF ME, LOVE,' Driver said, sitting forward and raising his voice. It was enough to make Malky's pulse jump, and he wasn't the one his eyes were locked on.

The girl froze. She may have blushed fiercely, or perhaps had the colour drain from her face were the hue there not an unadjustable artificiality. 'Yeah, I just mean . . . I don't know if he's in. I think he might be—'

'That's your Porsche outside, is it?' Driver sat back; his voice again sedate. 'Be a good girl, and go fetch him. And two sugars in the tea. Thanks, love,' he called after her as she disappeared though to the back.

'Get the door, Billy,' Driver instructed. Malky wished he hadn't just heard Brown Leather Jacket's name.

Billy flipped the 'open' sign on the door and pushed a bolt at the top. He examined the street outside before returning.

The man who entered through the door orange girl left through had to be Kelty. Suit jacket over black jeans and a light blue shirt opened nearly to the chest. The one who walked in behind him was surely this one's subordinate. Malky had been 'Wee Malky' since primary school, always a head shorter than his classmates, but he might just about be taller than this guy. He was maybe five-five if he stretched, but about the same again wide. The black T-shirt he wore looked painted on. He walked in a sort of muscle-bound waddle with his arms out from his body looking like he was carrying a pair of invisible carpets.

'I'm sorry, gentlemen. I'm going to have to ask you to leave. I don't know who you are and frankly I don't give a fuck. If you can't find the door, my associate here will help you,' Kelty said. His left hand flapped in a shooing gesture. *That's a mistake*, Malky thought. There wasn't really anywhere that might qualify as out of the way in this reception area, but Malky did his best to shuffle into a space next to a vending machine selling drinks.

'But I haven't had me tea, yet. Remind the girl it's *two* sugars, would ya?' Driver said. He made no move to stand.

This drew a small, humourless laugh from Kelty. He made a head gesture to his small associate, whose eyes were locked on Gorilla. His fists clenched and he stepped toward the far larger man with impressive confidence, but he wasn't the man he should be watching. It happened so fast, Malky's eyes struggled to make sense of it. Billy had circled the approaching man and in the same movement, pulled something from the sleeve of his jacket. He then slashed at the man's ankle, sending him onto his back and in a second movement Billy brought the thing down on the guy's stomach, emptying him of air with a loud 'ah-ouff'. He curled into a ball, clutching his torso. He wasn't getting up anytime soon. Billy pulled the weapon back into his sleeve, some kind of metal bar, or maybe a baton. The sort of thing cops carried.

'I'll forgive that,' Driver said. 'Because we're yet to be introduced.'

There was a loud engine noise from outside followed by braking and a little skidding. Seemed Kelty had made a call before he'd come into the room.

'My name is Nelson Taylor and I think maybe you have something that belongs to me.'

Again, Malky wished he hadn't been given yet more information. He was easy to dismiss and be sent on his merry way if he had nothing to taddle. The name meant nothing to him, but the look on Kelty's face, opened-mouthed petrification, suggested he'd heard it before.

There was a crash as two more painted-on black T-shirts collided into the door they thought unlocked. One of them chapped at the glass. Kelty was waving him away. There was a silent exchange that looked like *Are you sure?* And from Kelty: *Yes, just get back.*

'Mr Taylor, I'm sorry. I didn't know. What on earth are you doing in this town?' he said. And then through the door at the back: 'Kerry. KERRY, get this man a cup of tea.'

'Two sugars.'

'Two sugars.'

'Why don't you sit down, Mr Kelty. And can you do something about that?' Taylor gestured at the writhing, moaning henchman.

162

'Sandy, get up.' He pulled the man first to his knees and then to his feet. His face was an astonishing plum colour. He patted his back as he sent him, stooped, but walking towards the door to the back. He looked at Billy, who gave him a wink as he did. He almost collided with Kerry in the doorway. Some of the tea sloshed out of the mug she was carrying.

Taylor took the cup from her and nodded back at the door, sending her out of the room too.

'Thanks,' Taylor said, accepting his drink. He took a sip and said softly: 'Decent cuppa.'

'So, you were saying something about property, Mr Taylor?' Kelty said. He took the identical mustard-yellow armchair next to Taylor.

'You came into possession of a very large amount of heroin lately. A large amount of uncut heroin.' This was not a question, but Taylor paused for a reply.

Kelty laughed nervously and opened his hands and brought them together again in a small clap that suggested he had no idea how to respond to this. He wanted to deny it, Malky thought, but didn't think he could risk it. It was all the verification Taylor would need. Malky had been right, fuck, Dingo had been right. A first for everything, they say. What did this mean now? Was it good? Or really not? The men outside were staying that way, but could break that mostly glass door down in seconds. There was half a dozen, at least from what Malky could see out of the window, and more might be on their way. Probably on their way.

'Let's say, for argument's sake, that this is true, Mr Taylor. What of it?'

'That stuff belongs to me. I'm going to need it back.' Taylor said this matter-of-factly and went back to his tea.

Again, Kelty opened his hands and brought them together again, shaking his head. 'I don't know what to tell you, Mr Taylor. If I did come into possession of such a thing, it was bought and paid for, all above board.'

Taylor sipped at his tea. Malky had no idea what was going through this man's head, but Billy and the Gorilla were looking pretty relaxed.

'I understand. That's why I'm going to buy it back from you, at a profit.'

Kelty sat back in his chair. 'Well, I'm happy to hear you out, Mr Taylor, but it's a lot of product.'

'How much did you pay for it?'

From the look on Kelty's face, it seemed he'd been asked the most difficult of questions, but of course it was not the question, but which of the available answers to give which was the hard part, Malky thought.

'We're talking millions in street value, Mr Taylor. I—'

'That's not what I asked you. How much?'

Kelty sat forward again. He scratched first at his chin, then at the back of his head. 'Even double what I paid doesn't come close to what I can get for it.'

'And yet you're going to turn a quick profit and forget all about it. And I'll consider it a favour.'

'That's . . . generous, Mr Taylor, but—'

'There's another advantage to your cooperation in this matter. You see, that product was what you might call a start-up programme. My business venture north of the border. It was always my intention to secure a local distributor to assist my colleague here,' he gestured at Billy who was now sitting in Kerry's chair. 'My advice is to grasp this opportunity with both hands, Kelty. Because the alternative is you decline my offer and I come back at a later time for another chat with a few friends of my own.' Taylor leant forward to get a look out of the door to the men outside. 'And I have many more friends than you do. But let's not go down that road, eh? Now. How much did you pay for my gear?'

Kelty rubbed at his face. He was backed into a corner. 'Hundred and fifty-thou,' he said.

Taylor scoffed and slapped his knee. Billy was examining a bottle of nail polish at Kerry's desk and laughed too. 'I'm sure you're a capable businessman, Kelty, although I doubt you managed to get that kind of cash together, but you know what? That's okay. Three-hundred K, fair enough. That's settled and I'm sure we'll work well together. Now, one other thing. I need to know exactly who you bought from and where I can find the little bastards.'

There was talk of lock-ups, stutters and a telephone number. There were arrangements for a future exchange of the smack and Kelty's pay-off. All more information Malky thought it dangerous to own. He thought maybe they'd forgotten he was there. There was a shake of hands and soon Malky was looking at the Forth Rail Bridge again, this time through the left-hand window and in failing light. It had started to rain and the stress of the afternoon in addition to the steady rhythm of the wipers was sending Malky's chin to his chest.

He woke with a start as the car came to a stop. He had no idea where he was.

'End of the line. Out you get, Malky.' Taylor said.

Malky was still coming to. He began to register sounds. The rain against the windshield, the clicking of an indicator. He released his seat belt and reached for the door handle.

Billy had gotten out the other side and was circling the back of the car. He opened Malky's door. 'What about . . . you know?' he said to Taylor.

'Let him have it. Make it quick, I'm starving,' Kelty said.

Billy took hold of Malky's arm and drew him from the vehicle, not roughly.

'Wait. What?' Malky was still foggy. What had Taylor just said?

He thought he recognised the alleyway, Hope Street Lane. Right around the corner from where he first encountered this mob. It was the middle of town, but this tight rat-run was dark and relatively hidden away. Malky had his back to the boot of the car. Billy looked one way up the street and then the other. They were quite alone. He reached into that Brown Leather Jacket.

'Hey. Wait. I heard nothing, man. Saw nothing.'

Billy pulled his hand free and Malky was trying to decide which direction to run. He felt a thud to his chest. He looked down and took hold of what Billy had just pushed there. A lovely big bundle of cash.

'Don't go far, Malky. We might need you again.'

Billy gave his cheek a light slap and climbed into the Range Rover, which took off immediately.

Malky pushed the cash into his jeans pocket. It was going to be difficult to walk properly, but he knew better to stand and count cash in the middle of the street. He walked along the lane towards his usual patch, cycling through calls as he did. He again selected 'Pizza Hut' and dialled and left a message after he was encouraged to try the 'vegan options'. 'Sorry I missed you. Call me back. I have something, like I said.'

While he waited for DC Geddes to ring, he thought about what he could and couldn't say. Enough to get paid again, and enough to keep the boys in blue on his side, just in case he needed them, but not so much to get burnt.

CHAPTER 13

Paying Bills

Jeanette from Case Management was a godsend. I'd written up plenty of cases, some pretty serious stuff included, but never a murder case. With three accused, it was complicated, particularly as they were all being treated so differently. Priss Donaghy was singing from the rafters, and although a report to the Crown Office and Procurator Fiscal Service should read bare-factually and impartially, there was room for a little editorialising and I wanted to convey a sense of sympathy for her. Deek Williamson was saying everything and anything to save his own arse, but as eager as he was to provide statement after statement, his confusing and often contradictory accounts were not helping. Chances were the charge against him would be dropped, but that was up to someone further up the food chain. As anticipated, all attempts to interview Barry Tobin were met with tedious, arm-folded, 'no comment' exchanges, however there was enough from the other two to include him in the report.

I'd had to chap DCI Templeton's door when I found myself in an evidential cul-de-sac, unsure how to present the information and feeling unable to ask the subordinate DCs on my floor and thereby alerting them to my inexperience and possibly ineptitude. She'd seemed a little annoyed at the interruption (I'd been warned how she got when she was under pressure) but to her credit she'd said, 'Follow me,' and led me to a part of the building I hadn't been aware was there and into a room and Jeanette's desk. She was a civilian, a 'normie' as Rowan would have put it, but had been tidying up cases before final submission to the PF for over ten years.

'It's looking fine, Don,' she said on the other end of the phone, these calls becoming daily occurrences since that first day I'd sat down with her at her computer, as I sent draft after draft to her over email. 'There's a few references to the physical evidence that reads a bit unclear, pages . . . uh, eight and ten. Have a go at clearing that up and send it back.'

'Thanks, Jeanette. Will do.' I was about to query her on another section, but something, or rather someone had just caught my eye. 'Morgan,' I called.

The lad swung around on his heel. He looked lost and since I was the only one sitting in this large open-plan space full of desks, I was easy to miss. 'Sarge?'

'Grab a seat,' I said and pulled one over from the desk next to mine.

'Uh . . . thanks,' he said and came over.

It had been – what? – six months, maybe seven since I'd last seen him. He'd come to me as a probationer when I was still in uniform. He was tall and thinner than any copper should be. He was socially awkward and lacking confidence to the point that when I'd first come across him, I'd had my doubts about his chances of getting through his probation. However, in the short time I'd worked with him, he'd grown into a capable officer.

'How have you been?' I asked.

'Aye, fine like,' he said in his thick Northern-Irish drawl. He sat and adjusted the seat, sinking down to closer to my level with a hissss.

'Where are you working?'

'Same place, Drylaw. On the shift now, though, no more community policing.'

I wondered what his enquiry was going to be. Help with a complicated case a detective might be able to advise on? Maybe his career aspirations were to move into CID and he was here for some advice. I'd let him get to it in his own awkward time.

'You're enjoying it?'

'Aye, sure. I mean night shifts are a bastard, like, but I had my confirmation and I'm feeling like I'm getting to grips with it all.'

'Good, good.'

He sat with his hands on his lap. He was glancing around the room. Was he nervous about something? What was he about to ask me? A silence had settled and I was growing confused.

'So . . .?'

'Yeah?'

'What . . . uh . . . What can I help you with, Morgan?'

'I think he's here for me.' A voice from the doorway.

I peered round the gangly boy at Rowan, holding coffee. Morgan stood. 'It was nice to see you, Sarge.'

'Yeah. Nice to see . . .'

I drifted off as he reached Rowan and she nudged away his attempt to kiss her cheek. She grunted something at him that was not difficult to make out: 'I told you I'd meet you outside.'

'I was out there for twenty minutes. It's cold.'

'Just . . . go to the car. I'll be down in a minute.'

They both looked over at me. Morgan forced a smile. When he'd left, a red-faced Rowan brought me the coffee she'd gone out for.

'Do you mind if I finish ten minutes early? I have a . . .' she thumbed at the door.

I was nonplussed. 'You? And . . . You and capital M, small organ?' This wasn't my cruel play on his name. It was something he did, some kind of pre-emptive strike at his own expense when he introduced himself, and something I'd tried to convince him was a bad idea. This seemed to rankle Rowan.

'Well, Sarge, I can categorically confirm that there is nothing small about that boy's or—'

'That's plenty, Rowan. Thank you.'

'Well, I mean it stands to reason, doesn't it? He's like six foot five or something.'

'I get it.'

'I'm just saying he's, you know, proportionate.'

'I hear you. Unfortunately.'

'Well. Yeah, maybe you didn't need to know that.' She stood, staring at her coffee.

'So, this is why you left the pub the other night? When did this start?'

She lifted her coat and for a moment I thought she wasn't going to answer, but the jig was up. 'We were on the same driving course. It was pretty intense – the course, I mean. We were stuck in the same car for a week with a complete prick for an instructor. We hit it off?' She looked at me with a shrug.

I smiled. 'That's great,' I said. 'And yeah, go on. I'm just finishing up.' I meant it. As a couple they were a bizarre match, but there was something comforting about it. He would never hurt her; he was utterly incapable of that. As for him . . . well, good luck, Morgan, my boy.

She stopped at the doorway. 'You're going to take the piss out of me about this, aren't you?'

'Every chance I get.'

'Yup. G'night.'

'G'night, Rowan.'

The sight of those two together got me thinking. I checked the time, it was just leaving six, already dark outside. I texted Marcella, asking if she was free for a late dinner at mine. She rarely texts back immediately, so I put the phone away and reached for my coat.

I was almost out of the building. I had gripped the handle of the door to the car park when my name was called. I turned to see Adrian Geddes jogging down the hall.

'My CHIS has been in touch. Need to go see him. DCI told me to find you.' I was imagining the chat he had with her: *What the fuck are you telling me for? It's Colyear's case*. Adrian didn't trust me or he would have come to me without being instructed to.

There was no hot chocolate this time. It was too late for that. Instead, we barely stopped the car on George Street and he threw himself across the back seat. It was overkill, surely, but he stayed on his back until we were safely out of the city centre and into the New Town.

'I think you can relax, Malky. What have you got for us?' Adrian said. He was driving and cut his speed to a leisurely twenty, and began doing laps of the streets.

'I found your stuff. That's what I've got.'

'What? Really?' I said and spun to look at him removing a scarf from his face.

'I have the location of the lock-up it was being sold out of.'

Adrian gave me a look, one a proud dad might flash, as if this drug dealer was his boy, done good.

'Wait. What do you mean *was*?' I said.

'Well . . . the guy, the *person* I got the intel from is reliable, but it might be a few days old. God knows if the stuff will still be there. But it was, that's for sure.'

'How do you know it's our stuff?'

This, surely obvious, question seemed to stump him. Like it had never occurred to him we'd ask it. There was something off about this.

'People talk, eh? Look, I'm sure it's your stuff. Do you want the address or not? I want everything we agreed.'

'We need to verify your info's good. Are you going to show us this lock-up?' Adrian said.

Malky huffed in frustration. 'That's not gonna work,

boys. Look, you give me two hundred quid and I give you an address. Take it or leave it. Chances are you'll find it yourself. I mean, if I can find it, surely the fi—boys in blue, can. It just might take you a while and I can give it to you right now.'

He almost said 'filth'. I wouldn't have cared, but his confidence and derision made it clear this was no bluff.

'Fine, Malky. But if this turns out to be shite, that's it between you and me.' Adrian pulled his wallet and handed it to me. I fished out four fifties, folded them between two fingers and held it out, over my shoulder, to the informant. He snatched them up and replaced them with a scrap of paper.

'There's two rows of garages on this street. As you pull in, it's the first one on the left. You can drop me anywhere up here.'

'Wait. I need to know where you got this info if it turns out I need to get a warrant,' I said.

'That sounds like *your* problem. Here's good.'

The car hadn't quite come to a stop as Malky wound down the window and opened the door by the outside handle, bypassing the interior safety locks. Not his first rodeo. He was disappearing into the gloom of the evening by the time Adrian pulled out again.

'Doesn't seem like the kind of area,' I said as we pulled into the small section of road flanked by garages, maybe eight or so on each side. For one thing they were spitting distance from homes on the street, good homes. For another, we passed a Waitrose moments before we pulled in here.

I double-checked the scrap of paper Adrian's CHIS had

handed to me. 'This is it,' I confirmed. 'According to your boy, at least.'

'Now what?' Adrian said. He gave a light kick to the padlock secured to the ground by a hasp.

'Well, you weren't expecting it to by lying open, were you?' I thought about it for a moment, how best to deal with this. *Fuck it*, I thought. 'Adrian, look, you and I don't know one another very well. I'm new and some shit went down a few months back that might mean I'm difficult to trust. And so, if you want to do this by the book, I have no problem with that. Thing is, finding the owner of this lock-up might take weeks. Even then it's probably sublet, or sub-sublet and we'd go in bureaucratic circles trying to serve a warrant. Or . . .'

'Or?'

'Or we turn up here and that lock's already been forced. It's our job to secure any evidence inside.'

Adrian looked at me, looked down at the hasp and back again. 'That lock?'

'Mmm-hmm.'

'That lock that's fucked and lying in the middle of the road?'

'Attaboy – is there a tyre-lever in the car?'

'Doubt it. I have a baton in the glovebox, though?'

'That'll get it done,' I said and it did. When the lock was first installed, it would probably have been tight to the ground and near impossible to jemmy. Years of use had lent it some give. I had a quick look across the windows of the houses opposite and pushed the tip of the baton under the hasp. A one-two-three upward tug resulted in a metallic ping and the thing sprung right to where Adrian said it was.

'I have to say, I have my doubts. What madman stores his drugs in a garage a ten-year-old could break into?' I said, pulling on a pair of gloves.

Adrian was doing the same. 'Hopefully a desperate one. Ready?'

'Yeah, go,' I said and activated the torch function on my phone.

Adrian pulled at the door and it swung on its hinge with corroded complaint. Inside was as you'd expect of such a storage place. Some gardening tools. A foldable decorating table. I found a light switch and a single bulb flickered into hazy, amber life.

'Take a side each?' I said. Adrian nodded and began sifting through some paint cans to the left, while I pulled at the gardening stuff. It looked to be a bust, no hoard of drugs here, but behind a strimmer that looked big enough to clear a path through the Amazon, I found some plastic. It was taut and ribbed as if it had been stretched around something, but whatever that thing was didn't seem to be here. There were granules falling out of it as I lifted. Probably mud, but maybe . . . 'Look at this,' I said.

Adrian came over and pulled a little of brown dust onto his finger. 'Same shit that's on the plastering table,' he said.

He was right. Again, maybe mud, but what were the chances Malky the CHIS might send us here and apparently know that the drugs were already gone?

'I'll call it in,' I said.

'As you say, could take us forever to find out who's been using this.'

I nodded at the bulb casting its dull glow around the four walls. 'Someone's paying the electricity bill,' I said.

I returned to the car. Just as I reached the road a light caught my eye, or rather the sudden absence of a light that I could swear had been across the street somewhere. I froze and studied the houses. Maybe a bathroom light somewhere had just gone out? I reached into the car and withdrew the radio from between the front seats.

'DS Colyear to control.'

'Go ahead,' the radio responded.

'Can you please organise SOCO to the following location? Over.'

'Roger. What's your location? Over.'

I passed the address. As I did, a car on the opposite side of the road started up, roughly where I thought a light had gone out. I hadn't seen anyone approach a vehicle, at least I hadn't thought I had. It was a dark colour, big. It pulled out and passed by the entrance to the lock-ups, driving slowly. I could only make out a dark shape inside, but there was nothing wrong with the reg-plate lights.

'Control. Can you do me a vehicle check? Over.'

'Roger. Go ahead with your details, over.'

I passed the reg and waited for the response.

'To DS Colyear. That vehicle is registered to a business in the Liverpool area, but I'm just reading through a PNC note. Are you ready to receive?'

'Roger. Go ahead.'

My phone rang the second control were done passing the result of the check. I was about to ask them to run the name that had been attached via the PNC note on the car, seemed I didn't have to.

'Ma'am?'

'Nelson Taylor? Where in the name of fuck did you see Nelson Taylor's car?'

I'd assumed DCI Templeton had long since gone home. It was possible she had, but either way she was spending her evening monitoring radio traffic.

'At a lock-up in the Orchard Brae area, or at least near to it. Who is Nelson Taylor?'

The reply was a breath of frustration, then: 'Tell me everything.'

There wasn't much to tell, but I gave her the story, being careful not to mention either version of how we found the security of the lock-up. If she jumped to the conclusion this character, whoever he was, had gotten inside before us, it might muddy waters to the point a confession would have to follow.

'You think he was watching the place?'

'I don't know, but it would be my guess. Sorry to ask again, ma'am, but—'

'Morning meeting. I'll explain then. But really? You've never heard the name?'

A flush of chagrin burnt my cheeks. I suddenly felt like the guy at the dinner party who didn't understand the topic everyone else had a strong opinion on.

'I, uh . . . it sort of rings—'

'Goodnight, Colyear.'

'Goodnight, ma'am,' I said to the blip telling me she'd hung up.

Staring at the screen in the cold dark of the evening, I saw I'd had a missed call from Marcella. *Shit*, I thought. *How did I not hear that?* Maybe it arrived when we were being fleeced by young Malcolm.

There were also a series of messages from her:

6.33 p.m. Sure, why not. Just getting finished up at work. I'll head straight over.

6.48 p.m. What are you thinking? I'm guessing you're not cooking. Shall I grab something on the way?

7.05 p.m. Guessing you're busy getting finished. I'll make an executive decision.

7.28 p.m. We're having Thai. You better be in when I get there, Colyear.

7.37 p.m. Okay. So, you're clearly not home and you're not answering my call. Goodbye Don.

'Fuck.'

'What's up?' Adrian said. He'd closed up the garage, we'd wait in the warmth of the car for Scenes of Crime Officers to arrive.

'Nothing.' I clicked the phone into darkness. If I was going to call Marcella, it wouldn't be tonight. There was zero chance of her picking up. 'Have you heard of someone called Nelson Taylor?' I asked instead.

He scoffed, like I'd just asked him if he'd ever heard of a place called New York.

CHAPTER 14

Meet the Gang

First, I called Marcella. I hoped the cold light of day, in addition to the lengthy, repentant text I sent in advance might at least have her taking my call. Not so.

'I'm sorry, but' some computerised voice began. Followed by 'Marcella' in her own voice then back to computer voice: 'is not available to take your call. Please leave a message after the tone.'

'Hi Marcella. It's Don. Well, of course you know that. I just, again, wanted to apologise for last night. It was a shitty thing to do to ask you over and then forget to call you when things suddenly got crazy here. And I know this isn't the first time and I also know I was probably already on some kind of last chance with you, but I'd really like to see you and chat about this in person. I can do better. Anyway. I hope you're okay. Call me back. Please.'

I can do better. Was that true? 'Shit, I don't know,' I said to the interior of my car. Maybe I shouldn't even have called her, left it at that. Was it potentially cruel to try to patch things up, knowing if I *could* do better, it might only be a temporary gesture? I'd left the message. If she didn't respond, I wouldn't pursue.

Second, I called Rowan. I gave her a resumé of the previous night's exploits.

'You should have called me. I'd have come back in.'

'There was no need. It was mostly stale small talk with Adrian while we waited for the garage to get swept. Did you know he races model boats?'

'No, but sounds exactly like the kind of thing he'd be into.'

'He wasn't even embarrassed about telling me. In fact, it was the most lively I've seen him. It was all I could do not to nod off in front of him as he went on and on about it. How was your night?'

'Do you really want to know?'

'No, not really. Morning meeting, thirty minutes.'

'Be right there.'

'Hey, do you know who Nelson Taylor is?'

'Nelson Taylor? Like the Liverpool kingpin Nelson Taylor?'

'For fuck sake,' I breathed and hung up.

The room was busy. I'd assumed this would be a meeting between the DCI and us, perhaps Adrian too, but every DC and DS in Edinburgh were present along with a few I didn't recognise. Without getting a look at their warrant cards, I'd assumed them to be senior.

Rowan was in what was fast becoming her usual

spot. She was perched on the desk, feet dangling without appearing at all self-conscious about it. She handed me a coffee. 'Are we going to be pulled into this briefing as well?' she said.

As much as the audience with the bear king had tickled her, it was clear she was suddenly aware that it could happen to her.

'No, I don't think so. We're going to get the low-down on this Taylor character. She knows I don't have a clue.'

The room slowly filled as my cup drained. More DCs, this time from outwith the city. The DCI was worried about this guy.

She finally showed, opening the door with her elbow, her hands full with paperwork. The door crashed against the wall, making many jump and everyone shut up.

'Uh . . .' she started, looking around the room, over the tops of heads. 'Colyear, come here, would you?'

'Fuck,' I mouthed to Rowan. She smiled, that smile.

'Don't look so terrified, I just need you to click on the slides,' Kate said.

I sat at her desk. I clicked on the first page of the PowerPoint she'd prepared. *When does she do these things?* I thought. *Does she sleep?*

The picture I was looking at on the screen appeared on the board on the wall behind me. A mugshot. Rowan had described him as a 'kingpin' and this guy fulfilled the mental shadow that might be cast. Sort of square-looking head, bald and a slightly amused look on his face. A knowing one that said he'd be out of whatever police station this was taken in before they had a chance to organise an interview.

Kate cleared her throat, though she didn't have to, everyone was still silent and attentive. I couldn't imagine anyone else in this room with that sort of command. 'Good morning, everyone. Sorry to drag you away from whatever you're doing, but I felt this was important enough to justify the trip. For anyone who doesn't know, we're chasing down the heroin you will be aware of that has been killing off junkies and star students alike.

'We made a significant breakthrough in the case last night. We're awaiting some analysis from samples taken from a garage, but it seems we're close to taking this horrible shit off the streets. However, it did throw up an unforeseen development in the shape of this fat prick.

'I can't imagine there's many of you who don't know of this one' – she paused to glance at me – 'but this is Nelson Taylor. Perhaps the biggest drug lord in the Merseyside area, with links to Greater Manchester, Leeds, Birmingham and now . . . here. He's a horrible cunt, but an ambitious one, we have to hand him that, with an uncanny knack of staying out of custody. This despite the fact he's as ruthless as they come. His MO is to identify an area of interest and move in swinging both arms. Or at least his crew does. He sets up a solid base and lets the cash roll in.

'We are only starting to look at him as of this morning, but his vehicle was seen close to where we think this batch of heroin has been kept stored. Coincidence? I think fucking not. Anyway, when a rat infestation moves into your patch, you want to know about it, and that's why you're here.

'Taylor keeps his operation tight. He uses his reputation to franchise his dealings out to local groups and only steps in when they're threatened, and since those affiliated with him use that reputation, it's not going to happen often. However, when it does, you're looking at bodies. So, pay attention to this next part. Don.' She nodded at me and I clicked.

The face on the screen and the wall behind me switched. Another fat-necked thug appeared. Older than Taylor, with a boxer's nose and deep-set eyes. His thin hair was wispy and combed forward. In this picture his cheeks were showing that scarlet shine that glows before they fade to deep blue bruises. Looking at him you could only imagine what the other guy, or probably guys, looked like, and given he was in a cop shop when this was taken, you had to fear it was a couple of colleagues.

'Mark 'Macca' Morrison. Unlike his boss he has a record the Krays combined would have been proud of. Three stretches in prison for violent crimes, the last one overturned after a few months on appeal by a very expensive lawyer. If you come across this piece of shit, tread with caution. He's been Taylor's right arm forever and on the odd occasion Taylor himself has been lifted, guess who ends up taking the hit.'

Another nod, another click. A face flashed up on my screen and, for a second, I thought maybe DCI Templeton had made an embarrassing mistake. This wasn't the sort of face I was expecting. Indeed, there was a murmur from the gathered crowd that grew in confidence over the space of a few seconds, resulting in a wolf whistle from somewhere, which drew laughter. Rowan had her arms crossed, eyebrows raised. She had rocked back to get a better look at this character. I was expecting the DCI to put a stop to the childishness. Not so: 'Yes, yes. I know he's got a face you'd never tire of sitting on, but don't be fooled.' She waited for the laughter to subside and continued. 'This is William – Billy – Flaherty. Now, as dangerous as the last one was, this one needs special attention. He's a new member of Taylor's set-up and so far, he's only been charged with relatively petty stuff, but intel has him connected to four killings in the Merseyside area. All joking aside, this is the guy you need to be particularly cautious of. I can't stress it enough. If you see this guy, it's backup immediately. Is that understood?' There was a murmur of agreement. 'These three appear to be the core of Taylor's enterprise, but we're, of course, open to any new intel. I want to know what this bunch are doing on my patch and what their plans are. I want to know how they're connected to this heroin and I want any excuse to lock them up. I want a message sent. Loud and clear.'

'What's your theory?' Rowan asked.

'What makes you think I have one?'

'Because if you don't it makes me a little nervous.'

I tapped at the steering wheel, waiting for the lights to change. 'I don't know anything you don't at this stage. I'm going to keep an open mind, let's see what we get out of Mr – what was it?'

'Daniels. Paul Daniels.'

'Really?'

Rowan leafed through the report on her lap. 'Yes, Paul Daniels.'

I laughed and put the car in gear as the lights switched to green.

'What?'

'Nothing, just, you know, *Paul Daniels*. It's . . . funny.' Rowan went back to the report, as if the explanation lay there. 'Paul Daniels. You've heard of Paul Daniels?'

'Another drug dealer?'

I laughed harder at this. The sudden image of Debbie McGee in full make-up standing in a grubby kitchen measuring tenner bags of smack on a little digital scale jumped into my head.

'What?'

'Paul Daniels! He was a magician on TV. No?'

'Like Derren Brown or what's-his-name, David Blaine?'

'I guess. Though more card tricks and sawing people in half than suspending himself in glass cases. He had a catch phrase – oh, what was it?'

'I think we're here,' Rowan said. She tapped at the side window. 'Number eighteen.'

We were met at the door by a smiling woman who looked nothing like Debbie McGee. The smile was replaced by a pallid look of confusion and fear as I introduced us.

'Paul,' she called over her shoulder, though her eyes remained on my warrant card. A man in his fifties came lumbering through. This guy wore an expression of annoyance, presumably we'd disturbed him from something. His face dropped too when he realised we weren't trying to sell him something. It told me he had nothing to do with what was going on in the lock-up he was paying the electricity bill for.

He switched off the television in the living room, some rugby game, and left us alone while he went searching for paperwork. The lady whose name I never caught and would always therefore be Debbie brought us tea. We'd both finished by the time Paul returned with three shoeboxes filmed with dust and some green stuff that looked like mould.

'My dad had a number of these lock-ups. He sort of collected them as investments, even had a couple of parking spaces. I guess he saw how Edinburgh was expanding and thought there was an opportunity there. Anyway, he popped his clogs about ten years ago and they passed on to me.'

'I've been telling him to sell up, haven't I?' Debbie said.

'Aye, love. And after this I will. It's just so much hassle, you know? I mean look at all this crap, where do you start?'

'But you've been paying the bills for these properties, Mr Daniels?' Rowan said. She took a couple of sheets from the pile Paul emptied onto the coffee table.

'I just look at the bottom line. When my dad passed, I swapped his business account into one in my name. All I know is that more money comes in than goes out. As long as it stayed that way, I didn't want to know.'

'Do you mind if we sift through this lot?' I asked, though I had a heavy heart at the thought.

'Fill your boots,' Paul said. 'You better fetch these two more tea, love,' he added to his glamorous assistant.

I separated the pile in two and pushed half to Rowan's side of the coffee table. 'You'll like this, not a lot, but you'll like this.'

In total we were in Paul Daniel's living room for two and a half hours. It was Rowan who spotted a faded rental agreement for our garage. There was a name and an address, but the paper on which it was written was in danger of biodegrading in my hand.

We were already heading to the address, though a person check with the details we had revealed the Mr Jack Marshall who had signed the agreement, and had previously lived at the address scribbled in barely legible block capitals on the sheet, had previous convictions for petty theft and fraud, which might paint an encouraging picture, except that it also revealed he was now deceased; had been for the past eleven years. I left Mr Daniels with the lengthy task of checking his banking, a tedious exercise that would only confirm the thirty pounds-per-month he had been receiving for the rent of the garage stopped over a decade ago. The address in Wester Hailes was now occupied, according to a voters' roll enquiry, to a Mr Bhatia.

The street was much like the one where poor Danny Bakker drew his last breaths. A cul-de-sac of grim modern tenements, all four stories circling around a concrete play area with a high fence that promised a dose of tetanus to anyone silly enough to climb on it.

'We've got a welcoming committee,' Rowan said, drawing my attention back to the road. A group of kids had materialised from nowhere and two of them had stepped into the roadway, bold as brass. I was forced to pull to a stop. A soft whine sounded from the brakes. I lowered the window as the boldest of the bold approached, chewing gum and inspecting the interior of the car in a way the most intimidating of cops might. He was maybe ten or eleven years old, going by his height and slight frame, though his lined face and swagger aged him as older. His hair was cropped short and crooked tram lines had been shaved deeper still into the sides. I suspected one of these other kids was responsible.

'Can I help you?' the kid said.

I managed to restrain a laugh, but a smile poured over my face. 'That's very kind of you, but no, we're just fine thank you. Now if you'll kindly step out of the road so we can—'

'Who you here for?' he said. He looked past me at Rowan and winked at her. She sniggered.

'What makes you think we're here for someone?' I said.

'You're police. CID. If you tell me who you're here for, I'll tell you where they are.'

Warn them I'm here, more like. There was nothing obvious in the car that revealed who we were, though I guessed a couple of suits rolling into this street might be as obvious as sirens and lights.

'Again, very good of you. What's your name?' I asked.

He considered this a moment then said: 'Cammy.'

'Cammy what?'

'Cammy, mind yer ain business.'

'Is that Dutch? German? You must get asked to spell it a lot?' Rowan said.

'What?' It had gone over Cammy's shaved head.

189

'Never mind. Maybe you *can* help, actually. Which one these blocks is number seven?'

He turned around and threw an index finger at each building, clockwise, in order until he got to 'Seven. That one. It's the *seventh* one.'

'Right, thanks.' I said. *Touché*, I thought. I'd meet this one again. I was absolutely sure of it.

In my rear-view mirror I saw Cammy was straight onto a mobile phone, texting.

Mr Bhatia was less than helpful. We chatted briefly at the door with him constantly tucking a curious toddler behind his leg. He wasn't withholding information, he just had none. He'd been allocated the flat by the council six or so years ago and had no idea about who may have stayed in the place before him. This was a dead-end line of enquiry.

One positive thing was that the car's tyres were all still inflated when we returned. I unlocked it and had a quick look down the road. We were some distance now from Cammy and his horde of little demons. Except that one of them wasn't so little. He was chatting now to a large lad, gesturing in our general direction. They moved off when they saw me looking over.

CHAPTER 15

Stay in Your Lane

The dark red Peugeot pulled out of the estate at a snail's pace. Dillon watched from the doorway of block three, finishing a cigarette. The guy driving eyed him. He should barely be visible, but he would swear he was staring right at him. The car indicated right and was gone, but for how long?

He took a final drag from the cigarette and dropped it at his feet. He returned to his own flat in block two. The door to Davie's room was closed over. Dillon paused before pushing it open. It was bad enough to endure the soundtrack of his brother's sexual exploits, he didn't need the accompanying images.

Mercifully there was only one body cocooned in the duvet. The room had a stench, sheets that needed changing months ago, clothes recycled way too many times. Dillon pulled the curtains and sunlight invaded the gloom. There was a groan from the cocoon.

'Get up. We need to talk. Where's Sal?'

Another groan that contained muffled words that might have been 'fuck off'.

'The police were here. Detectives.'

The cocoon hatched in a hurry. 'What the fuck? Where?'

'They rolled in ten minutes ago. They went to seven and rolled out again a few minutes later. Where's Sal?'

'Big fucking deal,' Davie said and pulled the duvet back over his head.

'You forgetting that's where we lived with Dad?'

Davie huffed. He sat up and pushed the hair out of his eyes. 'It doesn't mean anything. Police are in this scheme every other day.'

'Detectives, D-Davie.'

Davie yawned and pushed a palm into one eye, twisting the tiredness from it. 'What door did they go to?'

'How should I know? It might have been a bit suspicious if I'd followed them in there. I think we should go.'

'Go? Where would we go?' Davie pulled himself from the bed and searched the floor until he found his jeans.

'We have money.'

Davie scoffed. 'We have a little over twenty-grand, Dillon. How far do you think that gets us, and for how long?' He was searching the floor again.

Dillon lifted his foot from a T-shirt and threw it over. 'People d-died. And other people know we were involved. Let's just get the f-fuck out of dodge. We can come back when the dust has settled.'

'You're paranoid.' Davie sniffed the shirt and dropped it to the floor, exchanging it for another that passed the test.

'Doesn't mean I'm wrong.'

Davie paused half in the shirt and half out. He sighed and finished the job. 'Okay, fine. Let's speak to Sal and Tavish. See what they think.'

'Where is she? She's not been staying so often. You t-two had a fight?'

'No, nothing like that. You know Sal. She's like a stray cat. Just because you give her a bed, doesn't mean she's going to sleep in it every night.'

'Where are you?' the DCI asked. Rowan held her phone high so we could both hear.

'Heading back from Wester Hailes, boss. Nothing to report. This lead is dead,' I said.

'Never mind that, get over to The Caledonian Hotel. Taylor's car was pinged on ANPR. I'll meet you there.'

'Roger,' Rowan said.

'Stay in the car, don't approach.'

'Roger,' she repeated and hung up.

She was quiet while I put the foot down and did my best to get through city traffic. *Nervous*, I thought. Maybe I was too, after the DCI's presentation.

The Waldorf Astoria, Edinburgh – The Caledonian, is situated in a particularly busy spot at the corner of Lothian Road and Princes Street in the city centre. One of Edinburgh's five-star jobs promising a superbly, and extremely tartan-y, comfortable stay for rich tourists, complete with a great view of the castle with a short walk from Waverley train station. Though if you could afford to stay there, you probably weren't walking or taking the train.

It was lucky it was so busy as it would otherwise be

impossible to approach the entrance discretely. I pulled in and was honked at by a taxi and shooed along by a doorman from the hotel. Another private hire car sounded his horn behind me as I hesitated, trying to look for a place to pull in. Still, every car pulling into this confusing corner was getting the same treatment.

'There it is,' Rowan said, pointing at the black Range Rover parked only just around the corner from the front door of the hotel. Automatic number plate recognition was a useful tool. The DCI had clearly requested the reg plate for Taylor's car be added to a lookout list. The windows were lightly tinted and I had to slow to confirm it was empty. I drove past a good distance before turning and taking up a position behind a white van liveried as 'Lothian Flooring – Carpet and Hardwood Specialists.'

'I can't see much from here,' Rowan said.

'Don't worry. I can see the driver's door. We'll see what the boss wants us to do. We can move if we have to.'

The DCI showed on foot less than ten minutes later. She wore a long coat and her hair was down. The stiff breeze lifted it from her shoulders as she strode. She looked very much like she belonged in a hotel like this. She took a brief look into the Range Rover as she passed it and then opened the door of our car before dropping herself into the back seat.

'Traffic division picked it up on their camera an hour ago.'

'Lucky spot. What's the plan?' I said.

The DCI was shaking her head and staring out at Taylor's car. 'I don't know. I'm not sure it does us any favours to tail him, and we don't have the authority as it stands, anyway. As far as we can prove, he hasn't done anything. If we take him in, he'll claim he's in Edinburgh on holiday and then likely bring down a lawsuit for harassment.'

There was a period of silence then. She held her radio in her lap and stared out at the Range Rover. Her eyes remained fixed when she raised the handset to her mouth. 'DCI Templeton for DC Geddes.'

The radio responded: 'Go ahead, ma'am.'

'Confirm you're in place, over.'

'Confirmed. Do you need us to move in? Over.'

'Negative. Stay in place.'

'Roger.'

She lowered the radio back to her lap and we fell back into silence. I could feel Rowan's eyes on me. If we'd been telepathic, she might have asked: *What the hell are we doing here?*

We sat in limbo for what felt like an hour, but was closer to twenty minutes. Then the radio crackled into life and the collective pulse rate of the occupants of the car jumped as Adrian announced: 'From DC Geddes, Taylor is leaving the hotel by the front door. Over.'

'Is he alone?'

'Negative.'

She paused, thinking. Then tapped my shoulder. 'Fuck it. Let's send him a message.'

I got out of the car and opened the back door. The DCI stepped out, straightened the fringe of her hair and said: 'Let's go say hello. Perhaps we can't pin anything on him, but I want him to know we're watching. Maybe it'll be enough for him to fuck off back over Hadrian's Wall.' She raised the radio 'To DC Geddes, move in. Over.'

'Roger.'

I took a breath and started walking. The DCI was reaching into her blouse to make her warrant card clear. I did the same. Rowan was behind, looking pale. I saw Taylor turn the corner. He was wearing a sharp suit and laughing. He was sharing a joke with a large man, one I recognised from the briefing. Macca Morrison. We were close to the Range Rover. The DCI cleared her throat, perhaps decided on the words to meet Taylor with.

'Don't you fucking dare.' The voice came from our left. It was a whispered yell, from way back in the throat. 'Turn around and go back to your car. If you have backup, stand them the fuck down.'

We stopped as one. The door to the white van boasting 'Twenty Years of Flooring Expertise' was open and a thin man stood there, his eyes on Taylor, approaching at a fat man's waddle, but getting closer with every second. He was still deep in jest with his ape.

'Just who the f—' the DCI began.

'OCCTU. No time. Stand down and fuck off.'

The DCI's face was glowing. Her lips were stretched thin. The teeth behind them were clamped and grinding. She looked at this man's face, then at the ID he held in his hand and then finally to me. 'Come on. Stand down.' I turned on my heel and guided Rowan by the shoulders back in the direction of our car. I could hear the DCI having a quick final word with carpet guy. 'You tell your boss to call me by the end of the day.' I could hear her walking now, behind us and back on the radio in a quiet, but urgent voice: 'To DC Geddes, stand down. Repeat. Stand down.'

The DCI didn't utter a sound on the way back to the office and so neither did we.

When finally Rowan and I were alone, she voiced what we were both thinking. 'I can't imagine anyone talking to her like that. There's no way she'll let that go, right?'

'Right. Unless that guy just happens to be chief constable, he's not heard the last of it. Organised Crime and Counter Terrorism Unit or not.'

I sat down at a terminal and checked emails. Rowan was doing the same. Before I opened my inbox I looked at my phone, seeing there was a message from Marcella.

Thanks for your voice message. Let's get together tonight and talk. Your place. Don't stand me up.

'Good news?' Rowan said.

I suddenly realised I was smiling. I washed it off. 'Mind your business.'

She laughed. 'Some emails back from the lab. From SOCO too,' she said clicking at her mouse.

'If it's not good news, keep it to yourself.'

'Actually . . . it is. Well, it's productive, at least.' She clicked and read silently from the screen for a moment. 'So, there's confirmation here that the heroin from Danny Bakker's bloodwork matches our stuff.'

'Not really news, but ties a bow around it.'

'Yes. But the really interesting thing is from SOCO.

Partial lift from the door matches a print on file. Sally Anstruther.'

'And what's interesting about Sally Anstruther?'

'Her last known address is what's interesting. Wester Hailes. Guess which street.'

'Piss off.'

'Yup. I wonder what it would take for charming little Cammy to tell us where we can find her.'

'Thumb screws, probably. Though a bit frowned upon these days.'

'We should head back . . . down?'

Rowan had trailed off. There were two men walking through the office. One of them was carpet guy.

'Can I help you, gentlemen?' I said, getting to my feet to intercept.

The one that wasn't carpet guy smiled. 'Yes, I'm DI Richmond, OCC—'

'TU,' I finished for him. 'You're here for DCI Templeton?'

'That's right.'

Rowan was already locking her terminal. She wasn't about to miss this and neither was I.

'This way,' I said.

'That was quick,' Rowan whispered to me.

'I imagine the phone call she made when she got back was motivational,' I returned.

I led them to the end of the room and chapped the DCI's door, which was open. She was typing away at her terminal.

'These gentlemen to see you, ma'am. OCCTU.'

'Right, yes. Come in. Rowan will you organise coffee?'

'Of course, ma'am.'

'Oh, not for us,' DI Richmond said, sliding around past me into the office. 'We're only here momentarily, as a courtesy.'

'Actually, you're here for as long as it takes to explain what the fuck you're doing on my patch without so much as a phone call. So, you might as well let DC Forbes bring you a refreshment.'

'Coffee . . . sounds good. Couple of lattes, DC Forbes, thank you,' the DI said and took a chair opposite the DCI's desk. Carpet guy and I stood near the door. The mirroring of the situation wasn't lost on me. Two lieutenants guarding their generals as they butted heads. Rowan didn't ask if the DCI wanted anything. This would be the quickest coffee run in the history of mankind.

'DI Richmond, ma'am. First, I should apologise for—' the DI began, but didn't get far.

'No, first *you* should apologise for being an unprofessional little prick,' the DCI said leering over the shoulder of the DI at carpet guy. He wasn't expecting to be involved and he stammered and fidgeted into life.

'I, uh, w-well. I am, uh, sorry ma'am. If I'd known you were a senior—'

'Rank has fuck all to do with professionalism. What's your name?'

'Uh, DC Sloe, ma'am.'

'DC Slow? Well, that's just too fucking perfect.' She flashed her eyes at me and it was all I could do not to laugh. *Oh Rowan, you're going to be so mad you missed this.* 'If one of my DCs had returned to me reporting the dog-shit encounter with you, we'd be having this self-same conversation. Is that clear?'

'Uh, yes, ma'am. And sorry, ag—'

'Now you. How is it possible, with all the protocols we have in place, that I tripped over your operation?'

The DI shifted in his chair. He began crossing his legs and then gave up on the idea. His attempt at looking comfortable was fooling nobody.

'I can assure you, ma'am, that the operation is entirely legal and above board, but you should be aware that it is also being kept as low-key as possible. If we might speak alone for a moment, some of this information is quite sensitive and it certainly could be described as need-to-know territory.'

Fuck. The DI was looking at me. *End of the show.* Or so I thought.

'DS Colyear is heading up this cluster-fuck heroin situation in Edinburgh. Now if you're about to tell me that your operation has nothing to do with that, then I will ask him to leave. Otherwise, by your very logic, he *needs to know.*'

'Fair enough.' The DI let out a breath and turned back around, which is when a puffing Rowan skipped back into the room. I wondered if she'd mugged someone in the hall for the four coffees she had balancing within a cardboard holder. She placed two on the desk and thrust another into the chest of DC Sloe.

'Close the door, will you, Forbes.'

'Ma'am,' she said and did so, remaining inside. The DI looked over and then back at the DCI and didn't bother protesting.

Rowan came to stand by me. I put my hand out for the coffee, but it went to her lips. 'What'd I miss?' she whispered.

'So much. It's Kate two, pricks nil.'

The DI cleared his throat and went on. 'We've had our eye on Nelson Taylor for some time. That won't come as any shock to you. We were alerted by our counterparts south of the border that he was making moves to expand his enterprise up here. Our intel suggests he managed to move a substantial amount of uncut heroin to Edinburgh a while back. We were then expecting to see a gradual distribution according to patterns we've witnessed previously. Our plan was to record this and push in to gather evidence that he was at the centre of it, only . . . well, either he got wind of our interest and pulled back, or something went wrong. We're now of a mind that it was the latter.'

'Given the deaths we're investigating.'

'Yes. It appears he lost control of his product. We don't know if he was double-crossed by a potential distributor or some other story, but it seems he's hunting it down. If he gets his hands back on it, our operation will continue.'

'Actually, ma'am, We have a name to go with the lock-up,' I said.

'As of when?'

'Well, just before this meeting. Rowan has an address. We were going to go check it out.'

'Lock-up?' the DI said.

'Where your "product" looks to have been held. Until recently,' the DCI said.

'Well, that's good. I'll need you to pass over everything you have.'

'Oh no, I don't think so. It seems we're further along than you are,' the DCI said.

'That may be, ma'am, but this is our remit. The case we're putting together traces Taylor's movements long before Police Scotland got involved. You can say no to me, that's fine, but when I pass this up, I'm sure you realise that this is *our* job. It would be a waste of both of our time.'

I was waiting for the rebuttal. Something sharp and damning, but she was tapping a finger on her desk. Her tongue was tracing her teeth behind her lips. She was considering the situation.

'Tell me why there was no OCCTU marker on Taylor's PNC file. If there had been, we would have brought you in earlier and I wouldn't have had to endure the situation with your colleague this morning.'

'Yes. Well, that's the sensitive part, ma'am. Every time we've moved on Taylor, he's been one step ahead. Once, even twice, you can put that down to bad luck. But he's slipped through drug enforcement's fingers at every attempt. We're now thinking there might be a reason.'

'You suspect he has someone on the force?' I said.

'Quite. It's a working theory, but we're running this operation close-knit. Hand-picked officers we're sure we can trust. I am sorry about this morning, ma'am, but this is our game and we're grateful for the assist, but we're going to need the ball back.'

CHAPTER 16

Stand Down

They left with the same swagger they entered with. While it had been fun to watch DCI Templeton rip them a new one, it was nonetheless bitter to watch the OCCTU officers leave with a boxful of physical evidence and all our hard work in a folder. DC Sloe, who would forever now be *Slow* in my mind, flashed a grin as the door swung behind him, a grin that might have been friendly, but I didn't think so. There was a sense of the triumphant in it.

'I'm sorry, Colyear, and you too, Forbes,' the DCI said as we were clearing up for the day. She was putting her coat on too. 'We still have the case to write up for Daniel Bakker, but otherwise we step back. And Colyear, I mean it. None of your bullshit. If I get wind you're looking at anything you're not supposed to be, well, you know the rest. Fire, brimstone, you're fucking fired etcetera.'

'Yes, ma'am, I understand. My concern, though, if you don't mind me voicing it, is that these guys aren't going to be interested in our drug deaths. In fact, I imagine they're so focussed on this Taylor guy that they will actively avoid working on any aspect that might interfere. I mean, where's the justice?'

'As much as I've never been a fan of the idea that you have to ignore a few cats to catch a lion, it's the way things are done. You've been around long enough to know that.'

'Yes, I do. I suppose I'm just a bit pissed off.'

The DCI patted me on the shoulder stiffly. I almost flinched. 'Sometimes you have to eat shit,' she said to Rowan. 'Doesn't mean you have to like it.'

'Yes, ma'am.'

We waited for the DCI to leave before we exchanged frustrated comments about being usurped on a case that was just getting interesting, a case we both felt we were closing in on.

The silver lining was that I got home, showered and was halfway through preparing a lasagne before Marcella rang the doorbell.

I turned off the ring on the bechamel and opened the door.

'Wow, you're here,' she said and handed me her coat and bag. 'And is that – dinner I smell?'

'I told you I can do better.'

'Ha. Yeah,' she said.

'I'll hang these things up. There's a glass of wine on the kitchen table with your name on it.'

'Now you're talking.'

As she went on to the kitchen, I hung her things. There were still two of Dad's coats taking up half of the pegs behind the front door despite the fact he hadn't done more than visit for an hour at a time in the past few months, usually removing another bag, suitcase or holdall of stuff when he did. I'd moved in with him after a particularly traumatic time working up north. Since then, he'd met Heather. She was nice enough, though, one of those yoga-patchouli-oil-unshaven-organic-types. Nothing wrong with that, but none of which described Dad, except the unshaven bit. Since they'd started dating his beard had grown full and his hair now was worn in a ponytail. The tie-dye T-shirt and sandals would surely follow, which was fine. He was happy. And the bonus was I'd sort of inherited his garden flat on Northumberland Street, which was more than I could have afforded to rent on my own and which I could never hope to buy.

Marcella had drained half her glass and was topping up.

'Dinner shouldn't take more than an hour,' I said. I gave the pot a stir, but she placed a hand on my wrist.

'Actually, I'm not hungry.'

My pulse quickened. Here was the break-up. Bizarrely, my overriding thought was that I was going to have to eat lasagne for the next three or four nights. I couldn't palm it off on Dad as he'd become a born-again vegetarian, or was it vegan?

I opened my mouth to speak. Something about making this easy for her. That it was no more than I deserved only, to my surprise, she was kissing me. Her teeth clenched gently on my bottom lip and then her back was against the wall with a thud that made the clock jump off its nail and onto the floor. She looked down at it and laughed. She took my hand and led me to the bedroom.

Dillon checked his phone. Message from Cammy:

Forget his name but hes bn before wants 2GMD.

Tell him I don't have anything. And anyone else who comes. No more until further notice.

'Sorry. What was I s-saying?'

'You were s-saying I'm a s-scared little bitch and we should all r-run away.'

'Cut that shit out, Tavish. It's not funny,' Davie said.

'Yeah, that's bullshit, Tavish. No taking the piss,' Sal said. She was sitting on Davie's lap at the kitchen table, but leant forward and mussed Dillon's hair.

'Fine. It was just a joke. Sorry,' Tavish said, though there was no sorry in it. 'But I stand by my point. If the cops or anyone else were going to bust us for that smack, they'd have done it already. It's long gone. Enjoy your cash. You can afford an appointment with a speech therapist.'

'Tav—'

'Kidding. Fuck sake, grow a sense of humour. Right, if there's nothing else, I'm out of here.' Tavish whipped his coat out from the back of the chair Dillon was sitting in. 'Later, dicks,' he called.

When he was confident Tavish was well out of earshot, Dillon jabbed a finger at the table and said: 'I. Hate. That. Guy.'

'You don't mean that. Tavish is okay, just a bit of an

idiot,' Sal said. She stretched again for Dillon's hair, but he pulled back this time.

'I do mean it. I meant it before the smack, now I really fucking mean it. One way or another, I'm d-done w-with this scheme. Done.'

'Dillon. Relax,' Davie said.

'Had it, Davie. Even if I knew for sure that detective wasn't on his way back here to throw us all in jail, I'm still done.'

Sal rolled her eyes and stood, giving Davie's groin a playful punch. She walked around to Dillon and even though he pulled back again, she insistently held his head and kissed it. 'You'll feel better in a few days. I promise. Your brother's right. Try to relax. I'm out of here too.'

'Really? You're not staying?' Dillon thought Davie sounded a little pathetic. Probably he would be thinking that too.

'I don't know. I have some things to do. Might be back later. Don't wait up, though, or whatever it is they say. Later, dicks,' she repeated with a smile and was gone.

'Don't pine. It won't help,' Dillon said. Davie was staring at the door.

'I'm not . . . Just – Fuck off,' Davie said. He launched a tea towel at Dillon, who was laughing.

'Seriously, though, if you get needy, it'll make things worse.'

'I'm not *needy*. And what the fuck do you know about women? How long since your last girlfriend?'

Dillon could feel the blood rise to his cheeks. 'I don't need a girlfriend, I have Tinder.'

207

'Oh yeah? And when was the last time one of these Tinder-birds ended up as a lay?'

The honest truth was never. He had been laid, though, but only once. It was in high school, literally in high school. People used to take the piss out of him for his stammer, until fifth year when he'd taken a growth spurt. Not just a growth spurt, but also a . . . thickening spurt. He'd discovered the gym at the same time he was growing out of clothes at an alarming rate and had gone from a wiry boy to a solid man in less than a year.

After that people kept their jokes to themselves. Actually, more specifically it was after the time Gavin Blair had made a comment in the hallway, something that used to happen a lot, but hadn't since the growth spurt. Dillon had made him repeat it. He recalled the turmoil on the prick's face. He clearly regretted it, but he had three friends around him and so felt he couldn't back down. He hadn't and had been punched once. Once was all it took. Dillon had left him there, curled in a ball, sucking in air, having taken a hook to the stomach he hadn't expected. Not one of the other three moved until he was gone. So, people left him well enough alone, except Becky Timmons.

He'd barely been aware of her existence, but she had set her sights on him. That had become obvious quickly. She was suddenly everywhere. Lunchtimes she would seek him out. He hadn't even known she was in his history class, but now she had moved from whatever corner she'd been in to be sitting next to him. She wasn't one of the popular girls, not really. Pretty plain, but also that, pretty. But she had a confidence about her. Which is just as well, as nothing would have happened otherwise. Big as he now was, Dillon would forever be that shy, stuttering boy. Even when he'd initially brushed her off, Becky just kept coming back. Her persistence had resulted in a friendship, which had quickly flourished into some kissing and then three weeks before summer term was due to finish, a summer that would see her moving into halls at Durham University and him spending most of it aimless before signing up to a mechanics course at Stevenson College, which he wouldn't finish, they'd had sex in the photography dark room. That was her thing, photography. The old-fashioned kind with film and trays of mysterious liquid. Her parents were strict and so going to hers was not an option. Neither was bringing this girl he liked to the shithole he shared with his brother. So, they'd fucked on a table under the glow of a red light. It was quick, it was clumsy, it was the most amazing afternoon of Dillon's life.

'I do okay,' Dillon lied. 'Don't worry about me.'

Davie smiled and thankfully let it drop, changing the subject back to the pertinent one, the reason for the collective pow-wow. 'Listen, I know you're sc—concerned, about things, but I have to say, I'm with the others. If someone was going to come knocking, it would have happened by now. We might have got a fraction for the gear we should have, but it's gone and good fucking riddance. You want out of the scheme, out of dealing? Then fine. We'll figure it out. I'll even give you some of my share, but at least do as Sal suggested. Sleep on it a few days?'

'Couple of days. And if I still feel the same, you won't try to talk me out of it?'

'Promise.'

'Fine.'

The sex was good. Better than good – I'd say great. Though surely to qualify, both parties would need to concur and she'd gone straight to the bathroom afterwards. She'd scooped up her clothes and now the sound of the shower hissed away faintly. It was difficult to say why it was particularly good, it was always pretty good with Marcella. This time, there was . . . an urgency? Not like she wanted it over quickly, more like she couldn't wait to have it. My jeans were still attached to my right ankle I suddenly discovered.

I lay in bed for a few minutes, wondering if she'd like to come back in and cuddle for a while, or whether I should get up, that maybe the bedroom antics might have jolted her appetite.

I pulled on a dressing gown and returned to the kitchen. A film had formed over the bechamel and it somewhat killed my own enthusiasm for food. I placed a lid on it and filled both of our wine glasses.

When she returned to the kitchen, she was wearing her coat. I suddenly felt very stupid.

She smiled shyly and took one of the glasses from me. Sipped once, twice and then put it down.

'Don, this was sort of a goodbye thing.'

'Yes, I'm starting to see that.'

'I like you, really. I mean, obviously,' she smiled and made a nod towards the bedroom. 'We're just not a good fit, logistically speaking.'

'Logistically speaking?'

'You know what I mean. I don't want you to feel bad about what you do for a living. You have an amazing job and you help people and . . . I'm, well, my life is more . . .'

Don't say normal.

'. . . normal. It's nobody's fault. If you like we can still get together for coffee? Maybe even the occasional . . .' She nodded again in the direction of the bedroom. 'Though I understand if you'd prefer to just, you know, draw a line, or whatever.'

I drew not a line, but a long breath and released it. 'I'd need to think about that. I guess this is goodbye? Or maybe see you later?'

I opened my arms and invited a hug. She moved forward, hesitated and then came into my arms. My dressing gown fell open at the front as she did.

For fuck sake.

'I'll see you,' she said and let out a little laugh as she pulled away and I hurriedly covered myself. 'You know what I mean.'

CHAPTER 17

Penny for Your Thoughts

You have everything you need?

Yeah, course

We'll talk again when you're done. And not until you're done. You understand what done means?

Yeah. I'll be here until I have all four

Then what?

You know what

Amuse me. Let me know you've got it.

Then I take a holiday. Two weeks, maybe three. Then, it's back to the ranch

Good. If you need another location check, get in touch with Macca.

I won't

But if you do . . .

Fine. But I won't. You relax. I'll see you soon

Alright. Happy hunting.

Billy smiled. He deleted the messages and powered off. He checked his watch, a quarter to nine. The 'location' was now twenty minutes old. He turned the phone over, removed the back from the burner and teased out the battery. He tutted as the SIM card refused to be gripped between forefinger and thumbnail, but then he got it. He spread the napkin his croissant was delivered on and snapped the SIM in two, laying the pieces in the middle of the tissue square amongst the butter crumbs. He wrapped it into a tight ball and placed it on the saucer next to his empty cup. This action must have indicated to the waitress that he was done as she came sidling over with a shy grin. She was looking at him as she removed his cup.

'Can I bring you another?' she said. She was blushing. These Scottish girls with their particularly pale complexions.

'No, I'm fine. Maybe just the bill when you get a chance, love.'

'You sure?' She leant in as she swept a cloth across the table. 'On the house,' she whispered.

'Well, when you put it like that, Chloe,' he said, making a show of leaning in to read her name tag, 'how can a fella refuse?' He smiled back at her, raising his hands in a what-can-you-do gesture.

That pale face flushed a deeper crimson.

Once she was gone, he returned to the phone. He pulled a further two napkins from the dispenser on the table next to the menu and wrapped the handset inside. The thing crunched and came apart in two uneven pieces without too much effort. He placed the bundle in his jacket pocket and the battery into the one opposite before straightening himself when Chloe returned with another latte and another smile. She placed the coffee in front of him and then the bill, making a point to touch his forearm as she left it.

'Thanks, love.'

'Any time.'

The bill, for the croissant and one latte only, had a little smiley face drawn in blue ink in the bottom corner. The reverse had also been written on he could see by the dark of the ink bleeding through and the score of the paper. He turned it over and smirked at the phone number and 'Chloe X' there.

'Shit timing, love, but thanks,' he said to his fresh latte and sipped. The 'location' would still be good by the time he finished his coffee and pulled on his baseball cap.

As he left the cafe, the low autumn sun hit his eyes. He took a moment to look up at the castle and the gardens below, taking it in. Soon he would leave this city and never return and he wanted to see it unobscured before he fished his shades from an inside pocket.

He stopped into a tourist shop on Princes Street and bought an overpriced A–Z. It surprised him they still made these things. Were it not imperative he steer clear of telecommunication masts, he'd have opened Google Maps like a normal human being.

Likewise, negotiating the bus system in a strange city is a piece of cake with hand-held technology, a piece of shit without. He had to endure, with his best, grateful smile two old biddies debating the best way to get to Wester Hailes when he'd enquired.

'You have to walk if you take the X-twenty-seven. No, it's the thirty-three you're wantin'.'

'He doesnae mind walkin'. He's young. He'll have to wait ages for the thirty-three, besides it's a lovely morning.' And so on and so forth.

It *was* a lovely morning, he *didn't* mind the walk and so the X-twenty-seven, it was.

It was on the bus he began to miss having a phone. You get so used to having the World Wide Web literally in the palm of your hand. Instead, he spent the twenty or so minutes looking out of the window. When that lost its charm, he pulled his rucksack onto his knee. He looked around and was happy nobody was watching. He checked the contents, though he'd carefully packed it the night before he'd checked out of the hotel. Everything he needed was here. One change of clothes, cash and his tools. No credit cards or phones. Taylor would be making sure someone was using a card in his name all over Liverpool for however long this was going to take. Someone would also be walking around his city with his registered phone, pinging masts like a champion. Of course, the arseholes in the van who had been intermittently following them since they'd crossed the border might know he didn't travel back to Liverpool with Taylor, but that was okay. Just as long as they didn't know where he actually was. He was being cautious, though not boring cautious. Chloe and the two biddies, for example. They could have been avoided, but this wasn't the movies. Police Scotland weren't about to start taking the statements of a horny waitress or two women circling the dementia drain. Besides, being overly cautious can itself be conspicuous. CCTV was another thing. He was being filmed on the bus for example, and there would no doubt be some camera picking him up when he stepped off. It was almost impossible to avoid, so why bother. The cap and shades he was wearing were not much of a disguise, but they'd worked in the past. Put even a little doubt in the mind of a jury with a good lawyer on your side and it's not easy to make grainy, stuttering images stick. Worse would be to make it look obvious you were hiding.

He hadn't been following the route in his *A–Z* and so had to guess where his stop was. He considered asking the driver, but thought that was a risk too far. He hopped off and walked until he found a street sign. Consulting his little book, he saw he'd jumped off a little early, but no matter.

Edinburgh was much like Liverpool, without castles of course, but similar idea. Charming city centre, but you didn't have to travel far to see where the working class lived. Close to the centre, but not too close. Same story everywhere, probably. He himself grew up in streets much like these.

According to the book, he was right around the corner from the 'location'. He hadn't asked Taylor where it had come from, you didn't ask Taylor where such things came from, but you didn't have to. As part of the deal to recover the dope, the three-hundred-thousand-pound transaction had also included a phone number. Someone had run that number and now he was a short distance from where that someone had told Taylor it had been used. There weren't many people who could run a number like that. Those that could wore uniforms and a uniform who would run a number for a man like Taylor only did so for an enormous amount of money.

He rounded the corner to the street. It might take minutes, but probably wouldn't. He settled himself in for the marathon, not the sprint.

What he hadn't expected was how neat the 'location' was. A series of blocks of flats circled around a shitty playground. A long pole sat adjacent to the play area. At the top of it, above a nest of barbed wire, four cameras eyed the crappy little estate, though who knew if they were working, or being manned. No point in worrying about what you can't control.

There was one road in and out of the street. On foot there were any number of options, but generally, this was good news. Very good. There was even a bench from where he could take most of it in. All but the furthest two blocks to the right. Billy didn't know exactly how triangulating a phone's position worked. This street was all he was given. Perhaps if someone were watching the phone constantly, they could pin it down to a specific building. As it was, he had one hit, and although Taylor offered another, it was best to keep it that way. Whoever his person was he, or she, would be not only expensive, but running an enormous risk each time. Billy considered himself a pro. He had everything he needed.

He went into the rucksack for the next item. A paperback. He wasn't much of a reader, but without a phone, he needed something. The cafe he'd been in this morning had a little exchange library. He wasn't able to leave anything, but he doubted Chloe would mind. *Where was she two weeks ago?* He would have kept that number for sure as opposed to dumping it along with the phone.

It was a well-thumbed novel. Slim, which meant it wasn't too intimidating, with a cover that was once mostly white, but probably published in the seventies or eighties and so gone a bit creamy yellow. *The Death of Grass* by John Christopher. For an hour he half read, half watched the street. Maybe a dozen cars passed, equally in and out of the estate. He kept in the front of his mind the only characteristics he had to work with – the blonde hair of the girl and the solid frames of two of the guys. Nothing matching that description so far. The car drivers ignored him, as did a couple of young mums pushing prams and whinging about something to do with a teacher at a primary school. The description of 'stuck-up bitch' was met with a concurring 'Uh-huh'.

The book was initially disappointing. It had nothing to do with executing snitches, at least not yet. However, it was actually gearing up to be pretty good. An end-of-the-world number with decent tension between the characters. Maybe not a snitch, but someone was getting shot for sure.

When the kid on the bicycle passed him for the second time, he lowered the book. The kid with the shaved head glared at him over his shoulder as he cycled away from him, back towards the buildings. He was the only one who'd clocked him and now that he had been, he was staying clocked. Again, he was reminded of his own childhood. When he was this kid's age, he had grown a sense of territory. On these tough estates, you just did. Something primordial that stays buried when you reach middle class or above.

The kid had stopped next to a few others on bikes. Now they were all leaning on handlebars and looking in his direction. So much for a marathon, he was going to have to speed things along.

On the boy's third lap, Billy lowered the book early and removed his glasses. He beamed at the boy, who slowed. He stood on his pedals and bounced a little. He had just enough pace to keep the bike upright and no more.

'Good morning,' Billy said in his best east of Scotland accent. The boy said nothing, he just stared and drifted, the front wheel twisting left and right to keep the balance with the sound of gravel being ground under it. 'Nice bike. Where did you steal it from?'

'No stolen, what you talkin' about?' the boy said, turning the bike one-eighty and now drifting and twisting past in the opposite direction.

'Just kidding. You live on this street?'

The boy didn't reply for a moment, he just bounced gently on the pedals, but then said: 'Is this where you give me sweeties and tell me to get in the back of your van?'

Billy laughed. There was no point in anything but the direct route with this one. 'I'm looking for my friend, maybe you can help?'

'Aye? What's his name?'

Dammit, Billy thought. 'I doubt you'd know him to talk to, but maybe you've seen him around? Big lad. Has a stutter. Know anyone like that?'

The boy's bottom lip was pulled down and he was shaking his head. 'Maybe you got the wrong street. Maybe you should go to another one.'

Billy laughed again. 'Aye. Maybe. Though I'm pretty sure this is it. Shame you can't help, 'cause I really need to see my friend and I would have paid big money to find him.'

The boy continued to shake his head. His eyes were concentrated on his front wheel.

Billy put his shades back on and stowed away his book. 'Oh well,' he said, standing and shouldering the bag. He'd taken maybe half a dozen steps when the lad called after him.

'H'much?'

Billy turned. 'Well, it doesn't really matter, does it? I mean, if you don't know him.'

'Well, maybe I've seen someone like that. But my memory isnae the best.'

'Oh, I see.' Billy started back. 'Maybe twenty quid will help jog it?'

The boy rasped from his mouth. 'Nah. Memory is still foggy.'

Billy returned to the bench and laid down his rucksack. He pulled his wallet from it and four notes from that. 'Eighty, then. But you need to be able to point at the door.'

* * *

Floor three and to the right as you look at the block from outside, Billy judged. And then the furthest flat. Billy reached the door and sank to his knees. With his sleeve pulled over his fingertips, he lifted the letter box. The smell of home cooking filled his nose. Roast chicken, maybe. The sound of a television. A coat rack lay behind the door, spilling over with jackets, scarves and hats. A precarious pile of shoes and wellies of various sizes lay at the bottom. *Little shite*, Billy thought. It was almost certainly a bum-steer, but he would make sure.

He straightened up and went into his rucksack. He pulled a bottle of water and poured a little onto his left palm before dropping the bottle, rubbing it now between both hands and into his hair, flattening it and pushing it forward on his head. He pushed the bottle along with his jacket back into the bag. He wore a thin, black jumper, which he now tucked into his belt. Next, he took his glasses and with a thrust of palm and thumb, removed the dark lenses and placed them on his face. He knocked twice on the door and pulled the rucksack on tight, using both straps so the bag sat high on his shoulders. He widened his eyes and wore the most gormless grin he could muster.

The woman who answered smiled warmly. The sound of children squabbling could be heard from inside.

Still with the accent applied, Billy said: 'Good morning, madam. I am so sorry to disturb you on this blessed morning, but I wondered if you had a moment to hear the good—'

'Sorry. Just gimme a—Would you two stop it,' she called into the back, though not harshly. There was a giggle from the hall and a little girl appeared at the woman's leg. She had the same golden hair and slightly turned-up nose as her mother.

'They're such a blessing,' Billy said, peering into the hall and now seeing a little boy, whose hair was darker, but not much, tucked behind his older sister.

'That's one word for it,' the woman said and mussed the hair of the boy. 'Sorry, what were you saying?'

'Oh, just that I was wondering if you'd heard the good news?'

'Ah,' the woman said, now pulling the girl from the door. 'I'm sorry, we're just not religious.'

'Perhaps I could just leave you with some literature?' Billy said and made a meal of trying to get to the bag on his back.

'No, really. Sorry, I better go. Have my hands full, as you can see,' she laughed. And began pulling the door.

'Of course. Well, God bless all of you and have a blessed . . . day,' Billy finished to the closed door.

From the landing Billy peered outside. It took a moment to find him, but there was the boy. He was still on his bike, now inside the concrete playpark, though standing, elbows on the handlebars. He was on his phone, apparently texting and intermittently looking up in the direction of block 2.

His phone buzzed for the fourth time. *Just fuck off*. Dillon pulled the pillow over his head. It had been a late one, even by his standards. Video games with Davie until 2 a.m. then he'd gotten lost in a YouTube spiral until his phone had reached one percent. That must have been around four.

He'd plugged it in, stupidly just out of reach of the bed. What time was it? And who the fuck was messaging?

'Fuck sake,' he growled at the ceiling as the phone went off again. A double vibration that was as hard to ignore as a dentist's drill.

He peeled back the duvet, pushed palms into both eyes and yawned. He got up and reached for the phone, pulling the cable from its arse before rolling back into bed. 'Told him not to . . .' Dillon said to the phone and trailed off as he read Cammy's messages. 'Fuck. Fuck, fuck, fuck.'

He leapt to his feet and had a brief moment of conflict whether to dress or call first. He did both at once, hitting the green symbol next to Cammy's name and pulling on his jeans. He glanced around for socks and gave up on them. He was hauling on his first trainer when Cammy answered.

'How long ago?' Dillon asked.

'Dunno. Five minutes?'

'What did you tell him?'

'Sent him up number five. Think he bought it.'

Dillon didn't want to miss a word, so instead of pulling a T-shirt over his head, he tucked one into the waist of his jeans. He banged on his brother's door. 'Davie, get up.' Then back to the phone, 'What does he look like? A cop?'

'Uh. I dunno. I don't think so.'

'What did he say? How do you know he was definitely looking for me? Davie. Fuck sake. Get up. Emergency . . .' Dillon pushed open Davie's door. No Davie.

'He mentioned the . . . Your, eh, stutter.'

The word turned Dillon's veins to icicles. He suddenly felt dizzy. Davie's bedroom swam around his feet.

'Cammy. Listen very carefully. What did this guy look like?'

'I dunno. Had a cap and shades.'

The phone was threatening to slip out of Dillon's now slick hand. 'What else was he wearing?'

'I dunno, Dil—'

'Think, Cammy. Was he wearing a coat?'

Then the confirmation came.

'Leather coat, aye. A brown one. Is he police? What do you want me—'

'Fuck, Davie where are you?' Dillon said as he hung up.

He thought about calling him, but right at that moment his first thought had to be getting out.

He pulled a holdall down from the top of his wardrobe, his gym bag. He tossed rancid socks from the bottom. He gathered a few items from his chest of drawers. In his haste, he forgot the top drawer was knackered and it fell apart on him, crashing to the floor, but amongst the socks and underpants was the envelope. He pushed it into the bag and went to Davie's room, picking a few items from the floor and stuffing them into the bag. Then he yanked the mattress up with one hand and snatched Davie's envelope with the other. He gathered a few items from the hall. The last was a jacket at the doorway. He stopped there, the door open in his hand. He took a look back into the flat. It was possible, probable, he'd never come back here.

Dillon peered both ways before darting from the flat, sure he was going to run straight into . . . *him*. He'd been in his dreams, a number of times. Always on the periphery, but getting closer. Now he was here, actually here. At the

224

landing window he looked down. At first nothing was moving, then he saw Cammy with friends in the playpark, pulling wheelies, oblivious to what was going on. Maybe he'd call him, tell him to get away, but first, Davie.

Dillon pushed his head over the banister of the stairwell, looking and listening, but nothing was coming his way. Davie's number wouldn't connect. Either he had no service, or the thing was off. Or . . . there was a third possibility, but it didn't bear thinking about.

Instead, he called Tavish. The number rang, but rang and rang. 'Come on. Pick up, you d-dick.'

He reached the bottom floor. The door to the outside had been wedged open with a brick, as it more often than not was. From here, sunlight spilt into the communal stairwell. He had a view, but not a good one. Nothing moved. If this guy had been sent to block five, maybe he was still there, going door to door, maybe?

'Fuck.'

The clever thing to do was run. Use the phone when he knew he was safe to warn the others. But Tavish was just in the next block, and on the ground floor. If Davie wasn't there, he could at least warn him, get him to get word to Sal and then run.

He laid his back to the wall and ducked his head outside. The light stung his eyes. He cupped a hand over his brow and let his vision adjust. If he turned to his right and ran full pelt, he could be out of the estate, out of Wester Hailes before his breath gave out.

'Fuck it.'

He darted left, keeping low. There was about twenty

metres between the doorways. 'Please be open, please be open,' he muttered. It wasn't, but he suddenly remembered how early it was. Not all of the intercoms worked properly. His finger trembled as he jabbed at the service button. He imagined *him* behind, a wire about to be slung over his head and around his neck.

The door buzzed and he pushed his shoulder into it, pushing it closed behind him and looking out through the slither of safety glass in the door with its grid of wire woven through. The bright morning looked back at him. Nothing else.

His phone was still ringing in his hand, evidently Tavish had no voicemail set up. He reached Tavish's door and was about to knock, until he heard the phone ringing inside.

Dillon opened the letter box and the sound intensified. In the brief pauses between the tone, there was something else. Sound of a struggle.

'Fuck,' he said again. There was a micro-moment when he considered running, but before the thought had fully formed in his head, he was trying the door and finding it open.

If they were struggling, that meant Tavish wasn't dead and there was a chance. He followed the sound past the living room where the ringing phone was coming from. He cancelled the call and pushed his phone into his back pocket. He continued on to the closed door at the end of the hall. Dillon pushed it open and balled his fists. Ready for whatever was on the other side. Only he wasn't prepared for this. He was struck utterly dumb in the doorway. Sal's bare back faced him. She rose and fell, her long hair swaying left and right. She had one hand pushed behind her for support as she groaned and moaned while she fucked Tavish.

'What the holy f-fuck?'

Sal let out a screech of surprise. She slid off her mount and hauled at a sheet to cover her breasts.

'Fucking hell,' Tavish spluttered, shocked too.

'Dillon? What the fuck are you doing in here? And why are you topless?' Sal said. She pulled the sheet around her as she turned properly to sit on the mattress next to Tavish who remained on his back, his erection still reaching for the skies.

Dillon had completely forgotten about the T-shirt. He snatched it from his jeans and pulled it over his head, talking as he did. 'What the hell are you t-two doing?'

'What does it look like?' Tavish said. His hands were now behind his head. He smiled and made no attempt to cover himself. Instead, there was a snap as he reached down and pulled the condom from himself. He tossed it to the side and his arm went back behind his head.

'It's not what you think, Dillon,' Sal said.

'Like f-fuck it's not.'

'Davie knows, Dillon. Look, it's actually none of your business.' Sal seemed to have just taken the events in and was now on the offensive. 'Who gave you permission to come—'

'Look, never mind – this, for now. You, w-we, need to get the fuck out of here.'

Sal was about to say something, but Dillon held his hand up, his head turned. There was a noise in the hall, coming from the outside. It was the service button, and looking back down the hall, Dillon saw that he had left the door wide open.

CHAPTER 18

What Goes Around

Billy found a spot between buildings seven and eight. He left through the back entrance that led to a patch of scrub and grass that qualified as a drying area to make sure the kid on the bike didn't get a look at him, though the little prick was sharp. It meant he was further than he'd like.

He watched the kid now as his shaved head bobbed from the phone to the building and back. Then something sounded above the noise of the other kids in the miserable playpark, a section of a song he didn't recognise. It was cut short as he answered his phone. It was his ringtone.

Billy couldn't hope to hear what was being said, not from this distance, but maybe he didn't have to.

The kid on the bike looked around with his right hand up, indicating he didn't know the answer to a question he'd just been asked. Billy sank back into the shade, but the little prick's eyes would have to be bordering on preternatural to spot him. Now the kid was pointing to the building he'd sent Billy into. The *I dunno* hand was back up again, and now was literally scratching his head.

Come on, lad. Eighty quid must have bought me something?

But now he was putting the phone away. What did that mean? He didn't seem too worried. He went back to his friends, pulling tricks on his BMX.

Of course, on his own, Billy could only watch one door and there were two ways out of each block. There was also the possibility that the kid didn't know stutter-boy and he was watching for no reason, though he doubted there was a soul on the estate the kid didn't know.

Then something moved. He wished he had a pair of binoculars, because what he saw darting from the door of number two looked like a blur of flesh. Billy straightened up to get a better look as the thing moved low to the door of number three.

'Hello, b-big boy. Good to see you again,' he breathed.

He dug into his rucksack and then readied himself to run, but he was pretty sure the lad had entered block three. 'What *are* you up to?'

He released his hand, secured the bag and pulled it onto his shoulder. He took the long way around, giving himself the best chance to avoid the kid's attention. He had to put himself into view though when he reached block three. The rear door wouldn't have service entry. It was a risk he'd have to take.

Billy bent and went into the bag. He pulled latex gloves from a side pocket and applied them deftly. The service button gave him entry and he was inside and out of view.

From here he went back to the bag. Shoe protectors first and then his tool.

It had been a gift from Taylor. The Maxim 9 mm looked like something out of a sci-fi movie. At its base it looked a lot like a standard Glock. But the business end had a built-in silencer that made the thing so much sexier. It widened into something Harrison Ford might fire at androids with.

Billy had been a dealer himself, though the days of scratching a living through miserable little drug transactions now seemed like a lifetime ago. The Norris Green Estate in north Liverpool had been his childhood, his adolescence and his adult livelihood. You didn't deal drugs in Merseyside without knowing who Nelson Taylor was and when he'd made moves onto his patch, he'd have been well advised to pack up and go find another. But that wasn't Billy and as far as he was concerned then, he'd only leave Norris Green in a box. The first altercation with Taylor's boys had been little more than a scuffle. Billy wasn't much to look at, but he was a keen boxer and if he'd ever been afraid in his life, he'd forgotten why. When two guys dropped themselves either side of him in his local, for a quiet word, he'd sent one toppling back off his stool with a broken nose and the other spilling blood all over the floor on his way out, holding what was left of his cheek together after the pint glass had done its bit.

The second visit wasn't going to be so straightforward. Taylor himself had turned up at Billy's gym with some acquaintances and the half-dozen or so there working out had quickly left. Taylor had given him the chance to apologise and presumably clear out without much more than a few bruises. 'My boys tell me they explained who it was they represented, Billy. But I imagine they're remembering wrong, or maybe you hadn't quite heard them. Either way, let's put it down to a misunderstanding and you get busy fucking off.'

Billy had calmly explained he knew exactly who he was and who his messenger boys had belonged to. Step forward Macca with a shifter-wrench and a proper fight had ensued. If a bookie had been in the gym, you'd have gotten slim odds on Billy, looking at the two men. But Billy had won that fight too, though had taken enough from the big man to ensure he'd be walking funny for weeks, and his smile would need some expensive repairs. As Billy rolled off the man he'd beaten, a man who would become a friend within a few months, he'd stared down the barrel of a gun for the first time in his life. Taylor had arrived with Macca and three other men and one, with a familiar-looking scar on his cheek, held a shotgun in his direction.

Taylor had placed a hand on that barrel and urged it low along with a proposal. 'Well, if you won't fuck off, you better come work for me,' he'd said. Not much of a proposal, really, more of an ultimatum. While Billy wasn't afraid, he was nonetheless a pragmatist and one way or another, he was no longer going to be dealing drugs in Norris Green.

Along with Macca, his main job was to stand around and look – menacing. Nine times out of ten, that's all it took. The other times he'd do what needed to be done.

He didn't exactly enjoy handing out beatings, but nor did it bother him. Taylor was a good employer and Billy was well looked after. He was enjoying being part of a team and when Taylor had come to him with a different kind of task, he'd said 'No problem' as always. It was only on the car journey to an industrial unit in Vauxhall that the enormity of that task had hit him, or more specifically when Macca had placed a handgun in his lap.

'You know how to use one of these?' the big man had asked.

Billy had shrugged, suggested it was much the same as a computer mouse. 'You point, and click, right?' Taylor and Macca had laughed and agreed.

That gun wasn't a Maxim. He couldn't say what it was. Well used and surprisingly heavy, but small enough to fit in his jacket pocket. He'd knocked at the door of the warehouse and had a full minute to think about what was about to happen. But when the guy had opened the door, Billy found that the gun slipped smoothly from the pocket. And much like a computer mouse, he had pointed and he had clicked and had closed the window on a man's life. Another first.

He looked now at the gift he'd received after that day. One he'd unwrapped just once before now. That trip had taken him to Wales for the first time. Taylor had expanded into Bridgend and a couple of big hitters out of Cardiff had temporarily closed down this particular arm of the enterprise. It wasn't closed for long. Billy had fired four times. Each one of the targets getting a bullet to the chest, before making sure with one each to the head. The effect of the Maxim was astonishing. The silencer subdued the noise of the gunfire, sure, albeit far from silent (not like the movies), but as the bullets landed into the bulk of each man the thud, which might have been inaudible under the crack of a normal gun, was tremendous. It was like an invisible car had slammed into the chest of each. The first time had preyed on Billy's mind for a few days; who exactly was this guy? Did he have kids? Did he truly deserve it? Billy was relieved to find that no such thoughts had haunted him the second time.

Now was different again. If he'd been reluctant the first time and numb the second, the third had him feeling – eager. They'd made a cunt of him and although Taylor had been outwardly understanding about that night in the breaker's yard, he was surely disappointed. Billy certainly was. He'd played the events over and over in his mind, varying little details to change the outcome into bloody, satisfying alternatives.

He couldn't change the past, but he could do this.

Billy cocked the Maxim and pulled the rucksack onto his back. He'd taken only a few steps before spotting the open door.

Another gift. Almost too easy.

The shoe protectors scuffed as Billy moved through the doorway. He stopped in the hall, listening, but nothing.

He moved quickly through the rooms, finding the place lived-in, but so far empty. Which left only one more door.

Dillon's first thought had been to go out of the window, but after three thumps at the bottom of the frame he took a closer look. The thing looked to have been painted shut, and then painted shut all over again. You could barely see the line that would separate window from frame.

He quietly closed the door to the bedroom and raised a finger to his lips, motioning to the two in the bed. Tavish had been about to say something, but Sal put a hand on his chest and his mouth closed. Dillon listened against the door, hoping whoever had entered the building was busy climbing the stairs to their flat.

He pressed his ear to the door. His right hand held in the air, urging continued silence. 'Fuck,' he said softly. There was a shuffling noise and it was almost certainly inside the flat. He looked around the room now and saw he had two options. Run down the hall towards whatever was coming or . . .

There wasn't time to say anything. Dillon moved away from the door, taking three long steps to the built-in wardrobe. He opened the door, sure the thing would be full of junk, but found only a few shirts and jackets hanging. He had to spin and twist and duck to close the door behind him.

The bedroom door slammed open before he had fully closed his.

In his own flat the doors to the wardrobes had just been removed. They were a shitty folding construction that only a few years of use had made unbearable, forever jumping out of their channels and the heavy mirrored doors coming away in your hands. Here it had been replaced by a cheap wicker alternative. It meant Dillon had a hazy view of Brown Leather Jacket entering. He wore a cap, but it was him. He had a gun raised and was laughing. The gun lowered as he guffawed.

'Well aren't you happy to see me, mate. I won't say I'm not flattered but I'm afraid your hard-on is wasted on me.'

Tavish was pulling covers over himself now, his penis visibly shrivelling as he did.

'What about you, love? You happy to see me too? You remember me, don't ya? No?' Sal was shaking her head. Dillon had never seen her anything but supremely confident, cocky, but the look on her face now was devastating to witness. She was ashen and utterly terrified. 'Oh, I think you do. I'd know that gorgeous hair anywhere. You know what, you're pretty n'all, what a shame. Make yourself comfortable. This will take a minute.' He shook the crazy-looking barrel of the handgun at her and she shuffled up the bed, clutching a sheet to cover her breasts. She came to a rest shoulder to shoulder with Tavish.

Dillion pulled his phone from his pocket. He couldn't risk the light of it showing through the wicker. He tried to use muscle-memory to open the messaging app. He pushed a thumb at what he hoped was the last message and that it would open a reply. He began typing unseen letters, on what might be a message, or might just as easily be a game of *Grand Theft Auto 5*.

'Where's the big one? Hmm?' Neither moved, though Dillon was sure a set of eyes would turn in his direction. 'Your f-f-f-friend. The big shirtless kid who came running this way?' Again, neither moved. 'No? Okay, I get it, you're not a grass. If anyone can respect that, it's me. In any case, I'd trade him for *you*. I'd trade the other three for *you*. I should check the calendar, because it might just be my fucking birthday.' He moved forward, the gun and his words trained on Tavish, his speech slow and gathering venom. 'I've had sexual fucking fantasies about seeing you again. I thought about what I would do to you when I finally got me hands on ya. But it's funny. Now that I have you here,' he raised the gun now to Tavish's face, 'I can't be arsed making it complicated.'

'Wait. Don't—'

Dillon dropped his phone at his feet as Tavish's body was sent back hard into his pillow with a strange grunt-crack of gunfire. His body then sprung upward, his arms rising and falling lifelessly. Another grunt-crack and another and Tavish's body was bouncing higher and higher. Bed stuffing and blood flew about the place. Sal was screaming now, but only for a second or two. Her shriek died in her mouth as a fourth shot sounded. She too was thrown back. Her body bounced gently a few times before coming to rest. Her left arm hung off the side of the bed, the other fell across the spattered, dead face of Tavish.

Her killer took a moment to inspect Sal, seeming to debate whether she needed another bullet. Then he lowered the pistol.

The light from Dillon's phone illuminated the side of his shoe and the piss running down the side of it. He wanted to move that foot and let the phone fall onto its front and kill the light but there was no control of anything. He stood and waited for the door to be opened and when it was there would be no fight in his arms.

Brown Leather Jacket was heading for the door. He fell out of Dillon's arc of sight. Hope was threatening to bloom, but then was gone as he returned. He stood in the middle of the room. Tiny specs of mattress or pillow stuffing fell around him, like some macabre snow globe. He was just standing there. The gun down at his thigh. He was listening.

After a moment he leant down and peered under the bed, gun barrel first. Then he stood and looked around. Then he was turning to Dillon. One step, then another. Gun barrel. And then—

Bang.

CHAPTER 19

The Lying, the Bitch and the Wardrobe

I won't lie, I had in the past wondered what Morgan Finney looked like in just his underpants, though I wasn't so curious that I couldn't have done without actually seeing it.

Rowan kissed him, flexing onto tiptoes as she did. Then she pushed a hand into his chest to urge him back inside while he stood in the doorway of the little house in Stenhouse he was renting, waving at me with a big smile.

Rowan walked to the car, red-faced and shaking her head.

The curiosity stemmed from the idea that he couldn't possibly be as thin as his frame in a stab-vest suggested. However, looking at him now, it was worse than feared. As his right arm tick-tocked back and forward the ribs under the elbow were visible. His legs were bordering on skeletal and he had only just enough in the way of hips to, mercifully, keep those light-blue boxers where they really needed to remain.

'You need to get a cheeseburger into that boy,' I said.

Rowan stretched for her seat belt as I waved at the lad and said out of the side of my mouth: 'You know, if the purpose of the exercise was to date someone not normal, I'd say it was mission accomplished. How's it going with capital M, small—'

'Don't. It's . . . fine.'

'Fine?' I gave Morgan one last wave and took off.

'Yes, fine. While we're on the subject, how's things with Marcella in *HR*?' She lingered on the initials like they were a dirty joke. I paused long enough for her to read into it. 'Shit. Sorry.'

'What?' I began, but what the hell, she'd guessed right. 'It's fine.'

'Fine?'

She was smiling at me.

'Okay, if I let Morgan drop, can we change the subject?'

'Yes. What do you want to talk about? How about dead bodies?'

'Good choice.'

'What do we have?' Rowan asked. She was staring into the mirror behind the sun visor with her finger at the corner of her eye, either adjusting a contact or fishing something out of there.

'Details are a little sketchy. The DCI was talking ten to the dozen and much of what she was saying was just swearing. But, we have two dead. Gunshot wounds.'

'Gunshots? What the fuck?' Rowan was wide-eyed, now lowering the visor.

'That's what I heard amongst the expletives. She said she'd meet us there.'

'Why are we on this?'

'You mean why have they assigned Edinburgh's finest detectives on a particularly gruesome murder case?' I got only a look in response. 'Fair enough. It's because of the address. It's a street in Wester Hailes.'

This didn't register with her immediately. She looked out beyond the dashboard, her eyes narrow. Then they widened again. 'No.'

'Maybe a coincidence. Maybe not.'

The street was full of onlookers. Families huddled together either looking grimly towards the epicentre of the action or else trying to capture a piece of it on mobile phone cameras. I tapped at the horn a few times to move the concerned and the curious out of the way. The press had gotten there before us too. A van sporting the STV logo was abandoned onto a grass verge. I looked around to find the crew. They weren't difficult to spot. A woman holding a microphone had her back to the cordoned-off building from a slightly elevated position. A camera guy was moving around her, perhaps trying to frame the best shot.

I parked up and approached the block of flats already well protected behind blue and white tape.

'Should we wait for her?' Rowan asked.

'She called us in. It's ours until she says otherwise. Let's have a look.'

A young officer stood at the tape. I flashed my ID and she raised the tape.

'Who was first on scene?' I asked.

She opened her mouth, then closed it. I was about to ask again, annoyed that I had to, when I saw what was going on. Rowan had figured it out before me and was rubbing the arm of the woman who was tearing up.

'Sorry. It's a tough scene in there?' I asked. She nodded. 'Has anything been touched?' She shook her head. 'All right. Look, tell your gaffer you need a break, okay. If they give you any shit, you tell them to contact me, Sergeant Colyear.' She wiped at her face and cleared her throat. We ducked under the tape and approached the building.

We stopped at the entrance and covered hands and feet. Rowan was struggling with her shoes and I took the moment to stretch my back. I looked first at the large crack down the pane of glass in the door, and then out across the street. At the playpark, there were a few kids standing on apparatus to get a better look at us, at everything going on. Beyond that I saw – or thought I saw – I shielded my eyes from the sun with a flat hand and looked again.

'What?' Rowan said.

'I – I don't know. Nothing.'

There was a common approach path set up already. The young officer, who'd had a shock at what we were about to go into, had kept her head and had done her job. Tape separated the communal hallway in two. While we had the whole thing shut down, we couldn't keep it that way for long. People needed to get on with their lives, irrespective of how serious the situation was. The tape

241

would allow residents access to their own places without compromising the scene.

I paused at the door. I thought about how hard that officer must have fought to hold back those tears, about how disappointed she'd be with herself later that she'd failed.

We entered and shuffled down the hall looking into rooms as we went. The door at the far end faced us the whole time and I knew that was where we would end up. It seemed to call: Look around all you want; you know it's in here. Come and see what I have.

I placed a gloved hand onto the handle, turned and pushed. I let the door swing freely and I took in the contents of that place.

'Fucking . . .' Rowan started, but drifted off, unable to finish her thought.

I entered the room, being careful not to step on a blood spatter or anything else that might seem important. However, the blood seemed to be contained mostly to the bed which was saturated; actually collecting in coagulating pools between the two bodies.

I went first to the left-hand side of the bed, to the naked man on his back sporting three obvious holes he hadn't been born with. 'Any theories on the cause of death?' I said.

Rowan looked at me, puzzled for a second, then realised I was joking. 'Looks like she only got one bullet,' she said.

The girl was on her side, her blonder hair covering her face, but Rowan seemed to be correct. There was a dark hole to the middle of her chest, like our fella here, though for whatever reason he'd also been awarded matching ones to the throat and forehead.

'We best not touch the bodies for now. SOCO will need to bring in someone who knows about ballistics. They'll want to see them in situ. See if you can find some ID, though I dare you to tell me this one's name isn't Sally Anstruther,' I said and motioned at the girl, then to the clothes hanging on the back of a chair and a pile by the side of the bed.

Whatever had happened here had happened pretty quickly. An execution. I'd never seen anything like it and to a degree I was guessing at the best course of action. The bit about a ballistics expert was something of a guess, but a safe one. Gun incidents in Scotland were rare creatures indeed, and we'd just walked into a double.

'You're right about her. Sally-Anne Anstruther, if you want the Sunday version.' Rowan was reading from a driving licence she'd plucked from a white wallet. I was looking at her face. Early twenties, pretty. 'What did you get yourself into, Sally?' I said to the young dead woman. 'And who's Captain Three Bullets?'

'Uh . . . Let's see. No driving licence in here, but a bank card and a . . . JD Sports loyalty card, both in the name of Christopher McTavish.'

'Do you think Mr McTavish maybe gave the shooter a mouthful before they got round to the trigger pulling?'

'What do you mean?'

'I mean, each one of these shots sends him to the next place. Three seems like he really pissed someone off.'

Mr McTavish's eyes were closed. His mouth was stuck in pursed position, as if he'd braced for the bullets. Sally, on the other hand, looked at peace. Her lips were slightly apart. Her eyes rested across the room. There was no expression at all. I followed her absent gaze to a built-in wardrobe. The door to it was open.

'Woof,' DCI Templeton said. I jumped a little having not heard her approach. 'This is where you tell me these . . . slayings are completely unrelated to our drug situation and I send you home to finish the weekends off I interrupted.' She stood at the foot of the bed in full protective gear, paper suit, the lot, peering up at the bloody mess at the pillow end.

'No such luck, ma'am. Sally-Anne Anstruther and – friend.' Rowan actually pointed at Mr McTavish's penis. 'Hers are the prints in our lock-up. Or rather OCCTU's lock-up.'

'Yes. Well, we will just have to see about that,' the DCI said. Rowan and I looked at one another. *What did that mean?* was the question I didn't need to ask. 'It will be clearer when we get back to the station, but this?' She drew the back of her hand across the scene. 'This changes things. In my mind, at least. Are you done here, Colyear? Let's fuck off and get this place sealed up for SOCO. We're going to run forensic strategy and let them get busy.'

'Yes, ma'am.'

I was last out of the door and closing it behind me when the action of it led me back to my earlier thought. 'Just a minute,' I said.

'What is it?' Rowan asked.

'Probably nothing.'

The wardrobe had a high shelf within. Various boxes were stored there. The main space was largely empty. The few shirts and coats that were hanging there had been pushed to one side, the side where one door remained closed.

'What is it?' The DCI had come for a look.

I didn't answer immediately. I was busy stepping into the wardrobe space and sniffing the air. I was thinking about the figure I thought perhaps I'd seen earlier. 'Why does it smell like piss in here?' I said to Rowan. I pulled the wardrobe door closed from the inside, not easy, but possible with some careful fingernail manipulation. I looked out at a hazy, but clear enough view of the bed. I opened the door and stepped out.

The DCI was eyeing me curiously. 'What do you have?'

'Maybe nothing, ma'am. But just maybe a witness to a double shooting.'

CHAPTER 20

Run to Ground

'Where the f-f-f-fuck have you b-b-been?'

'Dillon? Slow d—'

'Where ah-ah-ah . . . are y-y—'

'Dillon, take a breath. What's going on?'

He looked around at the street in Sighthill. Not a soul. He quickly found a piece of kerb between two parked cars and allowed himself to sit for a moment. He raised the phone to his ear again, relieved Davie had finally picked up, but couldn't form a word. His face stretched into tortured grief. He pulled at his hair and swatted the side of his head with the phone.

'Dillon? What's—Dillon, are you crying? What's going on? What's happened?'

He heaved in breaths. He hadn't sobbed since he was a child and the loss of control of his breathing was a shock to him. He dropped the phone at his feet and pushed his hands against the doors of the cars flanking him. He concentrated on the air coming in, remembering exercises the school-appointed speech therapist had taught him. As a child, when he heard the words getting stuck, the embarrassment, the panic it induced just made it all the more difficult to escape the loop. It was better to stop entirely, allow two breaths and go again. He did that now. He had something to say to his brother, and the message needed to be clear.

He wiped at his cheek and nose with the back of a hand and picked up the phone.

'Davie. Are you s-s – are you still there?'

'What's going on?'

'Tell me you're not at home.'

'No. I'm just about—'

'Stop. Don't go home. Where are you?'

'Uh. Fountainbridge. There's like a dozen missed calls from you. Now, tell me what's happened. Please, Dillon. You're scaring me.'

'I will. Just stay there. Bowling alley. It'll take me an hour, maybe a bit more.'

'You're walking? Just get a bus.'

'I'm walking. I'll see you there. And—I don't know, stay inside. Is there still an arcade there?'

'You mean like machines, videogames and whatnot?'

'Aye. Look, just stay there. Stay inside.'

Davie was playing air-hockey with himself, slamming the puck against the far side and letting it glide back to him, not quite letting it stop before batting it again with the paddle.

'There you are,' he said, suddenly looking up and seeing Dillon. He smacked at the puck one last time. It flew into the goal at the far side. 'What's going on?'

'Not here.' Dillon looked around the room. There were a couple of older kids racing each other at a driving game and a father and daughter trying to win a prize from a grab machine, but the place was otherwise empty. 'There.'

He led Davie to an enclosed arcade game. He seated himself behind a plastic crossbow set into the dash of the machine and pushed the holdall down at his feet. Davie climbed into the other seat.

'Well?' Davie said.

Dillon tried to hold himself together, but couldn't. A high-pitched whine left him through his nose. He gripped the crossbow and tried to compose himself, snorting back the sob and letting one more go, determined not to allow any more.

'Jesus Christ, Dillon. Spit it out.'

He didn't bother to even try to speak, until he felt sure he could. But even then, he wasn't sure how to say it. 'Sal,' he said finally. 'She's . . .'

'What?' Davie turned in his seat. He was no longer watching the zombie horde on the screen. 'Is she hurt? What?'

'Dead.'

'. . . *What?*'

'Dead, D-Davie. Tavish too.'

Davie scoffed, sniggered even. Then fell silent.

Ten seconds passed before Dillon continued: 'That guy from the car yard. Brown Leather Jacket. Shot both of them.'

'You're sure they're—'

'Dead. Yes.'

'How do you—'

'I was there when it happened. Hiding. I saw him kill them. I almost bought it too and would have b-but for Cammy.' Dillon would spare the details of the escape, though it was something of a small miracle. He'd inspected the text he'd somehow managed to send off to Cammy and the kid had done well to not just ignore it as nonsense. What was supposed to be 'get here block 3 make noise' had left his phone as 'Ge6 hrtr vki k3 make nose'. Cammy and the others had raced over banging and slamming at the communal door of three with anything they could find from the street. The blow that had cracked the glass had the shooter looking down the hall and then fucking off sharpish out the back way.

'Police—'

'All over the place. I first ran until I couldn't run any more. Got as far as the back end of Kingsknowe and had to stop.' Dillon was about to elaborate, to explain that the running in piss-soaked jeans and boxers had made the insides of his thighs raw and that the stopping had actually occurred on the golf course there, ducking behind a gorse bush prompting a few dirty looks from tartan-trousered fuckwits while he changed into the one dry pair of jeans he had packed and rolling the soiled set into a ball and abandoning behind said bush, but didn't. 'I tried calling you again and again and then, as stupid as it was, I went back. I'm not sure why. Think maybe I just couldn't quite believe it, you know? By the time I did, there were police everywhere, blue lights, vans, the lot. I stood and watched for a while, then this one cop showed up and—'

'What cop?'

Dillon shrugged. He wasn't quite sure why this one made him particularly nervous. 'A detective, spotted me before. He just seems—sharp. I got out of there and just tried to find somewhere this guy won't look.'

'The cop?'

'What? No. The fucking guy with the g-gun.' Davie nodded and then hung his head in his hands. 'I ended up just walking, trying to figure out what to do. I'd just about convinced myself he'd gotten to you first and I was going to have to do this on my own and . . . where the fuck *were* you?'

'Does it matter? Does any of it matter now? Fuck, I think I might be sick.' Davie was shaking. Dillon thought there was a good chance his brother might actually vomit.

They sat, not in silence – the zombies continued their groaning and rasping, with commentary designed to entice the passer-by to part with their pound coins by daring them to 'Survive the walkers in A-M-C's *The Walking Dead*' – but they said nothing for a minute, maybe three.

When Davie's spell seemed to have passed, he cleared his throat and sat up. 'I had a job interview.'

Dillon wouldn't have thought it possible, but his brother made him laugh – then he saw straight away he was being serious.

'Job interview?'

'For a restaurant here.'

'Seriously?'

Davie shrugged. 'Something about what you've been saying. Use the money to make a change . . . Fuck, where's the money?'

'Here,' Dillon patted the bag at his feet. 'Why didn't you say something?'

He shrugged again. 'Knew I'd probably tank the interview and when I did, I wouldn't be in the mood to talk about it.'

They'd both had jobs, though never for long. Dillon's longest spell in gainful employment had been working a door in town. Easy money, wear a black shirt and wink at the girls while talking shit to the other guy in the black shirt for a few hours. This was a year ago and had lasted all of six weeks until his employer had discovered he was seventeen and not nineteen as he'd told him and below legal age for the role. Davie's best had been some gig driving a van for a dodgy guy who ran a construction outfit, as well as a bunch of other stuff Dillon never fully got an explanation of. He'd let Davie go after he made a joke about not having a driving licence. Davie had been bitter about it. The guy had never asked if he had a licence and there was fuck all legal about any part of the operation. 'Don't need the attention, if you get stopped. Sorry,' was the redundancy announcement along with fifty quid in cash by way of a severance package.

'And you tanked?'

'Actually, went pretty well. Explained to the boss that I don't have any experience. Thought she'd send me packing. Instead, she asks if I'm a quick learner. I told her I was.'

'You lied, in other words?'

'Aye. I lied.' They shared a laugh. 'She seems all right. Offered me a paid trial shift next week . . . But . . .'

'Yeah. This sort of changes things. Fuck, Davie. I'm so sorry about Sal.'

Davie hung his head once more and drummed fingers on his crossbow.

After a time, he sat up and took hold of the plastic weapon. 'You got a quid?'

'It's two quid.'

'Well two quid, then?' There was some anger in Davie's voice, like it was on a loose leash.

'I don't . . . aye, sure.'

Dillon fished first into the pockets of his jeans and then into the holdall for his jacket. In an inside pocket he found some change. He slipped a two-pound coin into the slot and after some cheesy preamble from the machine, Davie was soon despatching the undead.

'Always knew she'd break my heart,' he said reloading the weapon and then double-tapping a zombie who burst into the screen from the right. 'Just assumed it would be because she'd fucked off with someone else.'

Dillon's mouth formed the question and then he thought better of it. Davie fired away. But Sal's last words to him were there in his mind and he couldn't stop himself even though he knew it was either pointless or worse, he was about to break his brother's heart all over again.

'Davie . . . Did you know, she was, uh, fu-, eh, sleeping with Tavish?'

Davie took his eyes from the screen for a moment and looked at his brother, long enough that he lost some energy from a walker bite. He turned back and took it out. 'I was aware – yes.'

'And you just let—'

'And I just let – yes. Look Dillon, I hope you never meet someone like Sal.' Davie laughed a little, reloaded, and went on. 'I hope you meet some sweet girl and you both fall in love so hard that the rest of the world and its occupants of weirdos just sort of fade into the . . . background.' Another bite and the machine was asking for another two pounds to continue the adventure. Davie looked again at Dillon. He checked his change, but he was coming up short and so shook his head. Davie sat back and let the crossbow go. 'Thing is, I was happy to have any part of her. This will sound strange to you maybe, but I didn't care if she slept with other people. Aye, maybe because it was Tavish, it was a wee bit – annoying, but when she was with me, she was *with* me. You know?'

'Davie, as I've mentioned before, the walls are thin in the flat, I do know.'

Davie smiled and drummed his fingers again. 'What now? I mean you were right, we should have gotten the fuck out of there, but the question is the same: Go where?'

'I've been thinking about that, mostly that, and, well, I don't know. Though I did wonder about one option,' Dillon said.

'If you're about to suggest handing ourselves in, keep thinking.'

'Davie—'

'No, Dillon. After what happened we'd go down, and not for a piddly sentence. People died. We'd be looking at a long stretch in grown-up prison. You're eighteen now, no juvie-pish for you. Hard time in a hard place.'

'So, what? We walk the streets until this guy finds us and fucking k-kills us?'

'I don't know, Dillon. What the fuck do I know? Only that going to the filth is Not-An-Option. Let's just . . . get something to eat. Maybe a fucking drink, and then see what we can come up with.'

Leith Police Station, home to this major investigation, was abuzz with life. Rowan and I entered through the public entrance after having to ask the various television crew members gathered there to *excuse me* as I pushed past. Two reporters, with front-of-camera-quality faces, simultaneously asked if we were working the double-killing case. I lied that I was not. There was a further crew inside having a heated conversation with the desk sergeant, something about the public interest and their rights as the press. The sergeant rolled his eyes at me and buzzed us through while telling the uppity young lady in his face that she had the right to wait outside with the rest of the ambulance-chasers.

If anything, the first floor was crazier than reception. People, some in uniform, others dressed smart, but not detectives, huddled in small groups, clutching Styrofoam cups of what smelt like bad coffee. There were a dozen conversations going on at once.

'Look,' Rowan said. She was nodding at the one person

not engaged in the circus. It took a moment to remember her name but it came to me as I approached. She was stood in a corner of the corridor clutching her crappy coffee to her chest, like it might deflect a bullet.

'Eileen, right?' I said. The woman jumped a little. I had roused the fiscal depute I'd met at the hospital from some kind of daydream.

'Oh, hi. It's, um . . . no, sorry, I forget your names. Sorry.'

'Don't worry,' Rowan said. She reintroduced us then took a position against the wall beside Eileen, taking in the rabble. 'It's a lot, right? This is your first forensic strategy too?'

'Yes. I'm glad I'm not the only one. What happens at these?'

Eileen was talking to me. I shrugged and looked around, trying to find my own crappy coffee. 'I'm not entirely sure,' I admitted. 'This is my first too. Are you representing the Fiscal's Service on your own?'

'No, my boss is here. I wanted to ask on the way over, but she's not the most approachable. Whenever I ask a question she sort of, huffs, or rolls her eyes, but I'm not sure how I'm supposed to learn anything if I don't ask.'

'Ugh. I've had bosses like that,' Rowan said, her face screwed in a bad-smell wrinkle. 'They make you feel worthless and nothing but a bother.'

'Exactly,' Eileen agreed. 'That's her.' She discreetly pointed at a short, red-haired woman, who was straining her neck upwards to talk to Kate. Their little huddle was at the centre of things. The other groups seemed to orbit around their discussion, which didn't seem altogether amicable and then I saw why. Within their group of four was the OCCTU inspector.

'I can tell you what I know,' I said to Rowan and Eileen, though my gaze was fixed on the debate in the middle of the hall. 'We're here to agree on a plan for evidence gathering. Of course, the police are here, but the fiscal's office too, clearly. Somewhere amongst this lot there will be some kind of scientist, like a biologist or chemist, though I'm not really sure what they're expected to contribute.' I looked around at the people present and saw nobody that fitted the cardigan-with-elbow-patches stereotype in my head. 'SOCO will have a senior representative here too to advise on—'

'The crime scene?' Rowan finished for me.

'Just checking you're paying attention. After we're finished it'll be back to the locus and some Crime Scene Manager will be appointed to make sure everything that is agreed here is carried . . . out. Hold on.' I trailed off as I saw Kate motioning. For a moment I wasn't sure it was me she was waving at, but now she was beckoning harder and not looking happy about it.

'I'll be back,' I said. I approached Kate and her group, though they were splitting apart and heading towards the conference room. I grabbed a cup of sludge from a tray I spotted. 'Ma'am?'

'We've got a bit of a sidebar here before the meeting. I want you in on this,' she whispered.

I followed her into the room and at her nod I closed the doors behind me. They were heavy and the place was plunged into sudden silence from the commotion outside.

'I really have to insist, ma'am—'

'What you really have to do is sit down and discuss this like a professional,' Eileen's boss said to a plain-clothes officer who must be the OCCTU inspector's boss. I was a little disappointed not to see DC Slow present, though the thought raised a smile I struggled to banish. 'Let's sit down, please.'

We occupied one end of the large oval table. The fiscal at the head, the opposing pairs either side. Kate's earlier comment of 'Yes. Well, we will just have to see about that,' was about to be played out, it seemed. The fiscal introduced herself as Patricia Ewing, the inspector next and then his boss who seemed annoyed at the break to indulge in niceties. DCI Owen Brodie gave me his name and went straight back to his point.

'This is clearly attached to our investigation, ma'am. An investigation dating back two years; involving thousands of man hours. OCCTU need to take ownership of this. To involve local CID, no offence,' he glared briefly at Kate and me, 'would be to jeopardise that operation.'

'What does that mean. Exactly?' Kate said. She wore a strange little smile and sat forward in her chair. Her hands were clutched as if in prayer. Her head was tilted in scrutiny. The fiscal's head returned to DCI Brodie and tilted just the same.

DCI Brodie's mouth opened and then closed. He pondered his next words and then sat forward in his chair. 'This case, this investigation is . . . sensitive. It requires special handling and frankly, ma'am, OCCTU are in a far better position to work this.'

'Ma'am,' Kate cleared her throat and seemed to be trying to contain some ire. 'I'm not sure how familiar you are with the type of investigation DCI Brodie here is putting together, but my experience of protracted evidence-gathering surveillance investigations is that they are worked from the background until the time is right to pounce, and right now we have a double killing which will be all over the evening news with a shooter still at large. Admittedly this link to Taylor is strong and it's the angle we will work primarily, but until we have gathered evidence to confirm it, we still have to keep an open mind. I have a community reeling and mourning and I need to be able to tell them that I am doing everything in my power to bring the person responsible to justice. Besides, DS Colyear here thinks we may have a material witness to the murders. We think we're in the best position to work this.' DCI Templeton mirrored the body language of her counterpart.

'With all due respect, Kate, I don't think you know the first thing about what kind of investigation I'm running.'

'I know you would be reluctant to move on anything immediately—'

'Is that true?' the PF cut in.

'Ma'am?' DCI Brodie's round, jowly face was beginning to burn. His gaze moved reluctantly from DCI Templeton.

'My understanding is you have suspects in mind for these killings and is it true that if you came across them in the line of your work, you'd be more likely to observe than to apprehend?'

'Ma'am. Again, with respect, I have been an investigator for over twenty years, I know how to work a case.'

'That's . . . not much of an answer,' the PF said.

DCI Brodie sat back, again clearly selecting his words. 'It is *imperative*, if these killings have come from the command of Nelson Taylor, that we can demonstrate a clear connection between—'

'That's a long way to say yes, but thank you. Look, I think there is scope here to have you both involved, but I have to agree with Kate. I want the suspects taken into custody as soon as is possible, without jeopardising the conviction, of course. As for a larger framework of criminality, well, that has to take a back seat.'

'Ma'am, this may be your call today, but I will be passing this up to the detective super and he will look to go over your head with the Crown Prosecution Service; an ace beats a king, after all. It feels like a waste of time to delay the inevitable.'

The PF mulled this over for a moment. It appeared like he'd struck a chord. 'Maybe so,' she said 'but as you say, this is my call today and I think we should get back to planning the forensic approach. Sergeant?'

I sat up and cleared my throat. 'Yes, ma'am.'

'Would you be kind enough to ask the others to come in.'

'Of course.' I stood, still holding the untouched sludge in my hand. *Wait until Rowan hears this*, I thought.

CHAPTER 21

Eyes Down

Dillon's relief, born from his brother's announcement 'I have a great idea', was beginning to fade, much like the daylight.

He'd been in Portobello only once, when he was fifteen. Winter that year had ended abruptly in early March when weekend temperatures had gone from close to freezing to seventeen overnight. He couldn't remember whose idea it had been, but four of them from the scheme had filled polybags with tins of cheap beer and headed for the beach. Most of the bevvy had been drunk on the same bus journey he and Davie had just taken this evening. It seemed everyone in Edinburgh and the surrounding area had the same idea that particular night. The beaches were full and the cafes and bars were spilling onto the promenade. Recollections were hazy, but there was trouble with a local group and a few fists had been thrown. Then suddenly police were everywhere and he was soon on a bus back on his own trying not to throw up. After that, the 'beach' held little appeal.

A public bus journey had not seemed like a 'great idea', nor had coming to a place that was not familiar, though Davie had argued in a shouted whisper on the bus that that was exactly why it was the best thing to do. No association with Portobello, nobody would be looking for them here. Add to that what Dillon was now looking at, having walked from the main street to this place on Bath Street, and it was all feeling like a decidedly bad idea.

'You're kidding?'

'What?'

'Bingo?' Dillon looked up at the building behind a moat of doubled Heras fencing, far bigger, surely, than a bingo hall needed to be. The blue sign for the 'Royal George Bingo Club' was flaking and faded. A bright new board sat across it announcing 'SUBJECT TO PLANNING: CHANGE FROM FORMER BINGO HALL TO RESIDENTIAL REDEVELOPMENT', though there was no sign that these changes were currently underway.

'Does it matter? A roof over our heads, that's what we discussed.'

'Yeah, but . . . bingo?'

'Come on. You'll be surprised.' Davie gave the street a look in both directions before pulling a section of the fencing from its concrete lower support. He bent, twisted and pulled at the thing until there was a gap wide enough to push through. It wasn't pretty. Davie got his head and shoulders through easily enough, but it took two attempts and made a lot of noise getting his hips to the other side.

When he was done, Dillon looked around and listened for anyone who's attention may have been caught. There were the sounds of construction in the far distance, but no sign of anyone, except for a dog walker further up the street, but even in the early evening gloom it was clear he was sporting white earbuds and his attention was on the screen of his phone and not his dog who was circling and lining up something the oblivious owner was unlikely to pick up.

Dillon tossed the holdall over and gripped the fence, giving it a tug, unconvinced he was getting through without taking the whole line of metal intersecting boards with him. Like his brother, his top half went without much complaint, but Davie had to help him the rest of the way, using his foot to force more room. He was soon lying on his back in the dirt on the other side.

'Come on, this way.'

Davie led round to the left where a small side entrance sat. It looked secure, but after two solid thuds with his shoulder, Davie had sent the door swinging.

'This was my last job for that prick I was working for.'

They stepped into a hall and then a little kitchen area. Thick dust covered every surface, but there was a kettle on the work surface. Dillon tried a tap and found that the water was running and then a light switch and that too worked.

'What is this place? I know it says bingo on the sign, but, like, originally?'

'I'll show you.'

Davie led through to the main section of the building. The room opened out and must have taken up almost all of the entire structure. Wires hung from the high ceiling like jungle vines and pieces of wooden flooring jutted up at them like fangs through thick layers of insulation felled from above. The false ceiling looked to have been brought down and now they had to wade through it. The place had been torn apart, but its former majesty wasn't hard to imagine.

'Used to be a cinema, back in the day. Developers have been trying to rip the place down for years, but the local council are having none of it.'

Dillion walked carefully to where the huge screen would have been, now a brick wall with exposed wiring, and looked up at the seating rising up in a semicircle, now broken and filthy, but it really would have been something. 'What was the job?'

'Huh?' Davie was pulling at some cabling.

'Here, the job, what did they have you doing?'

'Oh. Copper.'

'Copper?'

'Aye, like piping or whatever. I don't think we had what you might call *permission*, to be here, but someone was turning a blind eye while guys took apart the old heating system and I transported the metal back into town. Price of copper is sky high. Anyway, this place is empty and nobody's going to be in here until they sort out all the planning nonsense.'

'Where are we going to sleep?'

'Through to the other side.'

They trudged on through the fluffy fibreglass insulation to doors on the opposite end of the room. They passed toilets and entered into another hallway with a series of doors running off. Davie led into one.

'I think . . . yes,' he said. 'I thought maybe here?'

It was a square room and empty but for one sad, solitary chair. Dillon sat himself into it and looked around. The carpet looked filthy, but the last of the sunlight came in through the window and it wasn't too cold. 'I suppose it will do, until we figure out what to do next.'

'I knew you'd love it.'

I tried my best to explain to Rowan what had been discussed prior to the meeting, which was taking an age to complete. Various people had stood to give their opinions on a scene most of them had not yet actually seen in the flesh, and they were mostly saying the same things. I was aware of DCI Templeton rubbing her face each time SOCO or this guy from the university, or this Crime Scene Manager went over the same point. I was grateful to have seen the locus before the bureaucracy landed, it was unlikely I was getting in there again judging by how many people seemed to be spouting the importance of sterility.

After two hours of what could realistically have been condensed into thirty minutes, I stood, stretched my back and followed Rowan into the hall. As relatively unimportant in this meeting and with no contribution to make, we had been sat at the back, near the door.

'Can you believe I was actually excited to be part of this?' Rowan had placed two hands on the wall and was stretching out her hamstrings, pushing one leg back and forcing her heel down and then the other. She could easily ignore the looks as people filtered from the room, but I felt uneasy.

'It was pretty brutal. Do you have to do that?'

Rowan looked up to see the PF furrowing her eyebrows as she passed. 'My backside went to sleep an hour ago. This is the only thing that helps. So yes, I need to do this.'

'What the fuck are you doing?' the DCI said, though almost passively, not aggressively.

'Arse is dead,' Rowan said, making no attempt to stop the stretching.

'Fair enough. A word, Colyear.' The DCI motioned to join her back in the room. 'You too, Forbes.'

She waited until Rowan had closed the door over to speak and then it was in a hushed voice, that had us both moving in closer. She'd taken one last look at the door before addressing us. She was making me nervous.

'I've tried to keep you on this case as it's developed. There's nothing that's happened so far that's led me to believe you couldn't handle it and you've both performed well. If it was up to me, you'd stay on it to the end, but I think that's about to be taken out of my hands.'

'You think OCCTU are going to take over?' I said.

'That's my gut feeling, yes. Though even if we manage to convince those above me to keep it CID, we're going to lose control to the Major Investigation Team. In that eventuality I can get you in there, but you'd be pushed so far down the food chain you'd do little more than canvas neighbourhoods or trawl through endless CCTV.'

'Well, that's the job,' I said and I was okay with it, though the folded arms and puckered face Rowan was sporting suggested she was not.

'Yes, that *is* the job, but . . . I had a thought.' At this Rowan drew a chair over and set it backwards before jockeying into it, resting her elbows on the back. 'As far as I'm concerned, the number one priority is getting our hands on the fucker, or fuckers responsible and this potential witness. Who calls the shots, who strategises about this and that, who do we arrest or let go and tail for weeks, is all beside the point. I am detective chief inspector for this area and someone thought it was okay to shoot dead two of my civilians and now I might even be told I can't investigate it? Fuck that. Problem is, I'm going to be embroiled in all this tedious bureaucracy before finally being told to take a back seat. So . . .'

'So?' I said. I thought I might know where this was going, but I could scarcely believe it.

'So, I need you two to keep working. For as long as possible, but my advice is work fast.' I glanced at Rowan, she wasn't even trying to hide her excitement. 'However, and this should go without saying, but I will say it anyway, no corner cutting, at least nothing that might jeopardise the investigation that will be coming at your heels. If you do, we're all circling jobs in the newspaper next week.'

'How long of a head start do we have on the other detectives?' I said. I had to admit, to myself at least, the excitement all over Rowan's face was slowly creeping up my spine.

'I don't know. Three, maybe four days. So, don't waste your time taking lengthy statements from potential witnesses. Find out what people know and move on. Just explain that someone else will be coming along to take full details. I'll feed you anything we get back on forensics as it comes in, though don't hold your breath on that count. Chances are, by the time the lab gets back to us, our little side mission will have been spotted and you'll be back to shoplifters and scraps outside nightclubs. If you can, find that witness. That's number one. If by some miracle our shooter hasn't skipped back over the border, then proceed with extreme caution. That's where this stops. If you find anything on the killer, then we send in the cavalry and go back to doing this properly. I fucking hate guns, part of the reason I moved up here, so no risk taking. Is that clear?'

'Yes, ma'am. Of course,' I said.

'And you?'

'Of course. I got into this to catch bad people, not get shot by them,' Rowan said as she got to her feet, sensing this chat was coming to an end.

'Any ideas where to start?' the DCI said.

'One, yes,' I said. 'We speak to the big man on the estate.'

CHAPTER 22

Blood from a Stone

It was dark by the time we returned to the street. The glow from the street lights did little to keep the night at bay, though the television crews had set up their own lighting. Three separate groups, huddled together in their own little camps passing around thermos flasks.

The onlookers had largely gone home, though a small group lingered. Four women and three kids stood at the entrance to block four. Two of the women were in dressing gowns, all of them smoking and chatting.

We parked up and headed first for the playpark. No sign of our boy, but three older kids were sitting under a basketball ring at the far end. Even from this distance the smell of weed was unmistakeable. We were almost on them when they clocked who we were. The quiet conversation and laughter turned instantly to hushed swearing and fidgeting. Something small was launched over the top of the fence behind them. I couldn't help but laugh.

'Relax,' I said. 'In case you haven't noticed, we've bigger problems than a few joints.' The three stood, boys, all between sixteen and nineteen. They wore different tracksuits, but it was variation on a theme. In this light they might have all been wearing the same white trainers, though. 'Looking for Cammy. Is he around?'

The boys looked at one another, perhaps silently deciding which one was going to field this enquiry. 'Who's Cammy? Don't know a Cammy,' the tallest of the three said.

'Is that right? Well, Cammy's not in any bother, I just need to speak to him, but if you're going to stick to the *I don't know nuthin line*, then Constable Forbes here will keep an eye on you while I go fetch that lump of hash you just tossed before organising a full strip search for all of you down at the station.'

There was another round of silent debate amongst them, then the tall one said, 'Oh, you mean wee Cammy? He'll be around here somewhere. If you want, I'll go see if I can find him?'

'That's very public-spirited of you. Thanks.'

Next, we approached the women at block four. The kids at their feet seemed interested in our approach, the women not so much. Their conversation never faltered. Rowan interjected.

'Evening ladies. Just awful,' she said aiming a thumb at the scene across the way.

'A bloody tragedy, so it is,' one of the women said, one of the two wrapped in a bathrobe, hers thick and grey.

'Did you know the, uh, deceased?' I asked. There was a similar silent exchange between this lot. I tried not to roll my eyes. 'I'm just trying to learn who these people were.

269

The more I know, the better placed I am to catch the person who did this.'

'Course we knew them. Everyone knows everyone here.' This woman was likely the youngest of the group. Early twenties, her blonde hair pulled back in a ponytail. A young girl who was her doppelganger stood between her feet looking up at me, eating from a bag of crisps.

'I'm interested in who they were close to. Who here on the street would you say they knew well?' Another exchange of looks. This was why you didn't interview people in a group. 'Look, I get you're not really comfortable with talking to the police about friends you've tragically lost, but we really need—' I stopped. One of the women, the other bathrobe wearer, had scoffed. A single laugh and then the cigarette went back to her lips. We were all looking at her now.

'What?' she said self-consciously. 'Come on. They were no friends of ours.' She drew from the cigarette, her eyes fixed on the lights of the camera crews. Then she looked first at me and then Rowan. 'Drug dealers.'

'Karen,' the young blonde scolded.

'Och, come on. We all know it, and we all know that's why they're . . .' She didn't finish the line, just prodded her cigarette at the lights.

'We're aware of the drug angle. Don't worry, you're not telling us anything we haven't already found out.'

'Well, if you knew, why didn't you do something?' Karen said.

'It's only just come to light,' Rowan responded. 'What we need to know now is who else they associated with. We know that they were a couple, Miss Anstruther and Mr McTavish—'

'Couple? No, they weren't a couple. No, that Sal's seeing the lad from number two. *Was* seeing . . .' another woman said. She appeared to be the mother of the two other kids.

'Are you sure, because we found them . . .' Rowan trailed off. She'd just dropped the most delicious piece of gossip into the laps of these women who looked like they lived on it.

'Found them what?' the final woman said, a generation or so older than the others.

'You found them *shagging*?' the blonde said, holding the ears of her daughter and barely speaking the final word, but mouthing it exaggeratedly.

'I, uh . . .' Rowan looked at me. All I could do was smile. 'So, this guy at number two, that Sally was—'

'She's a dirty bastard that Sal – *was*,' the mother of the two said, making no attempt to cover the ears of the little ones. She said it not as an insult. The smile on her face and slight shake of the head were of admiration.

'I'm guessing none of you have any idea who might have done this?' There was a collective shaking of the head. 'But could you tell me who this guy is that Sal was seeing. Where can I find him?'

There was still no sign of Cammy, or the kid who'd offered to look for him either. He'd likely picked up his hash, if he managed to find it, and was sparking up a fresh joint further away from the police. I had a new name at least, David Marshall. Flat four, block two. It was information the detectives who would be following us would glean in the coming days and when they did, they might just get a 'I told all this to your colleague' and our little side mission

271

would be discovered. For now, we would be the first to speak to Mr Marshall and the brother he lived with.

'You don't think this guy might be the shooter, do you?' Rowan said, following me up the stairs to level one.

'You mean jealous rage at finding them together?'

'Well, yeah. People have been shot for less.'

'I doubt that very much. It would mean this guy walked around with a gun and had it on him when he walked in on them in bed.'

'Or, he found out about them and waited until he could confront them in bed.'

There was no part of me thought that as true, but I did hesitate when I reached flat four before knocking. I paused for a moment and then wrapped twice on the door. I'd intended three knocks but stopped as the impact from my knuckles was sending the door into an arc.

'Hello,' I called into the darkness of the hall. 'Police. Anyone home?' Again, I hesitated before stepping over the threshold, Rowan's thought infecting my instincts. 'I'm coming in,' I called. 'Don't shoot me in the face,' I whispered to myself.

'Are we allowed? I mean, shouldn't we think about a warrant?' Rowan said.

'At the moment, the guys who live here are potential witnesses and we've stumbled across an insecurity near to where a double murder took place. We wouldn't be doing our jobs if we didn't check everything was okay in here.'

The only light on was a bedroom. An unmade bed, drawers pulled out with clothes spilling from them and the smell of teenage boy, almost stifling.

'Check the other rooms. Let me know if you find a wallet,' I said.

'Why?'

'I have a feeling that you won't. I think someone left in an awfully big hurry. It will be one of only a few things they took.'

Rowan left the room as I continued to search while trying to get used to the smell. There wasn't much to find, other than a Tupperware box in a sock drawer with around two dozen assorted pills, separated into cellophane bags and held by elastic bands. Drug dealers, right enough, but barely qualifying as such.

I went looking for Rowan. 'Find anything?' She was trawling through the other bedroom. It was far worse than the previous one. It looked like it might have been ransacked, only the drawers were all closed. More likely the occupant was just filthy. The smell here was a concentrated version of the other room.

'Just that,' she said. I followed her pointed finger to a framed photograph on top of a chest of drawers. Two brothers (I'd have deduced even without the information gleaned from the neighbours, such was the similarity to their eyes and brow). It looked to have been taken on a bright summer day. I lifted the picture for a closer look. The older of the topless two had dark hair, the younger fairer. The younger held the head of the elder in a playful elbow clench, both had their tongues stuck out and middle fingers presented to the photographer. In the background a pair of legs could be seen, someone sunning themselves. It could have been anyone, but I thought about the blonde, still lying in her deathbed not far from here.

I looked again at the two boys. The dark hair was Davie, fair hair was Dillon. 'I've seen this kid. Maybe even seen him today,' I said.

'Which one?'

I tapped a fingernail on the glass of the frame.

'What are you thinking?'

'I think they were all in this together. The four of them, at least. What's not clear is how Nelson Taylor crosses paths with them. These guys deal pills, maybe weed too, but low-level stuff, nothing hardcore and nothing on a scale that seems to have been stored in the lock-up.' I felt like I was talking to the kid in the photograph, the subtext being: *how did you fuck up this bad? What happened?* 'Let's just close the door over, let the next team find what we already have. But here, keep a hold of this.' I passed the framed photograph to Rowan.

To my astonishment, Cammy was waiting for us in the street, his arms folded across his handlebars. He looked bored and put-out.

'You wanted to see me?'

'I did, aye,' I said. I looked around; he was on his own. 'Normally if I'm chatting to someone your age on an official basis, it would be in the company of a parent.'

'Well, good luck with that.'

'Folks not at home?' Rowan asked.

'Mum's working and if you find my dad, tell him I'd like to meet him and tell him he's a prick.' Rowan laughed.

'All right. What the hell. I'm looking for David and Dillon Marshall,' I said.

Cammy pursed his mouth and shook his head slowly. 'Who's Davie and Dillon when they're at home?'

'Well, they're not at home, that's why I'm speaking to you. And you know fine well who they are. Especially since I said "David" and you went with "Davie".' I took out my wallet and looked inside. I'd hoped there was a tenner, but there was only a twenty. I folded it and held it out to the lad between my first two fingers. 'I don't have time to fuck around, Cammy. I need to speak to them.'

He leant his head and examined the cash. 'I'll take your money, but really, I can't help you.' He reached out, but I drew my hand back. 'Cammy. Listen. You know why the policeman over there is standing in the cold, right?' I nodded at the young officer standing at the blue tape surrounding block two.

'Because there's dead people inside.'

'Because there's dead people inside. Did you see anyone in the street today?'

'Loads of folk.'

I rolled my eyes at him. 'Anyone not from here. Anyone suspicious?'

He shrugged. 'Just dodgy characters in uniforms and,' he nodded to my chest, 'suits.'

'I don't think you're grasping the gravity of the situation here, Cameron,' Rowan said.

'What's that mean?'

'It means, as if I have to explain it, that there are some very serious things going on here and you're in a position to help, but instead you're just being a wee wide-o,' Rowan continued.

Cammy shrugged again, a small smile on his lips. 'We done here?'

I sighed. 'Just about. But let me tell you one thing before we go. I don't know how well you knew the two people still lying in there, but I suspect you knew them pretty well. What would they think if they saw you refusing to help catch their killer?'

'I doubt they're thinking much at all.'

'The point is, if you know something, you should say something.'

Cammy straightened up on his bike. His right foot found a pedal. 'Well, since I don't know anything, I'll just be going now.'

I took hold of his handlebars with one hand. 'I get it, Cammy. You don't speak to police, no matter what. Kind of like a code you and your pals live by. I want you to think about it. Because you and your pals aren't going to catch the person who shot those folk. Now, take this. Take it.' He hesitated and then opened his hand. I pushed my card and the twenty into it. 'Listen carefully. If you have any way to get in touch with Dillon, I want you to tell him that I think he saw something. I think he saw something so horrible he had to change his trousers after. Tell him he's not safe, but I can help him. And tell him even though he thinks he's in too much trouble to call me, he has to, and I'll still do everything I can. Have you got that? All of it?'

There was the shrug again. 'If I knew who Dillon was, aye, I've got it,' he said. He stuffed the card and money into a pocket and took off into the street, pulling a wheelie as he did.

CHAPTER 23

With Friends Like These . . .

'Naan breads and rice? Are you trying to seduce me?'

'Of course. Is it working?'

'Tell me there's pakora in that bag and these knickers will be off before you finish the spiced onions.'

Malky reached across the table, opened the bag and waved it under Lainey's nose. 'Chicken *and* vegetable,' he said with a double-eyebrow raise.

Lainey laughed and caught Malky's face in both hands. She landed a lingering kiss on his lips and then let him go. 'How are you so flush?'

He was spooning jalfrezi onto two plates. 'Work. Been a good week. What?' He stopped, seeing the look on Lainey's face. The disappointment there was almost heartbreaking.

'It's fine,' she said, laying the pakora she'd just plucked onto the kitchen work surface. 'I just, I shouldn't have asked.'

'It's not. It wasn't, you know, dealing. Honest.' He put his arms around her waist and nudged her, encouragingly towards him.

'No?'

'Promise. Keep this to yourself, but I was actually helping the polis.' Of course, this was a half lie, particularly as most of the cash he'd come by had been paid by the other side, but this was the answer that would encourage her to stay.

'Really? No bullshit?'

'No bullshit.'

'So, you're done with the dealing?'

He was nodding, though he was struggling to make his mouth form the words. He wasn't dealing, at least hadn't, since his windfall, but how long would that last? It would last beyond tonight all right. So, he said: 'Aye, done with it.'

Lainey, a full foot taller than Malky, ran her fingers through his hair, then kissed him again. Kissed him hard. They continued kissing as they shuffled from the kitchen towards the sofa in the next room.

Lainey was less of an ex and more of an off-again-on-again thing. They'd first met at a nightclub three years ago and in the early days he'd told her he worked in graphic design. It was the first thing that had come to him when they'd met for their first official date (the nightclub and subsequent drunken sex at hers not counting). Fortunately for him, she'd shown little interest in his job and questions were sparse and easily fielded by guesswork and general bullshit. That was until she'd held a dinner party and the partner of a friend of hers couldn't fucking wait to talk shop with a fellow graphic designer. That was the first break-up. The second came about seven or so months later when he'd grovelled his way back into her good graces and she'd spent a few nights at his. Long enough to find the hole at the back of the medicine cabinet, where a string held in place a bag containing around forty small wraps of brown powder. Bad enough, though just as well she hadn't stumbled across the Tupperware box behind a loose panel under the kitchen sink where twice that many hid.

He'd assumed that was that and had, by the time another six months had passed, even deleted her from his phone. Then a message one Friday night, the content of which identifying it as coming from her, had led to another go. The dealing was a serious problem for her, but at least it was out there, laid bare. She'd tolerated it as long as she could, and they were soon apart once more.

This time it was he who had messaged her. His new-found wealth sparking in him the idea that it might somehow be possible.

His head was between her legs, her fingers in his hair when his phone rang for the first time. He fished it from his jeans, lying by the coffee table in an impressive manoeuvre which had allowed him to continue his circular mouth action, a tried and tested orgasm certainty, and toss it across the room. When it rang for the fifth time, he didn't need her tut and two-fisted thump of the sofa cushions to tell him the moment was gone.

'I'm sorry. Just ignore it.'

'If only I could. Just get it,' she said. She curled her legs up onto the seat of the sofa and pulled a cushion onto her lap, refusing eye contact.

If that's Dingo, I'll fucking throttle him next time I see him, Malky thought. 'What?' he yelled into the phone. He was only vaguely conscious of his nakedness.

'Is that any way to speak to your, most generous, benefactor, Malcolm?'

Malky was suddenly far more conscious of his lack of clothes. He glanced at the screen of his phone. It was an unknown number, but the voice was very known. He grabbed his jeans with his free hand and went into the kitchen.

'Mr Taylor. Sorry, I didn't realise it was you.'

'Better late than never. I hope I'm not dragging you away from anything important, or anyone important.'

'Uh, no. Sorry. I was, sleeping.'

'Course you were,' Nelson Taylor said.

Could he know he was with someone? Malky put the phone on speaker and began pulling on his jeans.

'Something I can help you with, Mr—'

'Never mind the formalities, Malky. No need for names,' he said, though it was okay for him to use Malky's name? 'I have a little job for you. One of an – urgent nature.'

'That's, uh, kind of you to think of me Mr, eh. But I'm a little—'

'I know you're not about to tell me you're busy. Since you were just sleeping. See, then I'd know you were lying and that would hurt my feelings.'

Malky looked at the mountain of food he knew now he wasn't going to eat. 'What do you need?'

'Good lad.'

The instructions were clear, though he wasn't allowed to write them down and now he was beginning to doubt himself. *Get a cab, don't book a cab, no Uber. Just flag one down and go to this address. If the cabbie asks why you want to go there, either tell him to mind his own business, or make some shit up like you broke down there yesterday and you're meeting a mechanic. Wait 'til he's gone and . . .*

What was it now? Walk down the road until you see floodlights? Which road? Clearly not back up the one the cab brought him down and there was another off to the left, although it was a small one with nothing signposted. Where the fuck *was* he? And did he really have to agree to this? Of course he did. He'd taken the man's money and there was no giving it back. And there was no getting Lainey back. Not this time. That ship had sailed, or rather that ship had laughed, a horrible little laugh that meant this was as far from funny as it gets, and stormed out after dressing in short, quick, angry motions and clutching her coat in one hand and the bag of pakora in the other. He'd called after her, a series of apologies and promises to call her later. He would try, but his number was probably blocked before she'd even found her own cab.

This wasn't a part of town he knew. Some industrial setting at the arse end of Loanhead. The cabbie hadn't asked why he was there, but Malky had asked the question of himself plenty in the past twenty minutes. He started walking down the road, because there was no footpath. A light drizzle had started and the coat he'd taken was too thin for this bullshit. He pulled the zip up as high as it would go and he dug his fists into the pockets.

His socks were wet at the toes on both feet since the street lights were too far apart here to warn him of the puddles. This was the last time, he told himself. He'd block every unknown number that appeared on his phone after tonight. The money was nice, but not worth it.

He was about ready to stop, turn around and go back and try the other road when he spotted a light through the trees to his left. A fence with a barbed-wire topping came into view and right enough, floodlights set at even intervals stood sentry at the perimeter of this place he was told was a scrapyard. After a time, the fence gave way temporarily for a gate. PENTLAND SCRAP AND HAULAGE the sign read. It was heavily padlocked. CCTV cameras bore down at him as he approached a smaller gate to the side meant for people rather than vehicles. He found the intercom he was told would be there. He reached for the button, his hand shivering a little from the rain, which he could now feel through his jacket and jeans to his shoulders and thighs. Shit, what was it now? Three long presses and then two short? Or was it the other way around? To hell with it. He went with his first thought. An electric buzz sounded with each press. A short pause and then two more. Nothing.

He swore under his breath and reached for the button once more, about to try the alternate option when the speaker crackled into life. There was no voice, just the crackle.

'Uh, hello. It's Malky. Mr – uh, a mutual friend told me to come by.'

Again, there was nothing, but slowly Malky became aware of another electrical noise. At first, he couldn't tell where it was coming from, then he looked up. One of the CCTV cameras was moving. It hovered on him for a moment and then began a rotation around him. It stopped and there was a moment when all that could be heard was the rain. Then a third electrical noise, one that made him jump. It was sustained and was coming from the gate itself. He pushed and it gave.

He walked into the yard, allowing the gate to swing shut hard behind him. This was where the directions Mr Taylor had given had ended. Towers of metal and piles of cars formed a sort of labyrinth in the industrial space.

When his eyes began to adjust to the glare of the overhead lights, he saw a series of portacabins he couldn't believe he had missed. He approached cautiously, not sure which, if any, might be the right one. Then a door opened. The guy, Billy, stood in the doorway shielding his eyes with a flat hand. In his other was a gun.

'*For fuck sake, Malky. Never again*,' he muttered to himself.

'The fuck you doin' 'ere?' Billy said.

Malky stopped walking. He took his phone from his pocket. 'Told you. Someone needs to speak to you.' He stood there in the rain while Billy eyed him.

'You better come in, then,' he said.

The portacabin was spartan, but it was warm. A desk was pushed against one wall with a rucksack on top. In another corner a sleeping bag lay open and a half-drunk bottle of beer along with a paperback sat next to that on the floor. A space-heater glowed and hummed and was the only other thing in the room. The CCTV equipment must have been in one of the other cabins.

Billy lifted the bottle and sat on the desk, Laying the gun down there by his thigh.

He opened his hands in a gesture of *okay, let's hear it.*

'I need to call him. Is that okay?'

Billy nodded and Malky went to the last number and hit redial. It rang only once.

'Malcolm. That was pretty quick. Is our friend there?'

'Yeah, he's here. Hold on, I'll put you on speaker.' Malky opened up the call and held his phone up.

Billy started: 'I'm 'ere, mate. What's going on? This wasn't the plan.'

'Plans change. We need to rethink.'

'Hold on. Should I ask this one to leave?'

'No, it's fine. Look, I think it's time for you to come home, Billy boy.'

'What? Why?'

'Have you seen the news? Your work made a far bigger story than I could have thought possible. Seems the jocks are a sensitive bunch. I think it's time for you to get your arse back down here. The other two will come again. Don't you worry.'

Billy rubbed at his face. 'I've never walked away from a job in me life.'

'I understand that. But you're not walking away, you're following orders. I know you could get it done, it's just the risk ain't worth it.'

'You're right about that, mate. I can get it done.'

There was a pause, on the phone this time.

'If they haven't linked us to these idiots, it's only a matter of time. They might be watching for you. Look, come on home and we'll have a good think about how best to play it. I'm thinking maybe we get someone on Kelty's crew instead.'

'That wannabe doesn't have anyone on his payroll could handle this, mate. You know that. Besides . . . I've just had an idea.'

Billy was staring at Malky now and Malky did not like it.

'What are you thinking?' said Taylor?

'You trust me, don't ya?'

'Yeah, course.'

'Then give me three days. If it's not done by then, I'll head home.'

'I don't know, Billy.'

'Three days, mate. I might need you to check on one more phone number after all, though. Is that still possible?'

Billy's eyes hadn't shifted from Malky.

'It is, yeah.'

'Great. I'll be in touch. Three days, mate.'

'All right, Billy. Three days.'

CHAPTER 24

No Pain, No Gain

Thanks to Davie's previous job, ripping the guts out of the heating system in this place, it was a bitterly cold night. The sleeping bag wasn't the best and the window in the room they'd elected for sleeping in was draughty. At some point in the night Dillon had awoken and had no idea where he was. Even when it had come to him, seeing Davie in his own sleeping bag next to him, snoring away, he had forgotten completely where the toilets were. By the time he hunted them down, relieved himself and crawled back into the sleeping bag, this time also wrapping his legs in his coat, he had been fully awake. He stared at the ceiling for what felt like hours, listening to the wind whistle through the gap in the window frame he promised himself he would fix before the next evening, just thinking. There was no clear path in front of him, no obvious way out. The words: *You're not going to be very hard to f-f-find, are ya?* echoed in his mind.

At some point sleep had returned to him, though he felt groggy when his phone chimed and pulled him back to wakefulness, despite the fact the room was full of sunlight and lacking Davie. The message was from Cammy:

Pigs looking 4 U

What U tell them? Dillon texted back. He stretched and stood. His back ached. They would have to figure out something to sleep on. Perhaps risk a trip into town, to an outdoor store for a camping mat, or maybe an inflatable number, if it wasn't too expensive. Part of the ache, he felt, was just the lack of exercise in the past few weeks, his body yearning to be put through a full range of movement.

The phone chimed again:

Can u talk?

Dillon hit the call button. It began ringing while he went looking for his brother. 'What's up Cammy?'

'All right?'

'Not really. But what's going on there?'

'Police all over the place.'

'Yeah. Who was asking about me?'

'Detective Sergeant Donald Colyear. I have his card. Told him I had no idea who you were, but he had a message for you anyway.'

Dillon had reached the room with the kettle and sink, but he stopped at the door. He could hear Davie making tea in there. 'What was the message?' He listened as

Cammy delivered it, then told him he'd be in touch and that he'd done well.

'How'd you sleep?' Davie asked. Bless him, he'd made two cups. He lifted one and sipped.

'Dog shit. You?'

'Same. My back feels like I slept on concrete.'

'We won't last long, living like this. Thought I'd take a trip into town, pick us up something better, maybe a few other supplies.'

'Sure it's a good idea?'

Dillon wasn't, but what choice did they have? Besides, he was aware he'd start to go nuts stuck in this coffin of a cinema. If he avoided Wester Hailes, surely it would be okay?

Davie was going to spend the afternoon making a few calls, adamant he could figure out something better for them.

It was a beautifully bright day. The cold of the previous night fading into memory as Dillon squeezed himself out of the security fencing and made his way across the street to where the sun was beating down. He dropped the bag Davie hadn't spotted as he left. He closed his eyes and pointed his face at the warm rays for a minute and for that minute he wasn't being hunted, there was nothing to worry about at all.

'What do you have?' I asked, looking over Rowan's shoulder at her screen.

'The brother has an Instagram account, but only two entries. Looks like he opened it and then abandoned it as

288

a bad idea over a year ago. If he has anything else, I can't find it. Dillon . . . on the other . . . hand,' she said, tabbing between screens, 'has Facebook and is reasonably active. Though nothing in the past month or so.'

'Well, this Wester Hailes lot might not be the smartest bunch, but we could scarcely expect him to be posting about his brush with death with a selfie showing us where he's hiding out. But it was worth a try. Maybe keep an eye on it.'

'Will do.'

'Mind if I have a look?' I asked.

'Sure. I was going to grab a coffee anyway. Want one?'

'Please.'

I took her chair and started to look through Dillon Marshall's posts. He was a normal kid, nothing too controversial on here. Themes of bodybuilding, videogames and Hibs. There was nothing in the background of the shots that might suggest favourite places, Easter Road Football Stadium aside. The faces in the few shots that contained more than just his biceps were the same characters he was already aware of. Another one of Sally Anstruther, this time winking at the camera with her arm around David Marshall appeared. I lingered for a moment. What a waste, what a horrible waste. My phone started ringing in my pocket. It would be Rowan asking what kind of coffee, or Kate looking for an update, but I was wrong.

'Hey,' I said to Marcella. I leant back in the chair.

'Is this a bad time? I can call back—'

'No, it's fine. Good, actually. Just doing some office work.'

'Taking a break from dead bodies?'

'Something like that,' I said. I looked again at Miss Anstruther winking at me. I clicked on the next picture to clear the screen.

'I'm sorry I haven't been in touch before now. I wanted a little time to pass before I did. I'm not sure how you're feeling about things?' I could hear the cringing in her voice.

'You can relax, Marcella. Really. I'm sure it was for the best. How are you?'

'Good, I'm good. Busy with work, I had something of a small promotion.'

'That's great. I, uh, guess congratulations?' I said. Rowan appeared at my arm, laying a coffee in front of me and quizzing me with her eyes. I pulled a sheet of paper from under the keyboard and searched for a pen.

'Thanks. It's nothing really.'

'You were just calling to see if I'm okay?' Rowan placed a pen in my hand. I scribbled 'Marcella' on the sheet. Rowan raised her eyes in surprise and went back to her coffee.

'Yeah, I guess. Though I suppose I did have a question.'
'Oh?'

'Yeah, well, I suggested we maybe stay friends, remember?'

'Yes. I remember and sure, friends. I can do friends.' Rowan's eyes were now rolling.

'I also suggested something else. Do you remember?' I could hear her cringing again.

I put down my coffee and sat forward, trying to recall the break-up conversation. 'Uh, you said, let me think, something about maybe getting together for coffee?'

'Uh-huh, and . . .?'

'And . . .' I was thinking hard. Then I remembered. 'Oh.'

'Yeah.'

'You mean get together to . . .'

'Yeah. What do you think? Could you handle it?'

Rowan's eyes were back to scrutiny. 'So, we're not talking about getting back together or anything – just . . .'

'Asking too much?'

'Well. No. I guess that would be . . . Wait. Just so we're clear, we're talking about sex, right?'

Marcella laughed on the other end of the phone. 'Yes, Don. Sex.'

Rowan clenched her fist and pulled her arm in, in a gesture of triumph. Now she was holding her hand up for a high five. I instinctively moved to respond, then glared at her and shook my head.

'Sure. Let's do it. Uh, so to speak. Tonight?'

'Could you manage, I don't know, now?'

I laughed this time. 'I can't right now, but maybe later this afternoon?' I was trying to ignore Rowan who had put down her coffee and was now doing the fist thing with both arms, imitating humping, or something.

'Great. See you later.'

'Yeah. See you,' I said and hung up. 'Grow up,' I said to Rowan.

I was about to turn the machine off when the picture from Sally had me thinking. Another muscle shot of Dillon, this time showing off his back.

'Where's that picture we took from his flat?' I said.

'The one in the frame? It's here somewhere. Why?'

'Just an idea.'

'Anything?' I asked as Rowan dropped herself back into the passenger seat.

'No. The only Marshall on their system is a Peggy. And the picture didn't ring any bells either. The receptionist showed it to a couple of other staff and nothing.'

'It was a long shot,' I said and put the car into gear. I drove out of the car park of the JD Gym, the next closest I could find on an online search of the Wester Hailes area. We'd tried a boxing gym first with the same result.

Although there was a lot on his Facebook to do with training, there was no mention of a gym, though it was hard to believe the kid grew those arms doing press-ups in his bedroom. Still, it was more likely, given his erratic drug-dealing income, some pal somewhere had a bench in a crappy garage or something.

'Who's next?' Rowan said. I looked at my watch, which made her snigger. 'We can finish early if you're eager to get over there?'

'It's not that.'

'Mmmhmmm.'

'Let's try one more. Where's close?'

Rowan consulted her phone. 'Mmm, nothing close, at least nothing you wouldn't have to jump on a bus for. She was spreading her fingers on her screen, widening the search. 'I guess there's two options. There's a Pure Gym out at Gorgie Road.'

'That is a trek.'

'Or . . . wait, there is something called Unique Fitness, arse end of Clovenstone, or maybe Kingsknowe.'

'Doesn't sound likely either. But let's go with that and call it a day.'

'Sure. That gives you enough time to get home and have a shower before you go meet your *friend*.' She planted her phone with directions on the dashboard.

'About that. Is it weird? Should I be pissed off that she dumped me and now wants me to come over for a . . .'

'Booty call, and no. I'm just teasing, but if you're not offended, why not? How do you feel about it?'

'I'm not sure. I haven't really had a moment to process. But, I suppose I'm fine with it. I mean I don't have the time to go dating again and frankly the idea is exhausting. Although I wasn't happy about being dumped, I have to admit at a certain release of pressure when she did. Like it's one less thing to worry about and – I like to think we're pretty good, you know . . .'

'In the sack.'

'Well, yeah.'

'Then maybe don't look the gift horse in the proverbial?'

'Why am I even asking you about this?' It suddenly occurred to me. When did talking about sex with Rowan become okay?

'Because I'm wiser than my years and I can give you a female perspective. And because you need the help.'

'Well, I – Yeah, fair enough. Is this right?' We'd driven into Drumbryden Industrial Estate. A shady corner of the city if ever there was one and just about the last place I'd expect to find a gym. I followed the line on the screen past a couple of run-down units being used as a repair garage. In the near distance high-rise flats loomed.

'It must be some shitty company selling gym equipment or something,' Rowan said. And yet, there it was.

A particularly large unit, the front doors wedged open, presumably because there were no obvious windows to open. I crawled to a stop and lowered the window. The sounds of bags being punched and the metallic, rhythmic clank of metal on metal could be heard. My earlier thought returned to me: *some pal somewhere had a bench in a crappy garage or something.*

Rowan lifted the framed picture and got out. 'I'll come with you,' I said.

I closed the door and turned to the makeshift gym. I almost dropped the keys. 'I don't fucking believe it,' I said.

Rowan said something, though I wasn't listening. My focus was fixed on the lad having a quick joke with someone at the door. He had a bag in one hand. I didn't need to see the picture again to confirm, though Rowan was comparing it.

'Fucking hell,' she said.

The lad took three or four steps towards us, still smiling at whatever was exchanged between him and the guy at the door. Then the smile was gone and he was no longer walking. Our eyes locked for a few seconds. Then, in a disturbingly calm motion, he pulled the shoulder strap of the bag and hauled it onto his back.

'Don't—' I started, but he was already off before I could say 'run'.

I tossed the keys in the general direction of Rowan and took off after him. He took a right at the entrance to the industrial estate, slipping slightly on the mud, but keeping his feet. He was quick for a big lad, even with the bag. I wasn't going to outsprint him, so I forced myself into a pace I knew I could keep, though this meant he was quickly putting ground between us. I followed onto a footpath and down beside a bridge crossing the canal. He was only just still visible as he hit the path next to the water's edge. The good news was there was nowhere to go. A high fence ran along the right and the canal was far too wide to jump.

The blue flash of his jacket was at the edge of my vision, which was itself drawing in through exhaustion.

There was a moment when I'd lost sight of him and my muscles and lungs begged me to give up. I almost did, but there was the blue flash again. I could make out that he took a left at a fork in the path, staying next to the water under a bridge.

He was still way out in front, but I thought maybe less so. I was slowing, but so must he be.

The canal path continued on. He almost collided with a cyclist who came to a stop to yell something at him. The cyclist was still muttering swear words when I passed him.

I was blowing hard, but definitely gaining. I watched as he had a moment of indecision. The fence to the right was gone and some scrubland was all that was between the path and housing in the middle distance.

He remained by the canal, looking over his shoulder now at regular intervals. When the next bridge arrived, he decided to change it up. He cut right, up and onto the road, turning left, now over the canal. The effort of the short climb had taken something out of him.

There was still fuel in the tank, though. We were heading into Wester Hailes. I wondered if this was intentional, or just some homing instinct. He turned left into Westside Plaza, still with a good two hundred yards on me. I didn't know this place well, just that it was a warren of the cinema complex and shopping centre. This was where he was going to lose me if I couldn't stay with him.

We were both at a fast jog now. A group of taxi drivers watched us with some amusement as I followed him, skirting around the plaza to the left. The road led into the large parking area for the complex. He was paying for the initial sprint he'd put on and I was gaining from the even-pace tactic. The gap was less than a hundred yards. If I'd had the oxygen to spare, I could have called to him, urged him to stop, but all I could do was keep on him.

He went left, and I could scarcely believe he had as it was up a steep set of steps. I was right on him now. I was thinking about what I would do when I could close my hand around his jacket, probably just let my legs go and trust he would fall too.

My foot caught on a step. I fell forward and felt my hand brush his ankle a moment before the concrete angle slammed into my shin.

I didn't even have the breath to yell in pain. I hissed and heaved in air. He looked back at me from the top of the steps with what might have been concern. I forced myself back onto my feet and hobbled up.

It was a small train station. I wasn't aware Wester Hailes had one. One platform either side of the single track. I looked around and for a moment I thought he must have found a second wind and run off. I knew I had no more run in me. But then I saw him, down on the tracks. He was clambering up the other side, tossing the bag up and pulling his frame over the edge.

'Wait,' I yelled. My hands were on my thighs.

When he got to his feet, he pulled the bag back over his shoulder. He looked unsteady. Then a torrent of vomit left him, back over the edge onto the tracks. He spat, once, twice and then threw up again. This might have been my moment – if I'd had anything left and my shin wasn't on fire – though I could hear a train approaching. If I'd been foolish enough to follow over the tracks, it was likely I wouldn't have had the energy to pull myself to safety on the other side.

He was continuing to spit and wipe at his mouth. I was about to try to talk to him, but the train cut past, Wester Hailes not included in its scheduled stops. In the movies there would be a nothing in the space where he stood, but as the last carriage thundered past, there he was. Looking reasonably fresh once more, but still standing there.

'Dillon. We should talk,' I said not quite at a shout, but voice raised.

He was shaking his head. 'Nothing to say,' he called back.

'So, what's the plan? Live under a rock the rest of your life?'

'I – I don't know.'

'If it's between me and the person who shot your friends, it's not much of a choice, is it?'

'If I go with you, I go to jail, right?'

'Not necessarily. I – It's complicated. It would be a fair trial.' In that moment I had considered a lie, but I had a feeling this kid was sharp enough to know one when he heard one.

'That can't happen. And p-people d-died.'

'I can do what I can. That I can promise – wait, Dillon.' He was walking off. He turned again.

I went into my pocket and pulled a business card. I made a show of placing it on the ground of the platform. 'You saw, didn't you? You saw who shot your friends?'

His head was nodding now. 'Yeah. I saw.'

'I promise you, I *can* help.'

I stood and raised my hands in an open gesture. I began backing away. Then I turned and made my way back down the steps.

CHAPTER 25

Candy from a Baby

The microwave pinged and Malky pulled his overflowing plate from it, jalfrezi spilling onto the floor as he did. He wasn't in the mood to clean it up and he wasn't much in the mood for eating either, but the curry wasn't going to eat itself. Another day and it would be risking a dose of the shits, so it was now or never.

He'd intended on eating it when he'd gotten home from his errand last night, but after hearing what had been asked of him, his appetite had done a runner, which was what he was now considering, had done most of the night.

Should have just said no. But how do you say no to a guy with a gun? Even without it, these were seriously dangerous people, the kind you don't take money from and then say, *nah, this has been fun, but I'm out.* He wasn't out, would likely never be out. It would always be, *just this one last thing, Malky.*

He had to do this; he knew it. Where would he run to

anyway? But after this he would delete all numbers. No, he would take his phone and throw it the fuck into the river.

Two mouthfuls and a single bite of a dried-out chicken pakora and he pushed the plate away from himself. *Let's just get this done.*

He took an Uber to Wester Hailes, still feeling pretty flush and, besides, he was getting a bonus for this fucking suicide mission if he came through it. He found the street and the bench Billy mentioned. 'If you can't see the little shit, just sit there, he'll find you.'

There was plenty to see from this bench. A block of flats surrounded by blue tape. A couple of TV crews milling around with cameras at the ready, locals too. All of them perfectly placed to see what Malky had to do. *This is so fucking stupid. Tell him you tried, but the police were there and given the situation, I felt it best to back off.*

Would that work? Would it fuck. Billy had been persuasive. 'I don't care how you get it, just fucking get it.' He wasn't holding the gun, but it was right there next to him. He didn't have to hear a specific threat.

What he didn't see was a kid on a BMX, tracks shaved into his head, 'rolling around the scheme like he owns the place'.

Malky looked over at the block taped up. People in white, paper suits were coming and going. Three in regular suits were chatting in the street right outside and another in uniform stood sentry at the door.

They never discussed what this bonus would amount to. Whatever it was, it wasn't enough.

There was a game of football going on in the playground

in the middle. The slam of a ball sounded every few seconds, followed by the gasp of a near miss or the yell of a goal celebration.

Malky checked his phone. No messages. He opened the last one he sent to Lainey and tutted. He'd had a few drinks after the trip to meet Billy and it was obvious. Overly grovelling and typos everywhere. He thought now about writing another to apologise for the last, but if the last, as yet not responded to, was desperate, then surely another on top would only be doubly so.

Raised voices seemed to suggest the football match was over. Kids were spilling out of the concrete oval, playfully shoving at one another. A few were on bikes.

As they drew closer, one of them seemed to fit the bill. BMX, shaved head.

Malky's pulse quickened. He waited for the kid to approach, as Billy said he would.

Five minutes passed and the group were thinning out. Not one of them had looked in his direction. They'd formed a circle and seemed to be generally shooting the shit. They showed no interest in the police at the far end of the scheme, probably old news by now. What if the kid went home? He'd have to sit here all day and see if he came back?

'This is bullshit.'

Another one in the group moved off, taking his ball with him. Now there was just three of them, two on bikes.

'Fuck it.'

Malky pulled his hoody up over his head, his scarf up over his mouth and got up, his heart banging in his chest now. He was forming a plan in his head as he approached and then, almost like fate, an opportunity. The two kids on bikes were comparing something on their phones. Malky was jogging now. He glanced at the cordoned-off block of flats. The suits were gone, but the cop at the door was still there. Malky was up to a run. This was going to work. The kid held the phone out, so the other could see. He couldn't believe his luck.

Malky lunged for the phone. The kid had been oblivious to Malky's approach but suddenly flinched at his clumsy snatch. The phone crashed off Malky's knuckles and spun out of the boy's hands and clattered to the ground.

There was a moment when the boy on the bike just stared at Malky. Then he said: 'Fuck's your problem?'

Malky lunged again, this time around the front wheel of the bike, but the boy was able to simply lean the frame of the bike and get to the phone first, though not before Malky got thumb and forefinger on its edge.

'What the fuck . . . are you doing?' the boy spat, trying to wrench the thing free.

'Just let go,' Malky said, his voice muffled by the scarf. He got a second set of thumb and forefinger onto it and pulled. The kid was freakishly strong and his grip remained, though the bike crashed to the ground in between them.

'Get off him,' the second lad yelled.

'Help. Paedo, help.' The kid got a hand around the edge Malky had and was about to reclaim the thing. He continued to yell. 'Paedo, fucking paedo, help!'

Malky had a quick glance towards the cordon. The uniformed cop there was looking over.

'Fuck sake,' Malky growled. He held the phone with his left, about to lose it, for sure, and released his right. He sent a fist into the face of the kid, once, twice. The second punch connected hard. The kid fell back, though Malky felt a shock of pain up through his hand. He pushed the phone into his pocket and turned to run but not before glancing again at the cop. He had a radio to his mouth and was walking this way.

'Shit.'

Malky grabbed the handlebars of the kid's bike and swung it back onto its wheels.

'Hey. Stop!' the other kid said.

Malky threw a leg over the frame and tried to catch the pedals but missed. He crunched down onto the saddle. He moaned in pain and tried again to get the thing moving. The kid on the ground was rolling around, clutching his face.

The bike now was in motion. Malky struggled with the handlebars at low speed as he kicked and pedalled. The cop wasn't far now, but Malky was already getting up to speed as the road ran downhill.

He didn't stop until he was into Gorgie. Here the footpaths were busier and he was getting yelled at by pedestrians.

His description might have been circulated by now and the most telling part of it would be he was cycling. He dumped the BMX next to a communal bin. He considered trying to throw it in there, but he couldn't bend the fingers in his right hand. It felt like someone had injected concrete in there. It hurt like hell, but he suspected that was just a hint of what was to come once the adrenalin started to fade.

He lowered the hood and pulled the scarf free of his face. He could feel sweat soaking his back.

He tried first to pull the kid's phone free of his pocket with his right hand, winced and went with the left. He pushed a thumb onto the screen. As suspected, it was locked. A Google search on his own phone showed a likely place just a few streets away.

Twice a police car passed, but showed no interest in him. Still, he was grateful to duck into the little phone repair shop. TRUETECH was empty other than the guy behind the counter. His attention was on his own phone.

'Awrite?' Malky said.

'Hmm.' The shopkeeper didn't look up.

'Hoping to get a phone unlocked. You do that, right?'

'Mmmhmm.'

'H'much?'

At this the guy looked up. 'Depends on the handset and your provider. Usually about twenty quid. Let's have a look.'

Malky placed the handset onto the glass counter.

'Who's your provider?'

'Uh, I dunno. Can you do it?'

The shopkeeper gave him a queer look. 'Aye. I can do it. You're looking to have the thing unlocked to be able to use SIMs from other providers, like?'

'Eh. No, I need to unlock the screen, then turn the security off.'

The shopkeeper put the phone down and sat back in his

chair, bringing his attention back to his own phone. 'Fifty quid,' he said.

'What? You just said twenty,'

'Twenty to unlock *your* phone, aye.'

'It is—' Malky began. Then had a rethink. 'Thirty quid,' he said instead.

The shopkeeper sat up again. He leant forward and tapped the phone on the counter with a single finger. 'You can do it for free,' he said. 'Just put your thumb on the screen, draw the pattern or type in the password. Won't cost you a penny. If you want me to do it, it'll be fifty quid.'

Malky heaved a breath and went into his jeans with his left hand for his wallet.

I hissed in pain and tried to draw my leg away.

'Oh, come on. You walked in here. It can't be that bad. Hold still,' Marcella said. I lay back on the sofa and gritted my teeth as she drew my trouser leg up. 'Oh shit,' she said.

'What? Let me see.' I sat up, but she urged me back with a hand on my chest.

'Just relax. It probably isn't as bad as it looks. I'll get some things. Don't look at it until I've had a chance to clean it up.'

When she left the room, I looked. I hadn't wanted to until now. 'Oh shit,' I repeated.

'I said don't look,' she called from the kitchen.

There was a huge lump on my shin and a gash in the middle of it that was oozing. My sock was soaked in blood.

Marcella returned with a basin and a first-aid kit.

'Why do you have a first-aid kit?'

'Are you hoping for a better answer than: *to administer first aid*? Why? Do you not have one?'

'No,'

'But – you're a cop. Don't you pick up little injuries all the time? Trousers off.'

'Not really. And do I have to take them off, it's going to hurt like hell.'

'Don, you came here expressly to take your trousers off. We just need to deal with this first. Now do it.'

I slipped them off gingerly. It felt strange to be fully clothed otherwise, so I removed my jacket and unbuttoned my shirt while she dabbed at the wound.

'What happened?' she said.

'I, tripped. No big deal.'

'This needs a stitch or it'll keep bleeding.'

'One way or another it will stop bleeding. I'm not waiting at A&E for six hours.'

She glowered at me. 'I'll put some steri-strips on, but if it's still bleeding by tonight, you'll have to go.'

'Where did you learn to do this?' I said. She'd cleaned the wound with an impressively gentle touch. It was already looking a lot better. She laid a patch of bandage across it while she began peeling the strips.

'I'm a first-aider at work. Pretty sure I mentioned that at some point.'

'You did? Why do they have first-aiders at an office? Paper cuts? Stapler-related incidents?'

Another glower. 'Don't be glib.' She began placing the strips. I watched with morbid interest. 'Last year, Alfie in my office had a cardiac event. I was able to recognise what was going on, raise the alarm and keep him comfortable until an ambulance got there. I even got an award.'

'Really? That's pretty cool.'

'Yeah. I'm pretty sure I mentioned that too. Right. That's the best I can do with what I have. I'll put a bandage on and then maybe we can – You're not in too much pain, are you?'

Her hands worked their way onto my thighs. I leant forward, pushed a dark curl behind her ear and kissed her. 'I think I can handle it,' I said. 'Leave the bandage for later.'

We lay on the couch after, her head on my chest, my aching leg raised on the arm. I must have drifted off as I was startled when she patted my shoulder.

'Right. Get dressed. You need to go.'

'I do?'

'Yes.' She sat up and started looking around, finally dragging her bra from under my back.

'Why? What's so important?'

'I have a date.' The pulse of jealousy that shot through me came as a shock. She must have seen it on my face. 'Sorry, that was a crappy joke. My sister is up with her husband and my nephew. They're coming for tea.'

'Nice.' I pulled my leg from its position with a grunt. The temporary stitches were holding. 'That's the one from, uh, Brighton?'

She smiled and patted my hand. 'Bristol, but decent try.'

I laid my head back. 'Ugh, I really was an awful boyfriend.'

'You had your moments. Now, out.'

'Yes, ma'am.'

I lifted my trousers, noting the lower section of the right leg was now stiff with semi-dried blood. 'I didn't leave any clothes here, did I?'

'Actually yes. A T-shirt or two and a pair of tracksuit bottoms. I'll get them.'

While Marcella left the room, dressing as she did, I reached for my phone. I'd been itching to, but didn't want to give the impression I had more pressing matters. No messages or missed calls. 'Damn it.'

I called Rowan while I hobbled to the kitchen.

She answered immediately. 'How was your afternoon? Full of ups and downs?'

'Fine, thank you. You were right.'

'Well, obviously. But about what, exactly?'

'He didn't call. He still might, but we can't afford the time.'

'Warrant?'

'Warrant.'

'On it,' she said and hung up.

We'd debated, after Rowan had caught up with me and then helped me back to the car earlier, whether to go straight to the gym. That had been my first thought, flash the badge and walk away with Dillon's number. Rowan had pointed out that, if they refused and we then had to wait for a warrant, given the sketchy nature of the place, his number, if they did indeed have it, might mysteriously vanish. She was right of course, the voice of reason. I'd banked on the lad calling me after thinking it over. Not so. Not yet, at least.

Now I would have to go tell DCI Templeton how close I'd come to our witness, and failed. But home first. I wasn't going to deliver the news in tracksuit bottoms.

CHAPTER 26

A Numbers Game

Davie was traipsing up and down the little kitchen area of the abandoned cinema-cum-bingo hall like a disapproving dad. 'Laying low was your idea,' he said.

'I know,' Dillon replied.

'What the hell were you thinking?'

'I – I wasn't thinking. I thought it would be okay.'

'How do the cops know what gym you go to?'

'Davie, I don't f-fucking know. All right. It was a mistake.'

'What if they followed you?'

'They didn't follow me.'

'How do you know?'

'Because the g-guy let me go.'

Davie stopped walking. His hands were up in the air. 'What do you mean? And what guy?'

'The cop. The one I told you about. I ran, he chased. He almost got me and – then we talked.'

'You talked?'

'Do you want me to tell you what happened? Or are you just going to repeat everything I say?'

The hands in the air now swept in front of him in a sarcastic gesture of: *the floor is yours.*

'There was a point at the end. I was busy throwing my guts up. I'm pretty sure he could have caught me, but he didn't. Said he could help. Said I should call him.' Dillon reached into his pocket and brought out the business card and looked at it before he handed it over.

POLICE SCOTLAND
DS DONALD COLYEAR
DIVISIONAL CID
GAYFIELD SQUARE POLICE STATION

Davie examined it. 'He wants to help you into a small cell for the majority of your adult life. Or maybe he wants you to call so he can trace your number here.'

'You're being paranoid.'

'Paranoid? We've had this conversation, remember?'

Shit, Dillon thought, walked into that one.

'Fuck,' Davie said. His hands were now on his head. 'Give me your phone.'

'What?'

'Give it to me. We should have done this straight away.'

'What are you—'

'The gym. Did you give them your number when you joined?'

Dillon paused, struck by the idea. 'I – I don't remember. It was a few years ago. Fuck, maybe.'

310

'You know they can find you with satellites, or whatever, if they have your number. Give it.'

Dillon reluctantly put his phone into his brother's outstretched palm with a slap. Davie went searching in a drawer and pulled a corkboard pin from it. With it he removed the SIM card and then the battery. 'It's the only way to be sure.'

'What about your phone?'

'My phone's safe.'

'Yeah? What if they go through Sal's phone and find all the lovey-dovey messages and probably pictures of your junk?' Dillon immediately regretted bringing her up. 'Sorry. I was just—'

'No. It's okay. You have a point. Shit.' Davie took his own phone and looked at it, as if he was about to euthanise a beloved pet. He reached for the pin.

'Hold on. We need a number before you do that,' Dillon said.

He was going to shoot him in the back of the head.

Even if he wasn't a whining little shit of a human being, he knew too much, but since he was obnoxious, it would just make the job all the easier. There would be no warning, no chance for grovelling or any of that shit. When he had the location, he'd tell Malky it was time to go and the second his back was turned – *blam*. Then one more in the side of the head to make sure. He'd dump his body in nearby woods and dispose of his phone in pieces. Then he'd finish the job before anyone even stumbled across this miserable dwarf. With any luck he'd be eating a good steak in Liverpool before someone walking their dog tripped over his corpse.

'What?' Malky said.

'What?' Billy replied.

'You're, like, staring at me. It's freaking me out.'

'Am I? Sorry, mate. I was miles away. Didn't realise.'

'You sure I can't just go. I mean I did what you asked, right?'

'That you did, Malcolm. A bang-up job. Really, Mr Taylor and I couldn't be more impressed. As soon as he calls back, we'll get you paid and on your way.'

'Okay. Sounds good.'

Or maybe shoot him in his chubby face. Give him a second to know it's coming and – *blam*.

Malky was looking uncomfortable, he scratched at his face with fingers that were crudely splinted together with a series of plasters. He was staring again.

Billy shook his head and stood. He looked across at the sleeping bag on the floor. Please let this be done today. Can't take another night on the ground.

Malky's phone rang in his hand. He answered and laid it on the desk.

'You there, Billy?'

'Yeah, mate. What you got?'

'Fuck all,' Taylor said.

'What?'

'Yeah. My contact ran the number, but it's offline. The kid's maybe not as daft as we were hoping.'

'Can we try again? Maybe the battery died and it'll be back on soon?'

'No can do, mate. This was the last time. Too risky.

Contact won't run any more for a while. Unless you've got another idea, it's time to pack up. See you back tomorrow? Billy? Still there?'

'Yeah. I'm 'ere. Okay. Let me have a think, but otherwise I'll see you tomorrow.'

'Good lad. Don't feel down. They'll come again.'

'Yeah. All right, mate.'

Taylor hung up. Billy stood in the middle of the room, running through options.

'So. That's it? I can go?'

He would look through the kid's phone again.

'I'll just, uh, go then?'

Go through each message and see if there was a hint of where he was holding up.

'Billy?'

'WHAT?'

'Sorry. I just, I need to go.'

'Then fucking go.'

'Okay. It's just—My bonus?'

Jesus Christ. You have no idea how close I am to killing you, you miserable little shit. 'Right. Bonus.' Billy went to the desk and lifted the gun. Gripped it hard, took a breath and put it back down again. Instead, he went into his bag and pulled a bunch of fifties from his wallet. He didn't even know how much. 'There's your fucking bonus. Now fuck off, but stay near your fucking phone in case I need ya. You understand?'

'Yeah. Sure.'

Malky walked quickly to the door. He let it fall closed behind him, bouncing as it slammed twice. Through the gap Billy could see the prick running on those ridiculous, stumpy fucking legs.

313

CHAPTER 27

No Cigar

DCI Kate Templeton listened patiently as I conveyed the story of my near miss with our one witness. I could sense Rowan was as nervous as I was as I finished and waited for her reaction.

'So, he confirmed he saw something,' she said.

'That's right.'

'But not what. You didn't ask him if he saw the shooting, specifically?'

'No. But it was, implied.'

'Implied?'

'He's our witness, ma'am. I promise you.'

'And you didn't call for backup because we're trying to keep this low-key?'

'Yes. Plus, I was confident he was going to come to us. In which case he'd be a far better witness.'

'But so far, no dice?'

'No. We have a warrant now to look at the books of

this gym he goes to, see if we can get his number. We were about to go execute it, but I felt it was time to update you.'

I hung my head a little, spelling the whole thing out like this was making me feel like I'd gotten the whole thing wrong.

'Well, that was a close-run thing. Thank you for trying and thank you for updating me. However, now I need you to tell the story again.'

'Okay,' I said, a little confused. 'But I'm pretty sure I gave you everything.'

'Not to me, Colyear. I have an update for you, too. Come on, there's some people I need to introduce you to.'

We were to take DCI Templeton to the Leith office. I guessed what that meant.

'We're losing the case to the Major Investigation Team?' I said, pulling out of Gayfield for the short drive down Leith Walk.

'Lost. Decided at this morning's meeting.'

'Does that mean we're off the case?' Rowan said.

'That's what we're going to find out. I won't lie, if you'd walked in with our witness in tow, I could have kept you in the engine room of this thing. As it is, well, we'll see, but the MIT does not play well with others.'

'What about OCCTU? Have they given it up?' I said.

'No. They're having to wait in the wings, for now. But they're still itching to take over. The update from them this morning is that they're sure the rogue batch, which we can pretty much confirm as Taylor's batch, is no longer in Edinburgh.'

'Do we know where it's been moved to?' Rowan said.

'Not really. They're continuing to play their cards close to their chest. The only certainty is that divisional CID are out. Now let's go see if that includes you two.'

I could feel my nerves on edge as we followed the DCI into Leith Police Station. It wasn't so long ago I'd walked in here to have a very frank conversation with Kate Templeton, one that I had been sure would be my last as a serving police officer. The memory of that day would never, ever leave me.

It was the same incident room too, though this time the doors were firmly shut. The same sign was taped to the door:

INCIDENT ROOM
AUTHORISED ENTRY ONLY

The DCI knocked and we waited. She huffed a breath as nothing happened quickly. This room had been hers last time I was here. Now she was an unwanted guest.

The door was pushed open by a woman in a grey suit. Her ID at her chest had flipped and so I couldn't tell her rank, though I was pretty sure I'd seen her before.

'Ma'am,' she said, so lower in rank than Kate.

'Inspector. I have some people I'd like you to meet. I think they can help you.'

The woman, the inspector, looked us up and down. Then her attention returned. 'Thank you, ma'am. There may well be a time to come when we will need aid from division, but right now we're still setting up. Give me a day or so to get a handle on things and then I'll be in touch.'

'You misunderstand, Inspector. This is Sergeant Colyear. He was working the case until this morning. He has some information on a witness that you need to hear.'

She scrutinised me again. Then the door she was holding close to her was pushed wide.

The room was similar to before. Banks of desks in the middle and a larger desk at the far end, where the DCI held court last time. There were boards with printed off pictures of the scene to the left and a large digital screen to the right. Many a face stopped to watch us enter.

Inspector Simpson introduced herself at her desk and I was invited to speak. She stopped me as soon as I'd gotten as far as the chase.

'Where is the warrant now?'

'I have it, Inspector,' Rowan said. She produced it from a folder she was carrying. The inspector held her hand out. Rowan looked to the DCI who gave her a small nod. She passed it over.

I finished my tale, ending at our arrival to Leith.

'You let him get away?' the inspector said. She sat herself on the corner of her desk and folded her arms, the warrant in its thin, clear protective sleeve getting trapped under there.

'No. Not at all. I could barely walk. He's a young lad in trainers with an encyclopaedic knowledge of those particular streets. I wasn't going to catch him. There would have been little point radioing it in, either. He'd have been dust before response or community could have attended.'

'I guess we'll never know,' she said.

'I – I chose instead to try to reach out to him. He hasn't

317

made contact yet, I admit, but I hope—'

'Hope is an indulgence Police Scotland can't afford, Sergeant. But we are where we are.'

'Sergeant Colyear's instincts have been beyond solid to this point, Inspector,' the DCI said. 'It's your investigation, of course, but my advice would be to keep these two involved.'

The inspector rocked back and forth for a moment. Then pulled the warrant from under her arm. She held it out to Rowan. 'Fine. I'm afraid this will probably be as exciting as it gets, but it'll save time if you do it, means we don't have to go back through the whole story again. We're already working on a strategy for the investigation. There won't be any room for you on it. But, serve this. If you get the number, call me immediately. After that I could use you canvassing the street.' She peered over my shoulder. 'Gail,' she called. A red-haired woman looked up from her desk. 'Do you have the canvassing schedule? What's left to be done?'

'There's eight blocks. We're doing the first four today. Nothing scheduled for the rest yet,' Gail replied.

'Mark Sergeant Colyear and . . .'

'TDC Forbes,' Rowan said.

'. . . down as working from block eight backwards.' She returned to us. 'Check in with Gail once you've done the first two, so you don't end up repeating work.'

I thanked Inspector Simpson, though I wasn't sure why. We were involved, sure, but being put out of harm's way. Door to door was a tedious endeavour at the best of times, but sent out to cover the furthest flats from the incident made sure we weren't going to interfere. This was a favour to the DCI, not to us. I might have suggested leaving it to MIT, but I was thinking of Rowan.

After dropping off the DCI we went back to the industrial estate. The place was less busy than before, perhaps due to the heavy rain now falling. Before getting out of the car I told Rowan: 'This is all you. You serve the warrant. You do the talking.' As the inspector alluded to, this was probably our last meaningful contribution to a double murder, she might as well have it.

It wasn't clear who was in charge. There was no reception, no desk. Just a unit fully open at one side and the place filled without much sense of order with equipment. Seven or so men and three women were either working hard under equipment, or breathing hard sitting adjacent to it. Rowan pointed over to where three of the men were gathered together at some free weights at the very back.

As we approached, a humour-filled conversation ended. One of the men alerted another with a nod of the head.

Rowan held out her ID. 'TDC Forbes. Are you the owner?' she said to the man who looked like an action figure; a swivelling head on a largely immobile body due to the muscle-mass. I had an image of him dropping a five-pound note and spending twenty minutes trying to figure out how to get at it.

'Aye. Can I help you?'

'You sure can. This is for you.' She handed him the warrant in its folder. He looked at it briefly and handed it back, or tried to. 'No, keep it. That's your copy,' Rowan said. 'Look, we don't have a lot of time so I'm going to dispense with the usual back and forth. Normally I'd ask for permission to look at the information you hold on file for your customers. You'll refuse, despite the warrant there in your hand. Then I'd mildly threaten you; pointing out that this place looks awfully – unofficial. Promise to check for licences, taxes, council permissions, blah, blah. That's when you start to soften up a bit. Then when I point out that you'll be arrested for obstruction if you don't let me into your files, you finally agree. So, can we just cut to it and save each other a lot of grief?'

The prepaid phone cost forty pounds. It left a bitter taste in Dillon's mouth to part with the cash, since his own phone, lying dismantled in a pocket of his bag was perfectly paid up. The packaging lay between them on the table as did the large cappuccino they were sharing. The phone itself lay charging on an empty chair nearest the wall, which was as far as the cable provided with the thing would stretch.

'What's it at?' Davie asked.

Dillon pressed a button on the handset. 'Eight percent.'

'It'll do. Turn it on.'

'Says to wait until at least fifty.'

'Leave it plugged in, but boot it up. It'll be fine.'

The instructions warned about having an insufficient charge while you register the phone, but then they had no intention of doing such a thing. Dillon lifted the handset. A flip-phone that might have drawn envious eyes when Dillon was in primary school. These days it was a piece of shit, capable of little more than calls and texts. No apps, no Internet. He pressed the power button and they were halfway through the coffee by the time the screen ran through its cycle of logos and PLEASE WAITs. Then he was invited to input his details. It took a moment of scrolling to find the little 'skip' icon.

The coffee was long since finished before Dillon was given over to a screen he could interact with. He selected messaging and carefully typed in the number he'd written down on the inside of his left hand.

Cammy. It's Dillon. Had to ditch the other phone. What's happening there? Tell me everything.

Before Dillon could hit send, Davie gestured for a look at what was to be sent. It wouldn't stretch, so Dillon read it to him. 'Is it wise? I mean, it's Cammy,' Davie said.

'Exactly, it's Cammy. Cammy wouldn't call the police if he was being held captive by terrorists. Don't take this the wrong way, but I trust him more than anyone in this world.'

'Ouch,' Davie said and forgetfully lifted the cup again. He lowered it, and hooked a finger inside for some chocolate-dusted foam at least.

Dillon sent the message and returned the phone to the chair.

'Get you something else?' the waiter said. He waited for Davie to return the cup to the saucer then lifted it away.

'No, we're fine thanks,' Dillon said.

'You sure? Share a tap water? Electricity bill?' The waiter winked as he said it, but the ire was there.

'We're going soon. But thanks,' Davie said.

They shared raised eyebrows as he walked away.

Passey's cafe was quiet. It was why they were there. It wasn't exactly laying low, but it felt safe enough. It was on Portobello's high street, which would, in most towns, make it prime-placed. Not so in Portobello where most visitors made straight for the seafront and ventured no further.

Five minutes passed and Dillon was beginning to feel the pressure of being a free-loader. The waiter only had one other table, but he passed by them half a dozen times all the same.

Then a four-chime ditty sounded from the phone. There was now twenty percent charge, so Dillon unplugged the thing.

He read it.

'What?' Davie said. 'What's wrong?'

Dillon's concern must have been written on his face. He placed the phone on the table for Davie to read:

How do I know it's you?

'What do I say?'

'You know him best,' Davie said and handed the phone back.

Dillon thought and then typed:

You fell off your bike when you were 8. I carried you home and waited with you til your ma got home. You made me promise never to tell anyone that you cried.

There was only a wait of a minute for the response:

Thank fuck. Thought you were dead. Bad shit here. We need to talk. Tell me where to meet. Not here obvs.

Davie read this one after Dillon and said: 'What do you think's going on?'

'I think we're in serious trouble.'

'Cammy's probably exaggerating.'

'The problem, Davie, is that that's not Cammy.'

'Eh?'

'The first message he sent, look.' Davie reread and shrugged. 'So?'

'Cammy types as little as possible. Never a Y-O-U, just a U. So, I made that shit up about falling off his bike. This guy is trying very hard to get to us. And fuck knows what's happened to Cammy. Now, what do I reply?'

Billy could barely believe his luck. The 08-plate Honda Civic was all packed up. The only debate in his mind was whether to pay Malky a visit before he left. Then the kid's phone had pinged and there was the stuttering little shit on the screen. *First get him on the hook*, he'd thought. *Appear suspicious. Then reel him in.*

He looked now at the last message:

Thought as much. Fuck. OK. Let me think. I'll get back to you with a time and place. Keep your head down wee man. Speak soon.

Billy put the phone down and went back to the car for his sleeping bag.

CHAPTER 28

Back in the Game

The bookkeeping was as informal as the rest of the set-up. The gym owner asked for the name and found the contact page on his phone. Rowan took a picture of it on her own phone and we were done. In and out in less than ten minutes. Not bad at all.

Rowan called it in and just like that, we were on the outside. It did not feel good.

Still, there was an upside. The sense of urgency was leaving me. That nervous tension I'd been living with since the DCI put us on this case was lifting like a fever. We even stopped for coffee, something we hadn't done in days.

The street was still a crime scene, though less of one. The TV crews were gone, chasing fresher stories elsewhere. There was little attention too being paid to the solitary uniform at the entrance to block two. A game of football was being played in the concrete enclosure. From over its wall came yells and the occasional glimpse of the ball.

It was with a slightly heavy heart I pressed on the top buzzer of block eight and began the repetitive process:

'Good afternoon, sir/ma'am. My name is DS Don Colyear. You're no doubt aware of a particularly horrible incident in the street last week. Could you tell me please if you noticed anything you think we should be aware of? No? Can I ask where you were at the time of the incident? Uh-huh – and did you happen to notice any vehicles in the street you're not familiar with? No? How about people? Anyone you remember at all? No? What's that? No, I'm afraid there's not much I can tell you beyond what the press are reporting. No, we don't think it's a serial killer. No, I don't know where you got that information but there was no black magic/cannibalism/ritual torture involved and, no, I cannot confirm they were in the middle of coitus at the time of death. I know it might seem like a waste of time, but would you mind if I come in and note a statement? It shouldn't take more than half an hour. Thanks.'

We worked our way down, taking turns to give aching wrists a rest. Twelve useless statements, six cups of tea, five *may I use your bathroom?* and a partridge in a pear tree.

Rowan had noted the last statement from a woman in her seventies while I tried to keep my eyes open. She asked, as we were trying to leave, whether we thought perhaps these killings and the disappearance of her cat four years ago might be related. I left Rowan to chat it out with her and walked to the street.

I looked up at block seven. Tomorrow's torture. I flexed my arm and yawned. I thought I might have to ice my wrist and hand tonight. I took my phone from my pocket. There was a missed call from a number not in my contacts, probably wanting to discuss the accident I hadn't been involved in last year, but a certain young man from this estate entered my mind. I cursed myself for missing it. Perhaps I'd try calling it in the car. There was also, a message from Marcella:

Hey. It was good to see you. Hope it wasn't too weird. Be nice to do it again sometime x

I would reply to this later too, reciprocating the sentiment. Something positive, but breezy.

It was starting to get dark, but not so much I couldn't see Cammy with a few others shooting the shit on the roadway. The three of them straddling the frames of their bikes and regularly spitting at the ground around them.

I looked back into the block, Rowan literally had one foot out the door, but she was still in conversation. I left her to it.

One of the young cyclists, the one who was able to see me coming, spun his pedals when he noticed my approach and took off. Too young to have a warrant out for him, so more likely something he was carrying, not that I cared.

The other two stayed put. Cammy's shaved head turned as I reached them.

'All right?' I said. Then, 'Woah. What the fuck happened to you?' Cammy was sporting a spectacular black eye. Not your typical darkening circle and puffy flesh – no, this was a Hollywood shiner. Deep plum from cheekbone to eyebrow. The eye itself was barely open from the swelling and the slit that was there was a cave to a bright red that should have been white.

He flinched away from my gaze. 'Nothin'. Fell.'

'Onto what? A fist, several times?'

'Into a door. It had a sign on it, said: "Mind your ain business".'

I thought about all the domestics I'd dealt with in my career. So many people had walked into that particular door.

'Fair enough,' I said. 'Though you know you can—'

'Yeah yeah. This the part where I start bawlin' and you make all the bad stuff go away?'

It's the part where I even up your face, ya wee prick. 'Never mind, then,' I said.

'That's what I thought,' Cammy was straightening his bike, ready to go, when Rowan joined us.

'Holy fuck,' she said. Cammy groaned. 'What did you get that for?'

'For asking stupid fucking questions,' Cammy said. He would have left, I think, but Rowan was right in front of him trying to get a better look.

'That is, hands down, the best black eye I've ever seen. Seriously impressive.'

'Ha-ha.'

'No, seriously. If there's some girl you have your eye on, no pun intended, now's the time to make a move, Cammy. You look like an action hero,' Rowan said. It brought a laugh from Cammy's friend.

'Shut up,' Cammy said to him, but he was starting to laugh too.

'You're ringing,' Rowan said to me.

She was right. I'd been aware of the ringtone, but thought it was coming from someone else.

It was the from the same number as before. I tutted, but hit the green button all the same.

'Hello?'

'Is this DS Colyear?'

'That's right. Who's this?'

'It's Dillon Marshall. Can we talk?'

'Of course,' I said, wheeling away from the group and pressing the phone harder to my ear.

There was a pause and I was afraid I'd lost him, then: 'I think I'm in deep shit. Well, clearly I'm in deep shit, but what I mean is, I think I n-need help. *We* need help.'

'You and Davie,' I said. Not a question. 'What's changed?'

Another pause, though I could hear Dillon breathing. 'A very bad man in a Brown Leather Jacket.'

'The man you saw shoot your friends?'

'Yes. I'd hoped maybe he was gone, but now I know he's not. And if it's a choice between you and him, then I choose you.'

'What happened?' Rowan was looking over at me, she seemed to be getting the idea of who I was talking to. She pointed a finger at block two and I nodded.

'I'll get to that, but I need you to d-do something for me first.'

'I will if I can.'

'There's a kid on the scheme. I think he might be in trouble. I need you to check on him.'

'Hold on,' I said. I couldn't help a small laugh given the situation.

I walked to Cammy and held the phone out to him. 'It's for you,' I said.

'What?' His face was screwed up like he'd just smelt something nasty.

'Someone needs to say hello.'

He reluctantly took the phone from me, first checking the screen and then holding it to his ear.

'Hullo?' he said. We listened to his side of the conversation.

'Aye.'

'Dillon?' Cammy looked over at us and turned his shoulder as if I didn't already know who he was talking to.

'I'm fine . . . Yeah . . . Defo wasn't me . . . Don't have it . . . Some cunt, dunno . . . Leather? No . . . Dunno, just some guy. Rushed me . . . Them? Fuck that.' Cammy was now looking at us. 'I am. I'm fine. Really. All right. Hold on.' Cammy pushed the phone out and I took it from him.

'Dillon.'

'I got a text message, from Cammy's phone. It was pretending to be him. Trying to set up a meet. I told him to tell you about who stole it from him. He's looking for me, DS Colyear, and I don't mind telling you, I'm shit scared.'

'I can understand that. Safest thing is for you to come in.'

'No. At least not yet. I n-need assurances.'

'Assurances? Like what?'

'I don't know. But there's no way I could persuade D-Davie to come in if we're going to j-jail.'

'Those kinds of assurances are above my pay grade, Dillon. But I'll take this to the top and see where we go. For now, I need you to tell me exactly what you saw from the wardrobe.'

We were the stars of the show. Quite the contrast from the morning meeting with Inspector Simpson. We'd gone from third wheel to taking the wheel in a single phone call.

The incident room had been cleared of all but those thought essential. In addition to Inspector Simpson and one of her DSs, representing the Major Inquiry Team, DCI Templeton sat with us at one end of the table. Her role presumably to ensure our parts in what was to come were assured. Our friends from Organised Crime were back, recent information confirming this investigation really did fall into their remit. They now had the floor. DI Richmond was being whispered to by DC Sloe. Really? I thought. Isn't it a bit late for cloak and dagger?

DI Richmond stood. 'Good evening, everyone. It's nice to be working this investigation with you all. I think this is the first time in my experience we have members of MIT, OCCTU and Division all working together. Let me also hand out a well-deserved pat on the back to DCI Templeton and her team for their part in gathering the information that has brought us together today.' Rowan was smiling for both of us. 'In the spirit of collaboration and in pursuit of the successful conclusion to this investigation, I have some information to share with you too. Uh, do we have . . .' he said, now leaning down and whispering to DI Simpson.

'Yes,' she said and nodded at her DS who flicked a remote at the screen on the adjacent wall. In a few moments the image I'd seen before of the man with the high cheekbones, cleft chin and knowing smile appeared.

'This is who we like for the double shooting. In fact, he's the only one on our list. Can I just confirm with you all that we're agreed?'

I nodded.

DI Simpson was nodding too, but she spoke: 'We can categorically discount both Taylor and Morrison? I appreciate DS Colyear's witness has described Billy Flaherty, but could there still be an assist?'

'Taylor is at the centre of it, absolutely no doubt, and our investigation will remain on that focus, however our observations confirm Taylor and Morrison to be back in the Liverpool area at the time of the killings. No sightings at all of Flaherty in their company despite what mobile data is telling us.

'There is something else you should know before we get into how we proceed,' DI Simpson interjected. DI Richmond sat. 'We ran a trace on the mobile number of Dillon Marshall, which came back as inactive. No surprise there, based on what he's explained to DS Colyear. But the interesting thing is that it was not the only check. The previous day a trace was made. The user ID attached is from Merseyside Police. Since we're sharing,' she said. This resulted in another hushed exchange in OCCTU.

'That's interesting, Inspector. We will get onto that, if you don't mind passing the information?'

'Of course.'

'He's desperate. That's what we can take from this.' DCI Templeton said. 'You said you thought Taylor had someone on the inside. This Merseyside check seems to confirm that. Assuming that check was also inactive?' DI Simpson nodded. 'Then he's shit out of ideas. Forces him into a ballsy move to steal the kid's phone right outside the locus in an attempt to set up a meeting.'

'Actually, ma'am,' I said. 'The description from the lad doesn't quite support that.'

'Please,' DI Simpson said, urging me to continue.

I did: 'Uh. As much as our witness was reluctant to get involved, once he did, he gave a pretty good account. This was corroborated by one of his friends and a response officer who was posted at the scene. Whoever assaulted the boy and stole his phone was well covered in a hoody and scarf covering his . . .' I drifted for a moment, something in the back of my mind scratching like a dog at the back door. 'Uh, his mouth and nose. The colour changed between accounts, but each description was unanimous in the assertion that the assailant was – in the words of the lad himself – "short as fuck". He's working with someone. That's what we think, at least.' I gestured to Rowan and sat.

'We've checked the witness's phone? The stolen one we think Flaherty is in possession of?' the DCI said.

'Yes. Inactive. He's being careful, though if he's going to use it to set up a meeting, with a potential opportunity to get at the Marshall brothers, then he will have to switch it back on at some point. We will be monitoring,' said DI Richmond.

'Is there a plan?' I said.

'That's why we're here,' said DI Simpson. 'I'm looking for suggestions, something that gets a violent criminal into custody without risking public safety.'

DI Richmond raised a hand and spoke: 'We have a suggestion. But you're not going to like it. But the way I see it, it leaves us little choice.'

'Go on,' the DCI said.

'The way we see it; if he has the foresight to keep this phone off until he needs to use it, then there's a good chance that if we ever do get a location from it, it won't be any good. Either on the move or somewhere public. We can't rely on it.'

'You're thinking of setting up this meeting?' DI Simpson said.

'Yes. Taking all practical precautions, of course. Do you think your witness would agree?'

'What?' I said. I couldn't quite believe what DI Richmond had just said. 'You're surely not suggesting we use this lad as bait?'

'He'd be in no danger.'

'You can guarantee that?' the DCI said.

'Ma'am.'

She turned to me, her face softening as she did. 'Don, I know it sounds insanely risky, but I can see where DI Richmond is coming from. It's this or waiting for a stroke of luck. Personally, I'd prefer to have some sort of control over it.'

I shook my head. *Was this really happening?*

'Of course, there's no such thing as a guarantee, ma'am, but yes. I am entirely confident we can keep him safe. This wouldn't be about getting our suspect and the witness together, simply getting eyes on the target. The second we have that we would move in. We'd be sure to set up somewhere that ensures that happens long before he could get close to the witness.'

'Then why need the witness at all?' I said.

'We'd be using spotters. My concern is that he could do the same. If he is working with someone else, he might wait for confirmation the witness is present before showing himself. What would your boy need to agree?' DCI Richmond said and then all eyes were on me.

He'd need a fucking plan where some maniac with a gun is not heading in his direction, I thought. 'He's already said he won't come in until this guy is caught. In addition to that he's just as scared of going to jail as he is of a bullet. My guess is we'd have to make certain promises in terms of his prosecution and liberty, but I will call him if this is the plan?' Now this nonsense was coming out of my mouth.

There was an agreement around the table that this was the direction to take. They discussed the DCI setting up a meeting with the procurator fiscal to see what might be done regarding charges being filed against Dillon when the time came, but I was only half listening. I was mostly trying to figure out how to get him to agree to any of this.

CHAPTER 29

The Mother of Bad Ideas

'I think it will be better coming from you,' I said.

'Oh, really? And why is that? Because I'm a woman? Because he's an eighteen-year-old boy and might be pulled off guard if I flirt a little?' Her fists were on her hips and she was looking up at me with an expression of *go on, I dare you.*

'That's exactly what I was thinking,' I said.

'Fair enough. I think it might even work.' Rowan smiled and sipped at her coffee. I laughed and lifted mine. 'If he even shows up. He's officially late.'

I checked my watch. Twelve thirty-two. 'No eighteen-year-old was ever on time for anything. Two minutes is nothing. He'll show.' I looked around at this cafe Dillon had chosen for the meeting, Passey's. An odd choice for a young man to suggest? It was a cosy place, decorated with obvious pride. More like someone's living room than an eatery, open to the public.

We were sitting at a table for four, Rowan and I taking the two seats facing the door. She had finished her latte and my cappuccino was all but foam dregs when the little bell at the door sounded and in walked Dillon, followed by his brother. He clocked us straight away, but scanned the rest of the room thoroughly before pulling out a chair and sitting.

'You were afraid you were going to walk into a room full of cops waiting to arrest you?' I said.

'It c-crossed my m-mind, aye.'

'I don't blame you, but everything I said on the phone, I meant. We need your help and the assurances you asked—' I stopped as the waiter came over with a notepad and a smile.

'Just a w-water for me,' Dillon said.

'Aye, same,' Davie said.

'You sure? It's on the—It's on us,' Rowan said, stopping herself from broadcasting the situation here, though I did wonder what this must look like to the waiter and the two other occupied tables. The age difference was an awkward one. We were too young to look like their parents, well, Rowan certainly, but beyond an age to be plausible friends. Add to that Rowan and I in suits and these two looking like they'd raked the bin outside of Sports Direct.

'That case I'll have coffee,' Dillon said.

'Do you do hot chocolate?' asked Davie.

'We do, yeah.'

'Then I'll have that.'

'Make it two,' Dillon added.

'I was saying that the assurances you wanted are being met. We've discussed the matter with the procurator fiscal. That is to say, the court. You will be reported for what happened with the heroin, but there will be no arrest. As for jail time, we think it's likely it can be avoided, albeit it will be up to a judge. But given your assistance so far and what we need to discuss today, it does your case the world of good.'

'What would we be looking at?' Davie said.

'Again, not up to me, but probably suspended sentences, community orders, fines maybe. That's what we're thinking. It does mean you can't put a foot wrong going forward or that sentence comes crashing down. But that's a discussion for . . . after.'

The waiter brought the hot chocolates and we waited for him to return to the kitchen before we continued.

'TDC Forbes here is going to run through our thoughts on how we proceed. I'll warn you, you're not going to like it much; I don't mind telling you, I don't like it either, but it's the plan we think works best. I'll ask that you hear the whole thing out before you tell us what you think. All right?'

The boys agreed and they sat back sipping at their cups as Rowan described a truly terrible idea.

The smell of the chocolate drifted across. As it did, the dog at the back door stopped scratching and started barking.

Either the idea didn't sound quite as insane to Dillon, or the tactic to have Rowan deliver it had done the trick.

The important thing was that he agreed. Davie had been plenty vocal, though, that he was not so convinced. However, since we only needed Dillon, it was his opinion that ultimately counted.

Dillon typed the text that had been agreed at the meeting the previous day and sent it before I paid the bill, and we left the cafe into bright sunshine. Dillon was staring at the screen of the phone.

'I wouldn't expect a reply immediately,' I said. 'Seems he keeps the phone off until he needs to use it. Call me the second it arrives.'

'I will.'

'Where are you two holding up? I know you don't like the idea of it, but we really can take you somewhere safe,' Rowan said.

'Thanks, but we're fine. No offence, we just don't trust you.'

Rowan smirked. 'Aye, none taken.'

'Not you, s-specifically,' Dillon hastened to clarify. His hands hovered over, but didn't touch the shoulder of Rowan. 'You seem nice. I mean, you know, fine. Trustworthy. But just the – police, you know?'

The lad was blushing fiercely. I suspected in that moment it *was* her delivery that had swung it.

'If you're sure,' I said. 'We can't force you, but you're our star witness, we need you to stay safe.'

'We're fine. Honestly,' Davie added.

'Okay. Listen, keep your phone on. We're not going to trace it, you made me promise and that's fine. Also, there's a marker on the number that means nobody else can. They'd have to call us for permission. The phone is safe, but I need to get hold of you at any time. All right?'

Dillon agreed and the meeting was over.

Less than four hours later his text received a response, and we were on.

We were back to bit parts, and this time it was okay with me. Not so for Rowan, she didn't seem to find any of this intimidating. Personally, I was only too happy to let OCCTU do their thing. The speed of the operation set-up was impressive. The first floor of Leith Police Station had been given over to a buzz of plain-clothed officers and those wearing more uniform than made me comfortable, all carrying firearms. There seemed to be a bit of a theme going on with at least half a dozen of them sporting denim jackets over hoodies with the hood hanging over the back, almost an alternative uniform.

Our job, it became apparent, as it was never overtly mentioned, was to make sure Dillon knew his part and also didn't decide that this was actually nuts and run screaming from the building.

The text to 'Cammy' had read:

Wester Hailes not safe. You OK to cycle over to Saughton Park? Picnic tables at the back of the cafe there. 6pm.

The reply had read: **Aye. See you there**

The location had been suggested by DI Richmond, apparently it had worked once before for them in the past. Plenty of space to plant plausible 'members of the public' and good vision from every angle.

Dillon would board a bus from Leith along with a plain-clothed officer and followed by an unmarked car, get off on Gorgie Road where a team would already be in place, including the armed unit in an unmarked van a short sprint to the location. Thereafter all he had to do was go take a seat at the table and wait. Rowan and I were given our roles and within minutes we were moving out.

We were back in Rowan's Fiat Spider, encouraged to take personal vehicles to ensure the car park there didn't end up full of similar-looking pool cars, which were all Peugeots and a red flag to a trained eye.

I hadn't worn body armour in a while, and never the sort you wear under a shirt, but I was happy to follow this particular instruction.

Every time I moved in the passenger seat, or rather each time Rowan took a bend too quickly, I could hear and feel the Velcro crackle under my T-shirt. I wasn't nervous as we swung into a parking space and exited the car, at least not for myself. I couldn't help feel somewhat responsible for Dillon, who would be getting close now on his bus journey.

Short updates came from DI Richmond via my earpiece, the radio itself tucked into the pocket of my jacket. I knew it was a bad idea to be constantly putting my finger to my ear, but the thing was uncomfortable and again, it had been a while since I'd worn one.

It was my first visit to Saughton Park, one of Edinburgh's many green spaces, this one on the western edge of the city. A collection of playing fields and a skateboard park sat on one side of a footpath with a more sedate section, with walled gardens, large greenhouse and a meandering walkway by the Water of Leith on the other. The little cafe there was still open. I must have looked like a slack-faced moron as the man serving asked me three times what I wanted since I was busy hearing DI Richmond in my ear update that Dillon had left the bus and was walking along the north edge of Gorgie Road.

Rowan and I began our circuit, hoping to look like sweethearts meeting for coffee. If I'd seen her before in her civvies, I had forgotten when. Even with the covert vest under her long-sleeved top, she looked trim. All too often we lost that athletic edge once the training college was in our rear-view mirrors, but Rowan was clearly hitting the gym on her days off.

We talked nonsense, occasionally bumping shoulders and laughing at nothing, all the time watching the faces of the couples, dog-walkers and parents shepherding children. Jesus, if this kicks off and one of these people get hurt, it will be beyond scandal, I thought.

One of these dog-walkers, a woman with short hair with a scruffy little black and white fella on a lead, passed me and did a double take. Her hair flicked a little as she seemed to spot the earpiece. I gave her a small smile and walked on. After a dozen or so steps I looked over my shoulder. She was in the same spot, eyeing me.

'Subject has entered the park,' my earpiece announced. We passed another pair of plain-clothed spotters and right enough, if you were *really* looking, the clear-plastic earpieces were not too subtle. My stomach was growing a low ache. Saliva starting to collect in my mouth.

'You okay?' Rowan said as I stopped to take a few long breaths.

'Fine. Just a little . . .'

'Nervous?'

'Yeah. Probably.'

'Subject at table. In position,' my earpiece announced.

Now my pulse was quickening, but my stomach was actually easing. Rowan was probably right, just nerves. We were at the furthest point now on the circuit from where Dillon was sitting facing the river. It was tempting to speed up to get eyes on him, but that would upset the rhythm of things and we'd been warned at the briefing not to. I reminded myself to do my job. I looked at faces.

There was a terrible moment, one shared by Rowan too as I sensed her freeze and go for her radio when a man, loosely matching the description, climbed out of a blue Mercedes as we were again passing the car park. The leather jacket was black, but he had the same dark hair and Mediterranean look. I clutched Rowan's arm as his dog and then his partner or wife climbed out after him. Still, we got a little closer just to absolutely confirm it wasn't our guy.

'Tie your shoelace and radio this in,' I said. 'We don't need everyone jumping when they clock this guy.' Rowan ducked down between two vehicles and delivered the message.

We continued our route, painfully slowly. Then, as we turned at the greenhouse the tables came into view. Dillon was sitting on the table itself, his feet on one of the seats. His legs tapped up and down nervously. As we passed him our eyes locked for a moment, then he forced his gaze away, back to switching between his phone and the river.

Forty minutes and perhaps ten circuits passed when DI Richmond called it. Unless Dillon had forgotten his own briefing, not only was it a no-show, but there had been no text message received either. If there had, Dillon would have stood and scratched his right ear.

'Stand down. All units stand down. Fuck, sake,' DI Richmond slipped into his radio before releasing the button.

We were closest to Dillon when the update came.

'It's over,' I said. 'At least for now.'

He blew out a breath and stepped down from the table. 'What now?' he said.

'For you? I'm not sure. Someone will come and take you out of here. As for us, we have to pay someone a visit,' I said.

CHAPTER 30

The Dog Barking

I ran my thoughts up the flagpole. That was to say I told DCI Templeton my tenuous theory and the problem I was likely to encounter.

'Fuck it,' she said. 'I'll make the call, get you the address.'

True to her word we had it within a few minutes and were spinning out of Saughton Park in Rowan's two-seater like – *what was it she had said? Scratchy and Hutch?* I laughed and told Rowan 'Nothing' when she asked.

Her frustration was clear, though not something I felt myself. She headed towards Leith, moaning at the result.

'I really thought this was it. Thought we'd be toasting a huge collar by now.'

'Nothing but good news, if you ask me. I can only imagine the shit-show if this guy had wandered in and found himself surrounded; dozens of civilians trapped inside too, not knowing what the hell was going on. Jesus, I can't even think about it.'

'Maybe, but this puts us back to square one.' Rowan sounded her horn at someone in front of her who had done nothing more than indicate a little late. 'Or worse, he slips away and the whole thing gets passed down to Merseyside.'

Oh, let that happen. Please let that happen, I almost said.

After a few minutes Rowan's ire seemed to lift a little indicated by her foot doing likewise from the accelerator. 'All right. Tell me about this angle. How sure are you?' she said. Her voice sounded tired.

'Scale of one to ten? I'd say – two.'

'Fuck sake,' Rowan moaned and hugged at her steering wheel. She might have been referring to the cars braking to a stop in front of us, but I didn't think so.

While we sat in traffic waiting to join Queensferry Road from a nightmare junction at Craigleith Crescent, I thought about the conversation DCI Templeton just had with Adrian Geddes. She shouldn't be interfering with his CHIS and he'd have been within his rights to say no when she effectively asked Adrian to hand him over to me. He would surely know that however this visit was about to be concluded, Malky would no longer be so willing to work with Police Scotland. Then again, I was trying to picture Adrian saying no to Kate and there was no plausible version of it I could find.

It was almost dark by the time we reached the flat on Dickson Street. Rowan pulled in and killed the engine. I had left the car when a thought occurred to me.

'Hold on,' I said. I went back and rummaged first through the glovebox, which was unexpectedly tidy, and then through

Rowan's folder, which was tucked between the seats. I pulled what looked like a crime report from inside. I folded it neatly and handed it to Rowan. 'Put this in an inside pocket.' She didn't query it, just slid it neatly into her coat.

The common close was choked with bicycles and bright, plastic children's toys. I tripped on a yellow tricycle as I entered, sending the dog who lived behind door number two into hysterics. Some enormous thing, by the sounds of it, and I was glad we were heading to a different door. Number four was directly above the abode of the hellhound. I spoke briefly to Rowan before I chapped. 'Maybe I'll do the talking with this one. Just go with the idea once I get going.'

'Roger.'

As always, I ignored the doorbell and went for three deep thuds of my knuckles.

The look on Malky's face when the door swung as far as the chain would allow it showed his experience, there was no surprise in his eyes. Only the cops announce themselves in such a way and he knew what, if not who, would be standing on his doorstep.

'What the fuck?' he shout-whispered.

'Evening, Malky. We need to talk.'

'The fuck we do. Seriously, go the fuck away.'

'Why, who do you have in there?' I peered over his head through the crack in the door, I didn't even have to raise myself onto my toes. 'Is it him?'

I was aware of Rowan sliding her radio from her pocket.

'Him? What the fuck are you talking about? It's my girl – Hold on.'

The door closed over, there was a scratch of the chain, and he was soon standing in the hall with us, closing the door back over gently.

'If she knows you're here, I'm fucked. It's a miracle she's here at all. You shouldn't be here. This is against the rules. Wait til I call DC Geddes, you two are royally fucked.' His face was turning an alarming shade with all the furious yelling he was subduing.

'Go right ahead. He'll tell you he can't help. As of right now you no longer have the protection of Police Scotland. No more blind-eye turning for you, Malky. Now, where is he?'

'What? Where's who? What the fuck is this even—'

'Listen. I'm about thirty seconds away from searching your flat. Girlfriend or no.'

'I. Don't. Know. What. You. Are. Talking. About. What the fuck? Come on.' A blood vessel was threating to pop in his neck. *Fuck*, I thought. *This is convincing. Might be time to climb down.* But then DCI Templeton's take on this returned to me. *Fuck it.*

I calmly placed a hand against the front door inches from Malky's head and leant into him. 'Assaulting a ten-year-old is the least of your worries right now, but I'm sure we'll get to that. Right now, if you want us to go away, you will tell me where Billy Flaherty is. I'm not fucking around, Malky.'

'Jesus Christ. Who the fuck is Billy—'

'Okay. Fine. Rowan, show this prick the warrant.'

She caught on quick, pulling the crime report triumphantly from her coat.

'This is for you. Now get out the way, or I'll move you out of the way.'

He stared at the folded paper, his eyes still wild with seemingly authentic incredulity. It was beginning to dawn on me that I had no next step, when he said: 'Fuck. Fuck, fuck. Look, I had nothing to do with—'

'Where is he?'

'It's just, they made me—'

'Malky, the next words out of your mouth better be an address.'

And they were.

'Ma'am, you're not going to believe this, but we think we have Flaherty's location,' Rowan said. She stood, moving her weight anxiously from one foot to the other in the street next to the car.

She had the phone on speaker and held it up between us in one hand and she was swishing the air with the pretend warrant with the other.

'Hold on, it's still going like a fair in here. What did you say?'

'I said, we think—'

'WOULD YOU SHUT THE FUCK UP,' the DCI yelled. The background buzz on her end ceased. 'Not you, Rowan. Now, again please.'

'We have Flaherty's location.'

There was a short silence on her end. Then she said, simply: 'Tell me.'

* * *

Rowan relayed the story. I had to admit to being a little disappointed not to get a 'well done' at least, but there were more pressing matters. The last operation was preparing for a debrief and hadn't yet disbanded. They were very quickly remobilised.

There was nowhere for us to go. Even in Rowan's rocket we would have been too far behind the rest to be of any use. Besides, from the radio chatter, it was clear this was being led by Operation Support Division, primarily firearms. A warrant was urgently requested, granted and the car yard in Loanhead was surrounded.

The chatter turned to whispered updates. The radio sat on Rowan's dashboard and we stared at it and listened to events unfolding. I wasn't fully aware of OSD terminology and tactics, but it seemed that Alpha were the entry team with Bravo and Charlie being two armed units at their heels. There was also some perimeter unit in place to contain if Flaherty fled.

'Alpha in place.'

'Roger, Alpha. Confirm Bravo, Charlie.'

'Bravo in place.'

'Roger.'

'Charlie in place.'

'Bravo team, you are authorised.'

'Roger.'

'Charlie team, you are authorised.'

'Roger.'

'Authorised?' Rowan whispered.

'I think it means safeties off. Weapons live.'

'Shit.'

'Yeah,' I said and pointed at the radio, urging silence.

'Alpha, what are you looking at?'

'Security cameras. If he's watching the screens, he already knows we're here. Gate secured by chains, shouldn't be a problem. Good to proceed?'

'Roger Alpha, proceed.'

There is a period of silence before Alpha team returns to the radio.

'Breach, breach!'

Muffled sounds of breathing and scuffing of clothes. I was expecting the sound of shots any second, but none came. Rowan had pushed her chair back so she could bring her knees up to her chest, pressed in against the steering wheel.

'From Alpha team, we're looking at three portacabins as advised.'

'Roger Alpha. Form three simultaneous entries.'

'Roger.'

'Bravo, Charlie, reform into three. Confirm, over.'

'Roger. Four-four and four-seven now Delta team, over.'

'Delta team, you are authorised.'

'Roger.'

A short pause this time, then: 'Alpha one, two and three in place.'

'Proceed.'

Slams and: 'Breach, breach!'

There was further banging and yells of 'Armed police!' I tensed, sure of shots. But all that came were three calls of 'Clear'.

There was confirmation that someone had been in one of these portacabins recently. One reported as warm, as was the space-heater there that was switched off. Beer bottles and other scraps were found. The sleeping bag described by our Malky was not there. Nor was the car he mentioned. A full search of the facility followed, but after a further thirty minutes of very little, Rowan was the first to talk.

'Fuck.'

'My thoughts exactly.'

'You think he's fled?'

I shrugged. What did I know? 'Maybe. If he's any sense, he has.'

'Do you think he was at the park? Maybe sensed a trap?'

'Possible. We'll probably never know.' I stretched and yawned, rubbed at my face and neck. 'Maybe we should call it a night,' I said. I reached for my seat belt, clipped it and waited for the car to start. Rowan wasn't moving. 'What's wrong?'

'Huh? Ah, nothing. I was just thinking. Doesn't matter.' She turned the key and the engine roared into life.

'Go on. What was the thought?'

She looked at me and then cut the engine. 'What if he *was* at the park. What if he knew, or at least suspected the whole time it would be a trap?'

'What do you mean?'

'I mean, what if the plan wasn't to get at Dillon there. What if it was just to get eyes on him?'

Her suggestion felt like a puzzle piece. For a moment I turned it around in my head, felt its edges. Then I tried it in the space. It fitted very neatly. 'Shit.'

CHAPTER 31

Beware the Fury of a Patient Man

It wasn't a great view from the window of the common close of 441 Gorgie Road, though it was far enough away from the cycle of fuckwits cramming themselves into Saughton Park and trying to look breezy.

The lad had arrived on the bus, that was a nice touch. It almost had him running out the door and ending this thing. The bus had stopped less than fifty metres from where he was bent over, elbows perched on the window frame. The binoculars, purchased for twelve pounds in a charity shop, were a little smoky around the edge of the lenses, but they were good enough. Through them he'd followed the boy along the pavement to a crossing. For a moment he looked to be genuinely alone, to the point where he'd checked the gun and was having one last look through the lenses before bounding down the stairs. A guy had appeared at Dillon's back. Hands in pockets, baseball cap, trying a little too hard. This was confirmed when the crossing went green and the guy in the cap had waited while everyone else walked. Just before the crossing went red, he'd crossed. Following the lad, but not too close.

There was disappointment, sure, but this was exactly what he'd expected. He'd let this play out, wait for the area to clear, and then head back to the car and back to Liverpool. He wasn't the type of kid to go to the police; there was a chance, even with a cross hair on his back, that he wouldn't, but he'd had to make sure. And now there was proof.

He lost sight of the kid for a good five minutes, but there was still plenty to see. A large Transit van on Gorgie Road, on double yellows. A couple in the park walking in circles, one small and auburn, the other, a guy with the dark hair fidgeting with his ear. He could smell bacon even from here. The longer he watched, the more of them he spotted. At least a dozen. Then the kid again. Perched on a bench watching out over the river. A rifle. If he'd had a rifle, he could do him from here.

Billy closed one eye, imagined one vertical line down the lens and one horizontal, got the kid square and centre. He imagined adjusting the scope for distance and again for wind, watching the trees in the park sway gently, the light gusts going right to left, not that he knew how, he'd never held a rifle in his life, but isn't that what they did in films?

Adjustments made, he waited for the shot. The kid never stopped moving, his feet dancing on the seat, his hands twitching around the phone. He could text him now, turn the phone in his pocket on and send a message.

What would that be? *Say hi to your friends for me. I'll see you in a few months when you don't have the pigs to watch your back.*

There. The kid raised his head up to warm it in the sun. 'Bang,' Billy said, easing down on the imaginary trigger.

It went on longer than he'd imagined. Eventually, though, the couple, the short one and the dark-haired guy, gave up the ruse and approached the kid. They talked for a while and were soon joined by others. One or two he hadn't spotted. The Transit on the double yellows moved off. Billy would give it another half hour or so, then he'd head out the back green of these flats and walk the quarter mile to the car.

There was the sudden sound of someone on the stairwell. He froze, all of him except his right hand, which found the handle of the gun. The footsteps scuffed on the steps, laboured. He relaxed; they were not someone of a law-enforcement persuasion. He released the gun in his right pocket and reached for the phone in his left. He pushed the powerless handset to the side of his face and began a series of *uh-huh*s and O*K*s while he tucked the binoculars under the heavy coat he'd purchased at the same time. He paced around the little landing between the two topmost flats. The woman rounded the last set of steps and barely looked at him as she passed and unlocked her door. There was the sound of it locking again and a chain being slid into place.

He returned to the window and his binoculars. They'd cleared out of the park. There was no sign of any activity at first, but then he saw a group of them walking towards him, removing earpieces, checking phones and . . . and something very curious. The kid. He was standing at the bus stop on the opposite side. Why bother with this now? The trap was a bust. Why—?

He watched on. Everyone who looked like a cop was either getting into a vehicle or walking away. The one with the baseball cap who'd tailed him was nowhere to be seen.

'What the fuck?' he breathed.

Thirty minutes, he'd told himself. That was the wise thing to do. Let the filth clear out and then give this up. But . . .

The heavy coat and the lensless glasses were all he had to hide behind. He could barely believe his legs were carrying him down the stairs and out into the street. He kept his head down and he walked. Not towards the kid, but away from him. Along the road the bus he would be boarding would come.

He reached the next stop, the one the bus would reach after it picked up the kid, half expecting the whole way to hear a yell to get down on his stomach and not move. It didn't come. Seven minutes later, according to the digital board at the stop, the bus did.

He couldn't be sure the kid would be on this particular bus. He could easily be waiting for the one after this, or the next after that. He'd board, look, and if he wasn't there, get off at the next stop and go again.

Only he *was* there, eyes locked to his phone, earphones inserted. Billy slid two pound coins into the slot and the door shut behind him with a hiss. The kid was seated halfway along the lower deck to his right. *Don't look up.* He walked past, sent into a jog as the bus took off. He scanned the other passengers, four of them downstairs and only one could plausibly be a cop. A woman in her thirties reading *The Metro*, or maybe pretending to. He watched her as he approached. She must have sensed it. She looked up, and in that moment, he knew he would have no problem in killing a cop. She smiled at him coyly and went back to her paper.

He took a seat at the back to his left where he could watch him.

The kid looked to be getting comfortable. He'd taken off his coat. He was taking this bus a good distance. Billy ran through his options. Follow him off the bus, hope for a quiet moment and do him. Do him here. Press the red button on the handrail and wait for the bus to just about stop. Walk up to him, two in the head and walk off. Nobody, even *Metro* lady, would be able to give more than the vaguest of descriptions. *CCTV, Billy.* Of course, most modern buses had it. One thing showing a video to a jury of a guy who looked a bit like him being on the same bus, quite another watching him shoot the kid in technicolour. *Relax. Marathon, not a sprint.*

Where the hell were they going? They'd left what he knew of the city behind a while back. Looking out of the window now showed more of his reflection than the world, now that it was dark out there and lights were on in here.

The bus stopped and *Metro* lady got up, she looked back and gave Billy a smile before she tucked the paper under her arm and left. What is it with Edinburgh girls and bad timing?

The bus was held up at some crazy junction for an eternity before it chugged on into 'Portobello', according to the sign, whatever that was.

The kid was putting his coat on. Billy uncrossed his legs. The kid hit the button, but stayed seated, so Billy did too. Then the kid was getting to his feet. He stretched and Billy just knew he was going to turn around. Only he didn't. The bus pulled in and as the kid reached the door, Billy was slipping down the aisle. He could have taken the kid's neck in his hands as they stepped onto the pavement. The kid turned right. Billy stayed where he was. He let him get perhaps a dozen strides and he began after him. The street was busy. It appeared to be the main road of this town, village, whatever. He could smell the sea, but not see it.

They passed a police station on their left and for a horrible moment he thought the kid might slip inside, but no.

Then the street was getting quieter. Not shoot a guy in the head and walk away clean quiet, but it was an improvement.

Billy wiped his hand on his trousers and slipped it back into the coat pocket, taking a firm grip of the gun's handle. Here we go, he thought. The kid had just turned left onto a quieter street still, Bath Street. He'd picked the location for this himself, but he hesitated. Dillon stopped and then returned to the main drag. *Damn it*. He went on a little further and Billy followed.

The soft ring of a bell sounded and the kid turned left into a cafe.

'All right, kid, everyone's entitled to a last meal,' he said softly as he took up a position across the street. 'See you soon.'

Ten minutes passed and Billy was congratulating himself on the jacket purchase. His leather coat was lying on the back seat of the car, which would now take him forever to return to, but what the hell. He loved the jacket, but it had always been a bit style over substance, and he'd be freezing his balls off right now were it not for this big, green ex-German army number.

The day had begun on a sour note. Then he'd allowed himself to hope, then those hopes had been dashed, only to be reignited. Now things were not just looking up, they were all but perfect. The other one, who could only be the kid's brother given the build and the face was walking into the cafe. *You little beauty.*

The plan to pop and walk was now looking a bit shaky, but what the hell. He had both of the bastards. Too risky to take both out quietly on the street, but it was getting late, the cafe would surely be closing soon and they had to go somewhere.

CHAPTER 32

The Curtain Comes Down

'This is based on what?' DCI Templeton said.

'Not an awful lot, ma'am,' I admitted. 'He's not answering his phone, so it's all I've got to go on right now.'

There were noises of some internal struggle on her end of the phone. A moment where it sounded like she was about to say something, but then it was released with a sigh. Then: 'I'll send a unit, Colyear, but without a sighting, or at the very least a more accurate area, it's all I can do. For all you know, the Marshall brothers could be on the other side of town, right?'

'That is true, ma'am. It's just that they have no obvious connection to Portobello and so why arrange to meet us there yesterday, unless it was in some way convenient for them.'

'Right now, we're watching routes south, based on the description of the car you obtained from your witness. That stretches us thin.'

'Understood, ma'am. Thank you for the unit, at least.'

'All right. Keep me updated. And Colyear?'

'Ma'am?'

'If you do spot something, no bloody heroics. We don't fuck around with guns. Understood?'

'Yes, ma'am. Of course.'

Rowan pulled onto the opposite carriageway for a double overtake. The bus facing us flashed its high beam before we had a chance to pull back in, leaving me with bright spots burnt into my vision, which probably meant Rowan had too.

'Take it easy,' I said. 'Remember, this is just a hunch. Besides, we have no particular destination beyond Portobello.'

I tried Dillon's number for the fifth time. It rang a dozen or so times and sent me to voicemail. I'd left two already, so just I cancelled the call.

The rush-hour traffic had since passed, which was just as well as the junction at the end of Inchview Terrace would have been backed up beyond the point we were doing nearly sixty on. Still, it wasn't long before the junction came into view and a healthy queue of brake lights met us. As we slowed to a stop, my phone began to ring.

'It's him,' I said looking at the screen. 'Dillon? You're okay?'

'Hi. Yeah, fine. Sorry for the missed calls.' I could hear Davie trying to speak over him in the background. 'We were sitting in the cafe and this phone kept ringing—'

'Dillon.'

'. . . and I'm thinking, would someone answer that d-damn phone and then later I realise it was mine.'

'Dillon, listen,' I said, but he wasn't.

'Forgot completely I'd changed it. Duh. Yeah, okay, Davie wants to know what happened after I left.'

'Dillon, I'm getting to that, but listen. Where are you?'

'Look, Sergeant Colyear. I know you're looking out for us, but I'm serious. We don't want—'

'It's not about that. Look, there's a small chance you could have been followed back from the operation. Now's not the time to insist on your privacy. This is a very serious guy we're talking about. I just want to make sure you're safe. After that, if you want to crawl back under a rock, I don't give a shit. Now, where are you?'

Billy watched the boys leave the cafe.

The street had a good amount of passing traffic and although it was now after 8 p.m. there appeared to be people still making their way home from work on foot, dressed as they were formally under their outdoor coats, though most were glued to their phones, just like the younger brother. Still, even a gunshot, even one through a silencer, would surely rouse them from their flirting over text or tweeting their inane epiphany of the day.

He was allowing a distance to grow between them before he followed, staying on the opposite side of the road. He was about to start walking when the young lad stopped. The screen of his phone lit his face. Then the phone was at his ear. With the distance and the traffic, Billy could only make out the occasional word or phrase.

'Missed calls . . . Phone kept ringing . . . Duh . . . Look . . . Serious.'

A bus passed and when the lads came back into view, they were looking around the place. Billy slowly dropped to tie an imaginary shoelace, but kept listening as best he could.

The boys were talking amongst themselves: 'Police . . . No way . . . Too dangerous . . . Fuck.' And then: 'Old cinema . . . Bath Street . . . 'obello.' Then the voices were gone and Billy stood. The lads were likewise gone, but only for a moment. A flash of movement further down the road. The boys were running, taking a right, down Bath Street where some old cinema would be waiting. He'd have to be quick. It wasn't clear what that call was about, but someone was coming.

Dillon looked up from his phone and scanned the street.

'What is it?'

'He thinks I could have been followed.' There were plenty of people around, but nothing obvious. 'He wants to know where we are.'

'No police, Dillon. We agreed. We do this ourselves.'

'It's too dangerous, Davie. Besides, if they really want to get hold of us, it won't be hard for them. All right?

'Fuck. All right.'

Dillon returned to the phone. 'Sergeant. We're heading back to the old cinema.'

'You have an address?' Sergeant Colyear asked.

'It's, eh, Bath Street. Portobello.'

'How far from where you are now?'

'Minute or two.'

'Then go now. Run. Don't stop.'

Dillon was already at a jog by the time he cancelled the call. Davie was at his heels and they were quickly up into a sprint. They reached the corner and Dillon almost collided with someone coming up Bath Street. His heart stopped in his chest for a second as he took in the face of the man who had ducked out of his way. *Not him. Don't stop.*

He wasn't kidding when he said 'old cinema', Billy thought. The thing was surely condemned. It sat incongruously on what was otherwise a residential street, like a great decaying molar needing pulled. *But how the hell did they get past this fencing?* He tugged at the Heras barriers. They rattled gently but were going nowhere without heavy tools or the ones specific to the erection and dismantling of this stuff.

He circled the building looking for an insecurity and saw none. He could climb, but it would make a racket, and there was no way those two heavy lads managed that in the time it took for Billy to find this place. He returned to what he supposed was the front of the building and reinspected the fencing to the far left, next to a wall. One of the junctions of metal joining one panel of fence to the next was missing and the one below it twisted. Separating the two meant you could step up over the twisted bracket and squeeze through the space. He left his rucksack wedging the gap. There was nothing in there he needed right now, and it would help with a quicker escape, not having to find this again when the adrenalin was flowing.

There was no way through the front doors. Great wooden panels had been screwed in there. But down the left-hand side of the building was a small side entrance. Billy drew the Maxim, taking pleasure, always taking pleasure, in the way it felt in his hand. The balance and heft of the thing, the potential and the promise of the thing.

He tried the handle, slowly, but there was no give. *Is it possible they had the key for this door?* Surely not, and if it was some other entrance, why force the section of fence on this side? He tried again pushed gently with his shoulder. The door was stiff in its frame, but there was the give, just a little. He gave a stronger nudge with his shoulder and the door swung, scraping on the concrete step as it did. Billy gritted his teeth, aware of the sound, but pushed into the building, into complete darkness.

Grit crunched under his careful steps. He held the gun against his hip with his right hand, his left was pushed out in front of him, feeling his way along the corridor. His hand found a door and as he pushed on it, voices floated to him from somewhere ahead.

He'd entered into the foyer, the area directly behind the boarded-up front doors. A little light spilt in from windows high above but he was still barely able to see his feet. The voices bleeding in from somewhere were spectral, reverberating against bare walls. He pushed through an oldie-style ticket booth and it was impossible not to imagine some girl in a little hat and a waistcoat handing you your stub and telling you to enjoy the film. Onward into the main auditorium and the voices grew louder and clearer. There were lights on in here, though only on one side. The brothers were discussing something, something about work. A job that the older brother had been offered, or missed out on, it wasn't clear.

Billy moved away from the lights and the voices to the far side of the main room. It was a riot of wires, insulation, piping and other detritus. He could see them now. Sat high up on seating, their feet laid up on the seats in front of them. He could fire from here, but a handgun was not accurate from this range, especially one with a silencer. It wasn't clear how best to get close enough without—

His foot caught on something, a wire or some shit, and he stumbled.

The voices ceased.

Billy stayed in the crouched position he'd been forced into to save himself from sprawling forward.

'Sergeant Colyear?' the younger brother said.

Billy considered for a moment, then pulled on his Scottish accent and said, 'Aye. Where are you?'

'You know an old cinema in Portobello?' I asked. The lights had gone green and it was touch and go whether we'd make it through the junction on this filter.

'You're forgetting this is your town, not mine. Hold on,' she said. The lights had switched red, had been for a few seconds when she overtook a black cab who had obeyed the signal. We speeded through the junction forcing traffic now entering to brake. There were blasts of the horn from four or five.

'Stay on the main street for . . . now.' I was trying to ignore Rowan's suicidal driving and focus on the map on my screen. 'Take a left after the next one.'

She did and I could feel my stomach beginning to churn from dealing with the movement while staring at my phone. It was a relief when she slowed as a building on our left came into view.

'I guess this is it. Unless there's another hulking, great unused building on this street,' she said. She pulled the handbrake and we stepped out onto the street.

I went to my radio while Rowan went to the boot of her car: 'Control from DS Colyear.'

'Go ahead.'

'For the armed unit attending Portobello, updated location is the old cinema on Bath Street. Is that received? Over.'

'Unit attending Portobello for DS Colyear come in.'

'Roger, from Four-Four, that's received. ETA ten minutes, over.'

'DS Colyear?'

'Thanks, control. That's received. You get that?' I said to Rowan. She was looking at the fence surrounding the place.

'Yeah, just need to keep Tweedledum and Tweedledumber out of bother for ten minutes. You seeing this?'

She had retrieved a good-sized torch from her boot and was pointing the beam at a bag wedged into the fence. I pulled it from its place and pulled the zip. Rowan angled the light and I looked inside where I found a bottle of water, an Edinburgh A–Z and a pair of binoculars that had seen better days.

Rowan was waiting for my reaction, evidently unsure what to make of it. 'No bloody heroics' was repeating in my head. 'We don't fuck around with guns.'

What I said was *ten minutes*, though I wasn't sure myself if this was a question or a statement. In some circumstances ten minutes is nothing. In this moment it was an eternity. 'Maybe you should—'

'No. No way. You did that to me once before. Practically pushed me out of a car in Dumbarton to go do something stupid. No, if you're going, I'm going.' It was probably unconsciously, but she was holding the torch like a club, daring me to leave her out.

For a few seconds I couldn't move I was so torn. 'Dammit.' A faint unease in my lower stomach, as well as my pulse quickening, told me some part of my being had already made its mind up.

I dumped the bag and climbed through the space. It was too high for Rowan to straddle, but she deftly hopped onto the bracket and through.

A door to the left hung open. I peered inside at darkness. Rowan pushed past me.

'Hey, wait,' I said as a pulse of pain shot through my guts.

'Who's got the torch?' she said, not looking at me, or sensing my discomfort. She moved on and I did all I could to ignore the burning in my stomach and I followed her in. We both jumped when the light came reflecting back from the glass of a door. She pushed through this and then stopped. A second later she killed the torch. There were voices, muffled and distant. Two options ahead of us. Stairs leading up and a door leading through. Rowan was indicating she was heading upstairs.

'Be careful. Any sniff of a gun and we go back outside,' I whispered. I could feel sweat filming my body. She nodded.

I passed a ticket booth and entered what would have been the cinema proper, grand but derelict. The place had a deeply musty smell that felt like it left a film on your tongue as you breathed it in. The pain in my lower stomach was sending saliva to flood my mouth. I swallowed hard and stepped over what looked like a ceiling panel either taken down or fallen there of its own accord. There was light to the right hand of the seating, rising ahead of me. One of the lights must have been angled in my direction as it hurt my eyes to look that way.

'Over here,' I heard. Dillon's voice and I opened my mouth to reply, suddenly thinking the bag had been a false alarm, but someone else replied.

'I cannae see you. Come down, we need to get out of here.'

I was confused. I raised my hand to shield the light piercing my vision. Two shapes were moving from the right. The boys. Then something from the left.

It happened too quickly.

All I could do was watch.

Billy Flaherty stepped into the room from the left. He calmly raised a gun and fired twice. The sound was muffled, but cracks reverberated off the walls. Davie fell back into the seats while Dillon stopped and ducked. A yell came from the seating above. Rowan shouting

'Hey.' She threw the torch, the light spinning as it hurtled towards the floor, landing impotently a full metre from Billy's feet.

'No,' I breathed. It left my mouth softly as I began to run, not able to believe what I was seeing. He was adjusting his aim and firing in one movement. I was focussed on the shooter, but I could still see Rowan in my peripheral vision falling backwards as if hit with a bat. The sound of the shot was in my ears as I collided with him. I made no attempt to hold him, just slammed into his flank as hard as I could.

His focus had been in the opposite direction. He hadn't seen me coming. I grunted as I rammed my shoulder into him.

He let out an 'Uff', as the wind was knocked out of him. He landed into a pile of plastic pipes and the gun skidded out of his grip, landing somewhere amongst some insulation.

I could hear more yelling. This time Dillon somewhere up and to my right. I looked up at where Rowan should have been standing and there was nothing. Billy struggled to his knees and made to crawl to where the gun had disappeared amongst the pink material. I kicked into his side as hard as the circumstances allowed. It was hard to get a steady step amongst the crap all over the floor. Another grunt escaped him, but he kept moving forward. I kicked again, but this time he sensed it coming. My foot landed hard, but he managed to get a grip of my ankle. I hopped once, trying to keep my balance, and then I was going backwards and I knew I was going to the floor.

I landed on my radio. I pulled it from my pocket and fumbled for the button. 'Sergeant Colyear, shots fired, officer dow—'

Fire erupted in my hand as Billy booted the radio out of my grip. I rolled to my left and tried to stand, but he was on me with a series of punches. Each one landed with accuracy and blinding venom. I tried to cover up with hands and elbows, but the blows kept finding spaces. I clutched at him once, twice, but he fended me off easily, although I did manage to get to my feet. Then, by some stroke of luck, I caught an arm as I deflected a left hook. Some move from officer safety training kicked in and I managed to lock his elbow.

He laughed, either from amusement or embarrassment, that I had him. My head was swimming. He'd caught me to the face a number of times and only now the pain was beginning to register. Again, I looked up into the seats for Rowan. Nothing. Dillon continued to yell from his position.

'Now what?' he said. I had his wrist in one hand and my other pushed at his arm above the elbow, forcing him into an L shape facing the ground.

My cuffs, I thought. *Where are they?* The inside pocket of my jacket, but I'd have to release one hand to get to them. *Need to get him to the ground.* I pushed against his arm and bent his wrist and urged him lower. He grunted in pain and went to one knee, but he was strong, far stronger than he looked. He pulled, pushed, spun and broke free.

I raised my hands in defence as he came again. I threw a punch and another and hit nothing. Then he threw his own. Three of them. The first landed square on my temple, the next to my stomach and the last square on my chin and I suddenly had no sense of which way was up. The pink stuff broke my fall. I was not getting back up. Could not.

All I could do was watch and wait for some control of my head, which I felt lolling. He looked at me, seemingly evaluating whether I was safely done. He decided I was and turned to look for the gun and found it immediately, staring back at him in the hands of young Dillon.

'You fucker. You killed him, you f-fucker.'

'Woah there, mate.' Billy's hands went up. 'Take a breath.' He took a step backwards, almost tripping on a beam of wood. 'This is that first night all over again, lad. And look how that turned out. Best put that down before you take your dick off.'

'Shut up.' Dillon was hissing his words through tears and through his teeth. The gun was shaking in his hands, which were covered in blood, probably not his. I saw in a moment how this might play out. I tried my legs. They rocked under me, but I stood.

'Dillon, easy,' I said, though the words were slurred, not from my giddiness but my jaw was not sitting properly in my skull. 'Don't do it. He's unarmed and no matter what he's done, this would be prison for you.'

'I don't f-fucking care.'

'Not now you don't, but you will.'

'It's not j-just Davie. If I don't, he'll keep c-coming. Soon as he gets out, he'll keep c-coming.' The gun was pointing straight at Billy's forehead now.

'Tell you what, mate. You point that thing somewhere else and I'll make you a deal. We'll call it even. All square, eh? I mean, fuck it. I'll do you a favour and you—'

'Shut up, just shut up.'

I thought then he would fire. His left hand had moved to the hilt of the gun, a large drip of blood fell from it and he looked ready.

Then sirens. Lots of them. Distant, but quickly growing in volume.

'Fuck,' Billy said. He looked at me, then at the door and then to Dillon. Then he moved. If the floor had been even, he might have had a chance. I was sure Dillon would fire, but as Billy clumsily charged him, he stumbled and as well as Billy Flaherty had punched me, the left hook from Dillon was better. Billy landed not in the pink stuff, but onto the same beam of wood he'd nearly tripped on. He'd landed with his arm underneath him. He rolled, clutching at it and sucking in air. Surely broken.

The sirens were right outside.

Billy blew out a breath and tried to sit up, winced and laid back down. He looked over at Dillon. The gun was now by his side. 'You know what, kid. You're right. Yeah, I'll go to prison, but not for long. I've got mates, mates in high places. I'll still be a young man when they let me out and when they do, I'll come for ya. You won't be able to sleep, eat, rest 'cause you know I'm coming. I'll fucking gut you. So, do it. Shoot me.'

'Don't, Dillon.'

'It's you or me, you little shit. I'll come for ya. No matter how long it takes, I'll come for ya.' Billy forced

372

himself onto his knees. Dillon raised the gun again.

'He's going down, Dillon. He shot a cop. I don't care who his fucking mates are, he's not getting out, trust me.'

Dillon looked over at me. I nodded. He wiped tears from his face, leaving a smear of red there and lowered the gun.

'Fucking coward,' Billy grunted and got to his feet. Dillon took a few steps back, but with a broken arm, this guy was no threat. Then Billy was walking. He stooped with his remaining hand and lifted my radio from the ground.

He raised it to his mouth and paused. He smiled at me and pressed down on the button. A Scottish accent spoke into the radio, rushed and harried. 'From Sergeant Colyear. He's coming out. He's armed, I repeat armed.'

He tossed the radio high into the seats and jogged for the door. I made no attempt to stop him.

There was the sound of internal doors banging and then from outside: 'Armed police, show me your hands. Armed police, get down, get down.'

And then three shots.

CHAPTER 33

No Good Deed

She came to me in the dream.

Some perfect version of Rowan. Her bronze hair flowed in waves at her chin. She wore a white gown that seemed to float around her as if bound by no gravity. Her smile radiated, and it warmed my face. She was so beautiful it hurt my heart.

'What are you grinning at?' she said.

'What?'

'Seriously, stop that. It's fucking creepy.'

'Uh, what?'

'Are you even awake?'

She slapped my face. Not hard, but hard enough.

'Hey. Stop,' I slurred.

'Oh, your jaw. Sorry.' She budged at my leg with her bottom until I moved it and she perched herself on the edge of my bed. 'Man, what drugs did they give you? You're wasted.'

I sat up and rubbed my eyes. I checked my phone while I sucked at the straw in the small plastic cup. It was quarter to two in the morning. I'd been asleep for an hour and yes, whatever they'd given me for the pain was potent. I looked at Rowan again. That 'bronze hair' was bed-head city. The smile was some weird scowl and the white gown was the same thing I was wearing, courtesy of Edinburgh's Royal Infirmary.

I cleared the drowsy sleep from my throat and said: 'How are you feeling?'

She shrugged that shrug. 'Only hurts when I breathe. Oh wait, you have to see this.' She leant forward and started lowering the front of her gown.

'Woah,' I said, putting out my hand and averting my eyes. 'What drugs are *you* on? Wait, am I still sleeping?'

'Oh, grow up. Look.'

'Oh shit,' I said and leant in for a better look.

'I know, right?' she said. Her voice was strained as she had her chin to her chest trying to look herself at what I was seeing. She'd lowered the gown only just enough to show a deep red mark in the centre of her chest where the vest had prevented a fatality but couldn't deflect the impact. From there a perfectly circular spiderweb of bruising was beginning to form. A few hours from now it would be extremely impressive, in a day, spectacular. 'I'm only still here because I lost consciousness for like a minute. I'll probably still get out before you, and I got shot. I mean, don't feel bad, but you only got punched a few times and I'll be walking out of here while you're still drugged up and sucking your water through a straw.'

'Hey.'

'I'm just saying. *Weak*.' She quietly squeaked this remark and gave me a wink.

'Don't make me laugh. It really does fucking hurt.' I attempted to rub at my jaw, but recoiled when my hand found the swelling. 'They said since this has happened to me before, that it's more likely to keep happening.'

'You mean since you've had your jaw dislocated in the past it will keep happening when someone punches you in the face?'

'What they said.'

'My advice would be stop letting people punch you in the face. But what do I know? I'm just a rookie.'

'What did they say about this?' I nodded at Rowan's chest.

'Small fracture in the sternum. Nothing they can do about it. Man,' she said and slapped my leg. 'I got shot.'

'I know, I was there.'

'No, but like for real, I got shot.' There was such a goofy smile on her face that I had to laugh. And it did hurt.

'Well now it's off your bucket list, no need to repeat it.'

'Agreed.'

'Have you seen the DCI?' I asked.

'Briefly. Kate popped in to check on me. She didn't come to see you?'

'No.'

'Is that weird?'

'My guess is she's pretty furious.'

'What? Why? That kid is alive because of us. They should be putting us up for some kind of award or something.'

'He's alive, but we were very nearly not, because I didn't follow protocol.' Rowan scoffed. 'And she's right,' I added. 'We never should have gone in there. If that bullet had been a few inches higher, well . . . doesn't bear thinking about. I think the good in this situation sort of offsets the bad. If I'm lucky, I'll escape disciplinary because we saved the kid. Still, another two dead.'

'But one of them was the bad guy.'

'The *unarmed* bad guy that was shot dead by Police Scotland. I can only imagine the shit that Kate's going to have to deal with.'

We sat in silence for a minute. Then I tried to move the conversation on. 'Does Morgan know?'

'Pfft, no. He'd have a heart attack. If I'm getting out in the morning, I'll explain it all in person.'

'But surely it's on the news?'

'The kid's brother and our bad guy, yes. Kate said they're keeping me out of it. Keeping it internal, if they can. Have you called Marcella?'

'No. I'm not sure we're in that place. I'll call my dad in the morning, though that's a lecture on career choices I'm not looking forward to. Anyway, you woke me up just to show me your scars?'

'Partly. But mostly because I can't sleep.' She was pulling at her gown again looking down through the gap. There was a slightly maniacal tone about her, the adrenalin was still understandably flowing. 'All right.' She patted my leg. 'Rest up, punchbag. I'll stop in before I roll out of here.' She kissed me on my forehead and left my little room.

Drug-assisted sleep found me pretty quickly, but not before I wondered at her reaction to what had happened. She was laughing about it now, but I suspected a time would come when the proximity to disaster would take her down a different path. *She'll need watching*, I thought.

I was ready to return to work after two weeks. Not just because I felt fine, the jaw still a little tender of course, but because Dad had all but moved back into the garden flat with me. He was on full Dad mode as well. He was like a mad scientist with his soup combinations. Even after I told him I was okay to chew solid food again, he was over his Bunsen burner nightly with such compositions as sweet potato, beetroot and mint, or broccoli, cheddar and chorizo, but the night he set out a bowl of turnip, sweetcorn and smoked haddock, it was time for a serious conversation. I wasn't about to quit my job, he realised that pretty quickly, though I did promise to take better care of myself and that was enough to send him back to Heather and me reaching for the phone for a takeaway pizza.

The investigation was now entirely in the hands of OCCTU; the nasty events in Edinburgh but a chapter in a far more complicated story. Still, it was Edinburgh that appeared to be Nelson Taylor's undoing, as far as DCI Templeton understood it. The net was circling around him and his arrest was imminent. Rowan and I would submit our operational statements, but likely never be called as witnesses. We'd follow the court case with interest, but from afar.

Still, there was one more job for Edinburgh CID. One that could have been completed weeks ago, but which DCI Templeton was saving for my return.

'You have it?' I asked Rowan. She patted her breast pocket and we entered the stairwell. The dog downstairs sensed our arrival and was apoplectic behind its door.

I knocked on number four and a woman in her early or mid-thirties answered, which took me a little by surprise.

I raised my warrant card from my chest to let her better see. 'DS Colyear, ma'am. And you are?'

As a cop, when you show up at someone's door unannounced, you get one of two faces. There is the shocked *who's dead?* face, or you get this one, the *what is it this time?* face.

'Lainey. Elaine. You're looking for Malky?'

'That's right. We have a warrant to enter, if you'd prefer to do this—'

'The hard way?' Her hands were on her hips, but she was swivelling, allowing us to pass.

'I was just going to say the official way, but thanks.'

'He's in the living room,' she said, pointing to the first door on the right.

She followed us in. Malky, lying on the sofa in his underpants, his socked feet up on the armrest while he watched football on TV, turned and had the shocked face on, but only for a moment before it switched to the other one.

'This is for you,' I said and thumbed at Rowan. She had the warrant in her hand. She placed it down on a sideboard by the door. 'Put some trousers on, you're under arrest.'

Malky clicked off the TV and stood. 'What for?' he said. 'I work for you, remember.'

This remark was clearly not for us. The idea his dealings with Taylor and Flaherty were about to be overlooked were laughable.

'I'm happy to list the charges, Malky, though you might prefer to wait until we get to the station, it's going to be difficult to hear.' I motioned at Lainey in the doorway, her face red, her arms crossed.

'I want to hear it,' she said.

'Love—'

'Don't "love" me. What is it? Drugs, right?' She looked close to tears, or perhaps murder.

There was no protest from Malky, so I let him have it. 'Malcolm Pritchard, you're under arrest on suspicion of the sale, distribution and supply of controlled drugs.' This didn't seem to unnerve him, though I was only getting started. 'For attempting to pervert the course of justice,' again his face was blank, I played the trump card: 'and for murder.'

'What?' he said and laughed a little. There was a gasp from the doorway.

'You're not obliged to say anything at this time, but anything you do say—'

'Wait. What the hell are you talking about?' He was talking to me, but looking pleadingly at Lainey.

'— will be noted and may be used in evidence. Now's the time for you to put some trousers on. It's more difficult to do it in handcuffs, Malky.'

'Wait. Just hold on.' He was backing up. His face was

ashen. Rowan had Lainey's arm and was guiding her to a chair, she was close to fainting. 'I didn't murder anyone. What the fuck are—'

'Malky. Just because you didn't pull the trigger on David Marshall, doesn't mean you weren't involved. And since you were involved, you get charged same as the one who did,' albeit Flaherty was beyond charging, but it would dilute the point to get into that. 'You don't get to play both sides and walk away into the sunset. Now. Trousers.'

'You might want to check under the sink for a little panel,' Lainey said. She was gathering her things as we led Malky out the door. The shock seemed to have passed, taking its place were stoicism and anger. 'There's a wee Tupperware box under there you might be interested in.'

'Thanks,' Rowan said. 'We'll do that.'

Malky was trying to hold back tears as we led him to the car, but lost it completely as I closed the door on him.

Closing the door on him and also this case, as far as we were concerned. I would find out tomorrow what the DCI would have me working on next. I'd been nervous of entering her office on my first day back, after the time off. I needn't have been. We talked only briefly about how I should have handled the situation, but she was surprisingly calm and understanding when I told her exactly how it had played out. I promised not to put myself, or others, in harm's way in the future and that was as close to disciplinary as it got. Contrastingly, there was no 'atta-boy', 'well done' or 'good job'; *the good offsets the bad*, as I'd told Rowan.

ACKNOWLEDGEMENTS

Thanks go to everyone at A&B for letting me tell stories and to my agent Joanna for spotting my efforts in the first place and taking a chance on me. To see a book on a shelf with my name on it draws a child-like thrill that will never leave me.

Thanks also go to Stuart Potter for fantastic technical advice. To Inspector Simpson for logistical advice and to Liam Rudden who stepped in when I needed an iconic Edinburgh building for some diabolical deeds.

Stuart Johnstone is a former police officer who,
since turning his hand to writing, has been selected as
an emerging writer by the Edinburgh UNESCO City of
Literature Trust, and published in an anthology curated
by Stephen King. Johnstone lives in Scotland.

storystuart.com @story_stuart